AVID

READER

PRESS

ALSO BY ISMET PRCIC

Shards

Unspeakable Home

ISMET PRCIC

AVID READER PRESS

New York   London   Toronto   Sydney   New Delhi

Avid Reader Press
An Imprint of Simon & Schuster, LLC
1230 Avenue of the Americas
New York, NY 10020

First Avid Reader Press hardcover edition August 2024

AVID READER PRESS and colophon are trademarks of Simon & Schuster, LLC

Simon & Schuster: Celebrating 100 Years of Publishing in 2024

For information about special discounts for bulk purchases, please contact Simon & Schuster Special Sales at 1-866-506-1949 or business@simonandschuster.com.

The Simon & Schuster Speakers Bureau can bring authors to your live event. For more information or to book an event, contact the Simon & Schuster Speakers Bureau at 1-866-248-3049 or visit our website at www.simonspeakers.com.

Interior design by Carly Loman

Manufactured in the United States of America

10 9 8 7 6 5 4 3 2 1

Library of Congress Cataloging-in-Publication Data is available.

ISBN 978-1-6680-1533-9
ISBN 978-1-6680-1535-3 (ebook)

To my brother, with Love

To all my traumas, big and small.
For breaking my eyes, heart, minds.
Which serves to open, open, open.

neither

TO AND FRO in shadow from inner to outershadow
from impenetrable self to impenetrable unself by way of neither
as between two lit refuges whose doors once neared gently close, once turned
*   away from gently part again*
beckoned back and forth and turned away
heedless of the way, intent on the one gleam or the other
unheard footfalls only sound
till at last halt for good, absent for good from self and other
then no sound
then gently light unfading on that unheeded neither
unspeakable home

SAMUEL BECKETT

Fuck narrative coherence, what about the dude is broken don't we understand!?

ISMET PRCIC

Obligatory Warning[1]

Translating feelings and experiences into language, as I'm attempting to do here, will ultimately fail my feelings, my experiences, and my language, not to mention *you,* the reader. Adding to that the fact that your language is not the same as my language shall make the matters even more difficult. The name of the game here is translation and translation is a war between two sides of one mind, the native side (B) and the tourist side (A). The life experience is thus ruptured in the absurdity of this war and becomes incommunicable to others in all its complex constitutions. The tourist settles for the gist while the native wallows in the intricacies of detail. Both sides lose, always: one misunderstands while the other is misunderstood.

Now that we all know what losers we are, let us at least try.

Hear:

---

1   Excerpt from *Bunnylove Savagery, or In Place of an Afterword* from **Unspeakable Home** by Ismet Prcic

Dear Billy Ol'-Freckles Burr,

I'm writing this super-slowly for ya because I know you can't read super-good . . . *Heheheheh, I'm just messing around!* I'm a longtime fan and listener, first-time douchebag. This is going to be a weird one, Bill, as you can't take a compliment to save your ass, but I'm actually writing to thank You, a famous comedian I've never met, from the bottom of my heart. Look, I know you're not going to read this on air during the podcast—because . . . I'm a nutjob and everything, *I understand*—but still, I actually had to write to you because I ran out of flesh-and-blood people in my real life. *It's a Hail Mary attempt* (to steal your own expression) to be heard.

I don't know why I'm sending this in to the *Advice* segment of your show, as I'm not asking for advice—*Overrated/Underrated* would perhaps be more suitable for my situation—but it's all really moot at this point in time because I'm writing after the fact. See, two years ago, my life *exploded.* My beloved ex-wife and I had gotten together when I was twenty-one going on eight and she was eighteen going on, like, forty. Too early to get married, right? *I hear you.*

Anyways, it was a foregone conclusion that one day mine and my ex's life philosophies would come to a clash, with me being a depressed writer of trauma, a refugee of war, obsessed with mere survival, and her being a computer coder from California and a dreamer of beautiful, achievable dreams, though with a tendency to keep her feelings bottled up in the way you, Bill, have been known to, from time to time, go on and on about.

Though the explosion had been coming for a minute, it still felt like it came out of nowhere, and I found myself living in our Prius (*oh, Jeysus!*) and pissing in plastic bottles, because I *had to* for a change. Back in Bosnia, during the war, I pissed in plastic bottles and used them to keep warm in those boom-boom winter nights that broke my mind and made me this way. I continued when I lived in my college teacher's attic in Moorpark, CA, because the collapsible stairs leading to it were super-finicky and trying to go down them to the bathroom, drunk in the middle of the night, was life-threatening. Eighteen years later, by the time I gave up on myself, I was depressed and a drunk and wanting to die for good. Pissing in bottles and forgetting them in stashes around the house was one of the reasons I was invited out of it to live in the car.

Long story short, I got divorced, and like five days into my *homelessness,* I moved in with a woman from my program, an alcoholic like myself, into this one rented room we started calling *the womb,* an achy joke that stemmed from my dumb attempt to sound like you doing Arnold Schwarzenegger. It fit just a bedroll and a dresser upon the beige shag and had a single window covered with a magenta duvet, daily washing its walls in pink. We'd been broken, left, and stunned in such similar ways that our ghosts just clutched at each other despite being otherwise mismatched. Both pragmatically clueless about how to live life, we slept on a bedroll under an AC unit and watched Netflix nonstop. I suffered through a bout of hepatitis, burning up and shivering, going in and out of consciousness, melting and losing over fifty percent of my muscle mass because I couldn't get up, couldn't stand. Though I thought I wouldn't survive, for some fucking reason, I kept watching your comedy specials and laughing until my nonexistent core muscles hurt.

I'd start watching one of your specials and wake up mid-another to feel like I hadn't passed out at all. I'd lose consciousness with you bald, in black and white, talking about helicopters, and come around to you with full head of hair, in color, talking about no traffic on the Serengeti, and the act still made sense to me even in that order. I don't know what it is about Your art that helped ease my mind and soul so much, but it played a huge role in my recovery efforts. I crawled through, Bill; I'm alive.

It wasn't until I did a deep dive online and dug up your NPR's *The Moth* appearance, in which you talked about your childhood trauma without being allowed to make jokes about it, that I *understood*. Once I heard *that* raw, clipped, throat-squeezed whimper coming from you of all people, everything fell into place for me too. I really don't mean to amateur-diagnose your work or make things awkward here, but I intuited that it is the trauma that is a *through line* in the voice of your comedy, which is why it seems to click into my heart's toothed receptors with such ease.

I'm *better* these days, though this post-divorce isolation is hard to take; I don't have *peeps* here in this country anymore. I live in a miniature apartment in the fruit-and-veg-packing district in Salem, OR, across the street from a rowdy dive, and only go there midday to eat jalapeño poppers and watch white people in micro-fleece sway in the same way to every beat. When knuckles and knives start to fly, around four–five p.m., I huddle my head down and trek over into my apartment complex that used to be a ropy motel, and I do what immigrants do: I hide there, thanking my fucking stars.

But personally, on the inside-like, I'm working on it; I'm working on myself. When I get in trouble, I write. It worked for me before. So, I'm writing again—revising and reimagining really, *foreverfinishing* (this) another book, trying to find bits from my life that can be of some personal meaning, perhaps even to others; I figure you have to do something similar, only for comedy. I break my life into manageable chunks and capture, dream up, and improvise therein. Every narrator is a version of me, every chunk a snapshot of a particular brokenness. And in that brokenness, I can go anywhere for meaning, anywhere for feeling, healing.

I can become homeless or fail at being a *punky* voice of a run-over generation, find peace in the painful memory or inhabit unlikely hypotheticals, call myself by any name, future-trip on worst-ever nightmares, all of it in preparation for that inevitable crush of breath and bone that is the big D aftermath, which, by the way, if I'm to be really honest, puts my war-memory shards to shame.

I make these chunks resemble stories and bits, but you of all people know that stories and bits don't do justice to the blood-and-guts anguish that gets us screaming about our shit in the first place, and neither do my jagged attempts. It seems that I just burn the body of my life for narrative heat and story smoke. I just don't know what else to do with the misery I've accrued over the years. It has to out. It has to transmute. It's hard to find humor in it, but I try all the time. Thank You for always insisting on it in your stuff, Bill. It's a strength like no other and a true inspiration.

I know you work your material and try jokes on your lovely wife, Nia, or some other first responder, but I haven't had that since my first roommate in the U.S. who proofread every assignment, every paper, I wrote, making sure I don't go out there embarrassing myself, as I wrote all of them in the vernacular of our bachelor pad, complete with swearing and slang and jokes I heard on late-night TV from the likes of You. These strange scribblings were left on the bathroom sink for my fatherly roommate to edit during the most important bowel movement of the day. All the swears were always cut, of course, but I'd find a way to sneak some of them back in.

Shit, now that I think about it, can it be that what I'm actually doing, by writing this letter to You, is just an attempt to fashion a surrogate father again, just a friendly consciousness that will hear my thoughts before everyone else, even if I don't necessarily end up taking the advice? *Who am I kidding, though?* In *real* reality this will (and should) be intercepted by your assistants, screening your incoming electronic mail, which I'm a hundred percent okay with by the way. I'm thinking: I'll even take placebo effect; I just hope the act of hitting *send* proves activating and therapeutic for me even if the missive goes unread. It has worked for me before, this kind of self-hacking to trick myself into engaging with the world at large, making this inner work feel like real work. Which it so is, if one exposes it and offers it to the world, no matter how painful it is, and polishes that proverbial turd into something that can be of help to others, right? Art can save your life and all that?! That was the damn thesis of my first book!

My ex started off liking that I'm this kind of writer but as soon as she recognized some of her own tendencies and traits in my characters, she balked at being seen or speculated about, cringed at what people might think about *her* as they read my pain, without having any control or input on the matter. She really didn't like the autofiction, the way I mix the real and the invented—my healing process.

So, I had to write this second book in two halves, kind of like a mix tape almost, a side A (merica) and side B (osnia). The first, the more palatable chunks that didn't have anything to do with her per se, Beloved was still willing to read and comment on. But the more personal stories from our life together, the ones in which the invasive, deep-rooted shit emerged into my voice and seemed to take over my narrative intentions—she wouldn't touch those B parts with a ten-foot pole. *Too close to home,* she'd decided, to shield herself from what my trauma processing unearthed about our marriage in the process, though both sides of the book were being written during the same period of time. The same time she was remarking on the stories from my youth that didn't shake up the official story of our life, I was writing the *weird and unhinged* side-B chunks that foreshadowed the end of the relationship. I was split: my daylight self was writing to keep the bond and build a home, while my shadow was digging up the dark truths that the official me was trying to drink under the carpet. There I was, trying to feel okay in a beautiful home while simultaneously rehearsing already being left and divorced.

But I'm oversharing now; I'm sorry, Bill. It is not your cup of tea, I know. You're right: <u>trauma shouldn't define us</u>. If you're really reading this, all I meant to say is Thank You and keep up the good.

Much love to You and Yours. And, as it is the custom on The Early Monday Morning Podcast, *Go fuck yourself!*

Smiles galore,

Izzy Prcic

P.S. I love the way you say "unreal." I love it so much that every time I go into a public restroom I unroll the toilet paper some seventeen sheets out and on the eighteenth I write THIS SHIT IS UNREAL, RIGHT? and roll the paper back up. A little something for the next fuck in there.

P.P.S. . . . I think I'm going to do a thing here now . . . Yes, I'm going to go all the way, Bill, and I'm going to attach the chapter that serves as the foreword to my book. I wrote it in *the womb* after most of the fiction chapters were already—at least—drafted, in an attempt to create a quick overview and a location map of my entire life so that, as *the narrators* change throughout the book, the reader can glean what part of my own brokenness I am trying to tackle with each chapter, what particular wound it is that I am writing from. The impetus for the foreword was a distinct memory one dawn of feeling like an imposter in the very house my ex and I owned, slinking out of our marital bed and fleeing into the gray streets of Northeast Portland and witnessing myself—as from above—making a map in my notebook of all the fruit-bearing trees in the neighborhood in preparation for what felt to me, for the first time, like an *inevitable* reality that I'm destined to end up homeless.

When I started to write it, I was looking at a photo of my pregnant mother. I continued by remembering vignettes from every other place I called home, chronologically. I omitted some of them, like when I lived in Croatia, in Scotland, with my theater teacher in Moorpark . . . because I've already covered them in writings past. Others, like when I lived with my in-laws for a year, I omitted because it was too traumatic at the time.

I also have to admit that there were way more pages about my beloved that I went and deleted in a huff when she broke it off. I nixed everything that was a good memory out of spite to myself, as I felt I didn't deserve to remember how much she loved me and how much I loved her. Back then I felt that the fact of the divorce proved me unworthy and I was adamant to lean into it and act the part, that I was destined for pain and death. How stupid does grief make us? How grievous does stupidity? Couldn't even use her name.

Bill, I'm sorry again. I can hear you go: *For Christ's sake, how many times is this motherfucker gonna apologize?* I hope you understand that my intent to connect with You is at this moment both real and unreal at the same time, both successful and doomed—like Schrödinger's cat—just like this book attempt. God, just look at all this bullshit I have to contrive in the absence of honest-to-goodness emotional support, something I'd had for nearly two decades and had been taking for granted. And yet note the absolute *lived* necessity for it. I actually had to write this letter out all the way to these very words to find out why I had to write it, and now, having reached this point, I feel like I had planned to make it part of the book all along. But I hadn't.

But you're in it now, Bill! Sorry.

Homo Homini Home *Est?* or
In Place of a Foreword

1.

I made myself at home in my mother. I drank her host-blood for nutrients, bathed in it for coziness and warmth, paying nothing in rent. I stretched out and elbowed for more and more space in her, imprinted my wanton shapes into her squishy organs as into a beanbag, leeched out and bogarted all of her accrued minerals. I tossed and turned, causing hot flashes and acid reflux, urges to vomit and actual vomitus. Her ribs were monkey bars, her bowel sack a trampoline. If she got merely near citrus, I secreted my alien chemicals which skirmished with her own, resulting in clusters of rash-bumps on her neck and breasts. I made her fart, snore, burp, and diarrhea at all the inopportune moments. In turn, I gained weight and sentience, got snug like a kidney in tallow, grooving to the muffled music of her inner workings.

I was called upon to exist and cherished into manifestation, growth, and, of course, just like many a spoiled human cub, I overstayed my welcome. Nine and one quarter months, ten and a half fucking pounds in American measurements, chiefly in the bum and noggin.

When the time came to move out, I threw untoward parasitic tantrums, boarded myself up in utero by willfully tangling up in the umbilical web, and hung in there for dear life. They did things to induce my eviction, and after a twenty-two-hour campaign, I was made to leave home via bruised and battered limen, made to breathe that homeless outside air all by my lonesome. I wept as my warm mush hardened against the cold into a body, the same one I have spent forty-some years now trying to make feel like my mother felt back then. But no go, so far.

I've been incapable, so far, of making myself at home in me.

2.

Out of the Gradina maternity ward in my father's drunken arms I was carted into an orange Fiat Cinquecento, where my mother, still hospital-gowned and with no underwear on, sat in the back, in tears from pain and exhaustion. These tears were characterized as pissy because she made a comment that her husband forgot to bring her a change of clothes in his selfish excitement at having a boy. Not a peck on the lips from him until the next day.

My father's sister drove and squealed, lambasting my mother for daring to be wounded in this way, in this particular moment, as if she weren't a woman, a mother of three, herself.

I bawled at all of them, especially Aunty, irked by novel sensations.

The two-bedroom apartment on Titova Street was full of strange relatives and sharp, hangoverish sounds and smells. A throbbing blur of kitschy late-seventies color palette—browns, oranges, and greens.

They plopped me on the fleece surface of a comforter in a darkened bedroom, and Aunty butted in to unswaddle me, dismissing my mother in her own home, her need to hold me. I promptly pissed right up and into her face.

Time passed in the two-bedroom on Titova Street, bringing staunch, everlasting, everloving, fucking change. In time I quit my sedulous fussing, realizing the fettle I was in, that there was no arguing with *is*, with *now*, that every so-called home was but a sojourn between changes, any way you sliced it.

Change was the name of the game and the game was compulsory so I made a home of my mother's breasts when they were near, my oaken cradle when I chilled, my blue blanket when I slept. I made a home of the orange shag carpet like a sprawling lake in the living room, my block toys—sampans in a storm—strewn about.

I made home inside my dreams too, hoping to bring back the good old times, prodding into the pliancy of *dreamstuff*, striving to conjure it into my mother's womb again, my ears wide open, hoping for the hum of her aorta. I'd send my protuberances out to goad, expecting sweet, loving push-back, just to find nothing but more and more of that flapdoodle dreams are made of. I did take note that the *dreamstuff* was just like the stuff of the two-bedroom on Titova Street—continuously mid-change.

At some point—when my turtle expired in a furniture-moving accident, I think—I was told of heaven, which sounded eerily like my first home—in the feel of it, at least—and I've spent years thinking of it that way, like it was a place to one day find again, go back to, somehow. But home, like heaven, is not a place. Land and walls have fuck all to do with home. We're born into lingering homelessness. Returns are as absurd as raptures. Who returns? To what?

The problem really lies with the nature of language. It allows us to call *home* places that only resemble it, to call *love* feelings that only come close to it, to round up 0.784 to 1 because it's easier to live in the world of integers. It's easier to live with ourselves when we can justify our selfishness by calling our *wants* our *needs*. We even limit something we call *reality* to a consensus of realities, rounding up intricacies of individual experiences into a common one that is more painlessly negotiated. Go us!

3.

When we were new growths, eager to escalate, to be big already, to have that grown-up power already, my cousin Eko—who didn't read or dread consequences or do any kind of arts and crafts but loved to throw aerosol cans we found in the riverbed into leaf-fires, eager-squatting at the base of some knobbed willow with his hands over his ears, waiting for that giddy *boom* that was to come—this troublemaker, earnestly believed that cartoonish U-shaped magnets we saw on Looney Tunes right before the evening news on Yugoslavia's Channel One would attract objects that were not necessarily made of metal, like, in this particular case, pigeon flesh.

We were outside of our grandfather's house on Jalska Street, in the country, where I spent my summer holidays and where he lived. It was a balmy, birdsong-choked, bugs-kamikaze-ing-into-your-head-holes, arachnids-trying-to-topple-you-like-in-*Star-Wars* kind of afternoon when a miscalculating country pigeon flew full speed into the next-door neighbor's living room window and thudded hard like you wouldn't believe. The birds, the bumblebees, the breeze, they were all stunned quiet.

We squatted behind the hedge-swallowed wire fence and through it saw the creature's gray breast heave then quit in the weeds between two properties. The way its wing fanned out in plumage looked like a curtsey.

"If I had that big Acme magnet from the toons," Eko whispered, "I could . . . zoom in that pigeon right here, get it right onto the spit?"

"What?" I spat. "That's not how—"

That's when the widow Umija, the next-door neighbor—a slatternly Baba Yaga and the reason why we really ducked behind the hedges in the first place—popped into the frame of her window to investigate. We went prone in time; she didn't see us. Just stood there, head on a swivel like a human turret, searching the scene for culprits. When she shut the lace curtains, it wasn't with malice but like a fisherwoman casting a net. One could still monitor through the lace.

We hated her because every time we played soccer in the commons in front of her house and our ball went over the fence and into her yard, she would *stoop and creep* through the overgrowth till she found it, raise it up into the air just long enough for us to see it and hope that it would be thrown back to us, then stab it to death against her thigh with a boning knife, muttering hate. It wasn't until recently that my mother told me Umija had lost her man, two of her three children, and eleven brothers and sisters to tuberculosis.

There were no homeless people in my grandfather's village.

Every madcap, certifiable, down-on-luck, heartbroken, disillusioned, abused, henpecked, handicapped, dead-inside, shell-shocked, disregarded, misunderstood, bipolar, fucked-with-during-childhood, can't-face-the-real-world fetid sot or poet, nomad-at-heart or piddler-about, village idiot or slut, they all had a home with a cot. Who paid for that? an American would have asked. Normies paid for that. Normies who knew that their normalcy amounted to nothing but luck. Normies who knew that they were two or three bad turns away from becoming just like that. They suffered them, paid for their meals, laughed at them, and thanked their lucky stars. They paid for it like they would a mulct. These were *their* lunatics, *their* fuck-ups. Unlike city folk, they knew their community and could tell a bad zit from a chancre.

During those hoary, slow-motion summers, Eko and I could hear the jangle of a horse-drawn buggy way before we could even spot it surface out of the green. We'd mad-dash to the turn in the dirt-and-pebble road to see if we could beg our way onto it for a jaunt. A carter would often just salute to us and keep the horse at a trot. But sometimes he'd slow down and let us clamber on and—for the stretch of the road from in front of Grandfather's house on Jalska Street, across the froggy Jala, through the neighborhood of Žabljak, all the way to where the dirt road met the asphalt leading either left or right into the world at large, which was where we knew we had to get off—we felt like something was happening, something was actually going on, in our lives.

Once, there was a tuber-shaped man in the back of the buggy with us, barefoot and crammed into a straining, buttoned-up coat, way too small to keep all of him in, and topped off with a French beret, of all things. He ponged of death and had a huge moist mouth like a beartrap and distinct grooves in the fat of his face. Some momentous *chompige* too—a toothy living-and-breathing caricature.

"The air-people will come in hives," he said, his black eyes burning, "and kill us all with their air-machines."

He was known as Idriz Belegija, a tediously familiar occurrence in the village. *Belegija* is a piece of rock or maybe metal (it'd be telling if it contained lead, because we all know how heavy metals impact sweaty human skin on a hat brim, though I don't know shit about agriculture) that reapers would wet and use to sharpen their scythes in the fields. During harvest time the hills around the village sounded like dozens of samurai continuously sheathing and unsheathing deadly swords.

"The locusts are gonna come and they won't be grasshoppers."

"C'moan, Idriz-aga," piped in that particular carter. "Shut that shit up in front of the kids!"

But Idriz beamed at us, his jowls slightly trembling. His eyes never left ours and we didn't know where to look but back.

By the carpenter's house Idriz spotted a covered woman working the pump at a well, stiffly bending up and down to keep the stream steady. He stuck his face in his armpit and took a coveting whiff. "I'd sure like to smell her personal exhaust before it's all over," he whispered, his shoulders drawn up, trying not to be heard by the carter. Eko and I couldn't help but look. The woman stood up and bent down, stood up and bent down, and was gone as the buggy made a right turn around a foundationless, slapdash little house with no facade, its two concrete steps leading to the front door at least ten inches separated from it, sinking into the yard.

"If you want to see a show," Idriz said, "and learn something," his eyebrows dancing, working the two-finger piston of his right hand into the raspy cylinder of his left, "that's the place."

And at the end of that year I *would* see, through a hole in the wall of the slapdash house, a mentally disabled man with a bony pelvis batter away at the backside of a mentally disabled woman, wearing a diadem made of corn husks, a show that I still cannot currycomb from my—child's—eye. I learned nothing from seeing this, except to stay away from sex as long as possible.

The real lesson came later in adulthood when, again, my mother told me the final chapter of their story, these two intellectually limited neighbor kids who fell in love, and whose parents couldn't keep them apart, and so built them a hovel where they could be the way they were. That they kept the woman medicated so she couldn't conceive, as her lover was a funny braggart who invited villagers to come and watch them make love. That love found its way and that they had a little girl who miraculously was born without her parents' afflictions, who raised herself and her parents while going to school, tricked her father, at age thirteen, into having a vasectomy, finished a vocational high school, joined the department of tourism and catering trade in Tuzla, and moved to Neum on the Adriatic Sea, sending money home on a monthly basis.

4.

Back in Tuzla, my family moved from the two-bedroom on Titova Street to a three-bedroom on Stupine Block just as I started high school. It was a clutch of parallel high-rises with parks and parking lots in between. People lived around and on top of each other like caught crabs, knew the exact moments when their fellow apartment dwellers celebrated birthdays and sport achievements of their teams, when and if their women came during sex, when they saw red and beat their loved ones, took their shits or fell asleep. Whole conversations could have been taped simply by pressing a recorder to a radiator pipe. They all bitched and moaned about it until the war started.

When that son of a bitch arrived on the scene, it came with a grand swelling of disharmony that wouldn't burst for years; imagine the opposite of a continuous Buddhist om. The sound of it was tangible and *wrong;* it juddered through human tissues with the power to rearrange, and it fashioned a sort of psychic ingot that shaped and contained any and every thought, emotion, and utterance. The dwellers all shut their fucking mouths afterward, their grievances made laughable in the wake of it.

In reaction, the grown-ups succumbed into their new roles and malformed into unhinged victims, perpetrators, onlookers, survivors, cowards, heroes, opportunists, reactionaries . . . People became their guiding archetypes. They leaned hard into every fear-soaked decision with absolutely every ounce of their being. Us youths, we did the same, only we were guided by our own limited knowledge and experience. Some of us aped the fearful, some fearless, without realizing that *fear* is the operating word.

When my guy friends started *going after pussy*—about age fifteen—I, in turn, fell in with a rogue theater troupe, head over heels, heart and soul. I fancied myself more enlightened, wanted ichor, not bodily fluids. There's time for that, I thought.

Boki was our twenty-five-year-old artistic leader, and he looked for inspiration for our troupe's pieces everywhere, both in literature (from holy books to Marquis de Sade) and in real life. He'd been sniffing around this thirty-year-old nurse. She had flirty hazel eyes and took minute drags of her cigarette as if milking the joy out of the last glass of posh cognac. We were in Café Galerija and he asked her to buy him a cup of coffee, since he was a starving artist and because women were emancipated. She fell for it. That's who got us into Kreka Psychiatric Hospital for a study of behavior, Boki's idea.

The building was cracking white and its cheap paint chips fell upon the courtyard like flakes of acute psoriasis. Like blossoms. Our troupe filed in through the dented gate into this otherness. The people in there had the consistency of unstirred sludge. An orderly was pulling someone's pants up. A man in a windbreaker zipped over striped pajamas and a pair of plastic slippers on bare feet clap-clapped over and asked Boki for a cigarette, avoiding his eyes.

"You can't smoke, Nermin," our nurse chided, shaking her head. "Your blood is like rice pudding."

"Where are your scrubs?" He smiled at her, guilty as charged.

We waited in the waiting room till she changed into her uniform. The grime on the checkered tiles was like glue to the bottoms of our sneakers. Yellowed radiators were redolent of fear. Barred windows at the end of the corridor beckoned to be smashed through with a washbasin like in that old film with Jack Nicholson. Every so often the draft wailed and went berserk like a bad ghost. I was scared. Somebody was praying in the doorless WC.

Upstairs, a blank orderly followed our nurse's direction and unlocked the psycho ward. The key clanged. I expected him to come in with us, guard us, assure us that everything would be fine, but he just let us through in silence and locked the door.

"How're we doing today?" our nurse broadcasted to the emaciated patients, lightly touching their biceps or shoulders, confident, in her element. They all wore their own pajamas. One young buck shambled over and showed us his flaccid thing through a pajama flap.

"Come on, Djoko," she rebuked him, "put it away. Nobody wants to see that." He did what he was told, snickering with pure joy.

The nurse took us to a lounge area with two tables and some benches. I sat down like a schoolboy, tight-assed, feet together, hands on knees. My eyes must have looked like ping-pong balls, for when she took my hand and told me to relax—at her touch—I was convinced that I was one of them.

Then Boki recognized Sasha Z. He'd been in *Do You Remember Dolly Bell?*, a hugely popular movie in the Balkans. He'd sung this heartbreaking song about having a dream in which he meets a blonde on a beach, in a pleasant breeze, who makes him so incredibly happy. He looked old but had the same bird features, and his hair was cropped oddly. Upon Boki's request, he sang a little bit of the song to us, without feeling, as if tired of his fame, as if bored with it all. You could see he wanted to be who he was now.

Boki asked him how it was to work with Kusturica, the director, and Sasha said he recalled someone giving him little chocolate bananas. Then he changed the subject and asked us why we were there.

"We're here just to visit *you* guys," Boki said. "See how you're living, what goes on."

"What's your diagnosis?" Sasha asked.

"We're not . . . patients."

"Yeah, right." He laughed, sincere-like. "Nobody's a patient." He looked out through a shrapnel hole in the window, through the bars of the window, and stilled.

Djoko, who had disappeared, returned to the lounge with a face full of cheese pie that he was trying to devour in a rush. Our nurse jumped in alarm.

"Hey, buddy, where did you get that pie?"

He faced the wall, trying to swallow an enormous wad of dough, and when she touched his back, he threw some elbows at her face, his screams muffled, his eyes squirting tears.

A squat, compact patient I had not noticed before ran up and pinned him against the wall, calling for an orderly, who thundered in, picked Djoko up, and simply carried him away. Our nurse followed them out and the squat man came to sit among us on the benches.

"What was that?" Boki said.

"Klepto."

The man turned out to have been the master carpenter in the Bosnian National Theatre. Small world. He held his hands clasped together while he talked. He told us that one day something came apart in his brain and he knew that he was crazy. It happened when he was kicking the shit out of his wife's lover when he found him squatting, half-naked, behind the barrel of sauerkraut on the balcony.

"Something just came apart," he repeated.

He said it was like the world turned to rust. His wife was gone in the morning, but he was convinced that she had left a small radio hidden somewhere in the house to drive him crazy because she was a bad seed, and that he shouldn't have married her in the first place, but that he was thinking with his pecker rather than with his brain back then, and did we know how it was.

We nodded like we did.

"That's life," Boki offered.

The man scoffed, looked right at him. "Life?" he said, chuckling in disbelief, at the stupidity, it seemed. He stood up. "Lives that sunder that easily shouldn't be called that."

×

Boki murmured what we should be looking for in the patients' behavior and gave us a goal to approach one patient and find out what they are about. We were to base our new characters on these observations. For art's sake.

I observed a blond man with rolled-up pajama bottoms pour water out of a plastic bottle of Pepsi Light onto his left foot, whimpering with horror. He stared at his wiggling toes, as if waiting for them to ignite again, then screamed and poured more water on.

Hell no, I thought.

Boki made rounds from patient to patient as if shopping in a grocery store. The rest of us meandered with fluttering hearts. There was something uncompassionate about this whole thing, as if we were there to steal souls.

I noticed a young man on all fours staring at the place where the floor met the wall. He susurrated, wrinkling his brow, tapping his forefinger against the plaster. After about a minute of that he got up, walked across the room, went down to his knees, and did it all over again in a different location. I followed him back and forth for the remainder of our time there, mesmerized. I didn't notice it was time to go home. Boki touched my shoulder, whispered: "We should go soon."

But I wanted to find out what this guy was doing, and so, with a huge amount of effort, fighting against my innate spinelessness, I went down to him and made myself present in his world. He looked at me, sensing my silent puzzlement, then pointed to a stationary ant on the floor.

"Look at him," he said. "That's Huso."

"What's up, Huso," I said.

"Come over here now." He lifted himself and waved me over to the other location, to another ant there. A lot of Bosnian jokes are about two guys named Huso and Haso.

"What's up, Haso," I said.

"Oh, you got it." He clapped me on the shoulder and kept his hand there. He seemed enamored with the insect.

"You like ants?" I asked.

"Not really. It's a scientific experiment. Although they are the same species, Haso possesses a significantly larger head then Huso, yet they are both invalids—I picked their legs off myself—and therefore unable to change their location without an outside device, in this case me. In other words, they are stuck in one spot. But one has a bigger head than the other. What does that tell you?"

"I don't know."

"They don't need to move because they live their lives in their heads. It's just that some lives are smaller than others, hence the discrepancy in head size."

This wouldn't make much sense to me until three years later. Not the part about head sizes and cruelty to animals, but the part about the fact that wherever we go, we're stuck with the lives inside of our own heads.

5.

At the age of eighteen, out of the war and into a SoCal gated community in the sun with American relatives on Garnett Lane, by the skin of my teeth, I started waking up in home number five, or rather the *home base,* an entirely New World concept for this Old World pilgrim.

Bald geriatrics sporting tiny white ponytails needed help out of their brand-new yellow Corvettes. Liver-spotted women in visors shuffled around the lake with minute hand weights, motioning like they were running but going two miles per hour. Zero kids in sight. Spotting a UPS guy running up to a mailbox was like seeing a cheetah in the wild. Wow, calf muscles!

Daily, Mexican workers cleaned the community pool in which I was the only community, ever. War-skinny as I was, lacking muscle mass, it was an effort to stay afloat. I tried floating on my back but would start to sink as soon as I exhaled. I persisted a couple of times and hyperventilated. Eventually I'd just hold on to the edge, position my crotch in front of one of the jets in the curved baby blue wall of the pool, and let the strong gush play with my balls. I'd close my eyes and right away be back on a buggy in Žabljak, and the covered woman was standing up and bending down, standing up and bending down, water surging out of the rusty spout into a bucket. Its chatter would change in pitch and when I'd open my eyes there'd be a fat seagull tussling with a squirrel, making a racket, and four or five community-watch zombies would emerge through the palms with loose fists ready to call the cops. They'd ask me where I lived, whether I belonged. Totally, I thought. I mean, look at my nineteen-year-old skinny ass. I fit right in.

In the community center on Agoura Street, I played pickup basketball and the Americans called me Kukoč or Divac, massacring either surname. I had no dribbling skills but had a decent mid-range fadeaway and would chip in a few points a game. I played hard—I'll-be-wearing-your-T-shirt—d-fence, and they called fouls on me every time. I'd say shit like *What's this, ballet?* pronouncing *ballet* like *ballot,* and they had no clue what the fuck I was talking about.

One time the game was canceled because in barged a horde of white couples armed with yoga mats, stipulating *they* had the court for the next two hours. The ballers staged an impromptu sit-in, and I couldn't handle that many people so close together and got the fuck out of there. Outside was a downpour and people ran for their lives in panic from this crazy water falling out of the sky. I strolled across the parking lot to the entrance to a fancy pizza joint where I was to meet my relatives in an hour. The staff looked unnervingly cheery and the couple in the first booth stared at their laminated menus with the concentration and gravitas reserved for those mariners on nuclear subs who have to turn their keys at the exact same time and end a civilization or two.

I hit upon a spot under the awning where the business kept their industrial recycling bins, put on my hoodie, took out a paperback, sat Turkish-style with my back against my backpack, and plunged into the text I didn't fully understand but could tread in okay, like the community pool on Garnett Lane, sans ball massage.

I was informed that the detective in the novel was eating a pizza and, sitting to the side of a pizza restaurant, I had to stop to think what that meant. The very next sentence and he was on the phone talking to his mother about borrowing her car because his transmission something-somethinged. I stopped, went back to the word *pizza*. What pizza was he eating? Something like what I would be eating in an hour? Or the real thing, from Italy? I thought of what my mom called pizza, this thick-dough rectangle made with ketchup and Poli *parizer* cold cut and smoked cheese. *Pica*, we say in Bosnia, slang also for *vagina*. A racially insensitive childhood joke popped in my head, a joke Japanese name that sounds like *Pizza Koyama* but in Bosnian means *pussy as big as a cave*.

"Excuse me," said an old black woman with a fancy hat, holding a pizza box in her hand, an offering.

I scrambled up, stiff and muddled, ashamed of what I was thinking.

"I couldn't finish all of this and was gonna take it home, but I think you need it way more than me."

And I knew my mother's pizza was somehow in that outstretched box. I could see her strong little hands knead the dough the way they did the tissues over my shoulder blades when last she hugged me, before I boarded the bus with the rest of my theater troupe in front of Hotel Tuzla in Stupine Ward. Her fingers dug into me, like *THIS is home!* That rickety banger of a bus took me away from her, out through and around the war, into Croatia, Slovenia, Italy, through the mighty Alps and into southern France of lavish green, onward across the La Manche to the *rosy shores of England* and farther northward into Edinburgh, and my back carried still the fraught depressions of her fingertips, like a fallen angel's scores. Even when I escaped my troupe and hid in kind people's houses in Scotland, and again in Croatia, while waiting for immigration papers to America, I didn't want those indents ironed out and slept on my stomach, my side, so that I felt hugged, loved.

The old woman stepped back at me, coming in for an unwitting embrace. I caught my arms halfway up and brought them back. I witnessed myself through her eyes and I took the box; I took what was actually offered. She saw through all the bullshit. I *was* homeless.

6.

Crestwood Chalets apartment complex in the old Thousand Oaks, CA, south on TO Boulevard, past the **Record Outlet Used**, left at the **Chef Burger**, and up the incline and into the grove of ancient oak trees. The Shade, my American roommate called it, our Apt. #3—my home number six.

Even now, in the hierarchy of places I called home, this little two-bedroom with cottage-cheese ceilings and beige shag carpeting, with a wooden balcony overlooking a grimy shitkick compound where poor, drunk white people yelled at one another about money, shines glorious and special—shines *transcendent*. It has to do with how liberated I felt there, out on my own for the first time, away from all that Balkan naysaying at my uncle's place, all the bullshit notions of what an immigrant should be studying, how a young man should be dressing, in what ways a thankful newcomer should be changing in deference to his benefactor and the host culture, for his own good, no less, *to fit in*.

When I called Bosnia and told them where I now lived, my father said: "Indian country, huh?"

I said: "Yeah, like the whole thing."

He said: "Yeah," but I could tell he was miffed that I'd leave the gated community and members of his side of the family (a sensible option) and move to a lowly apartment and work at a movie theater to be able to afford community college (a dangerous dream). He wasn't a person to understand me in any meaningful way; any *soultalk*, any mention of feelings or deeper meanings, or God forbid *premonitions*, sent my father into a distrustful and anxious sulk.

I didn't know what else to say to him, couldn't tell him a single thing that was really going on inside of me. I couldn't tell him that I experienced a miracle of love, that, while at my uncle's, I'd been secretly working on a book called "The Man from a Lightbulb"—in which a young man lives through the hell of Bosnian war, loses his consciousness in one of the last mortar attacks on his town, just to wake up tiny, inside of a lightbulb on the ceiling of a room belonging to a redheaded girl in an American suburb, where the only way for him to free himself from his glass bubble is to become pure light and the only way to accomplish that *is to love and be loved in return*, and he falls in love with this redhead, the only girl he can see, as she does with him, and in the moment they come together in a burst of light he's sent by the energy of their connection back into reality, into his conscious state, back into the hell of Bosnian war, where he finds himself truly disfigured by shrapnel but doesn't consider his situation hell any longer but a paradise of sorts, a stretched-out feeling of oneness with *what is*, all on account of the vision he experiences while unconscious—a book about enlightenment, and that the moment I left my uncle's, the moment I enrolled in Moorpark College, in the very first class I took there, I'd met *that* redheaded girl, the very one I'd imagined while writing (she even had the white-painted wrought-iron bed I'd described), and that the first time she hugged me goodbye after running lines for our scene together I didn't want her to ever leave the embrace.

To my mother, next in line on the phone, I told the truth, that I fell in love with a girl in my acting class, that she was my dream, my everything.

She said: "You just turned twenty. Be careful."

To Boki, married now and expecting a kid, I said that I *got* me a girl.

"S'wrong with you?" he said. "That hot sun get to your head? Look at *me*. I don't know what's worse: having to look at what I can no longer fuck, or having to fuck what I can no longer look at."

On and on he went, and I couldn't but feel sorry for him. Boki obviously didn't have what I had. He didn't swoon when he saw her coming out of the Psych Building with her hair on fire, her long green dress shimmering in the sun like wet dragon scales. He didn't open up his heart to her for three and a half hours behind the Music Building, making her miss her photography class altogether; didn't feel her take off his two-dollar gas-station sunglasses so that she could see the sincerity of his tears. He didn't plummet into that kiss in her Dodge Avenger after which it was impossible to find the door handle, to know how to use it, what a door handle actually was. He didn't know what it was to merge with her into a steamy human octopus, to have her sit naked in his lap inside a tent on a beach one night and become one being, with all these goading limbs, with two brains and a single heart. He didn't have a soulmate. He didn't know how to build her a home inside of him, how to enter the one she made for him in her. He didn't have . . . her . . . my Honeybee, my beloved sweetness with a sting. My dream. My everything.

God, I forgot; I'd written it all down, our love, and then deleted it all up in anger. Maybe it's for the best. Maybe the rest of this section would've been redacted anyway, for sentimentality and flowery adverbs, however earned.

7.

But after our year in community college together, Honeybee opted for a southernly migration to a feeder school in San Diego. Way back when, she had made a pact with her two childhood besties to live their college years together, have some fun, be each other's rocks. She up and left and we became *long distance*. Our homes we built for each other inside of ourselves became far apart. I couldn't stand for it, the fact that I had to fucking rapture or astral-project every time I wanted to go home. So, when it was my time to transfer, I applied to UCSD only and, a star student, I got in. I followed her from Thousand Oaks to a three-bedroom house she was sharing with her BFFs in what Ron Burgundy would later brand Whale's Vagina, CA.

I, refugee, a man in between homelands, packed up my so-called life— my bag of clothes, my box of books, my scribblings—into my silver 1980 VW Scirocco that would stall every time I brought it to a complete stop and, in what I thought was a romantic gesture, showed up at her door. There is no counting the number of red flags in that sentence. I did my best to assure her friends that I intended to have a life of my own, that UCSD was the best theater school on the West Coast for what I wanted to do, but it was clear they felt that the beehive was entirely compromised. Sensing an attack on the sisterhood, these girls turned protective and cold. They loved my beloved in a different way. What they couldn't stand was my following her, choosing her, and showing it so unabashedly, without reserve. When I wasn't around, they told her I was too serious for her, too old, too clingy, *what does he expect?* They told her she would regret staying with me and not living it up, not doing what they were doing, which was trying everything and everybody, being young.

Honeybee helped me find some roommates, gave me some of her furniture, helped me move into a Spanish-style little house on the corner of Dwight and Mississippi in North Park, and then she broke it off. Gone.

It was in this brick-and-mortar home number seven for me that I started to drink in earnest, because of my emotions, to get through the day, through the heartbreak, and not to have fun or lower inhibitions or blow off steam. I even started to perceive things differently, more like an observer, as someone around whom life was happening.

It got bad. One day I got drunk four times because I kept seeing *her* everywhere, kept seeing red.

The day before—it was the middle of finals week and she'd left me earlier in the quarter—I was drinking Albertsons vodka, openly in front of the skittish guppies of the living room aquarium and in secret after six p.m. when my roommates came home from work or outrigger practice or whatever the fuck. They said I ate too much mayo and that it was bad for me and I thought, If you guys only knew.

Later, halfway through a Steven Seagal movie, someone telephoned and I promised I'd be in the Porter's Pub tomorrow at nine a.m. and wrote it down on a Post-it and stuck it to my forehead. It seemed like a good idea, in sync with my current humor of bluesy self-pity to which only Tom Waits could give some credibility. Tight-lipped Seagal beat up on fools, and I swear to God one of the extras looked directly into the camera.

In the morning garbage trucks I thought Serbs were advancing up Dwight Street with tanks. The Post-it said: "Porter's Pub @ 9—be there!!!" and I got up to obey my own handwriting, ill-remembering everything. There was a red hair in the sink. I hurried out. Everything in my room was the stuff she'd given me. I brought my wallet with me because it was mine.

A morning walk, out of North Park and into Hillcrest, with painfully tightened calves. I slowed down. There was a guy shaving in the driver's seat of a PT Cruiser at the stoplight on the corner of Park and University and it hit me that I lived in America. It hadn't happened in a while. Someone honked and I gestured wildly.

A derelict Santa Claus was sprawled on his back on the concrete bed of flowers in front of Pick Up Sticks with a chunk of his late dinner as if carefully woven into his impressive beard. Next to a crumpled beer can, twisted out of habit into a colorful misfortune cookie, his hand laid tough and creased with wrinkles of something harsher than time and blacker than the dirt under his fingernails. For some reason I imagined a watch on his wrist.

There was a cloud of bees by the Scripps hospital parking lot, and they can smell your fear, so I crossed the street. A fat man walked out of Carl's Junior with a shake and I warned him about the bees. He proceeded, paying me no mind, the daredevil.

At the shuttle stop everyone was Asian.

The doors hissed open and my man Robert put the shuttle in park. People poured out. "How you doing?" he asked without betraying his style, the way I thought only a black man can. I sat all the way in the back. Some Barbie with a pierced navel tried to bring on a Styrofoam cup.

"Can't let you bring that on board," Robert said.

"But it's empty."

"Read the sign."

"But there's no trash can outside."

"I don't care."

She stood there with one fancy shoe on board and the other one on the curb, but he waited her out. She tossed the cup over her shoulder and climbed in, tsk-tsking her outrage. We got moving to jazz. There was still some latte in the cup. I saw it spilling out onto the pavement.

Eavesdropped on a conversation in front of me until the girl said "whatever floats your boat," which is what Beloved used to say all the time, and then it was like it was *her* sitting there, flirting with the guy, and I made a hell of an effort to care about the palmy scenery. Tons of redheads on the road too.

On campus, hard nipples through white tops and crusty eyes and running up and down Library Walk with blue books. I watched all this on fast-forward, gloating because I was done for the quarter—aced everything. I took a shortcut through the grove. Something invisible ran through eucalyptus leaves, making a lot of noise; I couldn't see what it was. Eucalypti are poisonous and nothing grows under them. There was a guy in Bosnia who in the wartime shortage of tobacco smoked oleander by mistake, his last mistake.

But there was Alan Wilson in front of Porter's with a greasy bandana on, baggy shorts, and sneakers on bare feet, sitting on a basketball.

"What's up, Monk-a?" He knew I hated when he called me that. He never explained it either, this verbal tic of his, this obnoxious little nickname. We were in a scene together earlier in the quarter. At rehearsals he would just start singing "Izzy the monk-a fish" over and over when he was bored. It used to drive me up the wall because it stuck. "Let's booze up!" he said.

"They don't open till eleven."

"Don't worry about that."

He had a buddy working there, and we sat in the back slurping down Old Guardians, and he thanked me for letting him stay on my couch next week. I was unaware of what he was referring to but kept my tongue behind my teeth and sucked down the beer kindly provided by him. Apparently, I'd agreed to this last night. Ahh, what the fuck, I thought. It was only for a couple of days.

Buddy brought another pitcher and the sun was just starting to poke out through the June gloom. They were pissed that the Lakers beat the Kings in Game 7 and I told them that NorCal hella sucked. They made fun of my accent and called me a commie fuck.

Another redhead passed the window, and another, and another, and fuck me if the whole world wasn't turning freckled and pale. I tried to mindpush her lingering specter out through the back doors, heard again the blistering words that had singed me. One, two, three gulps and the Old Guardian did its job.

Then Buddy had to open and Alan had an exam so I went to see the other half of my acting class perform their final scenes, applauded too loud, laughed too loud, generally overdid everything.

Afterward we all decided to hit Rock Bottom, the teacher and all. I met up with Alan and he drove me there in his truck. All his possessions were in the back, tied together under a tarp. There were at least three pairs of basketball shoes behind my seat and the air smelled like feet.

"How did you do?" I asked him.

"Two more to go," he said. I felt like a square, watching him wing his finals, envious of his lack of care for any good outcome.

He played this country song on tape and sang along, displaying emotions I'd never before seen on that face. Said it was for his Singing for Actors final. I detected stronger ties between him and the tune.

Rock Bottom was full and the first two vodka tonics were like rag water until I tipped the bartender five bucks and then they adopted the taste of lighter fluid, which was a good sign. My peers stuffed themselves with hot wings and salt-and-pepper calamari rings and artichoke-spinach dip and listened to the teacher talk about "the business" and what to expect. None of us will ever get a job, I thought, and spotted a redhead across by the pool tables and asked Alan to switch seats with me.

"What's up with you, Monk-a?" he asked, rather genuinely. I knocked back my lighter fluid.

The group slowly eroded and it was just Alan, Jose, and me around Jose's nachos and my barely touched sixth V-tonic (the first two were throwaways) that I couldn't even think of touching for now. The screen above the bar was green with golf and I bitched about Honeybee, which reminded Alan to call his girlfriend in Spain. Jose was a silent bastard from Guatemala with an aura of a Latin lover extraordinaire who never had a problem in the broken-heart department and even if he did, he was silent about it, and cool and mysterious, and even now I can't fucking shut up.

Alan came back and blabbed about his girlfriend with a mixture of dejection and hopefulness that was eerie. For the second time I thought him a closet country lover. Details of a long-distance relationship with a punk-rock chick.

"How do you do it?" I asked.

"Distance makes the heart grow fonder, Monk-a."

Jose scoffed. That last "Monk-a" went through me like a welding spark through a soft-toed shoe and I felt like swinging.

"Fuck off! You fucked Amber's roommate at Jackie's last week . . . and that Moroccan dancer at Ditko's way back . . . and that's only the ones I know of I'm sure . . . so don't tell me about . . . fucking . . . heart."

"I didn't fuck them."

"Fuck off!"

"We kissed and she gave me a hand job."

And in the middle of it I had to hurl. I ran through a shifting corridor to a restroom and deposited the first batch of Jose's nachos and liquor into a trash can and then hugged the urinal for the rest. When I came out, the corridor was shifting no more and I was neither that drunk nor that mad; it was amazing.

We moved to the patio so Alan could smoke and Jose left and everything was fine. I was hungry now so I ordered a four-cheese pizza because I needed something solid in me. Alan explained they had broken up before she left for a year with a possibility of reattachment if the coals were still burning. I apologized. He called me Monk-a again and I told him to quit.

The fucker started us again on brewskies and tricked me into going on a diatribe on avant-garde theater and once I started on the subject I couldn't stop and he dozed through half of it and I didn't care one bit because for a change I wasn't thinking of Honeybee. Soon we were buzzing again and he came up with an idea, scribbled it on a napkin, and slid it over to me, slaloming in between the wet rings our beer mugs left on the surface of the table. On the napkin it said:

ALAN & MONKA'S AVANT-GARDE THEATER PROJECT #1
Order of business:

1. Find a venue
2. Find a single spectator and convince him/her to come
3. Perform something off the top of the head (total bullshit)
4. Swarm around the spectator asking him/her if they liked it

As I was trying to make sense out of this, he said we should go up to the Theater Building and do this immediately. He said that his eyes were drunk but his hands weren't. He wanted to drive up. No way, I decided, but went.

"Your truck smells like shit," I told him. He drove up the hill with a window down, bellowing that song.

Nothing was being loaded or unloaded so we parked in the zone, right next to a dumpster, and went in to see if the GH157 theater space was open. We peeked through the back to see there was a performance going on. It was an invited dress rehearsal for an undergrad Page to Stage show and they were treating it like an opening night, there were like twelve audience members in there. Alan's parade was shat upon and we went to Studio D next door and dribbled his basketball until someone came in and told us to stop because there was a show going on. We broke into a prop closet and fucked around with the props.

"Dude, we should walk through their play," he said.

"No, man . . ."

"Dude, just find something to cover your face with and we'll just walk across the stage like we're part of it."

I felt insane but giddy too. There was an orange and white traffic cone and I put it over my head. I wrapped myself in a blanket and picked up a broom. He stripped down to tighty-whities and I made him a ninja mask out of a T-shirt.

We crossed the hall. A stagehand carrying a nightstand with a phone screwed to it performed a classic double take. The other one, the one with a potted palm tree, actually froze, her mouth agape. We passed them calmly and went backstage.

The show was in a transitional phase; they were setting up for the next one-act. "Cat Scratch Fever" was playing and Alan and I went on, did a little spur-of-the-moment dance, and left. Everyone was confused because we were ahead of our time.

Afterward, it was basketball with two freshmen under the sun. We were shirts. They were trendy pierced nipples. I was alcohol sweat and I didn't care and everything I tossed was going in. I wished I could play like that when I was sober. Then Alan took over. I was there only to get the ball inbound. My heart was zooming and my brain was pumping and Honeybee was there under the basket and I threw the ball too hard every time.

He drove us home drunk, singing his stupid song as I scanned the 5 South for Honeybee's red Dodge Avenger, which was one car in ten. Well, not really, but it seemed it. In my Spanish-style home I cooked some mushrooms and onions because Alan was vegetarian and we ate it with the leftover rice from takeout the day before. I was tired with drinking. Everything below my knees was slush.

"We'll get you laid," he said.

I didn't want to go but he wanted to meet up with someone so I went. Lancers on Adams had Waits, the Pixies, and the Pogues on tap, and I turned festive, drinking girlie drinks. I just ordered fluorescent colors and a Mexican bartender was a speedy gatherer of spirits.

Alan's someone never showed. He went silent. A barstool over, a short blonde kept smiling at me and making self-deprecating jokes concerning her looks and I shriveled away, not knowing what to do. Not my scene, I told myself, put my hand in pocket to give off the appearance of leisure, and found Honeybee in the lint there. But Alan effortlessly jumped right on, telling her she was full of it, that she was sexy, and soon we were in her apartment literally across the street smoking bowls.

From the patio we watched two white people fight outside the bar at closing, and stumble over curbs, and yell fighting mantras no screenwriter could manage, and try to run each other over with a Cadillac or something big like that. Alan promised he would drive us home when his swoon turned to buzz and I went to find some reading material to take a shit in this lime bathroom and discovered a collection of *Calvin and Hobbes* in the river of literary self-help, the one with a two-headed snowman on the cover. I got myself to reading.

But when I got out of the bathroom, the front door was locked and the patio was empty and I panicked, thinking *Twilight Zone* shit, and the blonde came out in a nightie with puppy eyes and Alan was in her bed without a shirt on, so I knew he wouldn't drive and got her to open the door.

"You guys have fun," I said, and plunged into the town with wailing sirens and wives that shrieked and androgynous creatures with Ralphs paper bags for shoes that threw kisses in my direction. It's quite puzzling how many redheads one can encounter on the route from Adams to Park to University to Mississippi to Dwight at four-thirty in the morning.

The next day I decided to slow down, that it was pure luck my grades didn't suffer, that this was my fucking life, that next quarter I should really commit. I buried myself into my theater major, took Business of Acting, and was told that I epitomized a goober, that the way I looked, I could maybe play a foreign exchange student on *That '90s Show*. In Art of Auditioning, I was taught that you never show up for an audition in costume.

The Theater Department was casting undergraduates for bit characters in four plays for their annual New Play Festival. One of the plays was
looking for a Homeless Man. I took a page of sides and went home to
memorize them. The day of the audition I dug up an old navy trench coat
and blotched it with peanut butter, put on a pair of ripped Levi's I dragged
through a mud puddle under the fig tree in front of the Spanish-style, stuck
a yard-long wooden slat through my jeans leg and into my sock (to give
myself a real-looking limp), used a phone cord for a belt, dirtied my face by
sticking two fingers into my car's exhaust and smearing it dramatically like
commandos on TV, put on a Pac-Man baseball cap way too small for the
crow's nest that was my head back then, and drove my ass up to the campus.
Five minutes before being called in, I slipped into the restroom and downed
the jam jar of vodka I'd brought with me. When I walked into the rehearsal
space chewing at my lower lip, whirring with madness, it was obvious to me,
to the playwright, to the director, to God Itself, that I was Homeless Man.

"Name?" the director asked, with a real click in her throat.

"The air-people are coming and they gonna kill us all with their air-
machines," I said.

The director left the box empty, hovering the ballpoint over her notes as
I launched into the lines. The ball at the tip of that pen never rolled, never
made a point on that paper, for three and a half minutes.

Hours later, the moment I heard I got the part, I stumbled into the Art
of Auditioning teacher's office hours in all of my hobo-chic glory to chide
her that everything she'd taught me was wrong.

"See," she said, smiling, shaking her thespian head, "even when you do
stand your ground and take a chance, you can't help being a *goober*. I had
you pegged. And don't you tell anybody what you got away with neither!
Jesus, this is a school still. You're sweatin' booze, Izzy!"

Month and a half later, during the tech rehearsals, I was outside on a
break and in costume, over by the faux Stonehenge across the way from
the Dance Studio, when I felt someone approach me from the left, and by
the strangeness inside my chest, by the way my breath waned and then re-
deployed, I knew it was her. Honeybee, my Beloved, materialized in front
of me, kind of looking down at her shoes. I had fingerless gloves on like a
real NYC hobo, and my character's beanie cost more than my own.

"You finally went shopping, I see," she said, and my soul grabbed for her. Like that, Honeybee came back to me, disillusioned apparently with hive life. The home I built for her in me was taken care of, still on the grid, utilities current. My home in her was also viable. She moved into the Spanish-style and we eased ourselves into each other once again.

Year later, I got a spot in a Theater Design course taught by a legend in the field, an Old World impresario notorious for making American students cry by dismissing their efforts as "shit," a word pronounced with such finality in his Romanian brogue that it patently crushed many a syrupy dream. He liked my production concept of Beckett's *Godot*, which imagined the world inhabited by humans as God's fourth-grade school diorama that earned it a B, was saved for posterity, but essentially abandoned to the caverns of a massive, shambolic garage in the sky.

The final we had to do was fully creative and I decided to make a short video.

A Day in the Life of Homeless Man

In the dark, "The Return of Jackie and Judy" by the Ramones, but performed by Tom Waits, roars. Camera scuttles out from under a pillow in the shamanic rhythm of Waits's rhythm section, goes down to the whorls of sheets on the bed, barely brushes them, then backs off to find another objective, a bulbless sconce with a moth gibbeting on a string of web, then back out, meeting doorjamb, telephone, side of an aquarium, and the television with a candle on it, in this fashion—all along taping "our" progression from a bedroom to a hallway to a living room to the kitchen of the Spanish-style little house in San Diego. It all looks like demented footage done by a spastic, sputtering drone, commandeered from who knows where by a tech journeyman who's never before operated a joystick.

In the breakfast nook it encounters an ashtray with keys in it and a pencil mug with a protruding American flag, propping itself over the lowly pens and pencils. Still in rhythm, the camera goes for a make-out session with the flag, then retreats, sticks its beak into the ashtray, going down to a key chain with a Bosnian wartime flag on it, then fucks away from it too. For three seconds it hovers, breaking the beat of the song, holding both flags in frame.

When it starts again, it's dancing no more. It descends in whirling fury and pecks at the colors of the flags, America, America, Bosnia, America, Bosnia, Bosnia, America, Bosnia, A, B, B, B, A, A, BABAABBAABABBBAAAB . . . We can hear the camera hit the actual objects—deafening thuds when the microphone connects— until it all comes to an abrupt rest, and we're left looking toward the perfectly framed kitchen.

Tom Waits wails, though nothing stirs the tight beige cabinets. It's a small kitchen with a midmost butcher block, a fridge to the right fended with shards of magnetic poetry, a sink to the left fended by a magnet-stuck range of knives above it. Beyond the block, the canopy of the air/smell intake contraption suggests the stove is right below it.

A nightmarish face moseys into view from the fridge side, swallowing the kitchen with its close-up. Its glossy, fat black makeup around the eyes clashes with the caked-on, crackled white of the cheeks, making eyes and teeth of the face yellow in the light. When the creature gawps, its face is still. When it leers, the paint flakes off into dust.

The creature beckons us into the kitchen, slips behind the butcher block. It waves, insistent. The drone elevates gingerly, inches in after it. The creature takes a cast-iron off the range and drops it on the wooden block. It starts to gag and curb, curb and gag, till a chicken egg plunks out of its mouth. On the egg, in black Sharpie, it's written:

YOUR NAME HERE

The creature is near cream-dream with exaltation. Its gloved hands crack the egg into the cast-iron, where it sizzles into splutter. It's like an anti-drug commercial, then cut.

Sudden daytime, and I wake up on that same pillow from the dream sequence, realize that Honeybee is taping me with a camcorder, sing-saying: "Wake up, sleepyhead, time to go to work."

I throw a throw pillow in her general direction, hitting the camera, prompting a cut.

I'm brushing my teeth when I realize she's back at it, taping through a slit in the door. "Come on, now!" I say like I'm angry, but curve my lips to show her I'm really not. I open a container of black clown paint and one of white, stick some fingers in the first, some in the second, and smear the mess on my face.

"I don't have time to make breakfast now," she says, and turns past the aquarium and deeper into the living room, shutting off the camcorder.

I've turned on the camera, grabbed a banana from the bowl on the butcher block, when I hear her honking. I dash out on the patio, shut the door, go past the fig tree and out the low gate. She's business-clad in her new Ford Focus, going: "C'mon, I'm gonna be late!" I point the camera at her face as I open the car door. "Don't shoot *me*," she says, no acting. I swing the camcorder on the neighborhood.

NPR is on the radio, reporting from India. Mumbai's background honks and toots, horn blasts and backup beeps, disagree with the chill glide down Mississippi Street in perfect California weather and no traffic. Past the Albertsons we make a left on University.

"Where do you want me to drop you off today?" she says.

There's an overpass on the corner of Park and I spot a loose shopping cart with my camera, overturned among some orange pylons.

"Up there," I say, pointing. She slows down, veers right, and drives up the mesa to the top.

"Here's good," I say. She stops the car and we touch lips, so my makeup doesn't ruin hers.

"Have fun at work," she says, then takes off.

"You too."

I place the camcorder on the bottom rack of the shopping cart, where the bulky items go, make sure it's aimed back at me, my nightmare face, my ripped jeans, my telephone-cord belt, my arms in a navy blue trench coat. I brandish the banana and eat it like an ape, looking around, waiting for the whir of my madness. With upper teeth I scrub my soul patch.

"All systems are go," I say, and plunge into the neighborhood.

As I push on, the camcorder pogo-dances, catching slices of sky and spikes of white sun, blurs of green and arbitrary details of the buildings, all non-sense but for the slog of my legs moving through the real world made jittery only by my presence, the state I'm in. Through the cart's clatter I deliver potsherds of monologues in Bosnian that make sense only given the circumstances: *"Kad sam bio nishta, bio sam svashta . . . A kad sam post'o ovo, bio sam samo ovo . . . K'o da nisam nishta . . . Al' opet sam neshta, a k'o da i nisam . . . Al' svi smo neshto . . . A k'o da i nismo nishta . . . Svashta . . ."*

Through the bars of a static shopping cart, I shunt into frame to wave to a jet in the sky, in the cactus garden in Balboa Park. Giddy but silent, I caper and jig, really wanting to be noticed by the faraway passengers. Waving intently. To the side, an old Latino man in a fedora looks on.

Erbes Road looks spastic as I plummet down it, the eye of the camera now facing forward. Dry scrubland coming to a wall of eucalypti.

"Amerika i Engleska," I sing with pomp and circumstance, doing a Bosnian Tom Waits, *"bice zemlja proleterska!,"* when a police siren burps and then aborts, with pomp and consequence.

I park the cart against the curb, and as it hits, the camcorder flips on its side, framing a dry shrub and the eucalyptus grove beyond. Wind against the microphone murders the hum of traffic on Florida.

"What's going on, guy?" a manly voice, off-screen.

"Nothing," my voice, all cracked. "Just shooting a video."

"Why don't you go ahead and take a seat on that curb for me."

Sunlit insects like tracers against the browns on the screen. A mild gust sounds like an explosion.

"Cross your legs."

"I can't, I have a . . . piece of wood in my pants."

"You pitchin' a tent?"

"No . . . it's a costume."

"You have any ID on you, guy?"

The branches of the brush barely rouse but, again, the sound of it . . . Like fuckin' King Lear.

Cut to dusk, behind Albertsons. My face in the frame but I'm looking elsewhere. I drink from a tall can. I look right at you, my eyes like oarlocks.

"Maybe," I say.

"Maybe not," I reply.

Cut and I walk up to the Spanish-style via Dwight Street and I can hear somebody playing *"Fikreta"* on an acoustic guitar. I flip open the mailbox but someone was there before me. I go through the front gate and up to the door. I try the knob but it's locked. I knock. The music doesn't stop. I ring the bell. I fucking drive my fucking palm into the fucking pebbled glass and the music still doesn't stop.

I swish through my roommates' plants and poke my camera through the living room window. In the green light of the aquarium my Honeybee is reading a cooking magazine, her feet neatly folded under her. And over there, on the love seat, there *I* am, strumming, singing:

Fikreta,
mi tresnje iznijela
a ja se sjetim nekog filma o pticama.
Kada je ptici
u losoj formi drug
tada ni ona
ne leti na jug.

It was a popular song in the old-old country by the Sarajevan band called Zabranjeno Pušenje: "Fikreta, she / brings some cherries out for me / and I remember a nature film about some birds. / When a bird's / partner is in a bad form / she then doesn't either / fly all the way down south."

From outside, I keep my camera on myself playing my guitar inside my living room. With the squeeze of my fingers, I zoom in on my face until its shapes and colors devolve into pixels, then fade to black. Acoustic guitar continues as the closing quote fades in in white cursive:

"The perceiver and the object perceived cannot be one and the same."

The quote fades too.

THE END fades in, then fades out as well.

The music doesn't fade but comes to a natural end. The black of the screen is alive with silent possibility, before the static brings "us" back to "our" regular lives, to "our" thoughts already in progress.

In the spring quarter of my second year at UCSD I was becoming dangerously eligible to graduate with honors, while Honeybee still had another two whole years of studies left. By that time, she and I were together-together; she was expecting a ring within the year. We were living a great little life within our means, sharing the Spanish-style with another couple, going to school, cooking together, hosting amazing, eclectic parties, traveling, going to plays, concerts. We drank every day, like all of our peers, me way more than most because I was suddenly petrified going into the real world with a theater degree. How was I thinking of providing for a family? Was I out of my mind?

Grad school became the only option. My university adviser was suggesting I take my GREs if I wanted to get in, thought me a shoo-in because of my grades and academic prowess. I bought into the hype and did like she told me, but when the time came, like a moron, I sent my application to only one school, UCLA—my top choice. Honeybee expected us to make our home in SoCal to be close to her family and wishfully believed I would get in too. But it was the thin envelope that came in the mail and I lost my mind.

She was on a trip somewhere and so were our housemates, and I spent an entire night failing at trying to drink myself to sleep. I played *The Phantom of the Opera* for the fish in the living room and bummed from room to room, opening doors, cabinets, touching objects, testing if they were real, found a whole turkey in the fridge. The Albertsons down the street had a deal and you got a free bird if you spent more than eighty bucks and I took the bird out, rubbed it down with butter and exfoliated it with coarse salt, stuffed it with fork-pierced lemons and put it in the oven on 450, had me a Thanksgiving breakfast by dawn, stuffed myself semi-sober, then made four giant sandwiches with the leftovers, left a note, packed the sandwiches and a handle of vodka into a backpack, and walked from North Park all the way downtown to Union Station, purchased a ticket to San Francisco, and got on the Amtrak train.

Around L.A. I came to my senses and got off, switched to a Metrolink line and headed north into the burbs, disembarked in Moorpark, and called my old roommate Eric from a pay phone to come and pick my drunk ass up. I spent two days with him and his pregnant wife in our old apartment in the Shade. The place looked different now, neater and with a brand-new blue couch instead of our old monstrosity. I was docile, full of tears and beans in turn, and Eric ministered to me like a father would, cracking familiar jokes, playing perfect music for every one of my moods no matter how fast or often they switched.

"You're having an identity crisis," he said. "If I was you, I'd figure out a way to stay in school. You're really good at it. Why don't you get a minor, stay another year?"

"Can I do that?"

"Can the pope shit in the woods?"

"What would I study?"

"Shit, if they didn't want you for playwriting, try learning something else. Give yourself time to breathe."

8.

My next home—during the grad school years at Irvine while I also taught English there three times a week—was in Los Angeles, Silver Lake to be precise, right where Micheltorena Street T-bones Sunset, in an apartment building that used to be owned by Gary Cooper, where he would stash his non-Hollywood and on the verge of Hollywood *friends*—the untouchables. How fitting.

The place itself was great, though, with hardwood floors, a mock fireplace, a Murphy bed in the living room wall, and a little backyard we could access if we jumped out the window. We were newly married by then with two cats, having lived a year or so with my in-laws, and Honeybee was exuberant about having a place of her own to decorate. She repainted all the walls to fit her sensibilities but I was adamant about choosing the color in at least one room, her pick. After our stint *living with parents,* I was in need of outward expression as well. Honeybee gave up the long hallway running the length of the apartment and I painted it a delicious primary green, the ceiling too—the Green Mile, I named it.

The neighborhood was old-school, haunted by broken phantoms of mortals who absconded their pain-filled before-lives and flocked to Tinseltown to become, to emerge, only to end up settling, staying hidden. And *settling* is another term for pain management, which is easier to manage with a dream, drink, dope. Though corporeally long gone, their initial dreams and potentials, their savvies and grit, their modes of surviving the pain of life, remained behind and still pulsed right over the hot asphalt, ready to latch on to any susceptible soul in transit. And if these boozy dreams can latch on to people, people can latch on to boozy dreams too, especially refugees, who already know all about dissociation and seeing your life as if it's happening to another.

It was here that I became a phantom, unrecognizable to myself, so dependent on booze that when I caught myself drinking in the mirror, I'd admonish myself, say, *What are you doing?* and the *you* in the mirror would just laugh and point to a bottle in *my* hand, and I'd clock myself swigging another swallow of fire, flipping the other guy off, watching him hatefully reciprocate.

One afternoon in the heartbreak of a sunbeam through the window, I had a moment of clarity, and when she returned from work—she was tired, I could see, and some bottles clinked against one another in the Trader Joe's bag when she set it down on the floor—I took her beautiful freckled hand and led her with tears in my eyes the length of the Green Mile and into our bedroom. She was ashen, perturbed. I knelt by the wrought-iron bed and dragged out the flat clothes-storage bag where she had previously "retired" my youthful clothes—my well-worn and well-loved punk (Dead Milkmen) and joke T-shirts (I heart picture of a beaver) and snuggles, holey favorite hoodies and emotional-value items she had promised to one day help me make into a quilt of our youth—and I showed her my stash. There were two bottles of bargain red wine, preopened and recorked, and three cans of Olde English.

"Malt liquor." She grimaced. "Gah!"

But there were deeper, unutterable-to-me, thoughts that percolated behind her brow.

I was broken and shaking, kneeling there silly in front of the mighty NOW, on the precipice of where choices become destiny, waiting for something: absolution, cure, guidance, kick in the head. My conscience was ratting out my ego by exposing my secret to another, to a loved one. I was saying, *I don't know how to get out of this, I don't see a way out of this, babe, I think I'm an alcoholic.*

Honeybee, she held on to my shoulder, squeezing. The silence was grief. Next to the hamper, far under the curtain, a pair of her underwear in military camouflage pattern with pink frill peered at me with fearful trepidation.

"How do you know?" she said.

And when I said nothing, when I just kept saying nothing, almost to herself, she said: "Does this mean that I would have to stop too?"

Within a week I was back at it.

And how do you know you're an alcoholic?

You know you're an alcoholic when you can't remember to call your mother in Bosnia—who awaits it like the sun—and you can't remember the idea you had just last night, the idea that would fix your book, but you remember that your father-in-law will be out of town for a couple of days, and that your mother-in-law works mornings, and that your car needs an oil change, and that you have one of those coupons to redeem, three oil changes at regular price get the fourth one half off, at that place near where the in-laws live, and they never lock their house, and that you have to return your father-in-law's suit that you've borrowed for a benefit and failed to dry-clean for weeks now.

You know you're an alcoholic when you remember all these things just so you can justify to your wife why you need to drive all the way to Thousand Oaks for an oil change, since there's not a drop of booze in the apartment, and she's in charge of paying credit card bills because you take care of the rent, and you don't want her to know, although you know she knows but doesn't say anything because her mother was an alcoholic for parts of her life, and she's afraid it might be hereditary and that she also might have to face the music one day and quit.

You know you're an alcoholic when you'd rather drive to Thousand Oaks, get stuck in traffic on 101, listen to *East of Eden* on tape, finally pull up in front of your in-laws' house around ten a.m., get in through the front door they never lock, leave the suit with your note on their bed, then go to their liquor cabinet and pour a little bit of every kind of clear alcohol they have in there into a water bottle and hide it in your backpack. You raid the garage fridge and take two English beers and a Japanese one for good measure, take a good gulp out of every open bottle of white, go to the sunroom and scoop up a big handful of coins from a box of change into a Ziploc bag, and rush out to the car. When you'd rather do all that than sit and work on your book, or take a shower with your wife, or play with the cats—yeah, you know you're an alcoholic.

You know you're an alcoholic when, tipsy, you drive to get an oil change, then back to Los Angeles, walk up what used to be Gary Cooper's stairs, get into your apartment and drink the English beers right away then start hitting the water bottle and are done with it before she gets home and brings three big fancy beers from the store, makes a dip, and reads about photography as you play your guitar, until she goes to bed and you take out the change from the backpack, count it on the coffee table, and wonder what all can you get for $11.79 down at the corner store on Sunset, tomorrow morning after she goes to work.

Tomorrow, around one o'clock, when the words are not enough to repel the whir of madness anymore, you go get that bag of coins, arrange them on the futon: two bucks in nickels, three in dimes, six in quarters, and the rest in whatever, step into your slip-ons, put a Lakers jersey on, and walk down to the corner store, pick up a seven-dollar bottle of white and four pints of Olde English (one buck each), say hello to a schnauzer belonging to the Mexican girl hiding herself behind her Miller Lite in front of the flower/lingerie shop, go back home, put the wine to chill, and drink the malt liquors, slowly, maintaining a bearable level of madness.

You'll take your first shower in six days, shave, and do the dishes before she comes home with a can of crab and two bottles of wine, press her into the wall with hanging pots, and make out with her until your eyes start to vibrate with dilation. Honeybee'll make some crab cakes and you'll make some slaw, and you'll watch some old *Daily Shows* on the computer, drink wine, and go to bed to read because it's that time of the month, and a ghetto bird will wake you both at two a.m. and you'll find both of your books face down on the comforter, amid kitties.

You'll struggle to fall asleep. *There's something grand about being nothing,* Fat Mike from NOFX will scream in your mind's ear, *there's something lame about being grand.* You'll get up and creep to the kitchen to finish a bottle and then sit there reeling in front of the screen.

9.

Fast-forward to now.

You moved to Oregon with her.

Apartment one in Portland, then a rental house on Fifty-Third, then another apartment, then—finally—*a house of our own,* though in your dipsomaniac's mind none of the four domiciles ever registered as home. Mere act of trying to picture them individually is impossible. They refuse to appear other than as an amalgam. The effort is an exercise in erecting a shoddy ruin atop the eerie basement of the house on Fifty-Third, utilizing the wooden beams of the house you owned, the walls and windows of the one-bedroom on Lovejoy and the glorious inglenook of the apartment number two—all materials instrumental, in one way or another, throughout the years, in hiding the bottles.

Dipsomania, that vampiric alcoholism, affords the sufferer a magical power of continuously sensing the entropy, being able to touch a brand-new door, for example, and in its very novelty, in that smooth factory patina, sense—know—that the door is already kaput.

"Maybe we should go to couples counseling," you said.

"That ship has sailed," she said.

She left for a Women in IT conference in Boston, sad-eyed and sans ring. You dropped her off at the Delta terminal at the butt-crack of dawn, got a peck on the lips, a stiffish hug.

"Be good," she said, hoping, though she doubted you even could, ever could.

"I will," you said through tears, knowing you wouldn't.

You wonder whether she would have filed for divorce if, instead of PTSD and alcoholism, your diagnosis had been diabetes or cancer, if your maladies were visible, measurable, if they didn't have to be communicated by words, if they didn't have to be *believed* to be true.

The last rainy night in the house, before you're to move into the Prius, hobbled by a heartfelt gout, fostered by American malt, having been pickled in the steady diet of American art that celebrates (though people to whom martyrdom is a four-letter word would say *romanticizes*) being a misfit, you know how a permanent tattoo can become transient, how WINONA FOREVER actually was WINO FOREVER first.

Through the sweats, through the shudders, you will couch-swim in and out of *Cheers* projected on the basement wall—different episodes of the show spliced by gummy, alcoholic slumber into a jagged narrative no sane person could trek—all night. You'll feel your blood scraping your vessels, thinning out their piping at every switchback curve. In the high window-wells, silhouettes of fern leaves will head-bang their coiled heads under the assaults of the rain. Norm will take a swig of beer on the wall. Canned laughter will sound exactly as delicious as the rain.

SIDE A(MERICA)

Dear Billy Ginger-Muff Burr,

So, I detected a lot of . . . judgment on your part when, two Mondays ago, you went off on punk rockers like it's *our* fuckin' fault you inherited a cloud of punky neon-orange pubes. *Jeysus!* what a rant!

Granted, there's something slightly lame, iconoclastically speaking, something straightforwardly unpunk to have to maintain a high-maintenance hairdo in order *to be yourself so hard.* I'll give you that. But the amount of disdain you showed in that short little segment for *my* people made me positively inconsolable, especially since your spandex-wearing, high-screaming, tease-haired '80's heroes (who all look like horror video game characters now) took that *statement* to another level of cocky glitz, don'tchathink?! I wrote a letter to my sweet mother back in Bosnia about you, I was so upset. I said: Oh, Mommy, this mean redheaded comedian was critical of my choices to dye my hair orange back in college and it hurt my feelings so! and made me cry bitter tears! She wrote that I should write you another intentionally overwrought and verbose letter, knowing that you get all tripped up reading it out loud.

I hope it's obvious I'm just failing at busting chops the way you bust chops, despite stealing your own words and rhythms, *appropriating your culture, man!* just like I did by dyeing my Mohawk back in the day. But *here's an olive branch* (now that you don't drink anymore), my ex-wife's recipe for a cocktail. *Go fuck yourself* ☺.

She's a fellow redhead, by the way, reclaiming this common insult.

The Fire-Crotch

1.5 measures of vanilla vodka

1 measure of lemonade

0.5 measures of grenadine

(or just enough to create a suggestive red triangle at the bottom
   of a martini glass)

1 measure of Bacardi 151, optional

(floated atop and set aflame)

P.S. I hear you, Bill; I hear your silence loud and clear.

This is not me bitching about it either. Not hearing back from you
is the perfect response for what I'm trying to do, what this exercise
(exorcise) does for me and my life's work. So, thank you, or the
Universe, or whatever runs this ecstatic algorithm we're all part of.
Whether you read my letter and/or dismissed it, or whether it's
sitting in your blocked mail and I'm truly only in communication
with myself, it's all . . . just perfect. I got no other option but to
believe that. Or, put more positively, I know one hundred percent
that it's a kindness that I'm really bestowing upon myself (I'm the
one who wrote everything and pressed *send,* and will again; I'm the
one who received it all too, and read it, and will again, tinkering).
So, yes, here We are, Me and You, at it again. I'm writing this for
You as if you're not Me. I'm writing this for Me, not knowing if
You are or if You are not reading this. It is a magical stretch of
inner space and time. Please, try to let go of what you think order
is and don't worry that first person is second, or third, that plural is
singular, that fiction is true, that truth is multivalent. Don't worry
where these words—no, these utterances—are coming from either.
We're all inside Here, talking and listening. Feeling.

But, just in case you're really reading, that's enough of that
kind of crazy for this missive. If at any time this creeps you out,
please tell me, and I will fuck off and stop hitting *send.* In the
meantime, in the absence of your cease-and-desist, on I go with

my original endeavor. Your punk-rocker rant is a perfect lead-in to this first chapter on side A, especially because—in one of the earlier episodes from 2012—you had responded to someone from my neck of the woods giving you shit for not performing in the Balkans, by admitting you don't know much about what happened with the breakup of Yugoslavia and expressed vague interest to know more. Here's way more than you bargained for.

Slouching Toward Pichka Materina

Two Bosnian-born Brits wait at a pedestrian crossing.

A man across the street from them bounds right into traffic, causing havoc.
Brakes squeal, horns scream, motorists raise bloody hell. The man somehow
makes it across alive, not without a certain clownish, apologetic charm.

"How much you bet he's one of ours?" the first Brit says to the other in
Bosnian. She giggles, shaking her head.

"Excuse me, sir," the first Brit asks the clown in English, "but where are
you from?"

"Iz pichke materine,"* the man says in Bosnian.

Both Brits burst into laughter.

The man's eyes widen.

"Just like the two of you," he adds in English. "Just like everyone."

*Pichka Materina = *Mother's Cunt*

—WITNESSED IN LONDON, UK, CIRCA 2005

"We're not here to answer cuntish questions."

—GUY DEBORD

"In America you vatch television; in Soviet Russia the television vatches you."

—YAKOV SMIRNOFF

0.1

We made it through what passed as childhood in Yugoslavia in the '80s
and into the gaucheness and ungainliness of adolescence just as our coun-

try was sent back into its mother's cunt. It happened in the early '90s. You probably saw some of it, spun this way or that, on your TV.

You and your *fucking* TV!

We loved you, though, still do, your cheery, mollifying sitcoms in which the TV set laughs at its own jokes, and your prescribed, moralistic dramas, the abridged binary worldview of good guys and bad guys, your representations of human conflict that can be summed up with the sentence: *You lied to me!* as if lying hasn't been the only reasonable evolutionary response to what we vaguely like to call "reality," your cultural exports that made the complex, fucked-up lives we in Yugoslavia both witnessed and lived feel easier to take, so much so that when we, the TZ PUNX (Tuzla punks), got pinched for, say, breaking into a newspaper kiosk to steal porn and cigarettes, we were so young and primed by your worldview that we actually believed we had rights, like you have in the States, and demanded said rights from the obtuse meat slabs that were Tuzla's cops—*kerovi*—who leered and kneed us in the ribs and, using our Mohawks and long hair, guided our skulls into various durable surfaces, bloodsplit our ears by pulling off our earrings, and full-on stole our stolen Doc Martens and leather jackets.

We really wanted to be like you. If you asked us TZ PUNX in the early '90s, we would have happily hung the Stars-and-stripes off of every Soviet-style balcony in our town. Shit, we would have tattooed them on our foreheads. Not because your stars and stripes are beautiful, not by a long shot, but because it would piss off our parents and grandparents and the other miserable commie and old and nuevo-nationalist fucks in charge of everything in our lives.

And yes, we sometimes made fun of some of your punks because they were "raging" against guitar solos that were too long in the '70s. Kudos for that noble effort and all but, with all due respect, suck it a little. Your Natives and your Blacks were way more punk than any of your so-called All-Americans. *Death,* baby! *Bad Brains,* baby! Right?

But let's stay on topic, shall we?

Mother's cunt, or *pichka materina,* as we say, is where the so-called Yugoslavs used to send a lot of things and people, rhetorically, on a daily basis. It was the national pastime. A footballer kicks a ball into a post instead of the goal; send him to his mother's cunt. A plate of *chevapi* slips out of hand onto the pine-needle-covered ground at some May Day celebration in butt-fuck Pozarnica; send it to its mother's cunt. A D string breaks in the middle of a *sevdalinka* in the early-morning hours of a party when only the true *raja*—only the cool, essential members of the party—are still up (read: true alcoholics with a built-up tolerance); *e nek se goni u pichku materinu.*

We could easily have said that "war sent our country to hell" and made more sense here, but we're not in the business of sugarcoating shit for you. It was back into its mother's cunt that it was sent, back into the uterus, back into the place where its pieces were first put together and made into a whole, and back there it was backward unmade. The so-called Yugoslavs shoved it way up there and unmade it so well that we, their children, awakened without a homeland.

We belonged nowhere, so we formed our own tribe, chose our own markings and names, our own rituals and sounds. We wrote our own story. Good riddance, beloved homeland; you can go fuck yourself now.

We emancipated ourselves with glue sniffing and laughter in the face of our parents' grave, fear-soaked talking-tos. Igor the Punk from Titova Street, who wore a giant encircled *A* on his T-shirt and who broke the communal light switches in buildings' vestibules with his forehead as soon as they were installed, and who one time, when his own father caught him red-handed with shards of cheap plastic at his feet, gave his father (he didn't know it was his father) a shiner in the darkness. He got his ass beat to a pulp, of course, but he kept on breaking the damn switches anyway, until somebody from the apartment-dwellers council thought to reinforce them in steel. Igor then started using a screwdriver on them, until his fed-up father sat him down and told him he had to stop or leave the house for good. Igor squatted on the living room rug and started to strain and grimace, as if in terrible pain. His father asked him what was going on.

"I'm trying real hard here to give a shit, Pops, but as you can see, no cigar!"

0.2

Before the war, we were kids who still somewhat respected grown-ups and gave a shit about getting together and playing games like football—sorry,

soccer. We would gather after school on the grass behind the boxy building called Furnace One, called that not on account of its incendiary little
apartments in the summertime, like everybody thinks, but because the area
on which our ward stood was in the time of the Austro-Hungarian Empire
known for distillation of local plum brandy using big furnaces. In our time,
it was considered a tough neighborhood.

Skojevska je oshtar greben,
dodjesh poshten, odesh jeben.

Or, "Skojevska Street is a sharp, gnarly ridge / you may come here all
honest but you'll leave here all fucked." This is an artless, unrhyming translation. You're welcome. (Also, the word *jeben*, or "fucked," used in this way
can be translated as both "to fuck," as in doing the fucking, and "being
fucked with," as in receiving whatever the fucker can unleash. Both are
powers.)

Once there on that patch of grass, we would divide ourselves into
cliques or teams, scream and kick soccer balls and each other's shins, get
kicked out of games for missing goals and pestered by resident drunkards.
There was this *birtija* called Snack Bar right around the corner, and the
lowlife inebriates who lived there would come out to take leaks right there
in full view of us children. The most insufferable of them, one Anto the
Hand—nicknamed that because he only had one—would always try to
play with us for a while, make a jackass of himself, and wouldn't leave us
alone until the soccer ball ended up in the river.

The river always claimed our balls.

River, however, is too generous a term for this stinky, pond-scummy
trickle of mostly sewage, forced by sun-bleached concrete embankments
into orderly flow through the town. Most of the time, after retrieving the
ball, all we had to worry about was wiping it on the grass to get rid of scum
and sludge and solids. But every once in a while, usually in spring, after a
snowmelt, this so-called river would become a monster.

One of us overzealous soccer-star wannabes would punt a mangy ball
too hard through a netless goal. The ball would bounce off the edge of the
embankment straight into the clayey, engorged river. We would all start
running downstream and the punter would sprint ahead of us, ahead of the
ball, climb down the sloping concrete to the water's edge, and try to recover

it with his extended leg or a stick. Often, if the ball caught a current down the middle of the river, the kids on the other side of it—attracted by all the hoopla—would throw helpful rocks, trying to nudge the ball within the punter's reach, often splashing him in the process with filth.

But sometimes it was the river that would reach up instead, nab the punter, suck him in, swallow him, and then tumble him downstream. The punter's best friend or older brother would run way ahead, climb down the embankment, and try to save his friend or brother in the same way their friend or brother tried to save the ball. Sometimes they would also get nabbed. Sometimes even grown-ups would get involved and some Good Samaritan—a firefighter on a day off or a soldier on leave—would jump in and save the boys or just one of them. And sometimes they too would succumb to the water's rush, leaving nobody whom we could later thank for saving our lives and/or blame for not saving our brothers'.

Skojevska je oshtar greben . . .

0.3

We were natives of our ward and newcomers and every mix and mutt in between: blue bloods and peasants, bruisers and cowards, lower- and middle-class latchkey kids. Our parents were teachers and miners, engineers and nurses, artists and lovable fuckups. Our parents were also drunkards and psychopaths, religious communists and secret nationalists, borderline personalities and depressives, but good enough eggs, we guessed.

The walls of our apartments were adorned with kitschy needlework and woolen tapestries, Arabic calligraphy and Orthodox and Catholic religious icons, portraits of Comrade Tito, or peeling yellowed wallpaper bubbling damply.

Once a year we piled into our families' sad Fiat sedans and endured pukey, serpentine excursions to the Adriatic seaside, stayed in our fathers' companies' trailers in Neum and Podgora, in Makarska and Bashko Polje and Orebich. We made friends with the locals, touched their boobies in the backs of theaters showing movies starring Steven Seagal and Eric Roberts, Bud Spencer and Terence Hill. We swam and fished *shparove* off the docks, pretended our pasty, peasantly parents were not our parents, and hoped that the Vespa guy with a cooler on the back would drive by the beach when our parents were still in the water and yell his customary *Pepsi-Cola, Mirinda, pivo!* so we could rush to him, beg him to sell us a beer.

In the winters—nothing. We didn't have money to go anywhere in the winters. We just stomached the cold and the snow and the Tuzla salt mines' briny industrial slush on the roads. We sniffled and sighed, dug our hands into our pockets of Spitfire and Levi's jackets, pined over girls who thought nothing of us. We went to crowded student clubs, sweated and swore, peacocked and thought that things could only get better or worse. We moshed to new American punk rockers and old American and British ones, watched as some of us who slipped on beer-soaked tile got kicked and punched in the mosh pits by peasants who came to underground clubs not because of music and strobe lights or to show off in front of punky girls but to anonymously kick fallen bodies when they were down on the ground.

In your movies, your male teenagers lose their virginity under the bleachers, or in the backs of gas hogs parked on dusty vistas in the middle of the night, or in dorms and Motel 6 rooms. In our neck of the woods your no-good cousin sits you down just as the first peach fuzz of mustache darkens your upper lip and plops hard-core German pornography in your lap and starts teaching you how to finger pussy. You ask him, *What does it feel like to be with a girl?* and he sends you to get him a jar of honey from the pantry, leaves the jar out in the blazing sun for a while, then calls you over, takes you by the wrist, and dips your forefinger into the honey to the second knuckle, and pulls it out. You scrutinize how the hollow in the honey closes as your finger tingles with warmth and newness. *See how it closes?* the no-good cousin asks, and you nod because you do. *That's how it feels.*

He also says, *Don't be a fool. All of your friends are gonna go around falling in love like greenhorns, getting their hearts broken by, like, four pretty-faced girls in the school. Fuck that. You have to go for the ugly ones. That's where the pussy is. You gotta blanket the market.*

Your twenty-five-year-old no-good cousin, who never finished high school and got a trucking route at sixteen, who lived in his parents' attic with his new bride—an unwed mother of two (one of whom was his)—whom he mercilessly squeezed and groped in front of children and elders alike (to the sallow woman's shame and chagrin), he, the no-good cousin, he promises the sixteen-year-old you he's gonna get you some this month, then plucks you off the street one day in his hearse (a side gig of his) with a cadaver in the back and takes you to the shores of the slightly toxic waters of Lake Modrac, where he introduces you to a woman who looks like the mother of the sallow woman he cohabitates with, pushes you into the woman's bedroom, and leaves the door ajar, turns on the TV in the living room. He watches a local derby between Sloboda and Chelik, narrating the action, as the woman who could be your mother opens up her robe and tells you to get in.

Malo vas je, malo vas je, pi!-chki!-tze!, your cousin, a soccer hooligan, chants from the living room as the dead man sweats in his penultimate hovel outside.

The prostitute puts your ear to her heart and rubs your head until the proximity of boobs gets you hard and then tells you how to go about it. You're in the incendiary honey jar for three seconds tops and then she's wiping herself with a kitchen towel, gracelessly.

Coming from a repressed culture and still confused about the birds and the bees, about love and sex, marriage and sex, you ask the woman for her hand in marriage—it's the least you can do, you think. She laughs and laughs and can't stop laughing. She beats the sheets on her side of the bed with her fists, and breadcrumbs, pen caps, and a pair of glasses bounce up into the air.

She informs you that it's not necessary to marry her to fuck her, that any time you procure a bottle of Vecchia and a ride, you're more than welcome.

You're confused and exhausted, disappointed and heady.

U pichku materinu! yells your no-good cousin at the TV. *Chelik just fuckin' equalized!*

0.4

We had city cousins who deigned to talk to us only—*preko kurca*—when they came over as part of the package to family parties, hosted by our parents, to drink our best *shljiva* and eat our *mezeta,* and who later acted like they didn't know us on the street, scraped the clouds with their haughty noses as soon as our eyes collided in the crowd. They wore Levi's with tucked-in polo shirts, aviator sunglasses and goatees, and other such horseshit.

Our demented country cousins, in turn, with their boxy LEGO dos and woolen trench coats, would give us a choice of spiderweb-sealed black galoshes from musty Siporex sheds that looked like serial killers' secret lairs. They would pick rusty hatchets and screwdrivers off the walls and stick them in the inside pockets, saying *perfect for the discotheque.* They would take us up a mountain to another village, through fields and forests to a secret brothel/club in the woods, painted pastel pink and yellow and called Rainbow, of all things. No windows. One entrance/exit. A stage with a fat fuck behind a synthesizer, and a broken woman in a too-short skirt behind the mic pole, and a sweaty accordion player religiously focused on his finger work. Intermittently the power would go out, and when it came back, sixty percent of the Rainbow's population was mid-coitus.

City rats, country rats, both we called family; both we called blood.

Until the war, that is, that ultimate prophet that roars at full blast and wakes up even the most comatose of citizens by educating them, by goad and by blow, that the rules they played by all their lives are just agreements that can be changed at any time, that society and reality, safety and money, land and power, law and order, God and country, family, LOVE, for fuck's sake—yes, LOVE—that these are stories alone.

As the agreement that was Yugoslavia became void, our parents, the "Yugoslavs," showed their true colors. Some right off the bat packed us up and fucked off with us, with jewelry and photographs, to the various suddenly enemy countries, or neutral ones, or, in one case, Guam.

Of the ones who stayed, some hoarded what they had while others shared with their neighbors, believing that good deeds get repaid. Some carved their existence out of the nonexistence of others. Some joined the army and eroded with war years into skeletons or drunks, or grew oily and bonkers on nationalist slogans, screaming, *Them or us.*

English and German speakers weaseled into interpreter jobs for the UN, the UNHCR, and world-loving humanitarian organizations up the ass, feeding their kids, squirreling away funds. Award-winning sopranos lost their aria weight, put on miniskirts and fishnets to sing dubious turbo-folk lyrics atop tables and bars, stirring their hips in front of men who were prospects suddenly—rich bus drivers, insane enough to drive the semi-privileged out of the Serb siege for ten thousand deutsche marks a pop.

Those with houses in the country were chased into the crowded living rooms of their urban kin or, if connected, "given" the apartments of some Tuzla Serbs who snuck out of the city on the eve of the attack with their families, promised by the *Chetniks* (Serbian uber-nationalists) via snail mail that all they had to do was leave and wait out the quick and inevitable fall of Tuzla into Chetnik hands, risk-free. In some instances, there were parties the night before the attack, and some Tuzla Serbs, though their cars were already packed and in the parking lots, warned none of their "fellow Yugoslavs," none of their friends and neighbors, none of their family members of different ethnicity, of the impending war.

Those with places in the city rented their own master bedrooms to foreigners and spies, so that they themselves could sleep on chaise longues and pullouts, piling the children at the bases of weight-bearing walls away from windows. They crowded together with refugee country relatives in suffering silences, three or four per room, bottling up diligent human grievances. They proclaimed their cheapo stand-up pianos off-limits to their rural kin but shit-grinned and cooed when blue-bereted Martins and Olafs two-finger-"Chopstick"ed the keyboards accustomed to Debussy and Dvořák, drunk on swanky bourbon they never shared with their landladies and landlords.

As always, life was easier for those who didn't give a shit.

A kid we called Masni, idiot savant on the bucket drums and a bit of a talker, told us a story. Masni's urban aunt, who lived in a two-story house near a park, housed a UN officer lodger and had no qualms about getting this tiny, mustachioed Swede blackout drunk and selling him, then stealing from him, one and the same ring, numerous times, this rare thirteen-carat diamond ring she first bought off of Masni's desperate mother for a fifty-kilo bag of flour and five boxes of powdered milk—courtesy of UN cash—who had bought it for the ruble equivalent of three thousand deutsche marks in Volgograd in the late '80s in hopes that her son might one day propose to his future wife with it.

Masni's rural aunt, on the other hand, gave so much shit that if she eked out a two-onion harvest she would get on a rickety, banana-seated bicycle and ride the ten-kilometer road to Tuzla to deliver one of them to her sister's family so they could have a taste as well, then pedal off back into the night.

0.5

We kept our Mohawks and long hair and were livid at the high-tech beasts on the hills around our town for having it in them to rain shells on zitty, malnourished civilians in bad shoes and with worse attitude, who inhaled paint-thinner fumes and shady spirits and exhaled blackouts and hangovers, rage, and nonconformity, all of it just to feel a tiny bit sane for a moment.

When the war started, some of us knew it was coming and some of us didn't. Some of us shaved our 'hawks and were sent abroad, to America, Australia, Europe, by our parents. Those of us who didn't have family elsewhere just hunkered down, trying to learn the new rules, opposite from the old ones. Now thou *shall* kill, and if you don't, it's jail for thou or digging trenches on the front lines, a human shield. The older ones among us were picked up by military police, given old rifles, and marched up mountains in our punky sneakers.

The younger ones among us once heard cats fighting behind the "Trans Servis" on Skojevska Street days after all the blood had been washed off, and we were curious and a little drunk and went to investigate just to find an ass—not an ass as in donkey but a human ass in Levi's 501s, red tab and all, and no torso or legs, just an ass—and somebody said it's perfect to park a bike in and everybody laughed and one of us poked at it with a stick wanting to see if it belonged to a guy or a girl but then we stopped and walked away in silence, and the cats, they were nowhere to be found.

Skojevska je oshtar greben . . .

0.6

Some of us were hard-core punks and some of us were wannabes, and either way we wore TZ PUNX handwritten on our T-shirts and spray-painted it on Tuzla's walls. Tuzla was named after a Turkish word that has to do with salt, which is mined but also used to be extracted from an underground saltwater lake directly beneath the town. Displacing the liquid holding up the crust on which everything had been built created growing pockets of vacuum or air under the town and made its streets volatile, and every once in a while, throughout the years, we witnessed asphalt imploding on itself, big sinkholes opening up like hellmouths, devouring citizenry, cars, trees, whole houses.

Those of us who were eighteen and over claimed we were seventeen and under because we didn't want to get drafted, freaked out by the increasing number of funeral announcements stapled to tree trunks and glued to poster boards, black if you were from a Christian family, green if you were from a Muslim family, and baby blue if you were "other" or just too young to give a shit.

At the beginning of the war, it was easier. People had stockpiles of food and the waterworks were largely undamaged. We had what we called Bucket Parties in our apartments when our parents weren't around, and the price of admission was alcohol. Those of us who were relatively well off would raid our parents' liquor cabinets and bring in a bottle of Brazilian coconut liqueur from the back of it, arranging the other bottles to hide our thievery. Those of us who weren't would scrounge or steal a bottle of beer or risk our lives and siphon slivovitz from our drunkard fathers' secret stashes into empty mayo jars and add water to the five-gallon canisters until it looked like they were untouched. At the party we would pour all of it into a plastic bucket, mix it around, pour it into mugs and creamers, and drink until we vomited into sinks and potted geraniums.

The New Year's Eve of 1994, at Frida's party in Super Blok, all we had was one canister of moonshine we'd made out of sugar and rice and aromatic herbs to cover the almost fatty taste of its high-alcohol content. We poured some of it into a communal soup bowl and slurped it with dessert spoons because Igor the Punk had told us it was easier to get drunk that way. Most of us blacked out before ten p.m. and woke up in the new year parched, lips dehydrated and puckered like sphincters, shivering on foreign tile or parquetry.

At midnight Masni woke up from a nightmare and, finding himself in the complete darkness, hightailed out of there, bounced around the building's stairways to end up on the deserted Titova Street.

It was snowing. There'd been no cars in years, no traffic to speak of except UN vehicles in the mornings, because the UN could ship in their own gas. He lay in the middle of the street looking up at gunmetal skies, pockmarked facades, shrapnel-chipped balconies, snuffed-out streetlights, the geometry of straight lines of human existence cutting nature into portions.

When he felt the water permeating his clothes, he got up. There was a mysterious coil of human shit steaming at the entrance to Frida's vestibule, a heartfelt, punk-rock-style sarcastic little nugget of joy.

Happy New Year, it meant.

That winter we used to sit in Galerija on bulky wicker chairs, eight of us around two cups of tarlike coffee, shivering, with crackling empty bellies and all the time in the world, making fun of the waiter with a gap in his teeth and the soldier by the bar who was looped up on grape brandy and livid at the command and his life and the mad dynamics of war and us youths too young to carry Kalashnikovs and hallucinate about pussy in the trenches full of mud and bullet shells. The soldier had no dough to pay for his bill, so to clear the way to the exit he hard-brandished a hand grenade, which slipped out of his hand and haphazardly distributed some shrapnel, the tiniest piece of which ended up in Masni's back and made him wail like a widow as the café filled up with the savory musk of gunpowder.

0.7

Every night at Club Stelekt, trying to find girlfriends though nobody wanted to have anything to do with us, we finally said *fuck this,* figured we'd do our own thing. Masni's father was a pretty famous Bosnian musician who, as luck would have it, had gotten stuck touring in Austria when the war started and so Masni lived with just his mother and brother in a big house on the hill, overlooking the old town center, and he had his own room where his mother wouldn't venture, and an acoustic guitar, and there was a mini recording studio in the attic and a huge storage in the basement filled with exotic musical instruments, Balkan and Scottish bagpipes and Senegalese drums, tooth-missing pianos, and, to our delight, a wine cellar to end them all.

Masni started sneaking out bottles of wine every evening and we would go to a remote place in a park, or to the old zoo—where, nightly, a ravenous lioness roared and roared to be put out of her misery—or down the embankment of the smelly, exhausted Yala River to pour wine into our empty stomachs, puke, and give each other shit for puking, daydream about starting a punk band, dreaming MTV dreams.

It went like that until the cellar was empty.

By that time, we were older. Our Mohawks were overgrown because the winter was bitter. Igor the Punk showed us how to get high off of paint thinner, the only other bottled liquid in the basement, and we haunted the streets of our city under siege, huffed under bridges, atop garages, in graveyards and ancient ruins, got in fights with soccer hooligans and lost, got our noses broken and our mouths burst, and cackled in the faces of our assailants to be beat on some more. Wracked and out of our minds, we raided people's war gardens and ate scallions raw in handfuls straight out of the ground. We blacked out and woke up in uncanny places with jaundice, TB, crabs. We stopped throwing ourselves down onto the pavement during shellings, felt shrapnel murmur in our hair. We stole our fathers' handguns and fucked around with them in the park and once one of us got shot by chance in the head by another one of us, and we went high to the funeral, smelling chemically of glue, laughed during prayer and wept during the reception, and a bunch of times we got picked up in army raids and, if of age, got sent to the front lines, where we got our limbs torn off by anti-personnel mines, and shot in the bowels and in the eye and through the jaws.

The Stelekt shut down and our group eroded.

Electricity was available for four hours every four days and hard-core punks stayed at home, slept all day. There was nothing to drink any longer, nothing to huff, eat. There was no point in going out, saying the same

words, soberly staring at the same faces, knowing you had nothing in common with the souls staring out of them, nothing but misery, psychosis,
paranoia.

Sobriety led to depression, boredom, thoughts of suicide.

We were spent.

In America, teenage punks die from overdoses and cancer, or wrapping
their momma's Mazdas around suburban oak trees, drunk, or just going
out with a busy daddy's BANG, out of pain or out of spite.

We died from boredom and shrapnel, from sharply broken hearts, from
slugs. When *kerovi* raided Stelekt, Igor the Punk, the hardest one of us, a
berserker who would crush bricks with his forehead for giggles, made a
stand with both middle fingers out. The rifle butts, though, proved harder
than even him. He was shoved out to the front lines, where, scrambled up
on paint-thinner fumes and who knows what, he stumbled out the mud-
fucked trench that very night, sans the gun, and zombied miraculously
across the minefield to the enemy side, thinking, I'm a Serb too, where,
summarily, Serbian Chetniks had him shot, Serb or not.

Masni's father returned from Austria and brought with him the newest
Ramones album, *Mondo Bizarro,* and the news of their new tour. When
Frida, one of the two girl punks we knew, and some others went over to the
house to listen to it, the father barged into Masni's room, wild-eyed and
wild-haired, said hello to them, shook their hands, and said rather genuinely but sternly as fuck: *How's it going, comrades? Would you like something,
a glass of wine, perhaps?* And they thought: Uh-oh!

Maybe some paint thinner in a plastic bag? the man continued in the
same manner, and their extremities felt like sandbags. Masni said: *Don't
mess with them, Dad!* and the man started to laugh, shook his crow's-nest
head, called them knuckleheads, and eventually left the room.

The moment Frida realized the Ramones, on their last tour ever, were
gonna play in Dom Sportova Arena in Zagreb, a few hours across the front
lines by car, she became obsessed. *We have to go!* she said to us, but it was
the third year of the siege and there was no way of getting out if you were
male, if you were close enough to fighting age. *I can't believe you!* she said,
gnashing her teeth. *You're a pussy hair away from getting rocked by a mortar
on a daily basis and you sit here and quibble. This is your life!* she screamed,

your last chance to see them! This is why you survived these three years! Punks, my ass! she moaned, then mooned us. *Aunties, is more like it.*

There was no way that we would put our asses on the line and try to cross the inflamed border illegally just to go and see a band—even if we knew all their songs by heart—lest we get caught by *our* side and sent to dig trenches in the line of fire, or by *their* side and get our throats cut, end up nameless in group graves, entangled with other gutless, nameless cadavers, or maybe get lucky and survive just to get locked up in a concentration camp and suffer a piecemeal devolution from an individual into a thing. No way.

But when the time came, Frida squeezed out of the siege in the trunk of a fake cab and managed to get to Zagreb in time and saw the Ramones play live (she had pictures and a T-shirt to prove it) and snuck back into Tuzla a week later, unmolested, alive, really alive, more alive than the rest of us ever were.

0.8

We all shaved our Mohawks and got jobs, got married, had daughters, sons. We became nurses, teachers, mechanics, religious zealots, hated and lovable fuckups. Grown-ups.

Those of us who stayed talked shit about the diaspora. Those of us who ran away talked shit about the motherland. Those of us who stayed couldn't wait for those of us who ran away to come back in summertime, in our fancy or trendily shitty foreign garb, to put the cowards in their place, Bosnia-style.

Hey, doctor, who're you pretending to be; I knew you when you ate boogers!

Hey, writer, how much do you make an hour at Burger King?

Hey, award winner, who do you think you're gonna satisfy with that dick?

On the trips back home, those of us who ran away avoided the old friends and mosh-pit churners, considering them triggers for our New World depression, PTSD, alcoholism. We pitied the fools who didn't have it in them to leave the safety of their own culture and make something of themselves in a different one, duke it out in the *real* wild world. We thought them cowards and peasants, thought because we lived in rented apartments in Chicago or Portland and could go see famous punk bands live that we understood *real* life better.

Some of us abroad, we still sported Mohawks—if our jobs, wives, let us—and got knowing nods in supermarket lines from balding, yam-shaped ex-punks who, upon seeing our the Exploited T-shirts, always said something sad, like *That's old school.* Desiccated, old white bastards in *USS Nimitz* caps, humping reduced-priced, guaranteed-tender good ole U.S. red meat in grocery baskets, asked us what tribe we belonged to and we said *Bosnian,* watched their faces smirk. Some of us walked away then, while others iterated that if there was a race war in the U.S. we just wanted to signal to the white American baby boomers that we're not gonna be on their side, despite our shade of white skin.

We had pigheaded, romantic opposition to change, though we gave in in all the important ways. We abandoned our old culture, our language, our family, and used our whiteness to assimilate. We showered every day even though our mothers back in the old country—living on fixed, always-late pensions—waited until midnight once a week, usually on Sunday, for the cheap electricity rate to heat up the water in the boiler. We cringed as we scraped our leftovers into bins, but scrape we did, to fit in. The originally Muslim ones of us celebrated Christmas and Easter, said grace holding in-laws' hands, complimented the succulence of dry turkeys. We were asked to teach the rest something in our language, told in tipsy human confidence that they were happy we had made it *out of all that mess.* The jokers among us made sure to get on video our spouses' extended families, kids and grown-ups, in reindeer Christmas sweaters, repeating the phrase *We love sucking dick* in Bosnian and shared it secretly on Balkan social media outlets to likes and likes and likes and likes.

When you Americans find yourselves abroad and stumble into one another at a pub or a stony foreign national monument with your cameras cocked, you recognize yourselves as expats, and even when one of you is a degenerate ex–meth head from Vegas and the other an evangelist from Michigan, there's a moment when you come together in your basic americanness. You exchange some familiar *damn right*s and *you better believe it*s, bitch about no ice in the soda out here, wherever here is, disclose hidden finds of the foreign lands you're in, and *have a good one* each other in the end.

Us, we hide in plain view. Those of us who ran away, we'd kill to fit in, to not be noticed. We are poster-child immigrants. We make self-deprecating jokes, are first to shit on commies, terrorists, Eastern Europeans, you name it, putting you at ease. And even when at Safeway we come across a couple obviously at each other's throats, a baggy-eyed woman and a gray man hissing at her in our homeland's lilt, we don't make ourselves known to them. We don't know what side they were on.

Instead, we pick an avocado off a pile and pretend to squeeze it in a knowing way, part of us wondering if our mothers would die without ever trying this buttery alien egg. We pretend we are you in front of our expats because we want to survive.

We don't *crave salad* or *smoothie;* we don't *cleanse* or *abstain;* we eat what's in front of us. We don't say *I need to get a run in,* or *a sweat in,* or *a nap in;* we do what we can as long as there are no eyes watching us. We don't *listen to our bodies* but commandeer them into the closest hiding places. Our aspirations and dreams are not particular or American. In our messed-with minds, in our traumatic lives, any life would do.

0.9

Those of us who dragged ourselves into our forties will feel older than our age. The ones who stayed will watch the unfathomable new generations in our constantly and exponentially changing cities and times. We'll watch and wonder how they can run marathons and open restaurants and care about regional theater, take their kids to basketball camps, join amateur folklore groups, learn languages, and have open minds—when we feel like *this.*

We will feel disgusted by them and cheated by life, tuck ourselves into unchanged and familiar city nooks of yore, and sneer at the verve and the élan of the people who grew up after the war. We'll blame our anger problems, poverty, loveless and sexless marriages, and inability to get work or an erection on the people who dare to believe in the future, these perky, tent-pitching, millennial fucks. We'll watch them out of our hazy, blood-shot eyes at closing times and use puny pretexts to start some shit every time, head-butt a youngster in the mouth for smiling too hard, for wearing a cap, or for not wearing one.

Those of us who, abroad, were weaned from the bosom of the mother-land, we'll change our names, our Tomislavs into Toms, our Mehmeds into Mikes, our Miloshes into Milos. We'll respell and repronounce our sur-names for the sake of generic English speakers. We'll chop up our fused consonants and squeeze foreign vowels into their gaping wounds. We'll neuter our rolling *R*s, to us vowel sounds, to accommodate our new friends and neighbors. Over time, we'll even umlaut our simple vowels, make them ooze or singsong, so much so that when we go back for a visit, our relatives will call us fags.

But here's the thing.

Those of us who stayed and got married to people who went through the same things as us, we'll somehow stay married. Despite the shit of life, we and our spouses will reach some kind of equilibrium, see each other not just as partners but as fellow sufferers, survivors of life, and though our children will grow up hearing hissed midnight fights about money and screaming drag-outs full of Mom and Dad's mother's cunts, mornings will somehow take care of themselves, and tears and apologies will be expressed or hinted at, and *chimbur* on *sudzuka* or *maslanjak*, coffee and cigarettes, will respawn all the players into a new day, new game.

Those of us who left and who partnered with people who didn't go through what we went through, we, God bless us, we got fucked. Try to explain to an eighteen-year-old Nordic Lutheran from the suburbs of California—who grew up with cats—that a car-squashed feline on the side of an American freeway is not just a stuffed animal, no matter how much she wants it to be, no matter how much it sucks that it isn't, just like nine plastic-covered mounds by the bus station in front of your high school back in Tuzla weren't just mounds of dirt.

1.0

But who am I kidding? It's not all of us who feel like this, just me.

If all of us felt like this, there would be none of us Bosnians left in the world. But we're still alive and kicking, becoming Miss Australia, a MacArthur Fellow, an Oscar winner, a restaurant owner, a miner, a truck driver, a fisherman, a policewoman, a psychiatry nurse, a PE teacher, a painter, a lovable fuckup, a grandma, a West Point graduate, a database administrator, a pole dancer, a Swedish politician, an inventor of some doodad that helps arteries get rid of fatty plaque.

It's just me, it seems, just me.

Yo! Billy I-See-Red Burr,

Check this out: last week I broke my finger, the left fuck-you one. I broke it taking off a hoodie too fast, I shit you not. That old disregard for my body. Can't be seen being gentle with it lest the guys take notice and jeer, smear, beat down, ridicule, kill. I was in my tiny closet/office working on edits and didn't realize I was getting angry at my hoodie for making me hot. My phone rang in the bedroom. I launched out of the chair; it's a rare occasion for a guy getting a real phone call post-divorce. But that same instant I realized I was overheating and the hoodie, this nemesis hanger-on, had to come off immediately. I shoved my erect hand under my arm with such force that my finger just *gave up*. It didn't hurt either, but for the snap, the sound and the surprise of it. And a limp fingertip now, no mid-hand grip, Bill; no guitar for Izzy, every jar's safe as milk. *Mallet finger,* the doc called it over the video conference.

If you haven't noticed from my last missive, I got some anger issues myself, sir. Only I don't have a physical outlet that lets me yell about it at listeners twice a week through a speaker. I used to do theater until I was in my mid-twenties and I remember how good it felt to push some of that rage out of me by pretending I was someone else: running around and chewing up the set, wielding the shit out of the prop swords, booming my lines out into the nosebleeds—giving everything to the physicality of the characters I was playing. I was in my body, you know, getting sweaty for real, my heart rocking out so hard in my chest. Afterward, I felt balanced because I spent and transformed that inner turmoil, and in a positive or at least tolerable way. Then I realized I was a foreigner with a fucking theater degree about to get married and enter the workforce! I freaked out and switched to writing (they can't tell your accent on the page, was the rationale).

I fell out of touch with my body then, and all that anger and anguish and angst that had no vent just kept accruing in my head, swelling it up and leaching into my jaw, my gut, my diaphragm. Mine is a whiny, self-hating anger; I always end up hurting myself, taking it out on me. Fuckin' A! I don't know about you but my whole life, voices going: *You're crunching my hand; this is supposed to be a greeting. You brush your teeth too hard. You scrub your scalp too vigorously. Do you have to slam the car door so much? Stop popping your fingers like that; it's loud! When your sleep apnea machine mask gets entangled in your ponytail, the violence with which you rip it off your head, you'd be charged with assault if you took it off of anybody else that way. You throw yourself around like a rag doll, Izzy. A rag doll you hate. Calm your tits, buddy. You're scaring me, hon.* This, my whole adult life.

But hey. I just think of that guest spot on late-night TV when you slipped into your patented *female voice*, Bill, going: *But honey, where is this anger coming from? Hahahah.* Shit. Even now, two years after the divorce, I'm still fighting with her every morning, sometimes for three to four hours, and I can't even raise my voice above a stage whisper. Who am I keeping it down for, my betta fish? It's uncanny how it happens: I get up at the crack to write and in the few minutes it takes me to make a cup of coffee I start defending myself from a criticism from like 2007. Next thing I know, it's eleven a.m. and I'm repeating a perfect retort to an argument with my wife that ended a decade ago.

I think this next chapter will be more enjoyable to You because the book veers from that *voice of the generation* macro view of the war and truly zooms in on just one particular night in Bosnia, in one particular town, from the point of view of one particular TZ PUNK. Now, is it true? I'm in my fifth decade of life and I'm still abased by the dreams about it a couple of times a year, at least. That's all I'm going to say about that.

Oh, and this is one of my ex's favorites. Good luck on your Scandinavian tour and go fuck yourself! Don't eat yellow snow!

Izzy

Curfew

Everything was so familiar it hurt.

After every rehearsal, the same people would go to the same café and say the same words. I would tell the same gross jokes and get pushed playfully by the same grossed-out girls. Masni would employ the same tactics to scrounge the same kind of cigarettes and Boki would talk us under the same table about the same things and the same winter darkness would fall the same way over everything and the same stars would come out in the same artistic composition and bear witness, terribly, that everything was the same.

Two years of siege in Tuzla.

The worst was the realization that I knew which chair I was sitting on. If the chair was a person, I would have known its name, where it worked, the size of its nipples. I knew that if I dropped my hand down and grabbed the right hind leg, I would be able to recognize the two bumps right underneath the place where the wicker winding made it fatter and fancier; it was unbearable.

A sickness came over me. No, I became aware of a sickness that I had been suffering for two years now, a sickness where nothing ever hurt but where life energy ebbed anyway as if drained by a constant, unyielding fever. That sudden awareness felt like an organic panic of some kind, where pain was not in the flesh but in the mere idea of flesh, in its initial blueprint. My skin was a Ziploc bag, and both material and immaterial chunks of me were astir in the violent marinade of disgusting juices. I got up and fled. The same people might have said something different then. I didn't hear.

The town was ruptured. The streets were gray lunatics. Black-marketers sold cigarettes and cooking oil off collapsible tables. Drunken freedom fighters sang heartbreaking songs about Istanbul's yellow quinces. Bearded fathers rode derelict bicycles one-handedly, puffing out steam. Dogs meandered looking for food in the slush. Darkness was merciless, just like the familiarity of every thing. Mechanically, I was headed home.

But Hotel Tuzla still had electricity. Its tenants were foreign journalists, humanitarians, adventurers, and spies, the only people who still had money here. It shone like a solitary porch light in the night, turned on just to attract the insects away from the real party going on somewhere inside. Mesmerized and dumb, I had to go in.

Bodies stood around purposelessly like singed moths. The punks snarled at the soccer hooligans and the soccer hooligans snarled at the punks. Both groups posed and ogled the slowly circulating girls. Every now and then the hotel's personnel in cuntish maroon jackets told them to disperse if they had no business there. They would start as if to leave, drag their feet, milk their goodbyes, and eventually just stay. I knew almost every person in the place.

I felt like my body was a rental, feeling the leftovers of somebody else's pain, muscle aches but I haven't done shit. Somebody else was going to scream through me. I let my eyelids fall like covers over the sameness of the scene and the reception desk imploded into a busy universe of shifting colorful circles. Organic nausea.

"Hey, long time no see."

Elvis. Elementary school. Last name . . . Something with a T. He slammed a skinny kid's head against the radiator in the school locker room once. I stared at his face, fighting off the rising acid.

"How are you?" he asked.

"Better ones than me are getting buried."

He laughed and pulled me by the sleeve through the crowd. He was talking about something. I didn't hear. People said hi. I shook a couple of hands. Then we were in the bathrooms. The stench in there would have made a plant puke. The tiles were but urine and dirt. A neon light flickered something awful. He stopped at the edge of wetness, pulled out his dick, and pissed in the general direction of the urinals, the whole time telling me how he got to drink whiskey with his Swedish boss and what an awesome job he had.

"Good for you," I told him, and went to wash my face.

I turned the faucet and nothing but air came out like a wail through the pipes. In the mirror I looked like this guy I know and my skin broke out in goose bumps.

"You still get high?" He smirked.

Wow. Gossip traveled far. Not that I cared. The only thing that mattered was that he got my attention. "What do you got?"

He showed me three white pills with jagged edges. I felt elation and hated myself for it, but at least the nausea started to subside at the promise of a high.

"What is it?" I really had no idea.

"The fuck I know. Olaf and his general buddies were handing it to everyone at the party."

"What does it do?"

"I don't know, you tell me."

His face was severe with probing eyes, something out of this world. I snatched the pills and dry-swallowed all three, eyeing him with livid apathy. For the moment they were on my tongue they tasted sweet.

"Wow. Must be desperate."

"Fatalism is my defense mechanism," I said.

"Whatever, man."

We went back to the lobby, away from the stench and the guy in the mirror. Things started to seem different because I had a secret. I was awaiting effects, a gradual slouch if the pills were opiates, a surge of power if they were amphetamines, wavering of outlines if they were hallucinogens. Elvis gibber-jabbered and I heard nothing of it. His eyes were cruel, constantly on me, gleefully expecting to see the outcome of his experiment. I could sense he wanted me to explode, strip naked, rip holes in cavities with my erect, crazy fingers, chomp down on some eyeballs, scrotums, titties; that would have made him happy, to see me lose it. I knew his kind and so kept my cool, out of spite.

"How is it?"

I just looked at him like he was a thing and then looked away.

The police were frustrated with a punk over there under the stairs. He was being flippant yet his eyes were shifty with fright. I knew him. Avdo Shupak, they called him. There are two kinds of dogs, I guess, nippers and barkers. He was a barker. They zoomed down on him, their uniforms mismatched, like amateurs doing a play. Only their guns were no props.

"Where did you get those boots?" the bad cop said.

"They're my boots."

"That's not what I asked you."

They went back and forth like that, getting heated. As for the boots in question, they were Turkish army standard-issues, black with green patches of waterproof material on the sides. The good cop tried to defuse him, but his colleague soon foamed up at the mouth.

"There are soldiers up there in the mountain fighting for your stupid ass in fucking sneakers and dress shoes, freezing their asses off, and you, you little shit, here you are parading new army boots in a hotel."

"Fuck you, that's not my fault."

"No, fuck you! Take 'em off!"

"You can't do that."

"Did you hear what I said?"

Click-clack.

Shupak pleaded with the onlookers to help him. His eyes were fuming hot, his knees bouncy with fury on the verge of spillage. We stood around, useless like hat racks. He called us cunts as he unlaced, yelled that his mother was a judge, threw the boots against the ground, and walked into the black snow in white socks.

I liked the fact that something had finally happened, but was suspicious of the easiness with which everything returned to routine. An hour probably passed and all I did was stand there and hate Elvis. I was starting to believe those pills were just placebos.

"Anything yet?" he asked, and I sensed ridicule in the way he shifted weight to his skinnier leg. I tightened my lips and smiled, raising my chin. That was so I didn't have to punch him.

"That's very funny," I said, and stepped back.

"What?"

"Take out your contacts."

"What!"

From where I was standing, I became certain that, behind his mask, Elvis had green eyes. But he wasn't going to admit that and we both knew he wasn't, so I didn't push the issue. I just backed up a few more steps since I didn't trust my fists and said:

"I just want you to know that I know."

With that I backed out of the lobby, pointing to my eyes. Deal with that, fucker, I thought. I figured it was probably close to the curfew hour anyway. I hoped I was going to make it home on time.

Outside the world was suddenly fucked. The curbs were higher; it was like climbing up walls. Everything was far away. The row of white buildings in my neighborhood was shielding itself from me, evading me. At the rate I was approaching them, I was surely due to violate the curfew regulation and end up in jail overnight. So I started running. It had to be eleven already. I remembered Avdo Shupak and pitied him running through this shit in his white socks. Ahead, humanoid shadows crept up buildings. The cops, as if they waited for me. I heard them say so. Their guns protruded from their shoulders. Shit, it had to be eleven already. That was all there was to it. I couldn't afford going to jail.

I threw myself under the quadriplegic blue truck sitting there since the beginning of war. Then I crawled the length of a parking lot, from car to car to dumpster to car to car to car to the bushes in front of my building, where I remained for some time because the cops started talking again. They sounded like jungle birds and the jungle birds they sounded like were no night jungle birds. That's how I knew it was them. I was aware that if I'd ended up in jail, they would have taken me into a round room and told me that they would beat me until I found a corner to hide in. After that they would have taken me to an office where the guy in charge would have put his keys on the table and told me to pick them up just to slam my fingers with a baton every time I reached for them—leftover communist policing methods.

There was no way I was going to jail. My eyeballs started to freeze in their sockets and if I wanted to look left or right, I had to move my whole head. My spine was already frozen rigid. I rotated my wrists and ankles to be able to spring into the dark mouth of the building when the time came.

But they were standing right there behind a van, sharing a cigarette. One of them had Avdo Shupak's boots. Fuckers. The ice was beckoning me to capitulate. If I waited any longer it was going to grip me, so I got up and ran, through the frostbitten air, soundlessly, without looking, my upper body like a puppet on a stick.

In there I knew where the staircase was and sure enough there it was. I knew that there were seventeen stairs per floor. Were they after me? I couldn't hear. Just my blood. My thoughts.

1 ok ok ok
  2 ok just
    3 be calm
      4 ok
        5 they didn't
          6 see you
            7 ok
              8 so dark
                9 that's piss
                  10 ok ok
                    11 a few more
                      12 be calm
                        13 you're almost
                          14 there
                            15 fifteen
                              16 sixteen
                                17 OH MY GOD!

One of them grabbed me by the wrist and I swear to God shot me with some kind of stun gun, because a surge of electricity ripped through me like death and all the ice melted into sweat over everything and I bucked insanely in all directions, my heart pushing against my throat, bulging out, until I stumbled over some soft tissue in the dark, some warm tissue in the dark, which told me he was just a man, he was just a man, and I bucked again but now I bucked only in his direction, and punched, and kicked, and the grip on my wrist became weaker and weaker as I became stronger and stronger and finally there was nothing grabbing me to take me to jail; nothing was touching me except the hard granite floor against the soles of my Reeboks, against the wetness of my socks, against my flat feet.

The hamster woke me trying to bite through his cage or trying to shave off the excess front teeth, whatever. Shutters were down and so was my mood, I could tell right off the bat. The little arm was between II and III and the big arm between VI and VII, closer to VII. Donald Ducks sleepwalked all over me in their pj's. There were pale dots of light on the wall, sneaking through the minute openings in the plastic shutters, which told me it was after noon. I tried to move and grumbled with pain.

I felt like ten thousand tiny, greedy treasure hunters had jackhammered into my body, burrowed into every nook and cranny of my bones, sifted through all the blood, dug through the delicate gray mass singed at places with paint-thinner fumes and alcohol, found nothing worth anything, nothing that could even be salvaged for pennies, grew pissed off, and in turn demolished the place, defiled it with their tiny poisonous droppings and urine and left without bothering to lock up. I think I had a fever too.

Routine of personal hygiene in the dark. It was an effort to squeeze some tasteless toothpaste onto my toothbrush and walk into the kitchen. There was water in an orange plastic barrel with a little makeshift faucet my father duct-taped at the bottom.

My mother sat at the table, cubing potatoes into a red salad bowl. The radio was hooked up to a car battery on a piece of cardboard on the floor. A dashing male voice reported on the aggression in Bosnia and Herzegovina. I zombied to the sink.

"You cheated the dawn," she said.

"I have a fever," I said.

"Somebody tried to kill Mrs. Abdic from the first floor last night. They beat God out of her."

I was going for the faucet when my raw, bloody knuckles came into stark focus. The radio played a jingle. I didn't have anything to say, so I turned around and went back to bed, where I hoped to sleep like a slaughtered child.

Dear Ol' Freckles,

Thanks for another Thursday-Morning-Right-Before-Friday
Monday-Morning Podcast, for your diligent practice of turning
darkness into light, anger into hilarity, and for giving naturally
occurring fucked-up swirls of human thought over to the
community by way of story so they don't start swirling cells inside
the old liver, or pancreas, or brain, or lung. Or, God forbid, heart.
Thank you for that. That's the genius of having an outlet for the
shit that most of us just stomach. Oh yeah, stomach is another
place you don't want the anger in. Or shit. And I know it's not
enough just to have the outlet; you still have to do it, still have to
get up and do the work, *keep plowing on.* Thank you for being a
bald-headed muse. I'm tired today, and sad and lonely, but here I
come at you with my shit too.

Not all of the anger is private and straightforward; some of it a
man takes on from family, community, country. Sometimes I get
so sick of combating personal phantoms of my ex or my family
members or life's numerous randos who *did me wrong* and my
anger morphs and becomes a psychic hologram that I can move
around like an energy puppet and send into anybody I've ever
encountered. That's how some of my stories arise, how I get to a
deeper level of myself. I take my personal shit and then I invent a
person outside of me to take it on and live with it through myriad
scenario'd possibilities. Living a life of isolation affords that kind
of endeavor. For example, I remember this guy I saw in theater
once. In my mind I keep calling him a shepherd, because in Bosnia
that's a funny and mean way to refer to somebody who didn't
grow up in the city—and this guy was the epitome of it. I was in
this children's theater recital and we were for some reason allowed

to stay and watch a performance of the real adult professionals. The play was some comedy of errors: a husband was about to fake his death so that he could be with his mistress, and his wife was coming over to view the body the last time. The shepherd was in the same row as us, all the way in the back of the auditorium, and didn't seem to understand that what was happening onstage was not real. He just sat there grunting and murmuring out loud. So, when the husband jumps out of the coffin, nails it shut, and hides in the wings and his grieving wife makes a wailing entrance shedding bitter tears into an oversize handkerchief, the shepherd just starts yelling out, screaming, warning her she's being bamboozled. He then goes apeshit that she's not heeding his warnings, starts cursing her and her very soul backward in time down her fucking lineage. He got kicked out; I don't know what they did to him outside.

That's how this next chapter came to be. I put *my shit* into this random person I've only encountered once in my life and by the time the experiment ended, I watched this amalgam hold way more of my own soul than there was, for example, in the narrator of the previous chapter, despite the fact that the other one looked more like me and told his story in first person.

I don't know what it is, Bill, but after twenty years of assimilating, learning, and showing deference to the American culture, lovingly I might add, being relegated to solitude in an apartment that used to be a motel room makes a man ponder why he did all that work.

Hope you're well. Don't forget to go fuck yourself today, it's Thursday!

izzy

At the National Theatre

Everything goes out like a light—the light, the fancy cave of a room with it, the packed fancy people in it, the fancy people's prattle—everything. It's the darkness that shuts up the gentry. It's a signal, remote-controlled. You're no idiot. You know that it's the part of the fancy dance in a fancy place like this. Lights out means *It is time: please be polite and refrain from talking.* If you're not fancy, this signal is not a signal at all but an order. It means *Shut up, you fucking peasant, and listen to what we have to say to you; you might learn something, though we doubt that that's even possible.* You *are* a peasant but you're no idiot. You're no sheep. You won't be remote-controlled.

So you scoff, audibly. In the darkness, in the cave, it sounds like a short burst of a chain saw, though these people wouldn't know what a fucking chain saw sounds like. You grin. You're not going to let these foreign players come to your capital and tell you how to live your life. And you're not going to let the gentry, these fancy sons of bitches who fancy themselves cultured, represent *you* in front of the foreigners.

So you scoff, audibly. Somebody somewhere coughs at you, polite-like. A man. You turn to see which one but cannot discern him. For all intents and purposes, you're blind. You squint but it doesn't help. You bulge out your eyeballs and still nothing. You let it go, this time.

The darkness plods on. Time lollygags, uncomfortably. Every once in a while, there's rustling of clothes. Somebody scratches short nails against hairy skin, and you think, Beard or pubes? Fanciness is contingent on being seen by others; in the darkness they all scratch their itches the same way. You grin again.

"Maybe the power's out," you announce, causing the crowd to sigh and tsk-tsk in disgust. They are all embarrassed, some of them of you and others for you. That man coughs at you again, less politely but still anonymously. You look for him again. Your eyes are the size of tennis balls now but still toothless in the dark.

"Hey, cougher," you call out, to more stirring in that dark, "cough again and I'll collapse you!"

Somebody else, another man, shushes you.

"You shusher, let me hear you do it one more time, by God! Just one more time!"

Then everything is quiet. You grin in the dark. You scoff again to break the quiet but no one stirs, no one comments. Your grin falters. They are changing tack. They're ignoring you. They are trying to erase your voice, now, when voice is all there is.

You have an idea. You scoff again then immediately, in a fake falsetto, say: "Oh, some people's nerve!"

Some woman in front of you is caught off guard and laughs but is soon shamed into silence by somebody next to her. You feel a kinship.

"Thanks," you say in your regular voice, "you might be a human being after all."

Something whirs up front, whirs and squeaks. You perceive a ghost of a horizontal line ascending. The darkness beneath the line, the expanding darkness, is more pronounced than the shrinking darkness above it. The bottom darkness seems more dangerous, more alive. There's no doubt that there's something in there. What will come out?

The whirring stops. The silence that ensues is frightening. It's superior to you; it will outlive you. It seems to say: *You are not. I'm alive!* you want to scream but the silence doesn't allow it.

Then an image explodes into existence with an audible bang. It's not your ears that hear it, though; something else in you hears it in the silence. This image clangs into your mind, and out of the darkness and the silence—out of this space of possibility—something distinct is materialized: a sliver of a visible and finite world.

A dumpster. It's a heaping dumpster with its wheels broken, off over there to the left. And to the right a concrete wall with entangled vandal marks in different colors, in American, presumably. In the middle of the space a charred metal barrel, white smoke wafting out, two crates, a red one and a brown one, on either side of the barrel. Right behind it all a dirty-looking couch with its back to you, the stapled fabric on it ripped here and there, exposing the wooden skeleton. Everywhere, covering every possible square meter of the stage, there is foreign trash—foreign newspapers, foreign discarded cans (the closest of them has a picture of peas on it, but the word above it is not *grashak*), foreign maltreated patio furniture, foreign rubble. Only the rags could pass for Bosnian but you bet if you go up there and check they would say *Made in America* somewhere on them.

This is what's pissing you off now. They have so much money that they can afford to collect a bunch of genuine American garbage, package it nice and neat, put it on a plane, ship it across the world, unpack it, and scatter it all right here in front of you, right here in the fanciest room that your capital has to offer. And you're supposed to be cultured and clap your hands for this, stand up and clap your hands for garbage. Maybe send some little brat with a bunch of carnations down to those who scattered it.

You look through your coat pockets for some Bosnian garbage and find a knife and a bus ticket on the left side and a half a coil of potato pita wrapped in waxed paper on the right—the remnants of the five coils your tetchy wife sent you away with this morning. You stop to think about it. You failed to ration today. You spent all your cash. This is your last bit of food until you return home tomorrow. *Is it worth it?*

You look at that can with a picture of some peas on it. Something inside you shifts.

You wind up and throw the half coil of pita over six rows of gentry heads and onto the stage. It hits the floor right in front of the barrel, bounces into its side, bounces off, and, in the air over the brown crate, like magic, splits into two things. The first thing, the coil of pita, twirls through the air and lands into some rags on the right. The second, the waxy wrapping, levitates above the crate for a moment, floats down upon it, tumbles to its edge, hesitates there for another moment, then slides gingerly to the floor.

Silence. Or rather the sound of hundreds of people not daring to make a sound.

Then the rag heap, what you thought was a rag heap beneath the concrete wall, the rag heap onto which the pita landed, starts to move. The soiled fabric assumes the shape of a human figure. It moves again, turns, and sits up.

A black man. Your first.

He rubs his eyes, looks around, looks about him, smoothing out the folds of his blankets, picking up their corners, and looking underneath them, looking for something. He finds it then—your wife's potato pita. He smells it, looks around once more, looks up at the Gods, comically, smells it again, and then devours it.

Thunderclap of laughter.

You watch this with your mouth open. You're the only person in the place not laughing.

The black man finishes your pita, licks all five of his fingers, and, with his sordid, moth-eaten rags, delicately dabs the corners of his lips. And just as he again makes himself comfortable in his rag bed, to the residual chortles from the fancies, a wild, terrified man comes careening in from behind that wall, a white guy this time, pushing one of those shopping carts from American movies, his hair and beard all patchy, his holey trench coat tied around his waist with a telephone cord. He hobbles over on one stiff leg and yells and spasms in American, pointing to the back of the stage like a goddamned demon's after him, and the black man gets so angry he starts to cough, and it's the cough you've heard before, that labored, wet cough that your father coughed a month before they put him in the black dirt.

They yell American words back and forth. The black man coughs in the American garbage. The wild man produces an American bottle from his cart and they pass it back and forth, drinking. They say more American words. American, American, American. Back and forth. Like you're not even there.

"*De sad na nashem malo,*" you say out loud.

That woman up front laughs. You can see her shoulders, lit by the stage, rocking as she stifles it. Others grumble, hating how easy it is to pop them back into reality, begrudging having to reinvest themselves. They would rather stay there under the bridge, in the garbage, as long as it's American garbage. *What was that joke when the war started? Exchanging a house in Bosnia for a sidewalk in America. Call Jasna.*

The players, the foreigners, they keep at it. American, American, American.

"*Sa Gradachca bijele kule,*" you sing boomingly, your voice cracking, "*Zmaja od Bosne.*"

Grumble from the fancies. American from the garbage.

"*Sokolovi zakliktali . . .*"

A man next to you—a bespectacled man in a bashful sweater—looks at you, his mouth sickened, his eyes glassy with fear.

"What are you looking at?" you say. "Eyes up front!"

He turns away, his upper lip trembling a bit. You start the song anew, even more boomingly.

"Everybody now!" you yell, clamping the bashful sweater at the shoulder. Some of the fancy ladies behind you get up to leave. Somewhere in the back a door opens, and then a beam of light shines on you from the side. A man in the aisle asks you nicely to keep it down or leave.

"Who of you is gonna make me?" you say. "I paid my ticket!"

You stand up. You are two meters tall. A family tent could be made out of your coat. Your gnarly, knotted hands are ruddy and swollen, capable of crumbling things into powder. Willing too.

"He smells of booze," someone claims.

"I'll call the police," the beamer of light says.

"Police?" you hiss, and reach for him. "Whose side are you on?"

The usher's light beam carves senseless arabesques into the darkness; he retreats, stumbles, and falls on his ass. You scramble over the couple of now-empty seats and you get to him before he has time to scuttle away. You grab him by the throat. His windmill arms beat you about the face, his knees trying to find your groin somewhere right about your knee—a little fellow, this guy, but full of beans. You maneuver him like a mannequin this way and that. His toes barely reach the carpet.

Then the house lights come on. For a moment you're blinded, but as your vision adjusts, you feel them—their eyes. You feel them on the back of your head, burrowing into your skull. Still holding the usher—a bearded man in his fifties, you now see—you turn around and face the fancies. Some of them are still in their seats; others are clustered around the exits, ready to slip out if need be, these sheep that allow themselves to be distracted by garbage in order to forget the past.

It's clear to you now why you left your tetchy wife and your skinny children at home—why you took the last of your measly veteran's compensation and came down your mountain first on foot, then on a buggy, then in a back-loaded van, then in a bus, down into the valley to see the capital where forgetful fancies make decisions about your mountain, your wife, and your kids, your veteran's compensation, your modes of transportation. It's clear to you why you decided to splurge and come to the National Theatre and see the fancy foreign players, Americans, put on a fancy play about the fake downtrodden. It is clear to you.

"WHAT?" you roar. The usher quiets, petrifies in your hand. "Go on, call the police on me! *I'm* the one who colonized the world, who wiped out the Indians, fucked their lands! *I* incinerated the Japanese, napalmed the jungle people! It was *me* who sat on my ass and watched you on television as you, you stupid sheep, as you dug shrapnel out of your walls, out of your children, your fancy pets! It was *me* who watched it all on television and didn't move my dick to stop it! You want to be American and have a freedom of speech? Put *me* in jail for speaking my mind! I, who fought for you, lost a kidney for you, who make food you buy at your fancy farmers markets! Put *me* in jail!"

As you're saying it, even though your eyes are filled with tears, you know it's not true. You were a cook in the army; you fired your rifle three times in three years and even that into the air while drunk. Your kidney was taken out when you were twelve because of a tumor. You haven't plowed your field in years. You know it's not true or fair what you're saying—but it *could* be. They don't know who you are. You just have to say it prettily, provocatively, loudly. None of them will have any idea.

"Call the police on *me* when they are the ones who robbed you, who talk down to you, who sell you their garbage? Why don't they learn *your* language when they come to *your* country to tell *you* things? Why do you have to learn theirs?"

Somebody whistles from the stage—the wild man, the one with the cart, thumb and index finger in his mouth. He says something in American and some of the fancies laugh. He thumps his chest and waves you over, pointing with his chin at you, pointing with his finger at you, then at himself, then at you, then at himself. He stands there in the garbage with his chest out, arms spread.

You drop the usher and thunder down the aisle. As you move, you feel powerful, elated. In a single leap you're onstage, and the wild man kicks down the barrel and a bag of something falls out, billowing cool smoke that spreads around you, covering up the garbage with white. He takes off his trench coat and reveals a tight black T-shirt that accentuates his hardened, fancy abs. His face is dirty and his beard looks real enough, but when he snarls, his teeth are calcified white, cared for. Faker, you think, and go for his throat.

The next thing he's on your back, his arms wrapped around your neck, squeezing, his heels dug into the inside of your thighs. You can't throw him off. You turn around and around, you bend and buck—all for naught. Sparkles light up in the corners of your mind, and then you're on your knees, disturbing the white cloud clinging to the stage. You see the fancies clapping, and hear it too, but the image and the sound don't match. The edges of your vision slide into darkness, the darkness that claims more territory with each nanosecond until your consciousness is a speck of white in the black—burning white-hot in the middle of everything for another moment. Then it goes out like a light.

The first thing you see is some fuzzy brown fabric on the floor where you're lying, face down.

Where am I?

You feel hot. You hear people talking, but it's mumbled, like your father playing his religious radio in the basement. Your eyes wander the folds and furrows of the brown rags beneath you. There is a white label on what looks like a shirt. You squint to read what it says.

MADE IN CHINA

Your heart bangs and everything comes back to you.

Slowly, imperceptibly slowly, you reach into your coat pocket and take out your knife. Your heart is banging so hard that it seems to be lifting you off the stage. You move your head a little and hear somebody approach. You look up; it's the man who humiliated you. He's apologetic, reaches out a hand, and even though he's extending the right one you give him your left one. He gives you his left, takes yours, takes your elbow with his right—you're a big guy—and when he gets you to your knees you plunge the knife into his chest. You feel his fancy T-shirt give, then his skin; then your knife hits the bone barring the entrance to the squishy stuff inside him but you twist the blade and finagle it in between two ribs. You beam at him when you see his eyes pop out, no longer confident, no longer the eyes of a man who thumps himself on the chest. Then he collapses.

All of a sudden there are other people coming out of the darkness. The black man is there, looking wary, but the others have tools and wooden planks. They are yelling, angrily. There are too many of them.

What did I do?

This thought cripples you faster than the wild man did. Your breath escapes you and your knees wobble and your head swoons and you have to sit down, down on the ground. Put me in jail, you think. You think of your skinny children getting skinnier, your tetchy wife getting skinnier with them. You can feel the knife in your hand, its handle made of rosewood. You look over at the wild man bleeding in the garbage, the smoke already dissipating around him.

Crazy ideas swoosh to the forefront of your mind. You clutch your knife because crazy is scary. You look about at the Americans surrounding you. What will they do? And what they do is suddenly get down on one knee in unison, their fists, hammers, planks raised in the air. *Thump* go their knees against the wood.

"BOO!" go their mouths.

Circus music starts up from somewhere. The Americans crack up and help you stand. They make a line at the lip of the stage and prop you up in the middle. The audience stares at you in wonder. They seem more befuddled than you. Some of the Americans start to encourage them to applaud. It starts off timidly but turns into a roar. Soon everyone is laughing and clapping, the usher, the man in a bashful sweater, the woman up front.

Still discombobulated, you glance backward and see the wild man spring up to his feet like a gymnast. He jogs, beaming, to the front of the stage and puts his arm around your shoulders. When the audience sees him, the applause becomes deafening.

"Good job," he says to you in the clamor, and you understand what he says. "And now . . ." he says, and you know you're supposed to bow.

But you remember how the rain hurt your face and shoulders the day your father died in the backyard, where he told you to take him so he doesn't die in bed. You can still feel your pregnant wife's hand burning on your cheek from that day when the war was coming up the mountain and you had to send her and the kid to Tuzla not knowing if you'd ever see each other again. You remember how Damir, the younger one, who was born toward the end of the war, was given a banana for the first time and, not knowing what it was, bit into it without peeling it first and how you all laughed.

You bow with the others. As you do, you come face-to-gaping-mouth with that can of peas. Your gaze slips to your shoes, then to the shoes of the wild man next to you. Blood—*is it?*—trickles from under his pant leg and into an already sizable pool.

You all right yourselves up in unison. Americans raise their hands in the air. The wild man's legs wobble a bit, and you feel his hand become heavier on your shoulder, desperate. There's a real slit in the sopping T-shirt where you stabbed him. Liquid seeps out of the wound. Trembling, you look down at your hand but the knife in it, your rosewood-handled knife, is a fake.

Dear Billy Can't-See-His-Rosy-Nuts-from-His-Stomach Burr,

Guess what I did yesterday after hearing your newest gut-busting rant on fat-shaming! That's right, baby: I went and signed one of those shitty contracts to help bust my gut down! I told you I've been working on myself—not drinking, breakfasting on beet and apple shakes, taking baths, pissing into a toilet like a normal person—but boy, did I have to swallow some old feelings about exercise before I drove my ass to this totally thrownaway part of Salem, to a gym right between a Dollar Store and a fucking speakeasy, which should tell you all about the quality of this establishment. I actually had to go past a blathering, thumbs-up-giving derelict woman who used her oxygen tank to prop open the door to the boozer so that her hammered ass could smoke.

My ex was always on my ass about diet and exercise and I was always like, *Listen, I'm not running in place, I'm not climbing forever-stairs, and I am not lifting up chunks of metal just to put them down just to lift them back up again. Leave me alone. I went through war and hunger and I know that energy preservation is paramount for survival.* And she was like: *You're not surviving anymore; you're supposed to find a way to thrive.* I had this stock answer for it every time, something I nicked from a Van Damme movie, I think, and I was like: *If you want me to run, hang a raw piece of carne asada off the back of my ass and sic a Doberman after me, then I'll run!*

At first her eyes would just roll, she'd shake her head and leave me be, just to be back on me tomorrow. But over the years I'd noticed that her face would get really deflated and bunched, really hurt, like there was a deeper reason why she wanted me to do it. So, once we settled in our house in Portland, I tried to compromise;

I went to her and said: *How about this? How about I just walk everywhere within the three-mile radius, to the store, to the post office, to the farmers market, whatever. Give me a real task, like go get a jar of mustard, and I'll walk a mile to Safeway and back. That's a good little stroll, right?* She considered it and said okay, and I started doing that. But walking the streets of Northeast Portland alone, having all this time to think about it, I realized that pretending to need a jar of mustard is also a hack, just as dumb as running in place at the gym, that I was tricking myself either way. I hated being tricked, and I hated being told to change by someone who didn't go through what I'd gone through. I felt judged, felt secretly pressured to mold into someone my ex could love. The isolation of my errand-walking also served to make me stay in righteous anger and resentment longer and find a way to "reward" myself with poison. I became an expert in sneaking little cartons of wine with every purchase, on every errand, and drinking them right in public, in the middle of the day, even in a crowd. I had this sixth sense and knew when no one was looking at me and I'd just take a quick glance and pound a carton in five to six seconds.

Today's offering is the last piece of my writing my ex ever read, a long attempt at a chapter about my father's side of the family, even though I don't know anything about it. My father was a person who never shared any stories from his youth, any of his feelings, any lessons he learned. Everything was vague and secret with this bunch, very protective, and I was always on the outside, *a fat little Prcic,* one of my cousins once called me, and it stuck. Aside from some stick-figure sketches of my father's relatives that somehow passed as family lore, these people might as well have been invented by me; they are strangers and thus characters, just like that shepherd in my story who goes down the mountain and loses his shit at the National Theatre. I know their blood runs in my veins, though, and I figure I owe the readers a little bit of a background and family history even if it's only gleaned and dreamed up, intuited to help me heal, help me at least try to explain to myself where my attitude, my anger, my boozing all come from.

Hope this is not *triggering, man*. Hehehehe. There are some funny parts in the mix, I swear. Anyway, I'm all sore from the rowing machine. Somehow rowing in place, even sporting a mallet finger, doesn't bother me because, in my mind, I see myself slicing right into the swell off the Oregon coast and rowing fast-forward across the thick of the Pacific all the way to the Adriatic, up the crack of the foggy delta on my peninsula, up the Neretva River to the very heart of my old land. Not country, mind you; the land, Bill.

Yourself go fuck! Love, Izzy

P.S. My father is such a mystery to me. I had a dream last night of a rotary phone ringing, like in a David Lynch movie. And, in the dream, they woke me; they said it was my father on the other line. But he's been dead since 2010 so I thought them mistaken and I yelped *Mom!* even before I picked up the phone off the cradle. The voice coming from the other side was stretched out and unintelligible like often the voices of the dead are to us living. But it felt like a warning when I woke up. It felt strange.

Bosnian Dream

I

Musa Music came to America skinny and bemused, and bereft of former edge, fearlessness, and swag. Though his punk attitude had served him well back in Bosnia—it was *the thing* that had ensured his mental survival through that shitty, shitty war—his father had panicked him into abandoning it for "a better life" at the *gripe* age of seventeen. Well, *the promise* of a better life, really—an assurance uttered by his American uncle into a telephone in a suburb of Los Angeles and subsequently heard and believed by his Bosnian father in Tuzla. *Desperately believed,* because it was the night of the Tuzla Massacre, when fathers in Tuzla had nothing else to do but be open to entertain and believe in perfect-sounding plans for their kids.

On the first day of his new life, instead of marching through the crowds with gusto and stomping his feet because he'd gotten away, Musa Music pitter-pattered through the LAX corridors, virtually unnoticed and willfully so. He moved out of everyone's way, dragging himself along the walls and avoiding human eyeballs. Even when nature so urgently called, he felt guilty for occupying a stall, but had to finally relent and undertook a stealthy, silent shit in a noisy chockablock facility that a fuckin' ninja would have congratulated him on had one been in the vicinity. He then joined an exit-bound current of sapped, wrung-out fellow long-distance travelers who looked like they knew what they were doing there.

As he approached the throng of loving families waiting for wandering loving family members to appear—staring at his face for a moment, then almost snarling because his face was not that of a loved one's, then pinning their eyes on some other exhausted fucker—he actually shuddered. Sweat seeped out of him, dampening his clothes. He was being plopped right into his new refugee life and had to wait to be recognized by a virtual stranger. That was the plan his father had made for him: Musa was to land in Los Angeles on such-and-such flight and his uncle Bahrija would pick him up and take care of everything.

Musa had met Uncle Bahrija only twice prior to this, so the dude might as well have been a stranger. The first time Bahrija had come to Bosnia, Musa had been only six, and all Musa remembered was this overly eager smile of boxy, calcified teeth. Bahrija had brought him a way-too-big T-shirt from Disneyland, which, weirdly enough, had ended up becoming Musa's favorite article of clothing early in his punk years because a Chinese manufacturer had ironed on Mickey Mouse upside down—a perfectly punk mistake with a picture-perfect message to boot.

The second time, Musa had been fourteen, and Bahrija had come for a visit with his first wife, a woman who was originally from then-still-Yugoslavia but had pretended that she wasn't, pretended she didn't understand the simplest words like *maslanjak* and *rospija*. She'd brought forty pairs of women's shoes in a checked bag, all for her own use, and all the other women in Musa's family had rolled their eyes and tsk-tsk-tsked their indignation on the sly.

Now lightheaded, Musa moved through the crowd with his old-timer hand-me-down luggage, apologizing profusely even if his bags only came close to colliding with someone else's. He made it all the way to the sliding exit doors without being seen or loved or recognized at all and had to stop because the glass doors revealed Los Angeles: the cars were crawling and honking out there in the sun; big-assed policewomen were gesturing with vehemence; the taxis were yellow like in the real movies; and yet somehow real life also was going on out there, a brand-new life he knew nothing about.

Uncle Bahrija drove his white Lexus with one hand, resting the other on the cartoonish belt buckle, which was shaped like the state of California. From the passenger seat, Musa hung on his every word out of fear and politeness. Bahrija, enjoying the attention, pointed out things through the windshield and talked about them as if he owned or invented them. He appeared slack, laid-back. *Look at how chill we are here across the pond*, his pose said. *Look at how good we have it. Watch and learn how to be chill.* The radio wasn't on and the engine's downy drone made the interior sound antiseptic and dangerous, like the hallway of a Hollywood spaceship. The car windows blocked the traffic noise and showed the languid Pacific Ocean, those beaches, the PCH, northbound—the goddamn beginning of every B movie under the sun.

"Your aunt is home trying to cook for us," Bahrija said in Bosnian, then looked at Musa, sticking his tongue out. "Maybe we should stop at McDonald's first."

That overeager smile of his again, false again, nothing but exposed, expensively burnished bone.

Musa felt fear for his new American aunt—for himself—but he smiled as his uncle had, only yellower. He felt as if he had to. His father had told him his uncle said not to worry about a thing, that he, his father, was no longer Musa's father, that Bahrija was now his father, that things were going to be okay again. His father had said Musa owed his life to his uncle and that he'd better behave, better listen. Better obey.

"You better believe it." Bahrija said the phrase like a real American, almost without an accent at all.

THOUSAND OAKS, a sign said, WORLD'S LARGEST AUTO MALL.

"Buck, darling!"

The woman, in her mid-sixties, actually dashed into Bahrija's arms. Bahrija smiled a Bahrija smile and carefully took off a cowboy hat he'd put on for the short trip from his garage to his kitchen. He gave the woman an Old Hollywood kiss, and one of her legs bent at the knee as they touched.

Musa stood, bag in each hand, and smiled a shiteater, wondering how long it would take him to learn *his* role in all of this.

Dolores hugged him and gave him the tour of their tasteful two-bedroom house, speaking as if he were deaf.

"Perfect size for an old couple like Buck and me," she apologized, and hipped open the guest room door. Wooden masks gawked and growled

from all the walls, crucified, forever carved in a single emotion. An orna-
mented tall clay pot in the corner housed three exquisite-looking spears
and some loud umbrellas. Next to the pot was a framed photo of an elderly
white man in a safari hat, balancing atop a felled elephant. A clutch of
saturnine black men in attendance suffered him. An array of newly bought
toiletries for men stood at attention on the bed stand.

"This dresser is empty." She pulled open a drawer, then pointed at Musa's chest. "For you. You can just drop the bags in for now, because *soup's up!*"

She mock-opera-sang this last part and pushed her husband toward
the kitchen. Bahrija pointedly nodded to Musa: *See what I have to deal
with?*

"Uncle," Musa said in a subdued voice. "My father told me to call as
soon as I get in."

"Let's eat first, or she'll start . . . you know. Let's eat first."

The dinner table was set as for a king's visit: bowls inside plates, decre-
scendoing silverware, napkin origami, the works. Musa felt unworthy. An
olivewood salad bowl held liberally olive-oiled, unevenly sliced tomatoes
peppered here and there with cubes of white onion. A wicker basket of
olive bread was still steaming. Dolores served him a clear broth with large
chunks of tofu, clumps of wilted spinach, baby carrots, and halved corn on
a cob.

"We're going *vegetarian today,*" she sang.

Musa thought of his late mother serving thin wartime lentil soup day
after boring day, holding back her tears during these breakfasts, lunches,
dinners by some miracle of self-control and parental stoicism performed in
spite of the chaos of war. Life, by definition, ends, he thought. It's the show
of life that must go on. So he *smiled* his face. And he kept it in a smile.

"Looks great, sweetheart," Bahrija said, and winked at Musa, who
brought a spoonful to his ravenous mouth and swallowed.

"So?" Dolores kneaded the kitchen towel.

The broth was savorless, the kind of elixir the devil slips to kids to make
them think they hate vegetables. Try as he did, Musa failed at supervising
his face, was unable to fend off the surprise of that taste. He watched in
panic as tears welled up in Dolores's eyes. He smiled, trying to retake control of his expressions.

"It is great," he said, grinning. "It just not salty."

His new aunt exhaled as if a spurned demon had left her body and ran through the kitchen and into the house's carpeted sleeping wing, holding a towel to her mouth. Bahrija sighed and stood up.

"I'm sorry," Musa stammered.

"No, no."

Bahrija went after his wife, who was now sobbing somewhere. Musa stared at the table, then up at a photograph of a beautiful woman (could that be young Dolores?), the stand-up piano, its teeth exposed. He looked down at the food and his stomach churned. He listened to his aunt crying how she wanted everything to be perfect and how everything was now ruined, and he snatched a piece of olive bread from the middle of the loaf so it wouldn't be noticed, dabbed it in the excess olive oil in the salad bowl, and added salt and pepper to it. He bunged the whole piece into his mouth like the refugee he was. It tasted like old times, before-war times.

Later, when things were again outwardly copacetic, when it was time to call Bosnia, Bahrija called his mother, Musa's grandmother, first. Musa couldn't believe it. His own father was probably going insane in Tuzla, staying up and waiting for his son's call, and his uncle was shooting the shit with Grandma, gossiping crudely about his wife's mental states right in front of the poor woman, in a language she didn't understand. Bahrija throat-laughed at some jokes, then hung up.

"Here's the number." He indicated a sheet of paper Scotch-taped above the printer in the kitchen nook. "Don't be long. Long distance is expensive."

Musa started to dial.

At the butcher block Dolores was trying to peel a melon to slice it for dessert. Bahrija deftly took the knife from her. "No, sweetheart. Let me show you. This is how one eats melon." He cut the melon in half, spooned its guts into the garbage. "This way you're using its skin as a bowl. Go ahead."

Across the world, Musa's father croaked a broken, beseeching hello. Musa told him where he was as he watched his aunt take a defeated bite of melon with the spoon. Bahrija petted her cheek and walked away. She chewed once, looking nowhere.

* * *

It wasn't even eight-forty-five p.m. and Musa's aunt and uncle were in their silly silk pajamas and getting ready to go to bed. Bahrija rummaged through the pantry and found a bottle of slivovitz, poured himself a shot. It wasn't homemade but a Croatian import, and when he asked Musa if he wanted one, Musa, for some reason, told him he didn't drink.

The three and a half years of punk life under siege in Tuzla and he'd pounded anything handed to him: wine, brandy, grappa, raisin moonshine, Bosnian sake made out of donated *Merhamet* and Red Cross rice. He'd huffed filched glue and paint thinner, sniffed sponges soaked in gas siphoned out of UN jeeps, smoked savory war-garden weed, pulverized Pharmacists Without Borders's downers into powder and injected them into his veins.

He'd left that guy behind, given up all those hard lessons, for a crack at what? Living in America with elderly relatives? Going to bed by nine o'clock? Barely watching barely audible TV so these old-timers could sleep? Pretending he didn't drink? Going to college if his uncle kept his word? What?

"Buck," said Dolores from the doorway, suddenly there. "I want you to tell Musa about the dream."

"I will, sweetheart," he said.

"I just think it's important. The spiritual side of things."

"Of course. I'll be right in."

She said good night and left. Musa glanced at him, expectant. Bahrija downed his shot, poured himself another half-shot, and retired the bottle.

The Bulls were beating up on the Cavs behind Jordan and Pippen. It was the third quarter, and Toni Kukoč was on the bench. Musa was waiting to see him come in. He'd watched the guy play since he was a kid.

"Jordan is a good-looking Black," Bahrija said. "But look at this Pippen. Like my uncle Vaha. You know Uncle Vaha, right?"

Musa felt uncomfortable, as if he were being tested. Uncle Vaha was half-Romani. "I don't see a resemblance."

"It's like there's some Arab in him." Bahrija pronounced *Arab* A-rab.

Dolores popped her head back in. "Did you tell him?"

"Yes, I have, Dolores. Why don't you just—" He made himself stop talking.

"Well, I just think . . . It's just so important. To hear about the other side."

"I know. I told him. He's fascinated."

She looked at Musa, and Musa readily nodded. This time he had complete control of his face. He looked into the woman's eyes, touched his heart with his hand, and said, "It is great."

She smiled, said good night again, left, then popped back in. "Sorry," she said. "Don't forget to give him the earthquake drill. We never know *when the big one's gonna hit*."

Earthquake drill? Musa asked with his eyebrows when she left. Up, up, up went Bahrija's eyeballs, like pinballs.

Pippen shot an off-balance leaner and clanged it off the back of the rim, slid around his defender, got his own gangly rebound in traffic, and flicked in an ugly, preposterous deuce.

Musa waited to use the bathroom until he could no longer hear them. He cajoled the doorknob, allowing no sounds to escape, used the smallest trickle of water to brush his teeth, pissed on the curve of the bowl almost noiselessly, and flushed the toilet with the lid down. Only when the water tank was fully refilled and again silent did Musa delicately open the door and tiptoe to his new room.

But closing that door, he was giddy. At last there was a door to close between Musa Music and the world, a private cube to be Musa Music in. Positively giddy.

He started to unpack, propping up his family photos and putting his art supplies on the dresser. The cottage-cheese ceiling had glow-in-the-dark star pushpins. He flipped the light off and on, making the constellation come in and out of existence. It clustered near the center of the room in no perceptible pattern.

Musa felt an exigent urge to occupy as much of this new space as possible. He walked the room's perimeter, jumping up and touching the ceiling over and over, Pippen-like. He didn't know why but the cat-tongue rasp of the ceiling against his palms, the click of his joints awakening, the rush of behaving in a way that no one was a witness to—the meaning of which no one was privy to, not even the behaver—helped him believe he was really alive. The room seemed to pulse with silent energy, not a residue of some prior life but a life's giddy potential.

Enough, said something in him—a scared, critical something. He stopped, a little out of breath, and found the book he was reading (Stephen King's *Misery*) and slipped under the covers, folded his pillow in half. This was the first book in English he'd ever tried to read. On the overnight layover in Vienna, it had taken him four hours to get through the first seven pages, as he had to look up every word he didn't know in his pocket dictionary. Discouraged by lack of progress, he'd started just reading right through the pages, even if he didn't understand everything. He'd gotten the gist, which made him feel like the rest of the people at the airport.

In the mirror on the far wall Musa clocked the granddaddy of all masks looming suspended just above his head: a considerable face with diamond-shaped eyeholes, a mouthhole of wooden fangs, with a head of a heron jutting from its forehead. If there really was an earthquake, the fucking thing would slide straight down the wall, its chin would thud against the headboard, the mask would tip forward, and that goddamned beak would peck him right between his eyes, braining him.

Respectfully, he shoved the thing under the bed.

While Buck-Bahrija worked, Dolores showed Musa around. First they went to the bank to open up an account in his name. A timid teller in an air-conditioned branch blushed as she said that she loved the fact that his name was really Music.

"That's why I took it too, when I married his uncle."

"In Bosnia, we say *Musich,*" Musa said.

"In the States, *it's pronounced Music!*" Dolores sang.

Musa deposited his four hundred dollars in deutsche marks, left over from the sum with which his father had sent him. "Two hundred more, and I can pay the bill for my plane."

"What?"

Musa showed her the promissory note he'd signed with the International Rescue Committee charging him six hundred dollars for the ticket to the States to be paid within six months of his arrival.

"No," Dolores said. "I'll pay this for you. I want to do it."

"Really?"

A committed hugger, she hugged him. "Don't worry. It's fine."

At Vons, in an empty frozen-food aisle which she made sure was free of shoppers, Dolores giggled, nervously covering her mouth, and said that his uncle wouldn't be caught dead shopping there because it was where "poor people" shopped. At the community gym she signed Musa up for yoga. From then on, weekly, he pretzeled and unpretzeled his body until his muscles trembled and drops of sweat plopped from the tip of his nose, and when the instructor sculpted him into Warrior Two and told him to relax, Musa said, "Relax, my ass," and all these white people cracked out of their poses and fell on their mats, laughing.

Dolores hired young Nathaniel to teach Musa how to drive, and Nathaniel and Musa drove around the neighborhood in a tiny Metro with two floor brakes, listening to music. Nathaniel had a ghoulish obsession with Janet Jackson and Paula Abdul and every day he asked Musa which one of these fine ladies was more popular in *his* country. Musa, being a punker and having a bad rep to maintain, claimed he had no clue.

When Musa passed the driver's exam and got his license, Bahrija told Musa he was welcome to drive his VW Golf if he kept it gassed. The Golf wasn't an automatic, and Nathaniel had to start all over again to teach Musa to drive a stick. One day in Westlake Village, as Musa made the car buck and spasm, gasp and stall, trying to manipulate its pedals—to find its G-spot, as Nathaniel called it—a cop pulled them over, checked them out, then apologized, said some white granny called in a suspicious vehicle rampaging up and down her street, driven by a Black man and probably a Mexican. The cop gushed with white guilt while Musa cold-sweated and shook at the sudden proximity of a gun and a uniform.

When one day Musa told Dolores he couldn't wait to start college as his father and Bahrija had promised, she acted as if she were hearing about this for the first time. (It was in fact the first time she'd heard of it.) Then she drove Musa into the dry foothills to the closest community college.

There, a kindly dwarf lady scheduled him for placement tests in math and English, and a man who looked like Santa Claus gave them a golf-cart tour of the fertile campus, a man-made oasis surrounded by the dry-beige rash and rubble of Southern California. The tour included a real zoo, a driving range, and a state-of-the-art performance arts center. On paved paths they glided past Americans Musa's own age—girls pressing binders into their tank-topped chests, dudes dragging their feet, barefoot sporty people pitching a neon-magenta Frisbee, and a single-humped camel on a leash being led by experts before the library. The camel was dribbling turds that gawky underlings scraped into square plastic buckets. Musa couldn't wait to run around all that stage space with a backpack on.

"They have great fine art and photography studios here," she said, pulling out of the guest parking. "I hear you're *quite an artist!*"

At home, in the interest of sharing, he showed Dolores all of his drawings, even the anatomically correct pencils of naked old people sitting spread-eagled on stools. She blushed some but recovered quickly and talked meaningfully about shading, continuously putting down her own humble half-attempts at fine art. When Bahrija came home, and he and Dolores went into their bedroom for him to change, they stayed in there longer than usual; and when he went for his daily walk around the lake, he went by himself, in Bermuda shorts, sandals, and a cowboy hat.

Second verse, different from the first.

The next day Dolores was cagey, inaccessible, doing things around the house as if everything were equally weighted. Each errand required a separate car trip. She walked into the house with a manila folder at eleven, a three-pack of paper towels at eleven-forty-five, and with a new haircut (the same as the old one) at two. Musa lay on his bed reading his English prep textbook, and though he left his door open to encourage conversation and show that he was working hard, Dolores passed it without a peep, looking at the carpet every time.

Close to when Bahrija was supposed to return, Musa stole a handful of cashews from the kitchen. A FedEx truck lumbered by, and when it was gone, Dolores was suddenly crying in the doorway. He asked her what was wrong, and she just whimpered and made a teeny step toward him. "I'm sorry," she said. Musa hugged her. "I talked to Buck yesterday." She went for a paper towel. "Your uncle doesn't think it's a good idea for you to go to community college. He's gonna have a talk with you tonight."

Musa held on to the doorway, stared at his thumb. The air tasted sour, shriveling his nose, throat, lungs.

"No matter what he says to you, you have to remember that it was *that* dream that brought you here. The one he told you about when you got here."

Musa looked at her, keeping his shit together.

"From the beginning I suggested we should bring you over, but he wasn't for it. Then one night . . . that dream. And he said to me, 'Dolly, let's bring Musa over.'"

The garage door begun to hum open and Dolores dashed to unlock the front door for her husband.

"It's important to know that even people like Buck have this other side." She bent to straighten up a pair of slip-ons on the welcome mat. Musa slipped into the guest room and closed the door. There was no lock, but he closed the door good.

He stood, palms against the door, listening to the house's noises and absence of noises. The door was constituted of atoms, which were mostly empty space, as the atoms of his hands were, and how strange only the parts not made of empty space were repelling each other, keeping the world at bay, keeping Buck from giving him this talk, and giving a mostly-nothing-Musa an illusion of safety.

II

The romance between the men from Musa's father's side of the family and the United States had commenced out of necessity more than true love. The first Music to escape the loving but overbearing embrace of Mother Bosnia had been Musa's granduncle Alija, who, having dreamed of forest fires and faceless peasants running harum-scarum with their throats cut, had awakened one night in 1938 in his rented room in a Jewish neighborhood in Paris (where he'd been a few months shy of getting his law degree) knowing that another big war was coming. The German occupation of Sudeten-

land and the subsequent resignation of the Czech government he'd read
about in a paper a few days earlier had prompted the dream.

As a child, he'd barely survived the aftermath of World War I, and so
Granduncle Alija, a small and myopic man (hardly soldier material), had
lain in the dark, emitting wheezy asthmatic whimpers, trying to calm
himself. But the more he'd tried, the more his mind had produced new,
bloodier images. When he'd seen himself in a uniform with stumps for
hands, trembling among frozen corpses in a trench, he'd bolted out of
bed and fumbled through the darkness to turn on his reading light. Then
he'd found his pince-nez, stepped shakily into his slippers, and gone
straight for the bottle of absinthe squirreled in a wooden coffer behind
the door.

The nightmare had come at the worst time. Even without the threat
of war mounting throughout Europe, he'd not been in a good place. He'd
grown to hate Paris and hadn't wanted to remain there after he'd finished
his studies. But even more frightening had been the prospect of moving
back home to work for his father. With a woolen comforter wrapped
around him and the whites of his eyes zigzagged with crimson and sodden
with tears, he'd conceived of a desperate plan. He'd written a letter to his
father (Musa's great-grandfather) Idriz-aga, a letter he'd known his illiter-
ate father wouldn't be able to decipher on his own. Thus it started:

"Please, read this to him when he's in good spirits."

Of course, he'd been asking for money, claiming he needed it since he'd
be receiving his diploma a little earlier than scheduled (which was a lie)
and needed to come back home as soon as possible to start helping out
with his father's numerous business affairs—from real estate to wholesale
to coffee roasting—as he'd promised years earlier. He'd believed he had,
roughly, a three percent chance of getting his fanatically frugal father to
send him anything.

Idriz-aga, though conniving and shrewd, had a soft spot for perfect-
sounding deals and so had let himself be tricked despite the too-good-
to-be-true alarm banging deep in his guts. He'd done so unconsciously,
because he'd been going through a change unbeknownst even to himself.
In the most hidden grottoes of his being, he'd been a novice dreamer of
dreams, and lately, more and more, he'd started to believe he could achieve

them. He'd dreamed of creating a colossal family-business empire unmatched on the Balkan Peninsula because he'd wanted to recapture the
wealth and the prestige his family had enjoyed before the Great War.

Before the war he'd been the richest man in Tuzla. He'd had properties
and businesses all over the county. He'd had so much land that he'd never
even seen, let alone ridden or walked upon, most of it. In his three-level
Nuevo-Moorish house, he'd buried in the basement a chest of gold that
Bluebeard would've been proud of. He'd been so rich his only daughter
practiced her embroidery using golden thread on Chinese silk.

When the war had come to Tuzla, Musa's great-grandfather, in order to
keep making money, had sided with the Austro-Hungarians and handled
the logistics for their nearby army base. This had proved to be a horrible
decision, as the Habsburg monarchy lost the war and the new regime—
people who'd been his employees and servants—had stripped him of
everything he had. He'd been lucky to walk away with his hapless head
still atop his shoulders.

However, little by little, people had forgotten what he'd done, and
Idriz-aga had wiggled his way back into Tuzla's business circles and started
making money again. He'd reacquired house after house in the town's core,
acre after acre of the best land on the surrounding hills. Which was when
he'd started dreaming up his dream.

Uneducated and distrustful of the learned, Idriz-aga at first had been
against spending his money on something as intangible as education. But
in the interest of fulfilling his dream, he'd let friends and advisers persuade
him to send his four sons to the best schools around (his only daughter he'd married off at sixteen to a widowed judge), reserving the right to
choose what they'd study. He'd arranged for his eldest son, Muhamed, to
study medicine in Istanbul; Hamza had studied economics in Budapest;
Alija law in Paris; and Musa (Musa's namesake and grandfather) engineering in Vienna. Once done, they were all to come back home to learn
the business alongside their father so they could one day, the joke went, *not
run it into the ground.*

Alija's letter had offered Idriz-aga a glimpse of that dream. When
Alija had received the money in gold via his father's personal messenger—
Idriz-aga didn't believe in banks—he hadn't been able to believe his luck.

He'd packed his coffer and treated himself to one last visit to Isabelle, his favorite harlot with the heart of gold, the only one who hadn't laughed at his physique but had smiled warmly and tickled his nipples with the tips of her dainty nails. In the morning—his eyes raw from wind and fear and his heart gashed in by sweetness and guilt—he'd bought his way onto a Spanish fishing vessel going first to Reykjavík, then Newfoundland, and then, finally, to New York City.

By the time Alija had finally made it to the U.S. (sans his father's blessing), his former neighbor Herschel Grynszpan had shot and killed a member of the German embassy as an act of vengeance against the Nazi treatment of the Jews in Germany. By the time Alija had finally written to his family, the Nazis were already methodically plowing through Czechoslovakia and the newspapers were filled with images of Arians marching through the streets. The first letter he'd received back said a ferocious stroke had made his father lopsided and there was no home for him in Tuzla as long as Idriz-aga drew breath.

III

One, two, three months of Musa's life in America tumbled down the drain to Buck's refrain of *College-shmollege* and *What can you do with a diploma? Wipe your ass with it.* Buck had somehow convinced Musa's father that Musa should cash in on his undeniable talent and enter the lucrative field of graphic design instead of going to college. And Musa's father now too bombarded Musa with his own mantra during their weekly phone conversations.

"Your uncle knows what he's talking about. He's been in your shoes. Go along with the plan."

Musa wanted to whine and scream, complain and manipulate, go berserk, do what teenagers do, but he couldn't—just could not do that with his aunt and uncle right there in the room, with his father in his ear, and with his body, alive, in the nook chair and not dead and bloated in a wet trench.

"One design a day," his uncle said. "To build your portfolio."

So Musa scratched pencil tips across white paper, blackened it with ink, primed it with primary, and shaded it with unnamable in-between colors. He dragged cursors across scanned-in drawings and photographs, set them against one another, got them to fuck, fight, cuddle, mix—to interact. Buck made daily inspections: Buck whose every fork bite had to have equal amounts of meat and potato and pea, whose favorite actor was Chuck Norris, favorite writer Michael Crichton, was the arbiter of what went into the portfolio.

More and more Musa couldn't stand the sheer sadness of this scrutiny so he avoided seeing his uncle (and Dolores therefore) as much as possible. He waited to start his day until he saw Buck leave in the morning, manufactured excuses to do his work at the library or adult learning center. He came home after Buck's bedtime and left his daily work on the nook table, waiting until the weekend to hear the reasoning behind Buck's Caesarean judgments. Weekends became a time to get through despite weekends being when they usually called Bosnia—Grandmother Fatima first, then Musa's father. Only once did they attempt to call his granduncle Alija in New York on his birthday but the man was demented and seven-eighths deaf and perhaps didn't expect to be addressed in the language of his youth so he feebly screamed racial slurs and hissed at them to learn English in a thick Bosnian accent before Buck shrugged, took him off the speakerphone, and ended the communication.

On Musa's nineteenth birthday, Dolores gave him an art book, a rare comic he'd told her about months before, a heartfelt letter, and a hug. Buck gave him a two-hundred-dollar gift certificate from Janss Mall, then drove him there in the Lexus and picked out all the clothing *for* Musa: two pairs of slacks, two white and two patterned shirts, one with a French collar, dress socks, undershirts, a thin black belt, and a vile tie decorated with flags. He excused this behavior by claiming Musa would soon get a job as a beginner graphic designer and didn't know what was expected of him in the American work environment.

"I had a shirt like that." He pointed at Musa's the Exploited T-shirt, laughing. "But then I got a job."

Waiting for Uncle Buck to get out of the public shitter, Musa saw a girl in green Doc Martens, black kitty choker, and double-XL Beavis and Butt-head tee that served as a dress. She had thick, healthy thighs and boobs like one big boob up front and a gorgeous face.

"'Sex and violence, sex and violence, sex and violence,'" she sang when she saw his shirt. She jumped up and down, her heavy bosom doing the same. Musa smiled ear to ear.

"That's old school," she said, and they talked for a minute about music. She asked him where he was from, and he told her. He asked her where she was from, and she said Encino. But her parents were from Iran. He asked what she thought about all this new trendy punk, and she said some of it wasn't too bad. She asked if he'd ever heard Sluts for Hire. He said he hadn't. She told him to shut the fuck up and pushed him in the chest with both hands.

"They play around here all the time," she said, shaking his shoulders. "You have to see them." She noticed Buck standing behind Musa, gave him an exaggerated nod, an almost curtsey. "At the Red Onion. Sluts for Hire. Say it with me."

"At the Red Onion. Sluts for Hire. Say it with me."

She guffawed and jogged away, waving ta, looking back.

Walking to the parking lot, Buck smiled an all-knowing smile. "That's not the kind of woman to pursue," he said in Bosnian. "What you want is a tall blond woman with long legs. That one probably wouldn't even let you see her naked during the day."

The first fun conversation with a girl Musa had had in the new country and Bahrija Music, in a cowboy hat and a fringe jacket purchased fresh from Janss Mall, was going to instruct Musa in *whom* he should find beautiful too?

He felt like shoving all the paper bags into his uncle's chest, and laughing at him, just *laughing* in his dumb, flat face. And he hated himself because he wasn't about to do it. He didn't have it in him anymore. Two years ago, if someone had done something like this—

He flashed to two years ago when, on a quest to lose his virginity and armed with a bottle of purloined moonshine, he and his wingman, Masni, walked into a pungent studio apartment in Super Blok to do the deed with a hammered fifty-year-old hooker easier to jump over than go around. He developed cold feet, declared the stench insufferable, but Masni said, *Open the window* in English and stood between Musa and the door. Musa faltered at the sheer size of her, but Masni quoted a poet, said, *Losing your*

cherry to a very fat woman is like graduating in the upper third of your class,
and made him go in first.

"What are you smiling about?" asked Buck.

From that day on, it should've been obvious Buck was up to something.
For a week he lauded Musa's talent, swooned over his new work, purchased
a black paper portfolio which he presented Musa one weekend. The portfolio had a laminated slot where one could slide in a business card, but
Buck thought a handmade one would better show off Musa's skills. Musa
designed a tasty one where the *s* in Musa was a swoopy violin key. But
Buck suggested Musa pick an American pseudonym and move the symbol
to his surname.

"You don't want, first thing, to be correcting a future employer's pro-
nunciation. You have to assimilate."

So under a new name, Musa Music—dressed in slacks, stiff dress shoes,
and a French-collared shirt already sopping with stress sweat—sat behind
the wheel of his uncle's gassed-up burgundy '82 VW Golf, uttered a prayer,
and started south in the direction of DreamWorks—yes, DreamWorks.
Buck's idea, of course.

In his shaky hand, he clutched a set of directions. With his art portfolio
carefully riding shotgun, he stepped on the gas and merged onto the freeway for the third time in his life. Five tense minutes later he was already
the farthest he'd ever been outside of Thousand Oaks on his own.

The card in the laminated sleeve of his portfolio said:

MOE MUSIC
ARTIST, GRAPHIC DESIGNER.

In the Monday-morning rush hour, Musa suffered a small nervous
breakdown. At the junction of several major freeways, realizing that he
was in the wrong lane and not being readily admitted into the right one,
he put on his hazards and slammed on the brakes, making a complete stop.
Eyes closed, Musa tried to breathe. Screaming vehicles careened around
him, their tires losing skin and tissue to the hard road. The fellow motorists
let him know in no uncertain terms what he was.

When Musa opened his eyes to reality that once again felt navigable, he saw an opening to tuck the little car in. He put it in drive and Tetrised its ass into the correct lane. As his panic attack subsided, he became aware he'd been squealing profanities in Bosnian.

DreamWorks was apparently located on the grounds at Universal Studios. A long two-way street led up a hill with a two-way guardhouse halfway up. Musa pulled up to the striped ramp and stopped the car. A truck stopped on the other side of the guardhouse was some kind of problem because both uniformed Black women were outside, standing tensely next to the truck's driver, holding giant walkie-talkies in their elaborately manicured hands. One made eye contact with Musa and signaled for him to wait.

And wait he did. For a long time.

Every so often a guard would look in his direction, point to her walkie, and shrug, her face tightening in an expression of guilt. Soon another car pulled up behind Musa, and another behind that one. The guard with bleached tips capitulated, ran to the guardhouse, and came out holding a sheet of stickers. She signaled to Musa to roll down his window as she approached. "You know where you're goin', hon?" she asked, exasperated.

Musa nodded, though he had no clue. She looked busy and he didn't want to complicate her obviously complicated day any further. She put a sticker on his windshield and manually opened the ramp. "Go ahead," she said.

Driving through the studios meant going from an East Coast American suburb to the cobbled streets of WWII Paris to a bodega storefront in the Bronx. Musa found an unassuming parking spot in the midst of these places and times, and with his portfolio under one arm, he started searching for DreamWorks on foot. Nobody asked him any questions, nobody cared who he was or what he was doing there. He was okay with that; being invisible was his cup of tea.

He passed a young blonde with a megaphone. She was a sorceress who kept some extras down the street frozen to their marks. When she yelled, they came alive and crossed the street, or emerged from the fake buildings, or took out their wallets and fake-paid the fake hot-dog guy. When she yelled a second time, they rushed back to the marks, back to being frozen.

In front of the first building, the building Musa was looking for, in fact, stood two hefty guys in white uniforms. They appeared to be special well-paid coplike people in sunglasses. They both had spirally white wires growing up their necks and into their ears, hairy arms, and real submachine guns.

There's no way, Musa thought. The guns, the uniforms, that he'd probably broken a law or two getting on these premises (the sticker on his car notwithstanding): all those things told him he should not go up to those guys holding his flimsy portfolio. But he was already halfway there.

"How can I help you?" said the closer guard.

"I'm looking for a job." Musa nodded toward the entrance.

The guard scrunched up his face at Musa's accent. "A job? In there?"

"In DreamWorks."

"Do you have an appointment?"

"No. I have portfolio."

The guy laughed—fatherly, good-naturedly. "Listen, man. I can't let you in without an appointment. Give them a call first, and if they say they want to see your stuff, then come back and I'll let you in."

"Oh," managed Musa. "Thank you so very much."

Musa walked to the car. He was emotionally kaput, yet corporeally his legs felt like skipping—as if elated by this mortifying failure.

He drove out of the fake town and into the real one but then got lost in its reality. A main throughway bottlenecked with construction and became a one-way, and there was no going back. In no time, hustlers ran up to cars at stop signs, signaling things he didn't comprehend. He remembered Nathaniel saying the next street parallel to a one-way usually went in the opposite direction, but when he chose a place to turn around, he ended up at a loading dock. An eighteen-wheeler backed in after him, blocking the only exit.

He had to wait for two hours until the cannery workers unloaded the truck. The air smelled of fish and wartime cornbread. Workers in white coats, their hair in silly nets, squatted in the courtyard like Bosnians waiting on rations, smoking and drinking out of paper bags. They smiled at him and shook their heads, came over and offered puffs of cigarettes, asked him in myriad lilts how he ended up there.

"Looking for Disneyland," Musa said, and they laughed. A short Mexican guy with a mustache gave him a can of beer with a wedge of unripe lemon. It was the best beer he'd ever had.

Eventually, back in Thousand Oaks, sobbing on his bed—even though it wasn't his at all—Musa, speaking in Bosnian, told Uncle Bahrija what had happened.

Buck listened, nodding, allowing for an appropriate amount of silence before saying quietly in English: "You're just not well equipped to sell yourself. You gotta learn how to do that if you want to make it in America. You can't let some guard stand in the way of your dream."

"My dream?" Musa said through a swollen face. And Bahrija misinterpreted the outbreak of uncontrollable sobs, ineptly patting his nephew's shoulder, not understanding that Musa was actually laughing.

IV

The second Music to come to America had done so out of blind love. Musa's uncle Bahrija, though born in 1940 and too young to really fathom at first what was happening around him, had inadvertently witnessed the birth of the communist Yugoslavia after WWII. This timing would've made him a perfect candidate to have been molded into a model communist had his older family members not taught him to equate money with happiness and success. As a child, he'd one time come home happy he'd received a piece of candy at school (just as all the kids had) until his mother, Fatima, had told him not to be happy about a mere token, that before the communists had taken over, it was his own family who had owned not only that candy but the store where it was bought, the building the store was in, and the land the building was on. She'd also been adamant about not letting him play with certain neighborhood kids, explaining (in a hush-hush way the political situation had mandated) they were not of his class; their parents had been nothing but their servants before the war. Bahrija's father (who'd never finished his studies in Vienna, having dropped out due to drink) had also sat him down any time it'd been safe to talk and had waxed *alcoholic* about how the fucking communists had ruined his grandfather's dream.

Bahrija had learned that growing up in communism meant you couldn't say what you mean. Also, that you could mean what you mean only if you knew how to keep it to yourself. Realizing this, he'd gone to the American embassy in Belgrade in the fall of 1964, hours before he'd officially enrolled at the university there. He'd known that leaving a communist country—even one not part of the Eastern Bloc—for a capitalist one required the delicate maneuvering of both bureaucracies. And as he was sharp and calculating, he'd set things in motion early and had then spent the next four student years talking to both sides, manipulating his way through both systems as one manipulates the gas and the brake so as not to stall in the middle of the road. He told no one in the family about his plans.

When, in 1969, possessed of a diploma and an American visa, Bahrija, a little fatter but definitely happy, had announced he was leaving Yugoslavia for good to stay with Uncle Alija in New York, his mother had shrieked and fainted. His father, already sauced on grape schnapps, had thrown a shot glass at his son's head—missing it by a yard—and stormed out of the house, cursing down the street. Also living with them was Srdjan, Tuzla's chief investigator of the notorious UDBA, the Yugoslavian Secret Police. (The regime had placed him to live with the family in 1945, deeming their house too big for one extended family.) He hadn't even stirred in his armchair but had puffed his pipe and, with his eyes cold and his mouth asimper, asked Bahrija whether he was going to New York to preach brotherhood and unity or to become another capitalist swine.

Bahrija had pretended he hadn't heard the question, aware that one whisker twitch from this man could have not only voided his visa but made him grow an extra hole somewhere or vanished him altogether. He'd simply hidden behind the urgency of trying to ease his mother back into consciousness. Musa's father and aunt had helped, spraying her with water and holding a fragrant quince under her nose. When she'd woken up, she'd asked to be helped to bed, which Bahrija had done, leaving his younger siblings to sweep up the broken dishes and scoop up the globs of meat and eggplant *musaka* off the carpet and back into the pot.

Prostrate on her bed, Fatima had clutched Bahrija's hand and cried.

He'd promised he'd visit often and would send money as soon as he established himself. Also, she could come to visit any time she wished. His voice had been even, unperturbed. For the first time, looking into his eyes, she had identified a certain foreignness and a cold resoluteness burning there that no amount of sarcasm or histrionics or passive-aggressive campaigning would've influenced. She'd then let go of his hand (or, rather, had made her hand limp so he'd had to disengage). Her eyes had instantaneously desiccated, and she'd told him she wanted to be left alone for her afternoon nap, that she needed it, that at her age one never knew when the angel Azrael might show up to separate spirit from flesh. For a moment he'd smirked, then had walked out, carefully closing the door behind him.

Ravenously, he'd looked around the cavernous, high-ceilinged grand hall of his childhood, needing to devour its details lest they disappear forever. The chipped white chandelier chinking in the draft like an elaborate crystal wind chime had made him remember the 1953 earthquake, when it had been cheerfully swinging, shedding shards of glass. High above the table, the life-size portrait of his sternly mustachioed and obligatorily fezed Grandfather Idriz-aga made the image of a drooling stroke victim Bahrija remembered that much more alive in his mind—this twisted, slurring creature who until his dying day had been known to smack his grandchildren around with his one good hand. The stuffed green parrot over the coat rack had been a farouche pet of his mother's, notorious for constantly screaming. Someone had shot and killed it through the open window with an air rifle.

Then he'd noticed it was ten to five, and he'd rushed out to Hotel Bristol to telephone his girlfriend in Belgrade. Seeing how his family had taken the news of him moving to America, he'd known he had to keep her and his future plans with her a secret for a little longer.

By the time Bahrija had moved into his uncle Alija's one-bedroom apartment in Queens, cancer had already been metastasizing in his father's expansive lungs. Some two years later, by the time he'd moved out and sent for his future first wife, his father was dead and buried, and he hadn't made it to the funeral. To his family's mortification, he wouldn't return to Bosnia to visit until 1983, fourteen years after he'd left.

V

The night after the DreamWorks fiasco, Musa didn't sleep. He sat naked in the dark on the carpet of the guest room, wondering where the fuck his punk attitude had gone, why the fuck he'd wasted months pretending he didn't know what he goddamned well knew when he'd first arrived. What he'd known for a long time.

At age seven, in Tuzla, Musa had learned—in the way children *can* learn abstract notions—that what people called *real world* didn't exist outside of people who perceived it as real, called it real, perpetuated it by believing it was real, molded their behaviors to fit their perceptions and beliefs of it as real. When the war hit, this lesson was confirmed on a larger scale. But these thoughts on reality had begun when Musa realized he couldn't hack it outside of his family's apartment—in that notorious Skojevska neighborhood—and had to invent a personality that could.

To get to school, he'd walk down Skojevska Street and every day bad, bigger kids—hoodlums in training, his father had called them—emerged from shadowy, piss-smelling vestibules and put him in "the machine."

The two biggest, most menacing kids would cut off his path. Musa would stop and turn back but the rest would've already been behind him. Within seconds they would have him corralled and herded behind a trash container or some bearberry bushes. Somebody would kick his backpack. He'd turn around. Somebody else would punch the back of his head. He'd turn around again. "Lardass!" somebody would hiss (because Musa was soft of gut), or "Peasant!" (because of his leftover country lilt from spending summers with his maternal grandparents), or "Pussy!" when he would start to cry, which was pretty much immediately. Once Musa was in tears, the machine could really get going.

After a while they didn't even need the machine anymore. Upon encountering Musa, they'd look him in the eye and nod in the direction they wanted him to go in, behind a newspaper kiosk or in between some garages. There Musa would empty his pockets and give them his money, his candy, his trinkets, and they'd spit in his face and push his head hard into a wall. After a while still, some wouldn't even waste their energy kicking his ass. They'd just make a fist, present it to him, and say, "Punish yourself!"

and he'd have to walk into it face-first, over and over, until they deemed his self-punishment adequate or when the damage equaled what he would have received had they done it themselves.

One time this one kid Vlado made Musa punch himself in the balls. He tried to fake it but Vlado knew where Musa's balls were and where Musa was punching.

"If you don't know how to do it, I can do it for you," he said in this cool, almost instructive tone, as if he *really* wanted to help Musa out. He took a bite of apple he'd taken from Musa's backpack and waited. Musa bit his lower lip and let himself have it.

As he lay writhing behind a rusty VW Bug that smelled of damp asphalt and motor oil, Musa recognized that he couldn't let this keep on happening. He had to initiate a change.

First he tried to find alternate routes to school. For a few weeks he went there one or the other roundabout way, hoping the new passage would stay safe, just to eventually always stumble into his tormentors. If they didn't see him in a while they'd turn the machine on the extra-special cycle, make sure he remembered the encounter.

For a month in the spring of his second year of elementary school, Musa used the river's concrete embankment to get to classes and back. The river was very thin, a brook of raw sewage being pumped into it from neighborhoods. A yard of relatively dry concrete on either side of the riverbed meant he could walk without getting soiled.

Every day he'd scale down the embankment and walk upstream. The walk to school took longer because the river didn't flow in a straight line but nobody in their right mind would've thought to look for him there. The stench alone was enough to make eyebrows curl. But he didn't mind that or the walking if it meant he didn't have to lie on the pavement with his mouth open and have assholes take turns spitting into it.

Then there was this once-in-a-decade snowmelt up in the mountains and the river rose up to the lip and he had to find yet another way.

At that time Musa took part in a school play, a politically sanctioned show in which he played one of six kid heroes—Tito's Pioneers—who knew where the communist partisans were hiding but had kept their mouth shut even when an SS officer, portrayed by a tall, gooberish-looking eighth-grader, had smacked them around and ultimately shot their parents. It was less a play and more a piece of propaganda, designed to remind the older Yugoslav generations of the need for and the power of Brotherhood and Unity. Six kids represented six of the country's federative republics—six South Slavic peoples standing together against a foreign invader and eventually thriving.

Musa noticed something. The play's audience—real, grown men and women—cried real, grown tears, clapped real grown-up hands. He thought if pretending to be a brave boy helping the partisans could fool grown-ups into crying, then Musa had to have in him a brave enough boy he could play to survive that treacherous stretch of Skojevska Street.

There was some trial and error. First Musa pretended he was somebody's son. He'd catch up to a random passerby and strike up a conversation as soon as he noticed Vlado or one of his goons. Seeing him with an adult, they'd grudgingly let him pass, though not without dragging their thumbs across their thin necks at him. Bright and streetwise, however, they became suspicious after seeing Musa accompanied by so many different adults day after day.

The last time he was ever put in the machine, the day he truly found his punk attitude, Musa was "helping" an elderly lady carry her groceries to her apartment in return for her escort. He kept her talking and kept Vlado, Klempo, and the rest in the corner of his eye. They were all leaning back on the windows of the Snack Bar, a local booze hall where senior citizens played chess and drank brandy all day long, where bus drivers ran in for a quick one for the road, and where middle-aged hoodlums would call kids to them and make them run and buy cigarettes at the kiosk because they didn't want to stop drinking.

As Musa and his parent of the moment walked past, Vlado nudged his friends and they all peeled themselves from the glass, put their hands in their pockets, and started to follow at a safe distance. Musa knew that the jig was up.

The thugs followed Musa and the woman way past Skojevska, way past their turf. At her building, the woman pressed the intercom button, then took a caramel from her purse and put it in Musa's hand: "Young man, you deserve this."

Vlado stood there in the periphery, his hands clasped behind him, waiting.

"Do you need help up the stairs?" Musa tried, but the intercom buzzed and the elderly woman pulled the vestibule door open.

"Thank you, son, but there's no need. Really." She took the plastic grocery sacks from him and, holding the door open with her hip, said goodbye. The door hadn't even latched when the machine was already upon Musa.

"Was that your girlfriend?" Vlado said. Others hooted and scoffed.

They surrounded him. Vlado had actually stopped to pop each of his ugly, long fingers when something inside Musa's head split. He decided to act exactly the opposite of how he usually acted in this very familiar situation. Brutal *degenek,* at this point, was inevitable anyway.

He started to cackle, earnestly somehow, naturally—Stanislavski's wet dream of a cackle—which stopped the gang in their tracks. Their brows bunched up in the center. Musa feigned trying to stop laughing, feigned being unable to stop, burst into another deranged round.

Klempo and others looked up at Vlado. Vlado raised his left hand and waved. When Musa's eyes followed the wave, Vlado drove an overhead right into Musa's face—a man's punch, with follow-through. Its smack rang, orgasmic, bursting lip against fang, bringing Musa to his ass, turning the laughter off.

But only for a moment. When Musa, on all fours, raised his head, he was smiling a maniacal smile, all his teeth outlined in blood. The power of pain surprised him, as did the power of spite in the face of pain, damage to flesh and psyche be damned. He laughed truly, from the heart, because Vlado couldn't touch him.

"'*Po shumama i gorama, nashe zemlje ponosne,*'" Musa sang through his smile, his fist pressed against his head in a WWII partisan salute.

Vlado kicked him in the chest, couldn't touch his chest. Musa sang on. Klempo kicked him in the ass, couldn't touch his ass. Musa sang on. The other *machinists,* seeing they couldn't shut up his song, bolted.

His face a petrified grimace, Vlado kicked at Musa the way people keep pressing elevator buttons in a blackout. He didn't notice somebody meaner than even he was right behind him. A hand grabbed his poof of hair, yanked him away from Musa, lifted him, then forced him down, topsy-turvy, helping out gravity. Vlado's neck and upper back collided with the ground, thudded and sighed, and his extremities awoke into a twitchy, demented life of their own.

Musa recognized the guy immediately: Igor the Punk, from the third floor of his building, a certifiable youth whose own father had kicked him out of the house, a notorious high school dropout, a guy who even legitimate hard-asses didn't want to mess with because he was relentless and crazy—sans code, with nothing to lose. Normally Musa would've squeezed himself into a mousehole before willingly encountering him, but this time he looked Igor in the eye and started the second verse.

"Hey, Boshko Buha." Igor smiled, revealing a graveyard of teeth. "Nice balls on you, kid."

Jackknifed in the grass, *O*-mouthed Vlado managed some wheezes of oxygen.

"And you"—Igor grabbed his leg, pulled him closer—"five on one and you still can't kick a little fatso's ass. That kid has more heart than all of you wannabes."

He went through Vlado's pockets, found a few folded notes and a pocket-knife, and pocketed them. He found a baggie of assorted glass marbles too, snorted, took out the biggest one.

"Boshko Buha, come over here!"

Musa marched over, singing, like real Boshko Buha.

"Stop with the partisan songs. You've made your point."

Musa stopped.

"I'm gonna show you a way for people to leave you alone. Hold his arms."

Musa stood above Vlado, and when Igor forced the gasping boy's arms over his head, Musa found himself stepping on Vlado's hands with his full weight. Vlado squealed but Igor forced his mouth shut, then parted Vlado's lips with thumb and forefinger.

"You're never going to touch this kid ever again," Igor said. "Because—" And he hit the boy's front teeth with the big marble. "Every time—" The enamel, dentin, started to chip. "You look in the mirror—" And split and crack. "You'll be reminded of what—" Crumbling teeth started to fill his mouth cavity. "Happens to little wannabes when they come against the real thing."

Horrified, Musa stepped away. Vlado spun to his side, coughing up bile and spitting up blood and cementum. Igor let go of him, stood, and showed him his own fucked-up teeth.

"Now you look like me. Say thank you."

"Dlyenyklyau," said Vlado.

VI

At the beginning of April, Bahrija filled up the Golf's tank and wished Musa good luck at DreamWorks the second time around. Musa thanked him with the heartiest of heartfelt smiles, then drove to a nearby shopping plaza and applied for a job at every business in the vicinity instead. He shook hands earnestly, held eye contact, cracked lame jokes, said things like *Better believe it* and *Only in America* and smiled until his cheeks ached.

In a musty, near-dormant stationery store between a bagel shop and a notary public, a twentysomething assistant manager, a dude with a soul patch whose tag said Clint but who said he preferred to be called Jenkins, looked over his application. When he read that Moe Music's place of birth was Tuzla, Bosnia-Herzegovina: "Mo' Music? I'll eat this here cash register with mustard and fuckin' relish if your real name is Moe Music."

"You are right as rain. It is Musa Musich."

"Why the shit would you call yourself Mo' Music?"

"It is my uncle Buck. He say it is more like American."

"Fuck Uncle Buck." Jenkins put his palms out. "Sorry, but that's ridiculous."

For an hour nobody came into the store and Musa answered all kinds of questions about war and language and communism. Then some woman returned a lamp because the cord was too short.

"Aren't Americans stupid?" Jenkins said when she walked out. Musa smiled, carefully, but he was already looking down at his application again. "I'll put it on the top of the pile on Patricia's desk and leave her a little note."

Breathing with ease for the first time in a long while, Musa drove back to his uncle's house, put on a sad face for him, described in detail an imaginary conversation with a low-level manager at DreamWorks who'd told him the company was not looking to hire anyone at this time, to try again at the end of summer.

"Okay," said his uncle. "Next week, Disney."

Next week, instead of Disney—because *fuck that!*—Musa drove Jenkins to a record shop in Ventura as a thank-you for hooking him up with a job. There was all of Buck's gas to waste, and they ate KFC, drank giant sodas, and licked the mealy mashed potatoes and gravy right from the Styrofoam because they'd forgotten sporks at the drive-in. Jenkins had a fur-covered flask in imitation calico. He wore a weathered porkpie hat and had brought a battery-operated boom box to play some road tunes, as the Golf had no radio. Jenkins played "Ski Bunny" by Boss Hogg at a deafening level and they couldn't converse over it, so they punched out the rhythm on the car's ceiling and slapped it onto their knees.

His shift started at nine a.m. It took Musa fifteen minutes to walk to work but he'd still wake up at six every day. He'd dress in the darkness of his room, then sit waiting, tracking his aunt and uncle through their morning rituals, listening to doors, bare feet on carpet, bare feet on wood, muzzy voice boxes, fridge and cabinet doors, liquid splashing into receptacles, microwave buttons beeping, microwave churning, microwave ceasing to churn, spoons against china, water against sink enamel, shod feet on carpet, shod feet on wood. Last was the garage door and the Lexus down the street. Then Musa would run into the bathroom, do bathroom things, and within minutes, with his wallet in his pocket and a book under his arm, he'd hurry off to wait for his work to open. He wouldn't touch their food any longer, wouldn't drive their car.

At work he'd daydream about dismantling the store's motion sensors so he could come in after closing to camp overnight in the break room or make a little burrow in the attic space above it, where the dusty Christmas garlands and the spiders lived. He'd eat one meal a day at lunch, a giant grocery store sandwich or Taco Bell. At five p.m. he'd help close the store, then run like a fiend to get to the house while it was still empty, change out of his work clothes, maybe give Jenkins a call, and scuttle out before Dolores would drive Bahrija back from his carpool spot. Every once in a while, he'd still be in the house when the garage door would open, and he'd flee, scaling the stucco wall in the backyard patio or hiding in the guest room, until they went on their daily walk.

Evenings he'd spend with Jenkins, if Jenkins wasn't with his girl, or at a chain bookstore that had comfortable couches, or at the movies. He'd walk back or get dropped off past Buck and Dolores's bedtime and sneak up the driveway. If he saw the light on in the living room or the TV colors throbbing on the walls, he'd lie face up on the concrete before the garage door and stare at the bullshit California stars like a character in some sad, sugary film until the house was still and dark.

One night in May, as Musa sneaked, sneakers in hand, from the front door toward the guest room, Bahrija flipped on the dining room light, all dramatic-like. *Gotcha,* the act said, but Musa wasn't amused. He looked up at the ceiling, about to start laughing.

"Where have you been these days, Musa?" Bahrija asked in Bosnian.

"Out looking for a tall blond woman with long legs," Musa answered in English, dropping his sneakers on the floor.

Bahrija's eyes were capable of puncturing holes in human flesh. "Listen," he started, then proceeded to say he was disappointed with Musa's behavior, that Musa hadn't assimilated, that he'd settled for a shitty job, that he'd heard from Musa's father, that Musa's father was still embedded in the old communist system: finish high school, go to college, wait for the state to give you a job. "That system doesn't exist in the States," Bahrija said. If Musa's father thought Musa should go to college first, if that was the decision, then the best thing for Musa would be to study in Sarajevo—

There was more. Bahrija's mouth kept turning out talk, issuing decrees and instructions, but Musa knew for sure now he'd not get to attend college in America, that he'd traveled across half the world just to be sent back. He knew this and hated that in life you had to go through the motions and hash everything out, put things into words. He knew his next set of lines, and now he had to deliver them.

"But you guys said I was going to go to college."

Bahrija smiled, recognizing the scene to come. He shook his head meaningfully, condescendingly. "I don't know what your father told you, but I never promised that."

Musa smiled, looking him in the eye. He was thinking how awesome it would've been to march over to the piano and start singing an old partisan march in a piercing fake baritone.

"Dolly and I are going to Mendocino County at the end of the month and you should be—"

"Why did you bring me here, then? So I can go to college in Sarajevo? What am I doing here? I'll tell you what I'm doing here. I'm here to make you look like a hero back in Tuzla, a kindly uncle who saved a boy's life, gave him a chance to make it in America, did everything in his power to help him, but the boy was just too weak, too timid, to make something of himself. He would've been eaten alive here in the real world. Isn't that how you phrased it in that letter you sent to my dad?"

Bahrija sat there like a block of particleboard.

"Yeah, my mom found it and sent it to me."

"Dolly and I are going to Mendocino County at the end of the month and you should be gone by then. I told your father I'd help with the ticket."

"What am I doing here?" Despite his best effort, Musa's voice trembled.

"Exactly."

VII

Historically, the Balkans—that gorgeous, ungovernable, godforsaken peninsula always in turmoil, always on the fringes of civilizations, always a broken-up borderland—had for centuries been a place to survive, endure. It had also been a place to fail to escape from and—both because and in spite of this—to love fiercely. If you were from this lush volatility, chances were you'd in some way participate in at least one war—two or even three if God really had it in for you and gave you a long life.

Musa Music was the third Music to flee Tuzla and seek a warmer place under the foreign sun. Musa's relationship with the United States had been partly an arranged marriage; at first he hadn't wanted to come. The funny thing about war was that, like a dreadful marriage or a damaging job, people got used to it, grew to count on its dynamic, and soon enough lost the ability to imagine their life without it.

Musa's immediate family had made it through the war winters sleeping in a piling burrow of his mother's nutria furs and loose winter clothes all in one room and in a row, like some musky mammal sardines. By five, it would have turned dark. And bored brainless without electricity, they'd watch the insides of their lids or steam coming out of their mouths. They'd retell old jokes, celebrating with appreciative laughter the heat of every fart.

They'd subsisted on bread and more bread. And fried dough and public assistance and sporadic humanitarian packages of flour which, provided water and electricity had been on, they'd make into bread. Public assistance had amounted to one quarter of a loaf of 750-gram bread and 250 deciliters of milk per family member. They'd had to get up early and wait in line for hours to receive them—until even that program had been discontinued. They'd played hours of card games in the candlelight or under a small neon tube hooked to a car battery until they'd gone nearly blind from the monotony and the quality of light.

For the first few months of intermittent shelling, they'd run down to the basement and sit around other dreary, disillusioned apartment dwellers. They'd count explosions until that too became tedious and turned into a routine, after which they'd just wait out these devastating projectile attacks at home, caution be damned.

Come spring of 1995 their food stash had pretty much melted away. Musa's mother starved herself, claiming no need of food, and served what they had on smaller and smaller plates. Musa foraged the town's grass surfaces and street islands for edible greens, hunted down after-rain snails, picked dusty crabapples, blackberries, dandelions. Musa's father tutored would-be grad students in math for a pittance but once received a good-size long-finned *deverika* as payment, which they'd savored for a week, sucking fishiness and oil from every last numerous fish bone. They drank chamomile tea to fill up their stomachs and stood up slowly from chairs to stave off the head rushes. They still went through the motions: went to school and work, worried about Musa's upcoming draft.

That had been when the war-torn phone communications between Croatia and Bosnia had been repaired and reestablished and when their cousins from Karlovac had called, asking how they were doing, if everyone was healthy. Musa's mother had told them the situation and the cousins had been first flabbergasted, then confused, and finally outraged.

"What?" Musa's mother had asked.

According to them, Bahrija had been sending the equivalent of one thousand deutsche marks to Karlovac every month since the beginning of the war. They, the cousins, had then sent it through reliable couriers to be delivered to Grandma Fatima's address in Tuzla. The money was supposed to be split down the middle between Fatima and Musa's dad.

Finding out that for years, *war years,* Grandma Fatima silently had kept the entire sum for herself devastated Musa's father and almost killed Musa's mother. The woman had already been anorexic and dried up, and this was the last straw. The news sent her into a quicksand of acute depression which she'd never manage to crawl out of. Her husband's memory had been markedly shorter and, after consistent histrionics and nagging pleas from his sister to forgive their mother, he'd caved and started talking to his mother again. In a few months' time the two women had him wrapped around their little fingers once again, and he'd been back to inhabiting his betrayal, making peasant jokes as if he hadn't married one.

Musa spent less and less time at home, living for his company of punks, for the punk band they'd imagined they were in, for the mosh pits at Stelekt and glue sniffing at the Orthodox Christian cemetery. He'd come home late after curfew, when the police were done raiding, just to sleep. His mother whimpered in the darkened bedroom and his father got in his face when red-eyed Musa ran into him in the streets.

Then, in May, in Café America, Musa and his friend Masni encountered someone called Banana, an ex–basketball center and a member of a Bosnian special forces unit popularly known as the Black Swans. This soldier was beside himself with what he'd known and what he'd seen, and had been doing his darnedest to *unknow* and *unsee* it by cursing and pouring grape brandy down his throat. They'd messed with this man, egging him on to tell them stories and saying they couldn't wait to join and fight.

And even then—a week before the Tuzla Massacre—Musa started to think panicky, *unpunk* thoughts about his future. He'd just watched Banana lose it, take out a hand grenade, pull out the pin, and demand more booze cure from the establishment. The soldier then fumbled the device. The grenade *thunk*ed heavily on the floor, then wobbled over in between an empty soft-drink refrigerator and the closest table, where it exploded and sent little metal balls all over America, some of which had ended up in Masni's back and shoulder.

That night Musa went home unscratched and sat next to his mother's bed, silently holding her hand, listening to a tinny tone ringing continuously in his ear. The massacre in downtown Tuzla a week later only further cemented his bones in fear and took away his attitude—the thing that had been keeping him sane. In that state he'd been no match for his father's plan to send him to live with his uncle.

In 1996, months after the Dayton Peace Agreement for Bosnia had been both initialed (in Dayton) and signed (in Paris), Musa was waking up from nightmares in his uncle's spare bedroom. He was surrounded by his aunt's collection of African masks, sick for home, shocked by culture, and already broken, just weeks in.

Seeing it in his eyes, even Bahrija had felt a twinge of humble fear and finally shared with Musa the dream Dolores had gone on and on about that first night, the one in which Bahrija's own father, Musa's namesake, had reached out from beyond the grave to ask Bahrija to forgive him, to take him in.

And Musa felt like crying then, felt he was safe under this roof, that blood indeed wasn't water, that everything that happened to him was preordained and made sense in the larger scheme of things. And Musa *believed* everything he felt.

But another inside of Musa, the punk, the punk *knew* better.

SIDE B(OSNIA)

Dear Billy Road-Raging Burr,

The weirdest thing happened to me Tuesday. This whole week I've been watching your little YouTube videos on Driving Etiquette because you're making some fancy movie and can't do a podcast for a while. Fuck us little people, right! ☺

Kudos BTW! Go get them, Curly!

Anyway, there's this gardenless compound I pass on the way from the gym—I'm talking real sad, like bare gravel and dirt—with a fucked-up midcentury house on it. All the other houses are lush and lined up perfectly with the street and this one is doing a Lisa Simpson solo. There's some American muscle car elevated on cement blocks right in front of the porch like a damn statue, black with a red stripe. Don't ask me which one, a Mustang maybe. I don't know. The porch is stripped, none of the windows have curtains, and there's a single decrepit chair facing this automotive shrine. Well, I saw an old man sitting there on Tuesday and I swear to God it's your crotchety doppelgänger from your worst nightmare, straight up from that bit in your special. So, if you want to see who you would have ended up becoming had you not chosen comedy, that old dude lives in Salem, OR.

But that's not the weird thing I was telling you about. Something happened to me. That same day, I stopped to drop off my rent check at the office, and as I pulled into the street, I got turned around. I don't know how it happened. I thought I was on Commercial, which is a one-way, but I was on this other street which is a one-way going the opposite direction. Yeah, exactly! By the time I saw this Plymouth coming right at me all I could do was brake and pray. And it was exactly like in the movies: the smoky screech, the fucking slow motion, the random useless details burning themselves into my mind, like the yellowed dog-eared triangle of the oil-change sticker on my windshield flickering in real speed while everything else was chilling, suspended in this moment of near-death. Inches! I'm telling you! We stopped inches away from each other, me and the Plymouth. The woman behind the wheel had her mouth collapsed and she didn't know where she was. It was like her soul was already on another plane and her body was trying to figure out if it should continue living or just slump over. Here's the weird part. I felt nothing. Not a goddamn thing. I just reversed a bit, then drove past her driver's side (she never changed her expression, never turned to look at me), circled around her car, and drove off heading in the right direction. I got home, drank a bottle of water, ate an apple, and watched a movie. I told the whole thing to a poet friend of mine and he immediately asked if I was on antidepressants, and I was like yeah, almost 40 mg of Lexapro. And he was like, *Shit, buddy, you should go see someone. That's not a normal reaction at all.* But it's only through my ex that I had ever had insurance. Now, if I want to use this Community Health thing, they make you take the whole physical and everything takes forever. But I should do something, right?

In other news, you might actually like this next writerly offering. There are immature characters in it, crude jokes; it has a blue-collar feeling to it. I wrote this chapter a long time ago and my ex quit reading an early version of it after only a few pages. I don't know what excuse she gave me, but I knew I had to file it under side B, things she didn't want to bother with. But just now, as I was editing, I think I figured out what might have been the culprit. The narrator, even though I made him an illustrator and not a writer, has a sexual relationship with a woman he meets in Bosnia. I didn't remember writing that. I know the real person I was writing about though and nothing like this ever happened between us. My ex-wife was my first. But why did I write it like that? Then I realized I did it twice earlier in the book, told stories of punks losing their virginity that could be interpreted that they happened to me, the writer of the book. This usually doesn't bother me; I write fiction all the time. I change details from my life to fit the needs of the story. But my heart got snagged here for some reason. Reading those segments caused me pain and discomfort way bigger than coming grill-to-grill with that Plymouth. I left it in because the chapter works fine, but still. Sometimes, when you play the game of exploring your life through art, the subconscious sneaks in some shit you've never intended. Who the fuck knows why?—I'm sure it has its reasons.

Hope you crush it on set, Bill. Go fuck yourself (in your trailer, please, because nobody wants to see that)!

izzy

Nimrods

Hunter Lopez, my boss, he likes to talk. He likes to talk about guns and anal sex, about monster trucks, about the chances of getting away with murder by taking advantage of an antiquated California law—still in effect, according to him—that allows white men to shoot an Indian without fear of prosecution if the Indian is found to be atop a white man's wagon. Hunter dreams of the possibility of this law applying to station wagons as well.

Today he's talking about his plans to raise his truck so high that the exhaust pipe can shoot noxious fumes right through the open windows of *nimrods* wretched enough to get stuck at a stop sign next to him. He has also admonished my immigrant sensibilities by telling me that I should stick to one brand of clothing, that no self-respecting American would ever wear a pair of Reeboks *and* a T-shirt sporting the scissor-legged silhouette of Michael Jordan suspended mid-dunk. I hate this asshole. But I need the job.

The theater lobby is empty at the moment. Hunter has propped open the Employees Only door to the box office so he can sermonize at me—a routine. The door to *his* office, on the far side of the box office, is open behind him. He's in his managerial garb, ironed and pleated, ponytail neat, goatee hairs scarce but indispensable for furnishing his face with the appearance of a chin. From my post behind the concession stand I watch him buzzing around, holding a lit joint out through the ticket window. With his other hand he's keeping the smoke out with a generically Asian-looking fan. Every thirty seconds or so he lowers his face to the hole in the glass, takes a toke, holds the smoke in while turning to make deranged eye contact with me, then exhales out the hole again, fanning away fervently, his face agleam because, once again, he has succeeded in not activating the smoke detectors while smoking in the splendor of an air-conditioned theater.

"These fucking nimrods," he goes on, "these so-called bank robbers who rob some branch in the burbs at noon and get caught in front of their house by five p.m., right on time for the evening fucking news, these dumb motherfuckers in wifebeaters being cuffed in front of their own fucking houses, looking like somebody stepped in their breakfast burrito! How retarded can you be? If I wanted to rob a bank, I would get a sick crew and silence-shoot dead every motherfucker in there. The tellers, the guards, the managers, the . . . those sour-faced fuckers that process loans, whoever the fuck came in, kids, rat-faced grannies, soccer moms, I don't give a shit, man. And when my crew gets all hungry-eyed eyeing all that cash, I'd mow those sick motherfuckers down too. Set up some pipe bombs on some major beams, douse everything in gas, drive off, and detonate that son of a bitch. That's how you rob a bank. No clues, no witnesses."

He goes down to the hole for another toke. He's been tweaking since we opened at noon—he smokes weed only to alleviate whatever the hell the speed does to his system. I wait until he's holding the smoke in his lungs and then, innocently, smiling my best refugee smile, ask: "You ever saw a dead man, Hunter?"

He chokes a little, trying to keep in a cough, then doubles over to exhale through the hole, fanning twice as hard. When he looks up at me, he seems capable of cutting me open—keeping me alive, taking out organ after organ, showing each one to me before squeezing it until it oozes dark liquid. Hunter's rants are monologues, soliloquies at best. My job is to be an admiring audience member, not an interlocutor.

"Here we go again," he says. "I am Bosnia. I survive war. I see dead people on the way to schoolroom. Boo-hoo. Try growing up half-whiteboy half-Mexican in Culver City, motherfucker! Shit. In war at least you know the general direction the bullets are coming from. Where I grew up, you never knew when some nimrod schoolboy with his daddy's Colt would unload in your gut over a pair of fucking sneakers, man. So, no, I've never seen a dead man, but at least I never ran away from a fight like a pussy. Your own fucking family, friends—your *people*, man, are getting killed out there, and you come over here to butter popcorn and help loaded cottontops in pastel leisurewear find their fucking seats in the dark. Cry me a fuckin' river!"

Something ignites in me. It sizzles all the way up my back, as if my T-shirt's on fire.

Hunter, still fanning, kicks the box office door shut, granting himself the last word, making sure to come out on top. The sudden silence is galling.

"I was not eighteen, man!" I yell at the door.

It's true what I say. But it's true what he says too, at least to me. To me, his truth is beefier than mine.

I take in air but my lungs can't seem to absorb it. Their bronchial receptors are apparently already occupied with some other substance, one you can't breathe. I stand there, leaning on the counter, the back of my neck aflame, like a spurned lover's.

Through the theater's tinted windows, the plaza, its parking lot, and Vista Road beyond it look docile and cool. The only evidence of the scorching weather, the only movement at all, is the uncanny but dulcet shimmering of the SUVs parked outside.

"I can leave any time," I say to myself, and as I do, inexorably, despite all the roadblocks I've erected against her, Halida crashes back into my mind with an audible crunch.

Two summers ago, on my annual two-month visit to the motherland, I had gotten my heart caught on an arresting brunette with an elfin face and a mouth on her that could shame a longshoreman. Halida. I had emigrated a virgin in 1994, midwar, when I was seventeen, and it was something of a novelty, four years later, to meet a Bosnian girl who was so uncomplicated about sex. They say that libidos thrive in the presence of death, but the girls I'd known before I'd emigrated were almost neuter in their prudishness, despite the daily violence.

By the time I met Halida, I'd had a few discomfited and feverish encounters with community college girls in the U.S., generally on the flattened seats of their parents' minivans or in their childhood rooms while, just beyond the wall, their grannies napped sitting up, large-print Grisham paperbacks in their frilly laps. I had grappled in the dark, hushed and hamhanded, stress sweat abounding.

But Halida was in a league of her own. When we were introduced, on a Monday, in passing, she grabbed my ass despite our mutual friends being two feet away. On Tuesday, during a chance meeting in the park, she reprimanded me for not finding a way to get in touch with her, and demanded my number. On Wednesday, when she called, we went out to a café overlooking some tennis courts, where, as I leaned sideways in my seat trying to get my jacket off, she leaned into me and stuck her tongue down my throat, her slight hand burning on my inner thigh. "Cradle of Love" by Billy Idol was on the radio.

That same night, in a different park, as I was still trying to figure out who I was and what world I was in, she said something like: "Now we have a cock to play with."

I had no clue what to do with her.

I kissed her like I'd seen men kiss girls in the movies, dramatically attacking her mouth from the right, then from the left, then from the right again, then from the left again, all in a span of two and a half seconds. Her hands clasped at my shoulders and squeezed, slid down my arms, and, finding no discernible musculature, climbed back up to my neck, to my hair. She arched her back and my right hand slid to her ass, flew somewhere else, fluttered back to the ass. I tugged hard at the back of her T-shirt, making the shape of her breasts more visible in the front even though my eyes were shut tight. She took my hand and put it on her crotch and then grunted like she meant it, grunted like I'd never heard anybody grunt. It was the grunt of someone who had, miraculously, been reunited with a long-lost limb.

It scared the shit out of me.

I kept my eyes closed as if love, passion, and performance depended on it. I felt stupid and outside of myself. It was obvious that I was faking the passion, that I had no idea what it was or how to use it. I had created an aura of vehement urgency, hoping to lose myself in it, hoping that something inside me would tell me what to do next.

Halida figured out pretty quickly where I was at. She led, and I followed until we were both sodden and grimy and bushed, until my arms were not my arms and my breath was the cool of the night and my heart was dancing a tarantella.

"Yo, nimrod!"

Hunter has the entrance door propped open for me now. He's smoking a cigarette, of all things. I snap out of my trance, start to wipe the concession counter with a rag. It's nighttime already.

"I don't pay you to scratch your balls. Go change the motherfuckin' marquee while I'm still here."

Red-faced, I take a box of letters and a rubber-tipped stick from one of the cabinets.

"You're cutting into my pussy-eating time," Hunter says, and chortles, as I walk by him and out.

We do a midnight movie every Friday. A manager is supposed to stick around, but Hunter routinely leaves me to close up the joint in his stead. It's always me, because he "doesn't trust that Gabe nimrod with Gabe nimrod's own dick." It feels slightly comforting that I'm not the lowest of the low.

Our only marquee is in the back, positioned to greet people as they exit the freeway on Vista. Behind the building, semi-hidden by some dense low-maintenance thicket, I find the flimsy aluminum ladder I risk my life on every Friday, when we set up the signage for the next week. I secure the ladder against the slapdash wall—as secure as that death trap can be—find the letters for the next movie, put them in order and in my pocket, put the stick in my mouth, and, mutely praying, start my climb. The cheapo rungs bend and creak under my weight. I stop two rungs from the top and, using the stick, slide the old letters out of their slots, letting them fall into the shrubbery, my knees ready to buckle even if the ladder doesn't. Then I put the stick back into my mouth, pray again, and step on the penultimate rung so as to reach the slots with my hand. As swiftly and as carefully as I can, I slide in the new letters.

When I'm back on the ground, I'm drenched with sweat. I look up and read:

FRIDAY MIDNIGHT CLASSICS
@ VISTA TWIN THEATERS
PILP FUCTION

I stand there for a half a minute, catching my breath, feeling disgusting and dumb. Then I saunter over and clutch the ladder again, looking up at my handiwork, my right foot disobeying me, unwilling to step on that rung again.

"Yo! Hurry up!" Hunter yells from up front.

I stand there for a while longer, exhale into the night, then lay the ladder back behind the bushes, pick up the fallen letters, and put them in the box.

"I left some extra garbage bags in the box office," Hunter says with glee when I'm back inside. "You're gonna need 'em tonight."

I give him a shit-eating grin. He gets into that ridiculous truck of his, revs it over and over in the parking lot, then peels out onto Vista Road, his bumping bass rattling everything.

For a time, everything's quiet. Then the freaks in theater B start to go off in ecstasy at something or other in the film. I walk to the doors and listen to the chanting, the laughter, the screaming the likes of which you might encounter at a professional wrestling extravaganza. The poster on the wall reads *The Rocky Horror Picture Show*. I've never heard of it.

On Monday I park my joke of a car at the far end of Vista Plaza and scan the entrance to the theater, detecting no signs of calamity. This past weekend was my first whole weekend off in a while, so I hadn't been around when Hunter found out about my spelling fuckup. I spent it playing *Delta Force* on my roommate's computer and procrastinating on my take-home philosophy final. But Gabe—whose mother lives two doors down in my apartment complex—has told me that the coast is clear, that Hunter is convinced some "nimrod from the *Rocky Horror* crowd thought he was being really funny" and that he, the nimrod, won't be laughing when Hunter catches up with him and collapses his trachea.

When I approach the box office Hunter is in there all lovey-dovey with Tracy, his underage girlfriend, whom he employs just to sit on her ass, sell tickets, and keep him company. He's living in her ultraprogressive parents' house nearby, a live-in boyfriend of their seventeen-year-old daughter, and I guess the job is a quid-pro-quo type of deal. She and I are paid the same, but she has never had to clean the popcorn machine, or sweep the outside area, or Windex the windows, or do inventory, or change the titles on the marquee. When Hunter sees me, he goes: "Yo, commie, the upstairs bathroom is in need of your assistance."

He says this through the hole in the glass and goes back to molesting Tracy. She slaps his chest and runs into his office and out of sight. He follows her with an unhinged jaw, a smile of sorts.

I remember Halida one morning, late for school, running harum-scarum around my parents' weekend house in nothing but white panties, trying to locate her clothes. I remember grabbing her and picking her up and her slapping my chest until I put her down. We had spent a month together by that point, and then I'd had to come back to the States for school and work and we'd made promises to meet up again the next summer, maybe go down to the Dalmatian Coast and pretend we were natives, spearing cuttlefish and selling the catch to high-end restaurants for top dollar to finance our stay. In the meantime, we promised to write, to call.

Tracy screams playfully, snaps me out of my little moment.

Tracy is a loudmouth know-it-all beach bunny to whom the world is owed. Her hair is green with chlorine, her earlobes, lips, tongue, what-have-you pierced with metal rings and studs, her lower back stamped with the word WICKED in a Gothic font, a word she claims really means a world to her. When Hunter first gave her the job, she went out and leased a brand-new black BMW to get her from A to B and sank most of her paychecks into the payments. What she didn't do is change the oil in the thing. Ever. I look at it now, still parked right there under a tarp, in what would otherwise be the Jesus spot in front of the theater, its engine cracked, still sucking up her money.

You deserve each other, I think.

Inside, I lumber up the narrow stairs to the projectionist's/popcorn-making room and catch Pamela, a grown woman who has an unhealthy obsession with Xena, the Warrior Princess, eating a PB&J sandwich with the crusts cut off. She swallows with gusto, then makes a face. "It's disgusting in there," she says.

I turn on the bathroom light and swing the door open with my foot. For a second I don't see anything wrong. The tiled walls are clean, the sink . . . and then I look down at the rat, its body broken oddly, its innards out, like a spilled container of fatty noodles. The mop that was used to dispatch the creature is broken in half and jagged.

"Get rid of it, please," Pamela squeals.

"I don't touch this," I tell her, and walk back downstairs.

I go to the soda machine and pour myself a Mountain Dew—free soda, one of the perks of my position. I'm gulping it down as Hunter emerges out of the box office.

"Did you see him?" he says, childishly revolted. "I got him good, didn't I?"

"I don't touch rat," I say, to my surprise, my palms signaling the end of the conversation. "Not my job."

Hunter scans me for a long time, his brow ribbed, his lips compressed. Then, lo and behold, he shrugs, smiles, even. "All right, man," he says. "I'll make Gabe do it. What time is it?"

I'm stunned. It takes me a second to look at the clock on the wall above me. "Noon and fifteen."

Hunter sniggers at my reply and shakes his head, but somehow more respectfully. He doesn't whip me with his laser look, doesn't threaten my job. For a second it almost feels like we're on equal footing. I feel my status in the company mushroom.

"Okay, then," he says, handing me the inventory sheet clipped to a clipboard. "Let's get her ready."

Our storage area is a diminutive and abnormally shaped room dominated by an industrial-size ice machine and metal shelving with long stacks of soda cups and popcorn containers in a range of sizes, wrapped in plastic. On the floor are cardboard boxes full of individual packages of candy: Red Vines, Mike and Ikes, Raisinets. The staples, I'm told. There's only enough space for me to take a single step in. I count every goddamned thing in there out loud, in Bosnian, and write down the numbers.

When I come out, both Hunter and Tracy are in the lobby, leaning on the concession stand, eyeing me. There's a weird energy about them, as if they were having sex and managed to get dressed just in time not to get caught. I hand him the clipboard and they walk off through the box office and into his office. I hear Tracy giggle before Hunter shushes her.

It's twelve-thirty, and I have half an hour before the start of the first matinee. I gulp down some more of my Mountain Dew and check on the ice in the soda fountain. It's half-empty, so I go to our ice machine and scoop some into a bucket. There is a twelve-pack of Sam Adams sitting in the ice.

Gabe, a youth with a touch of a weasel about him, comes in. Hunter makes him spit out his gum, shows him where the heavy-duty cleaning supplies are, and sends him upstairs. Hunter's stern with him, eyebrows furrowed, but as soon as Gabe turns to go up the stairs, Hunter grimaces and smiles at me. I can't help but reciprocate. He extends his soda cup in salutation, and I pick mine up too. We noiselessly chin-chin.

Zero patrons show up for the first showing of either movie. But it *is* Monday, and this *is* a tiny independent movie theater in a well-to-do bedroom community, nothing more than a tax write-off for our moneyed owners somewhere in Bel Air. Gabe descends the stairs seeming scarred, then spends forever in the restroom, water humming in the pipes in the wall. When he emerges, he opts to watch one of the films, which we're allowed to do if there are no customers.

I don't touch rats, I think, my chest filling with elation and something like pride. I'm in charge of me, my body, the space I get to occupy. I'm in charge of this shit. I get the Windex and a rag and put them on top of the candy display in case Hunter comes out, so I can pretend I'm busy. Then, immediately, I think: Why the fuck do I have to worry about what Hunter thinks? He sucks at being a manager. He sucks at being a human being.

I feel my soles sticking to the black rubber mat and I'm surprised that I find it disgusting. It bothers me so much that I peel it off the tiled floor, the octopus suckers on its underside going *smack-smack-smackity-smack*. I have a sudden urge to see it up close. It's fairly new, but it's coated in a sticky syrup of dried soda sugar. I pick up the whole thing, take it outside, and hose it down against the side of the building until you could eat off of it.

The forceful heat and the physical effort make my heart bombinate, but I don't want to stop yet. I put the mat back, pick up the Windex, and give every window a twice-over from the inside. I'm in the storage room getting a new thing of Windex when, in the lobby behind me, Hunter and Tracy burst into laughter. She slaps her forehead cartoonishly. Look at these dumb fucks, I think.

"Dude, I should do this more often," Hunter manages through his spasms. "Look at this motherfucker *work!*"

Tracy smacks herself again.

"Do what?" I ask.

Now both of them are doubled over. Hunter holds to the counter in earnest as he fights for breath. Their eyes are leaking.

"How're you feeling?" Tracy asks. "High?"

"Yeah, you want some more Mountain Dew, man?"

I look at the cup. I look at them, my heart sputtering. I finally connect the dots.

I feel it coming again, the heat: from my neck up into my face, and from my back up the back of my neck. I feel the panic crop up, and the rage. My heart is a machine-gun nest now, and the gunner is wasting all his ammo. The empty bottle of Windex is vibrating in my hand, like in the movies when ghosts take over an inanimate object. I hurl it at Hunter but it hits the doorway, ricochets off, and starts poltergeisting around the storage room, missing me every time. Right before my knees crumple in panic, I take the door and bang it shut. Then I lock it, curl down in between boxes on the cold cement floor, lay my face upon said cement, and watch the shadow puppetry in the lobby through the crack under the door. A busy, urgent kind of play, by the looks of it.

The gunner doesn't stop. For a long while.

It's Friday again and I'm on the ladder, teetering, sweating. Hunter is below and behind me, supervising, and Tracy is just out of my line of vision, sniping at him about how they're gonna be late, how she's waited so long to see this band live, how she will get him kicked out of her house if he makes her miss them. He goes on a diatribe about responsibility, about how his "taint" is on the line if he gets caught trying to take a seventeen-year-old to a twenty-one-and-over show, X-rated at that, not to mention leaving "Bosnia boy over here" and "that nimrod" in charge.

"I DON'T GIVE A FUCK!" she screams, and I almost fall down.

I spit out the stick and hug the wall with my outstretched arms, abrading my cheek against it. I stay like that until the ladder steadies.

"Is this . . . good?" I say.

"Never move in with a girl with a tattoo on her tit," he says. "Come down."

I do, and look up.

FRIDAY MIDNIGHT CLASSICS
@ VISTA TWIN THEATERS
BUTCH CASSIDY AND SUNDANCE KID

"We should get a new ladder, huh?" Hunter says, patting me on my moist back.

Ever since Monday's "shenanigans" (this is what he calls it), he's been extra nice to me. He may be tough, but he's not tough enough not to sweat what would happen to him if I went to the cops and told them what he did, what he keeps in his office. On Tuesday I had asked for a Thursday off and had gotten it—a first. He even offered me a baggie of weed to take home, to implicate me in his criminal activities, but I declined.

We go back to the front of the theater. Tracy honks thrice from the parking lot, each honk longer and more painful than the one before it.

"Just follow the list," Hunter says. "And don't forget to deposit the cash."

He goes leisurely down the steps, stops, and lights a cigarette.

Tracy starts to honk in a wicked, demented rhythm, like a goose being tortured with a fork. He ignores it, turns back to me, and grins. Slowly, prolonging every movement, Hunter gangsta-walks to the truck.

Inside, Gabe greets me with a lewd gesture, his tongue out, his curled hand bobbing in front of his crotch. "I'd fuck that bitch and wouldn't take a dime from her," he says.

"After Hunter?"

"Oh, that would only make it sweeter," he groans, then abandons jerking it and starts to mount the concession counter, thrusting his hips at it. "Christ, to fuck that asshole's girl!"

"You know she only has seventeen . . . I mean, she's only seventeen?"

"Me too, man. Me too."

He laughs like he's gotten away with something. I try the box office door and it gives.

"Listen, Gabe, you want to go home? I will do everything."

"I need the hours, dude."

"I'm not gonna say anything. Put whatever hours you want on the thing."

"For reals?" he says, and cocks his head.

"For reals."

"See ya," he says, and runs out of the place, bucking and pumping his fists.

I walk into theater B: thirty or so people watching John Travolta take a sip of a milkshake. Nobody seems antsy, no popcorn tub is empty. I walk out, peek into the bathrooms, scan the parking lot for unusual activity, then slip into the box office, walk through it, and try Hunter's door. It's locked.

Motherfucker.

I go back behind the concession stand and count all the money in the cash register, minus the hundred dollars we start the day with. Then I count the popcorn containers and the soda cups on the cabinets behind me and all the candy in the glass display and check the numbers against the day's inventory to figure out what was actually bought. Fridays are our busy days, and I see we've made over five hundred dollars. Doing calculations in my head, I stroll into theater A, which I've yet to clean, and start looking for clean popcorn tubs, the ones that a customer didn't soil with our butter substitute or completely cover in salt. Luckily, our daytime clientele is made up of old folks worried about their cholesterol levels and soccer moms worried about their calorie intakes, and I find half a dozen containers that can pass as new. I take them back to the stand, wipe them off with paper towels, and put them on the bottom of the stacks. Four small popcorns for $2.50 apiece, two large ones for $4 apiece. I take $18 out of the cash register and put it in my sock.

Who's a nimrod now?

I watch the end of *Pulp Fiction,* stand up, and prop open the doors. Suburban creatures of the night emerge out of the theater in Korn T-shirts and hoodies, hugging their pink-haired girlfriends. None of them use the bathroom and I'm able to lock the doors immediately.

Having done the inventory and with the box office money already in the deposit bag, all I have to do is add the concession money and deposit it and clean theater B. I dash through the auditorium with a garbage bag, picking up the big things, then do another sweep with a sweeper, getting rid of the spilled popcorn. I throw it all in the garbage and then, propping the entrance doors open, I run across the plaza to a bank and drop the deposit bag through the slot in the wall. Then, elated, I go back into the theater.

With the box of letters in the lobby, I take the scrap of paper out of my back pocket and look it over.

<u>BUTCH CASSIDY AND SUNDANCE KID</u>
NUDE SASSY BITCH AND DICKHEAD CUNT
DYKE ASS IN THE SAND
BITCHASS NANCY
TIDYASS BITCH NANCY

Although NUDE SASSY BITCH AND DICKHEAD CUNT uses all the available letters and although, English being my second language, I am most proud of that one, I decide it is a bit too much for the good folks of Vista Falls. I double-check my work, take the rubber-tipped stick, and go outside to do the deed.

FRIDAY MIDNIGHT CLASSICS
@ VISTA TWIN THEATERS
NASTY DANISH DICKSCAB

When I went to Bosnia last summer I did so with glee and trepidation, with all of Halida's letters in my carry-on, proud that I'd stayed true even though I'd had two occasions to do otherwise. True, I knew this only in retrospect, because I'm kind of—well, for lack of a better word, let's call me a nimrod when it comes to deciphering what is a come-on and what is not. I don't speak body language.

Once, late at night at a party, the girl from my Women's History class whom I ate lunch with three days a week and who laughed at everything I said pulled me upstairs, saying she wanted to show me something. We went into a room and she locked the door, sat on the bed, and told me she'd had her nipple pierced and did I want to see it? I said sure, and she patted the bed next to her, then popped out a perfect boob with a young-moon stud through the nipple. I asked her if it hurt, and what the procedure was, and why did she pick that shape, and kept up my inquiries for another half an hour until the person whose party it was gonged for us to leave. We stopped having lunch after that.

On the airplane I reread all of Halida's letters. She had written them in pencil, on graph paper, and I had retraced every letter of every word in ink for fear of the graphite fading or being smudged away. I zipped through pages about her university life, about her going out with friends, about her tumultuous family, and loitered on the ones about our plans to go to the coast, about how much fun we'd have, and how happy she was when she received my letters. I signed off every one of mine with *Love*. She signed every one of hers *XO Halida*.

On July 15, when she was supposed to return from her aunt's house in the Netherlands and give me a call, I moved my parents' rotary phone to my childhood bedroom and sat there waiting for it to ring, trying to read Dostoyevsky's *The Idiot*. My childhood friends called, inviting me out for drinks, concerts, paint-thinner sniffing (like in the olden times), breaking my heart because they weren't her. I told them I was under the weather—a summer bug. I waited until midnight and gave up, figured there was a snag in her travel plans, that the promised phone call would come the next day. I reread the letters in bed, only the good parts.

The next day I started to experience chest pains. Certain segments of her letters, the non-fun parts, started to gnaw at me, certain phrasings about going out with friends and just having fun, the myriad ways one can interpret the words *friend* and *fun*. My fingers tingled, my eyes watered, and I paced the room in a square formation, tracing the outline of the design on the carpet compulsively. I felt like something was growing in me, filling me to capacity, and growing still more. I wished I was able to let some of the pressure out through my nose or my ears, like a cartoon character, or from under the cap of my cranium in the form of fire and volcanic smoke accompanied by the sound of a train horn.

On the third day I found her father's number in the phonebook and called around eleven a.m. He was curt and sympathetic at the same time, said that Halida had gone to the seaside with her boyfriend. He seemed miffed by it. I thanked him in my highest voice, as if through a sphincter, and hung up.

On my childhood desk in front of me was a model of a Mack truck that I'd used to draw my first comic, a Skeletor action figure holding aloft the wartime Bosnian flag instead of a weapon, a beat-up Rolodex containing the name and number of every kid I'd met since first grade, a mug of pencils for penciling, a mug of Rapidographs and a mug of brushes for inking, a flesh-colored model of a human foot (as those are hardest to draw), a ninja star I'd bought with my own money through mail order from Gornji Milanovac and that I'd once stuck into the side of my cousin's knee, an orange lamp with a heavy base and an expandable neck that I'd gotten from my mother for my thirteenth birthday when she'd realized I was serious about drawing, a pine cone given to me by the first girl I'd ever gone out with during the war, plus all the marks of youth, the familiar nicks and scratches in the wood, moisture rings where my juice glasses used to sit without coasters, arranged like inebriated Olympic circles, and of course our red rotary phone—but none of it, not one thing, mattered to me. You could have burned all of it right then and I would have raised my hands and enjoyed the heat.

On July 18, I found myself on the roof of a building where I'd lived as a little kid, sitting on the knee-high wall, the metal guardrail burning my hands and my ass through my shorts, my feet on the gravel on the roof, my head leaning back over the ledge looking down onto a parking lot, hazily trying to identify car models from my bird's-eye point of view. Thinking, breathing. A thought came to me up there, a mind-voice saying: Why don't you just go back to the States? If this shit doesn't get better, you can always kill yourself over there.

I'm cleaning every inch of the popcorn warmer, inside and out, and doing it thoroughly, because Hunter is outside smoking a cigarette with two guys and monitoring me through the glass. He's calmer now, as opposed to earlier in the day when he and Tracy were going at it. It started out circumspect enough, behind the closed doors of his office, until she yelled that he was "fucking impossible" and stormed out into the box office, talked to herself there, banged some drawers, then went back into his office and—with the door open this time—told him to apologize. He laughed, said he didn't have anything to apologize for, she asked him to apologize again, he said, "What for?," she called him an "infantile child," which I thought was a little redundant, he called her (surprise, surprise) a "nimrod," she said, "Fuck you," he said, "You act like your pussy is golden," she said, "I quit," he said, "Good luck getting your dad to throw his money at that Beemer," she said, "Good luck moving in with your mom," and then he ran out of his office and she ran outside while he yelled, "I gave you a fucking ride this morning, you octagon-head." Then she turned around and marched back inside and used the phone in his office to arrange for a ride as he cackled and cackled, using all his energy to pretend that he was okay with this.

I finish cleaning the warmer and keep busy so he doesn't give me shit. I don't mind working for real today, because I'm sweating my little stunt from last night. I took the freeway over here on purpose and saw that the marquee had been fixed. By the time I came in, Hunter was already fighting with Tracy, having bigger problems, I guess. It couldn't have turned out better for me.

A model employee, I pop a new batch of popcorn upstairs, ask Pamela to monitor it for me, come downstairs, get more ice for the soda machine, rub the metal edges of the candy display with a rag until they're almost fulgent, then pop back upstairs to grab a huge garbage bag of warm popcorn for the warmer. As I come back down, I hear the screech of a car braking outside. I turn and see this big black Bronco alongside where Hunter and those two guys are talking. The driver pulls out a neon green squirt rifle and opens up on all three of them, laughing and *wooooing*. They jump up and scream but the Bronco peels out onto Vista, away from the freeway, and speeds off. The two guys bolt across the parking lot and into a sedan and go after the Bronco, with no regard for human life.

Hunter yells: "GET SOME!"

I peek outside. "What is going on?" I say.

"That cockpolisher picked the wrong guys to squirt with piss, man. Those motherfuckers are training to be marines. If they catch up to him, they'll fuck him up, piss in his mouth."

"Wow!" I say. "Shit."

"I said piss, not shit."

We stand there staring after them for a while, then watching Vista Plaza sink back into monotony. Hunter finishes his cigarette and puts it out in a dish of sand on top of the stand-up ashtray next to the door.

"She fucking kicked me out, man," he says.

I'm stunned. I have no clue what to say to him. Is he confiding in me? Did he forget I was there?

"What happened?" I manage.

"Nothing." He snorts. "She's fucking certifiable if she thinks she can manipulate my ass."

It's nine-thirty when Hunter comes out with some kind of newspaper, holding it open, and walks up to the concession stand. "We're empty, right?"

"Yes."

He swings the paper onto the counter so I can read it and, using a Sharpie, points to three girls' faces on page twenty. There's a name and a phone number under every black-and-white photograph. "Which one?"

I look at the spread, all pouty lips and perfect hair, cat eyes and manicured hands, most of them showing a bit of tongue in the corner of their lips. One toward the bottom looks like Halida and something tugs at my lungs, tries to collapse them. I do a double take but it's not her.

"Come on, douche."

I look at his choices. They're all blondes like Tracy. I pick the one who looks nothing like her and press my finger on the girl's picture. He smiles.

"Cynthia it is."

The rest of the week passes in monotony. Hunter talks shit about Tracy, her parents, says he would marry Cynthia if only she would take care of him like she did that day and keep her mouth shut. He seems to be serious. I think of Halida, imagine seeing her on a night out in Tuzla, yapping with some girlfriends, and me, hiding behind beer mugs, acting like I don't give a shit but really wondering what's in her heart. Wondering if she would have been worth killing myself for.

On Friday I put my life in jeopardy once more to advertise our showing of *The Good, the Bad and the Ugly*. I keep waiting for Hunter to leave so I can work on jumbling the letters again when he calls me into his office. The only time I've been in there is some two years ago, when a long-departed assistant manager gave me the job. I come inside and realize that Hunter lives here now.

His desk is pushed all the way into the corner, with a TV on top and a sparse beard of cords leading to a VCR, a Nintendo console, and two or three controllers. Next to the desk are a small microwave and a toaster. There is a gargantuan open suitcase under the desk, like a head of a yawning hippo with neatly packed clothes in it. On a clothesline tied around a pipe on one end of the room and to a random rivet sticking out of the wall on the other hang three pressed outfits—his managerial clothes. Leaning in the corner is a rolled-up foam mattress.

Hunter's in his office chair, packing a huge bowl into a six-foot magenta bong. I think back and realize that I haven't had to wait for him to open the doors for me at noon since Saturday—a common occurrence, previously. I try to pretend I'm not surprised, but he can't be fooled.

"What was I gonna do? Sleep in my truck? Move in with my fucking mom?"

I look around, nod my head. "Do owners know?"

"Are you limited? What's wrong with you? Don't ask bombastically moronic questions. Shit, man, think! Everybody is in B, right?"

"Yeah."

"Let's go. I need you to help me light this."

We go to theater A, and staying close to the wall so we cannot be seen by Pamela in the booth, I light the weed and he gets himself high. The theater's high ceilings and the ventilators take care of his exhalations in seconds.

"You wanna hit this?"

"Maybe next time."

He shrugs, then sees something on the back of one of the seats in the last row. "Check this out," he says, giggling. "Remember Cynthia?"

I walk over and look at a white stain on the dark blue fabric, like Lewinsky's dress. He moves his hand in front of his crotch, suggesting fellatio.

"Remind me not to watch movies here," I say, and he smacks my shoulder with hilarity.

"Hey, remember Isidro and Pat? The other day with the piss gun and everything? They're in jail. They caught up to that dude at a red light on the corner of Vista and Century, the busiest fucking intersection, knocked on his window, and when the motherfucker didn't open it, one of them just smashed it with a claw hammer, broke the guy's shoulder with it. And his fuckin' cheekbone too. On the corner of Vista and Century, like, by the mall?"

I nod, smiling, thinking of what he would do to me if he knew I was behind the marquee shenanigans.

"Then the cops caught them," he adds after a pause, lamentably.

We go back into his office and he wraps the bong in a blanket. Then he produces a tab of pills of some variety and pops three or four of them.

"Hey, you wanna stay up tonight and wait for the joker?" he says, an aluminum baseball bat appearing in his hand by some kind of magic.

"I don't know, man."

"Come on. You can add it to your hours. Overtime. Come on!"

"Overtime?"

"Good, backup," he says, and punches out two more of those pills. "Take these. They'll fuck your ass up real good."

I take them. What the fuck.

"You think I can have one of those beers in the ice machine?" I ask.

"Shit yeah, take them all. They were Tracy's. That's the only downer she would take. But you should see her on speed, man. That girl is spinning. Ass like a jackhammer. Bongitty-bongitty-bongitty-bongitty!"

He smiles, but he's too high, and as soon as he's not talking it's just an empty grimace. He sits down, stares glassily at his hands. He doesn't move.

"You okay?" I say.

He looks at me like he didn't even know that we just had a conversation. He nods.

It's four in the morning and I'm with Hunter on the side of the Vista underpass, in the shadows, not even watching the marquee anymore but lying on the dirt and looking at the anemic sky and listening to the big rigs going by on the freeway. He's slurring, going on and on about how beautiful Tracy is, how they met at a fancy rehab in Arizona when she was only sixteen, how they fell in love in sobriety and how they slipped up and how it all turned to shit. He describes their first time, under a piano in her parents' living room while fancies were rubbing elbows by the pool, and every time afterward, every new place riskier than the next: while driving, in front of some industrial building, in her father's office, in the pool where she trains. And he sobs and the tears pool in his earlobes and he says that everything is over.

He tells me everything except why she kicked him out.

I sit up.

"Don't go yet," he says.

I show him that I'm only taking a sip of my beer. He takes his hand off my elbow. He clonks his head back against the ground, like someone giving up. Lying there with his shirt unbuttoned, he looks emaciated and thrown away.

"I love that fucking bitch," he says.

"Why did you break up, then?"

He looks back at the sky. "It's stupid."

"Tell me."

"Nah."

"What did you do?"

"Nothing."

"Come on."

"You'd laugh."

"What is it?"

"It's dumb."

"What is it?"

He says nothing. I wait. He says nothing still, his eyes rolling from one part of the sky to another, searching. I realize I have to piss. I move to stand up and he goes: "I want her to die."

"No, you don't."

"Yes, I do."

"Why?"

He points at the overpass above us, flops his arm back on the ground. "See this goddamned street? Every gangsta-ass fucking day she has to drive down this goddamned street when she goes to school and on the weekends when she has training. She's a diver. Did I tell you this?"

"Yes."

"Well, I saw her with some . . . fuckin' asshole . . ." he says, and chokes up. I look at him and he might as well be a cadaver, with lips pulled away from bared teeth and hollow sockets with eyes closed—a gruesome mask of ancient, candid, lonely human pain.

I drink until he opens his eyes again.

"Why don't you just apologize?" I ask him.

He looks at me like manager Hunter for the briefest of moments, then turns back to gushiness. "I can't do that."

"Why?"

"Because then she wins."

"She wins what?"

He snorts, sadly. "You wouldn't understand," he says, and turns away from me.

"Just call her and say, *Baby, I am sorry. Please take me back.*"

"She doesn't like those imbecilic terms of endearment."

"What do you call her?"

We say nothing for a while. I think of the first time I met Tracy, how much I hated her and her stupid whiny voice, her sense of entitlement, the way she looked down on me. And right there, as I think of her, something gets illuminated by a spotlight in my head, makes me smile.

"I have to go number two," I say, and stand up. My limbs feel heavy and full of meat but at least the world isn't spinning anymore. "You left the back door open?"

He grunts.

I go down to the theater and take a leak in the darkness. I go into the cabinets and pull out the box of black letters, spend some time choosing the ones I need. Outside, right by the back door, I hide them behind the little brick wall along with the rubber-tipped stick and make my way to the overpass.

I remember the aftermath of Hurricane Halida, the ferocity of my hatred for her. Every time I'd been in love before and the love had been lost, I'd still been me, miserable, broken, but still me. But there's something about betrayal that for a while turns love to hate, while the intensity of the feeling remains constant. I remember thoughts, vivid scenarios that would spring into my mind out of nowhere, as if someone else were putting them there. Someone evil. These palpable flashes that soiled me forever.

I wished Halida brokenhearted. I wished her poor. I wished her anorexic. I wished her obese, in one of those fat-people-wheelchair-carts with a flag on them. I wished her broken under a car. I wished her decapitated. I wished her toothless. I wished her legs amputated. I wished her bald and blind. I wished her wrecked at the bottom of a flight of stairs. I wished her overdosed. I wished her floating face-first down in a river. I wished her buried up to her neck in a desert. I wished her dangling off a beam. I wished her poisoned. I wished her sorry. I wished her dead.

I wished these things against her for making me have these foreign thoughts in this foreign land when I first came back from Bosnia and for three months carried a jar of random pills in my backpack just in case.

My friends say she's in a band these days.

When I get back to the shadows Hunter is dead to the world. I half-wake him and then half-carry him into his office, where I lay him down on the floor. I lock the back door and with my stash of letters and my trusty rubber-tipped stick I stand under the marquee.

Tomorrow some other asshole will drive that bitch Tracy to an early-morning diving practice. Puffed and groggy, she will look up at the marquee. Hunter will still be passed out on the floor inside, with no idea what I've done, and I myself will be long gone, but what she will read is this:

**FRIDAY MIDNIGHT CLASSICS
@ VISTA TWIN THEATERS:
I LOVE YOU, WICKED GIRL
I AM SORRY, TAKE ME BACK**

Dear Bill,

I got the sneakiest of letters today. A doozy. One of those unassuming pieces of data that upon making a landing on the old noggin at once capsizes thought, upsets all the colors, and snuffs out the sun like a birthday candle . . . I fled inside, went to the john to die, or not to. When I turned on the light and flushed the toilet, its hole kept on sucking everything down, swirl-swallowing my entire body, headfirst, twisting it and somehow folding its image into the curving shapes of the inward-caving bathroom, circling these elongated, ever tightening cavatappi of image that just seconds ago was matter, and collapsing it all into a speck. Boy. I'm sitting here struggling with how to tell it to you in this format. Sometimes I really wish writing was enough. Or translating into writing. Sometimes I really wish you were real.

And I woke up singing this morning! Singing *dzigera*, to be exact, but still, singing. I fed my betta fish next to the bed, made some faces at it, thinking of the phrase *drinks like a fish*, checked on the orchid on the sill, and on the way to the bathroom, I caught myself humming this overly sentimental shit: *I tebe sam sit kafano!*, which means "I'm sick of you too, my tavern," the high example of this boozy kind of music derogatorily called *dzigera* back in the old country—kitschy and regrettably unavoidable in the Balkans. I washed up, thinking, Where's this coming from, Izzy?, but it kept coming again and again as I put on my gym clothes, made my shake, grabbed my keys and wallet: *I'm sick of you too, my tavern / I pray to God you catch on fire / She's left me because of the wine, blah blah blah*. What the fuck? I'm a punker, right? *Dzigera* shouldn't even be in my vocabulary!

Then an image of the word alighted in my mind. I was walking through the parking lot to the Prius, twirling my keys, when I remembered the yellow room in our rented house in Portland, the one my ex designated as my office because of the primary paint job. She got me this dry-erase board that she hung above the desk and wrote the words **TO DO** on it. **DZIGERA**, I wrote underneath in big block letters. She asked me what it meant and I told her it was a private word just for me, a warning to myself, a reminder of what I needed to do.

I usually get the mail on the way *back* from the gym, but for some reason I stopped by the mailboxes and checked mine, found two flyers and a letter from Community Health. I had done a mental evaluation, a physical, an ultrasound, and some basic bloodwork after my last missive to you (what was it, a month and a half ago?), but nobody ever called me like they'd promised. I was over it and would have just tossed the envelope into the passenger seat for later but it kind of looked like a bill and I didn't need another bill, Bill.

The letter itself looked like it was written by robots, like a four-page form crammed into one to save paper. My eyes didn't know what to read, kept looking for the dollar amount they were undoubtedly asking for. There was a logo, some medical disclaimers in separate shaded boxes, bold text galore. And then I saw this single, cold, and unassuming sentence as a bullet point, hidden in the mess of all the other useless language, under a diminutive heading of "The Results of the Ultrasound." I read it forward and backward, I looked away from it and read it again, I cursed and read it again, and when its meaning dawned on me, when it reeeeeally landed, I knew exactly why I woke up singing that song, why *dzigera* haunted me all morning.

Liver.

She wasn't exactly happy about me keeping the meaning of the word *dzigera* to myself back then. She did let it go, though, for good. But hey, she's a computer whiz and maybe she looked it up, I don't know. If she <u>had</u> found out, she didn't mention it to me; it was always a bit taboo for her, the topic of alcoholism and what it does to the body. We never talked about it other than when I brought it up over the years, when I was unraveled and crying for help. So, I could only just write about it, imagine in fiction what our future could look like if we didn't address it head-on. We were thinking about kids back then and I had asked her to read this next chapter but she couldn't.

I'm sorry. About the whole thing.

i.

Teletović Grills Lamb, Defensively[2]

BEFORE

You pass out and—at once, it seems—a pointy knee lands in the place where your ass and spine meet. As you come to, you do catch the tail end of your own loud snore.

"Seriously?" she hisses with lament.

She does this to the darkness, the universe, not you. Her fists flop up, then kamikaze onto the mattress, righteous and driven.

Your body starts to do it even before you think to, and you turn to your away side, slide your right hand under a yeasty pillow, open up your breathing passages by pushing your left shoulder away from your chest. Then—here it comes—her hand pulls and yanks at your shoulder a little bit more, helping out.

She has taped you snoring (*honking*) on her phone and made that your special ring on it. You imagine her away from her desk and purse and her coworkers going up to her in the office kitchen, saying: "Oh dear, your husband is sawin' your desk in half, hahahahah!"

You lie there, twisted and guilty, listening to her breathe. When the air intakes are no longer angry-seeming and exhales strained, you dare an *I love you.*

It ricochets right back in her whisper, fast. At once, in fact.

2　Taken out of context from a YouTube NBA Highlights clip by an unknown announcer, commenting on Teletović blocking Lamb's ill-advised runner.

Too fast?

Automatic?

You swear to God you're not going to fall asleep until you hear *her* snore. You stretch your spine, open your eyes, and fuck you! if you're ever fucking going back to sleep ever again! That'll show her! A sacrifice on your part. That will make things good and even.

You stare at the bed stand in the grayness, a silhouette of your eye-glasses against the wall.

Eye-glasses. What a language!

In English they come up with one word for something, and every time they find another function for that something, they just add another word to the original to specify what they mean: window glass, glass of Scotch . . . glass eye . . . hahahaha (eyeglasses for my glass eyes—glasseyeglasses?)— hahahaha!

You can't tell if she's still awake. No sound from her side, just the rattle of your own preposterous thoughts. It seems safe though to close your eyes in the presence of it. So you do.

—fake glass, stained glass, pebbled glass . . . *bulletproof, my ass!* you watch Mishko say, lying in fatigues in the mud next to you mid-enemy-onslaught, tracers doing a clinic on Doppler effect right above your heads *I worked in security for fifteen years, in Sarajevo, in Ljubljana, all over the country* and now a mortar hits close enough and you hear the hissing spray of shrapnel puncturing holes in the fabric of his diatribe *I worked for banks and treasuries and I'll tell you one thing, none of that shit is bulletproof, not in this fucking country it ain't, in America maybe but they're too cheap here so they make it look like it's thick and strong but you put a nine-mil in that sucker and guess what? there's a nine-millimeter hole in it, that's what . . .* and the way Mishko is lying on his side there, cleaning his teeth with a twig, his face propped up on his left hand while yours and every other soldier's is pressed into Mother Bosnia, swallowing it while praying not to be swallowed, until you have to breathe again and crazy Mishko is on his back now and he has his dick out and he's pissing up into the air yelling *kill my piss! come on, kill my piss* and the piss is going everywhere *you can't kill my piss, you assholes! kiss my piss* and now he's trying to catch it in his mouth, laughing, not like a hyena at all, because when hyenas laugh you know they are in there, in those bodies, emitting sounds for a reason, and you turn your head away to the other side to find your son, Haris, there, skeletal in his System of a Down T-shirt and a beanie and he is getting ready to advance at the enemy with no weapon, no training, no sense and you scream *HARISE NEMOJ!* and he doesn't even take the buds out of his ears and without looking at you he screams *MY NAME IS HARRIS!* to the wet mound of earth in front of him, he crouches and cocks his body for a sprint, and you scramble for him, for his calf, for his sneaker, but he is up and over the mound and you wake in your bed, poached under the comforter, sodden and mealy, your heart a pump in distress.

And it's four-thirty, of course, like every other morning.

Your heart labors to thrust panic out every corner of your body, pushing grainy blood, scrubbing out deep unreachables. Separating your jaws, you gauge the vibration quotient of your morning shakes. Chatter go the teeth.

MY NAME IS HARRIS! nobody screams for real. Not really.

You know better than to lie there any longer. Keeping silent, you put on your eyeglasses, step into your sweatpants, and sneak out of the room.

You want to walk into the kitchen next but the kitchen door is closed. And you . . . you just can't just open it.

You stand in front of the obstacle, wondering whether you should just reach out your hand, grasp the doorknob, gently twist it, let the door swing open, and enter. Or if it's easier to go the long way through the living room and the dining room and enter the kitchen from the south, where there's no door.

And you go the long way. You go in through the living room and open the fridge.

Tupperware upon Tupperware, neatly dated and labeled with masking tape. You squat and pick up three-day-old leftover steak and two braised leeks, a dozen eggs and a half bottle of vermouth from the door. You dump the cut-up meat and leeks into a baking dish, whip up six eggs in some half-and-half, mix it all together, and drop the dish into the toaster oven on 350. As you watch the countdown start, you open the bottle of vermouth and pound it, wash it out in the sink, discard the screw top in the trash, and delicately place the bottle in the recycling.

The recycling is full.

You remember Himzo, a guy who lived next door to your grandparents' house in the village who waited for downpours and snowmelts to dump trash can after trash can of beer bottles off the bridge and into the little river, right there where in the summer you and his own barefoot kids would swim around and try to catch chub with your bare hands. Recycling, Bosnia-style.

You grate some cheddar, pour some salsa into a bowl, arrange the hot sauces for her and the ketchup bottle for Haris at the table, and you stare out the window. The old woman across the way has one of those fake wells in her manicured yard. The sky above her house, hedges, is ruddy. Birds fly fast and planes fly slow across it.

The toaster oven beeps.

You got this down to science. You take out the dish, make sure that every part of the surface of the egg is covered with cheese, than put it back in on warm. By the time they get up, it'll be perfectly melted but not burnt.

Job done, you make your way down to the basement. Haris calls it Little Bosnia, jokes with his one friend that you need a passport to enter. It's just a normal little basement, washer, dryer, workspace with the wartime Bosnian flag sporting lilies on a shield push-pinned to the wall above, and the smaller postwar flag draped over the vise. Some of your memorabilia is down here too, photographs and trinkets, and also your new 1.75-liter bottle of cheapo vodka, down on the shelf behind the spider-infested coils of Christmas lights that came with the house.

You unscrew the top slowly, making long pauses in between the clicks when the perforated plastic pieces of the cap snap as you twist. Somebody stirs upstairs. The bed creaks. You're frozen, waiting, the bottle open. Whatever sound escapes next will determine your course of action. You're all ears.

But the stirring stops, and you take a pull on the bottle in slow motion so there's no slosh. You swallow and gag, manage to keep it in and down. Inebriation boggles the mind. Here it arises, the certain calm that comes from feeling the effects of going through the motions of a ritual. You take another sloshless pull, stash the bottle.

There was this brutalist TV relay on top of Mount Majevica that everybody wanted, this, artillery-wise, strategic point that you saw at least seven people die fighting for in your brief stint in the Armed Forces of Bosnia and Herzegovina when you were eighteen. The trenches were manned by civilians, really, grown family men with people to lose, constantly on the verge of crying or losing their minds. There were also these seasoned near-psychopaths, already not human anymore, cracking up at things the family men found unbearable, yelling truly funny, soul-blackening observations at the enemy and shitting and masturbating in full view of whomever. Of course, there was always a sampling of you greenhorns, geeky students whose parents didn't have enough money to send abroad, who were picked up in street raids and sent up the mountain in your jeans and Converse, with semi-automatic rifles from WWII with five to ten bullets, largely impotent against cannon and mortar shells and a much richer army up the hill that stopped firing projectiles only to literally "cool off the pipes."

You zone out for a while.

Upstairs, the bed creaks again, creaks some more, then heels on the wooden floor, over your head and to the bathroom door, shower on, tinkle of piss, flush, laundry chute open, and you look up and wait for it, and here it comes: a tank top with a built-in boob support falls down into the laundry basket, camouflage panties with pink frill, two balled-up ankle socks, in that order. Bath curtain screeches and the sound of the shower changes with a body in it. You take another swig for posterity, fast now, not worried about the slosh with all that water splashing around her ears up there. You gather your giddy legs to climb the stairs.

The door to Haris's room is covered with posters: apocalyptic horrors, fat bloody clown faces sticking out their tongues or gnashing yellow teeth, freaks with smiley-face irises, ornately designed words written in symbols that resemble letters yet are unfathomable to you. You place your ear into one of the clown's mouths and listen for the signs of life. You knock lightly, then regular-knock after a second.

"*Ustaj radni narode Bosne i Hercegovine!*" you say cheerfully into the door.

You hear him grunt in there before a wall of music informs you the message has been received. Another task accomplished, you walk your giddy legs toward the sanctuary of the bathroom and have to curb their giddiness when Beloved blurs by across your way and into the bedroom, her face now even skinnier with wet hair. She's in a bathrobe.

"Good morning, you," you say from the doorway.

"Good morning, hon," she says, pulling clothes out of one of the lower drawers and tossing them backward onto the bed. "I'm so late."

"Should I make your breakfast to go?"

"Nah, I'll wolf it down here. Let them wait."

"You done with the bathroom?"

"Oh! You know you shouldn't sit in there that long, right?"

Her boobs are out and you chance it, go over to touch them.

"Cold, cold," she whimpers even before you touch her, continues like that when you do. It's good to see a smile, however tired. You hug her and she responds and it feels so good—the best feeling in the world—but then her body stiffens. You don't let go.

"Honey, I'm late."

You make sure not to exhale when you kiss her on the lips, then break off to the bathroom.

"I'm serious about sitting in there forever!"

"Let me do my thing!" you project through the door.

"It's gross!"

You go straight to the mirror triptych hiding two medicine chests, open them, and arrange these mirror doors in such a way that, when you sit on the toilet, you can't see your reflection in any of them. You cover the bowl because you don't really have to go, open the stained-glass window a smidge, sit down, and wait for your family to leave.

The magazine rack is obscenely full and you pick up a random one and flip the pages, stop on a picture of a stylish funeral—lots of black-and-white contrast with just enough sepia. You find yourself smiling because what pops in your head is this forever bachelor back in Bosnia who would go to all the funerals in town—atheist, Muslim, Orthodox, Catholic, all of them—and sneak into the line of grieving family members just so that people who were going down the line offering their condolences would pity him too, shake his hand too, pray for him too. When townspeople came upon the impostor, they all politely pretended and gave him honest-to-God condolences, saving the snickering and gossip for when he was out of earshot.

You lean your head on the wall tile and stare through the turquoise window slit at the visible sliver of the street. Somehow it's that forever bachelor who drives by in a Saturn.

"Bye, honey! Have a good day!"

"Bye, love!" you say with a voice of a man. Your eyes are wet, maybe from vodka.

When you see her SUV pass, you get up and close the mirror doors, staring at the sink. When was the last time you washed your face? Just the thought of being in contact with water terrifies you.

In the kitchen you find out that both of them have eaten because one of the plates is in the sink and the other, the ketchup-smeared one, is still on the dining room table. You check the time on the microwave and hop over to Haris's door again, bang on the images. You do know the names of the bands, you're familiar with what your kid's into—you're not that old—but you feel like it bothers him that you do and so you keep playing your role.

"*Hajde vec jednom! Harise! Zakasnicesh!*"

"I know!" Haris yells out.

It now sounds like there's a baby rhino in the room, lumbering across parquetry, smashing into walls, running over furniture. The music shuts off before your first-and-only-born opens the door, backpacked and bean-ied, his skinny arms almost pellucid sticking out of his pitch-black T-shirt sleeves. Mad-eyed, like in your dream.

He weasels by, closing the door behind him.

"*Shto che ti kapa po 'vakom vremenu?*"

"I like it, Dad! I like my beanie."

"*Ne kazem ja . . . nego biche ti vruche, bolan bolan.*"

"Then I'll take it off! Jesus!"

He's finally running out and down the street, late like his momma.

You shut your eyes and the door against the guilt. You breathe it in like a flower, hold it until it burns, and let it out. You have to imagine the relief as you do.

At some point in the morning, you become aware you're just strolling around your place with a handle of vodka in tow, dragging a forefinger over everything you come across and claiming it for yourself, saying out loud, in Bosnian: *. . . this is my wall . . . this is my doorway . . . this is my corner . . . and so is* this *wall . . . this is my carpet . . . and that right there is my light switch* *too* . . . until you're again in front of Haris's door. You quiet when you notice (can it be the first time?) a white sticker on it that says: PRIVATE.

You recall a dirty magazine by the same name that, when you were a little kid, the bigger kids would send you to buy for them. They'd write a shopping list in their best grown-up handwriting and entrust you with their pooled money. You'd go over to the place they called the Three Kiosks, go up to one of them, get up on your toes so that the woman working could see you over the shelf of newspapers, and you'd hand her the list and the money, turning up the innocence and cuteness. She'd ask a stern *Who's this for?* and you were instructed to say *My dad!* in your natural falsetto, no acting necessary there. She'd grumble but pack the magazine and whatever else random shit was on the list, the decoys—Ping-Pong balls and lighters, a political weekly or a trashy thriller paperback—into a plastic bag and tell you to run it straight home.

"Private, my ass," you say. "This is my door."

You walk into your son's room. The BO is pubertal. The bed's unmade. The sliding closet doors bulge. You twist the shutters open some, take in the creatures on the walls.

"This is my room."

You ease into Haris's desk chair, rotate in it to face the computer, set the bottle on the desk, and lean back.

And right when you're ready to claim the chair as well, in the slight crack in between two extinguished full-screen monitors, taped to the wall, you recognize a face. Bemused, you separate the monitors and stare at an article from a newspaper and a photograph of a white basketball player with floppy blond hair, in a white jersey, number 33, midair, sideways-leaning, *just out of reach of Vince Carter's outstretched hand.*

"TELETOVIĆ SHUTS DOWN MAVS WITH 34," reads the headline, and you're crying now with some kind of pride and shame, some kind of hapless happiness, because despite the fact that your son hates you for driving him and his only friend to school in a downpour on the wrong side of the road for a full minute, blotto and brazen and downplaying the danger after the fact, there's still some Bosnian pride in there, somewhere. You didn't manage to fully sour that half of him yet.

Going for the bottle again on this, your only day off, you brush the cordless mouse in the process and awaken both screens to a suspended game, an old-school first-person shooter by the looks of it, its pixels extra-rectangular on a high-resolution monitor. There's a sky with circling vultures and below is the beige desert with rudimentary bushes and cacti, blocky man-made buildings. Superimposed and gaudy are red and blue letters, lists, representing scores and percentages: 1. AARONSTAR_CA, 2. LITTLE BUDDHA, 3. I_KILLED_SADDAM, 4. MYSTERIOUS LADY COCK, etc.

In the bottom-right corner: PRESS ENTER TO JOIN THE MULTIPLAYER GAME.

"This is my game," you say, and you press the button.

There's a countdown and when it reaches zero you find yourself in the beige desert mid-enemy-onslaught. You stare at your pixilated hand holding a pixilated pistol you wouldn't know how to cock in real life—a fancy Hollywood thing, this. You don't know how to move in this world so you just stand there in the desert, listening to the bursts and cracks of automatic weapons, watching what you assume are your fellow comrades (since they don't shoot at you) wondrously respawn in front of your eyes, become corporeal out of thin air, check their weapons, and jog into the battle as into a soccer game.

It's something in the way the instant messages pop up in the upper-right-hand corner next to a clock and a countdown that you realize that this war is live, that it's being fought as you sit there with a bottle in your lap. *Kind of like in the real war you brag about being in, that you use as an excuse for various shitty behaviors, drinking to name one of them.* You shake your head at the thought, concussing it away.

"*HALO BA*, LITTLE BUDDHA! *DE PROBUDI SE!*" one of the messages reads.

You gather that this is meant for Haris, that your son has chosen LITTLE BUDDHA as his avatar, that LITTLE BUDDHA is a female soldier with a beanie on, face camouflage-painted, that someone out there in the world knows that your LITTLE BUDDHA, your son, is half-Bosnian, and speaks to him in his mother tongue. It makes sense that it's an old '90s first-person shooter too because the guy writing to him is probably in Bosnia, which is ten–twenty years behind the rest of the world, or more. You can't sway the tears that Haris is practicing his Bosnian, can't help but spin the story this way.

Some pixilated soldier with red on his arm pops up from the horizon, takes a shot at you, and you're dead apparently, your prone body spinning in a circle in the center of the screen. Soon the countdown starts again from ten and you respawn in a different environment now, but with the same pistol, same choppy hand.

There's a mesh tent to your right and bullets are zooming by, and in the messages ORGANSKI_TE_NE_MOGU writes: I BRAINED LITTLE BUDDHA, so you bring the keyboard closer to you, and in Bosnian you write: WAIT-WAIT-WAIT! I LOST MY CONTACT LENS BY THE MESH TENT. HAS ANYONE SEEN IT? Since you're clueless about how to move LITTLE BUDDHA around, the message board feels like the only place you can make a difference.

"HAHAHAHA," writes ORGANSKI_TE_NE_MOGU, and then you're hit again, in the thigh this time, and back to twirling stiffly in your death grip as again the countdown starts anew.

ORGANSKI_TE_NE_MOGU killed LITTLE BUDDHA, the message board announces.

"HEY ORGANSKI, WHAT'S THE WEATHER LIKE IN BOS-NIA RIGHT NOW?" you type in Bosnian, hopefully.

"WOT DE FAK IS RONG WIT YU BUDDHA? LET'S GO!"

"I'M A LOVER, NOT A FIGHTER."

"YOU'RE A FAG," ORGANSKI_TE_NE_MOGU types in Bosnian.

A soldier sidles over to you on screen, same blue emblem on *his* arm too. He stands in front of you, sleeves pulled up over meaty forearms, week worth of digital stubble, Stallone sunglasses. He goes through his arsenal, showing you his knife, his pistol, his submachine gun, his M16, his LAW, his satchel charge, his frag grenade.

"YOU WOULDN'T SHOOT A WOMAN IN A BEANIE."

The soldier drops a frag grenade in front of your feet, runs to safety. He turns to watch.

You know what a hand grenade does to a human body, to a soldier you knew by the name of Sanela D., to be precise . . . this portly young woman all of whose male relatives perished in Eastern Bosnia, who was then allowed to join the army but only because she was a junior women's air rifle champion in 1989, who in the first week of trench time took out two enemy soldiers from a great distance with a rickety semiautomatic rifle—two shots/two kills—graduated immediately to Dragunov sniper rifle to became a sharpshooting star, who then got friendly-raped one night by her own spotter, a fellow Bosnian soldier, and washed him out of her vulva in a trench pond as he wept and rationalized what he'd done to her, blaming war stress, the Balkan curse, and life.

She killed with him for two weeks longer, listening all the while to his apologies, each one of which insisted that he was a victim too, and at some boring but insane point in their day she had to walk away from him and she did, to some blackberry bushes—alive and abuzz with clueless insects that day—just because she couldn't abide suffering that narrative any longer. Kneeling among the bloom-brambles in the streaking sun, she realized she couldn't bullshit herself no more, that his narrative will never be unclaimed, unheard, that what he did will never be undone, that fucked-up things never get unfucked, just endured, that she might as well be done with knowing and pain, and the pain of knowing.

She went prone, pulled her hand grenade close to her chest, put it between her heart and the soil that would receive it, and brought it to life with a click, not certain at all, yet stoic enough in her action.

You were on military police duty that night even though you were a greenhorn and didn't have a proper uniform yet. The sergeant in charge was miffed about this goddamn complication in his life, a destroyed rifle, his rotten luck, and he ordered you and Mishko to guard the body until the morning—all of the body. Somebody was apparently en route to photograph the incident, investigate.

Mishko, that psycho, picked himself to guard Sanela's head, which was some twelve meters into the wood from the body. He spun a yarn for your benefit as he worked on himself behind the blackberries, conjuring up disgusting scenarios with a fantasy female form that could complete the severed head at his feet, a form that would allow him to *love* it, as he put it. He grunted and gagged, made overzealous faces, in the end ejaculating onto some leaves. He went to sleep then and there. The whole night you could look at *your* charge only once. Her torso was bloody and angled downward into a small crater. A solitary vertebra glared wet and white in the moonlight.

She looked as if she tried to burrow and bury herself by chewing her way into a grave to be out of sight from the likes of you. You know what a hand grenade does to a human body, and you gladly let this one burst in between your feet. You deserve it.

AFTER

You get up the moss-grown stairway of your new underground domicile, a new Little Bosnia, its memorabilia still in boxes and Trader Joe's paper bags for more than a year now. The front door you still lock, though, your key chain strangely light with only two keys on it. You say goodbye to no family, feel the pang of it, but the voice in your head says an equivalent of *Fuck you, asshole!* in that weird mixture of thought and utterance displaced bilingual people have to stomach in their heads their entire lives.

What they call a gorgeous summer day in these parts, in Vancouver, WA, is straight-up blinding, positive in an offending way. You hang in the shadow until the truth-voice is finished, until you can first hear the sound of and then finally locate a woodpecker plastic-pecking a box atop a pole, going at it good. In the shaggy yard below, among car seats and IKEA bed skeletons, a red, white, and blue sign says: THIS LAWN IS TREATED. You walk to where you parked the Mighty Max.

"Like shit," you mumble into your chin.

"Like your wife and kid," your brain chimes in. *No.* No jokes for you.

It was Beloved's spring cleaning that got you here and got her to Idaho.

You were on your way back from your sporadic second job, a weekend delivery gig in California, and got stuck in traffic near Woodburn for four and a half hours and couldn't make it home, had to drive straight to work, worked the closing shift at the largest meat department in the city, dragged your exhausted ass home at one in the morning, kicked off your animal-fat-covered rubber anti-slip slip-on booties on the patio, stumbled into the house to an artful display on the coffee table of some thirty to forty bottles of booze and boxes of wine in various degrees of annihilation that were stashed and/or forgotten in the nooks and crannies of the house over the years, to the tear-bloated face of your sniper-eyed wife who thought (or made herself wishfully think) you were done with all that.

Zero words.

In fear, in tears, unable to bear her fear and tears, you went back into the living room and moved all the bottles and boxes to the kitchen, dumped them out in the sink, watching the garbage disposal devour pungent liquids, a part in you crying for every spilled drop.

You stomped the wine boxes into cardboard and recycled the bottles with defeated but angry, capable hands, did what you should, knowing how futile it was to should-do anything, what an outward performance this act was, an attempt to cover up inner stink by doing outer perfuming, knowing how unchanged you were by this act, how broken you were, always had been. That your grandfather was broken in the identical way but that your family hid this fact from the children and the cousins and the community at large and instead spun tall tales about a jovial man who played the shit out of an accordion, laughed with abandon, was the life of a party, was a legendary basketball trainer, bighearted and barrel-chested, and not a wife-beater, and not the recognize-him-passed-out-in-the-river-embankment, fat-livered drunkard that he was. That despite this fact your father never told you about it, even named you after him, never saying, *Hey, this drinking shit runs in the family, maybe you should watch out for it.*

"Boo-hoo," said the truth-sayer in your head, says it still nowadays, on a loop. Only malt quiets it and only for a spell.

And back then you just couldn't stop crying, couldn't stop coughing and gagging and fighting for air, and then she was next to you, barefoot on tile, not touching you but standing there holding her elbows, her boobs pushed together.

"Come to bed," she said, and it destroyed any feeling in you that you might have merited this kindness, this love, any love.

You stared at your hands spread on the tile and the following thoughts appeared in this succession: This is not your tile. You don't deserve this beautiful tile. Get your hands off that tile. But fuck this tile! Why tile, and beautifully at that? Why the need to tile? To make it easier to clean the dirt? Like we're not it? Like we don't end up in it? Boo-hoo! Boooooo! Hooooooo!

She helped you to the bathroom and you washed your face in half-darkness, blew and inverse-blew your nose. She stepped out and closed the door. You swaddled your face in a towel, dared, and looked at this hell creature in the mirror triptych, this unholy trinity of you.

Boooooo! Hooooooo!

You then slowly knelt at the laundry chute and opened it, silently, of course. You reached inside and up on the little shelf made by the foundation beam and you found what you knew was going to be there, the last-resort bottle of vodka. It was half-full so you took two long gulps, made sure there was some left for tomorrow, for the shakes and the sweats and the like, you Listerined your mouth twice, and went to not-your bed.

Now, on the way into Portland, they raise the fucking bridge. You call in, tell Isidro you might be late and why. Isidro is a cruel boss who's secretly afraid of you because you're the only person in his employ who's been to college. Community college, but still. He calls you Professor—a flaming anti-intellectual slight—and makes fun of the thinness of your arms, their inability to throw a baseball out of a paper bag or some such macho American spiel. You can't wait to check this week's work schedule to see if he heeded your concerns, ready to kill him if he didn't or, most likely, go up the chain of command. Or finally just give up.

The only reason you applied for the job was because Beloved was into cooking and you wanted to learn where on an animal certain cuts come from, to become a good sous-chef for her. But, guarding his managerial position, Isidro is yet to let you open, scared to have you around at the start of day when real butchering is going on.

"Get in as soon as possible," he says.

You curse at the wheel. A motorist next to your truck is openly staring and you turn away from her. In a pool of rainwater on the bridge's bike path a lean crow ducks its head in, shakes it off, unfolds its wings up in the air, and starts cawing, standing there like *Come at me, bruh!*

You went cold turkey for Beloved, though you said it was for you. Cold turkey under her watchful eye. You trembled on the couch like a child, sweated through sheets and cushions and decorative pillows, starting one

TV show and waking up tangled mid-another, trying to make sense of the narrative. You drank pitchers of water and Gatorade and listened to your heart mosh around in your chest, hating you more than your brain does.

The shakes eased after two days and you went back to work where the produce department suddenly went blurry (you were walking to the break room from lunch) and you said something like *I don't think this is right* and woke up ten minutes later as they were loading you into the ambulance with your tongue chewed raw and bleeding, and your work pants soaked with urine, and the technician saying that your blood pressure is 222 over some other apparently crazy, impossible number and Marcy from produce was reporting to Beloved on your phone, holding your wallet that she'd shoved into your mouth when you passed out because she's an epileptic and could tell a grand mal when she saw one.

And still you went to drinking. Medicinal drinking, you called it in your head, keeping just enough alcohol in your system so that you don't have another seizure. Booo-hoooollshit!

This time, though, Beloved was the one crying and coughing and gasping for air and you were the one standing mutely. And she said that you could go to court and make it complicated or she could just take Harris (she called Haris Harris this time even though she always tried to pronounce it in the Bosnian way before) and go back to Idaho. That if it went to court you probably would never be allowed to see him. That she loves you, that she always would, but that she is not going to do this anymore.

You cried and pleaded but she cried harder and pleaded not.

Both of your tear ducts went dry.

Haris went with Beloved gladly, no fuss. You gave him some pictures of Bosnia, of the family back there, and he threw them in the pocket of his backpack.

"I hope you wake up" is how he put it before they drove away.

The work schedule has you closing six days in a row.

Isidro is hiding in his office but you march right in there and ask him about the schedule. You try to talk like the rest of the butchers, try to be macho. You ask about the opening shift, he says *seniority*. You ask about the middle one, *seniority*. You try to joke, say that this schedule is seriously cutting into your *fucking* time. He laughs and laughs. You say that there's always two extra hours of work, every night to close; he says that you're receiving your overtime. You mention going to Michael, the store manager, another man who went to college. Isidro stops laughing.

"Do you like booze, Professor?"

"Huh?"

You didn't see it coming.

"Because you smell like it."

"So fire me," you say, though you know he's reluctant, has been before, for reasons probably having to do with politics.

Couple of months earlier you were so done with this job, so wanted to get fired, that you started breaking all the rules. You parked in the customer parking lot, came in without the no-slip booties, would go on your break and, in full butcher regalia (store logo prominent), walk across the parking lot to a Tex-Mex boozer in the same plaza, drink three White Russians in an hour, and come back swaying. The motherfucker would see it and still put you on the bone saw.

"I defrosted a bunch of turkeys this morning," he says now. "They need to get cut."

You fuck around in the back room, moving as if with purpose but not doing any work. When you're done with that you go to the Prepared Foods to see who's manning the meat stand and there's Kevin the comedian, in his white coat, flipping thick pieces of bacon on the Foreman grill.

"C'moan, Professah. Dig in."

"I don't dig on swine," you quote Samuel L. Jackson.

He laughs, at your accent, it seems. "This is lahmb bacon."

"Lamb?"

"Yeah, man. New item."

You go to the bowl and pick a good-looking, nicely caramelized chunk and put it in your mouth. It's salty and fatty and the best thing that happened to you your whole day and then Kevin starts to cackle, says that it seems you do indeed dig on swine, hahahahahahah, and who ever heard of lamb bacon?

It's suddenly wintertime 1994 and you haven't had nothing but thin lentils for months, yet every day Mishko is slicing smoked meat on the butt of his rifle with a hunting knife, sharing it with whoever asks to partake. Since you don't eat pork, you ask him if it's pork. He says no. Beef? No? Lamb? No? Chicken? No? Fucking . . . kangaroo? You're getting closer now, he says. Other soldiers in the trench figured it was probably rabbit or squirrel, and they tugged on the jerky with their side teeth or cut it up into their lentils for fortification and protein until a guy you all called Popeye found out that, on his weeks off, in town, Mishko harvested the clueless dogs that the populace under siege kicked out of their families for lack of food. He shot them in the street, strung them up in his garage, then smoked their haunches in a makeshift smoker in the back of his house. Alsatians, poodles, pugs, bulldogs. Ex-Lassies. Ex-Fidos.

When you all asked him why? oh, why in the fuck! did he do it, Mishko said:

"Jebo meze i rakiju bez suhog mesa."

You stand, staring at Kevin, this twenty-three-year-old single father of a seven-year-old daughter, good-looking, a hard worker (rides three buses from downtown to open at six) . . . And there's no malice in his laugh. This is just how guys he knows do. A healthy prank. A bit of ball-busting. No big deal.

And you step toward him, and then you back away. You look at the entrance, the ceiling, your sordid booties, his face again. His smile is gone now. He looks worried. Things go splotched and blurry in your eyes and you think: So much for micro-dosing alcohol to prevent seizures.

But it isn't a seizure. It's a . . . miracle, an epiphany.

It comes into your head that in about forty-five minutes there's a decent chance that, though in Idaho, Haris might spawn up to fight a war in a fake beige desert in the form of a female soldier named LITTLE BUDDHA and that is the only thing that has ever mattered to you in the history of time and space.

People yell your name from behind but you glide out of the store and to the Mighty Max, through splotches and blurs of reality, looking like it's already changing to pixels of the video game you can't wait to enter.

* * *

You make it to Little Bosnia in record time. Your heart's beaming when you kick the booties off your sneakers and abandon them out there on the curb, finished with that shit. Downstairs, you unlock the front door, grab and gulp out of the first bottle you see, so you don't have to taste anything until you're at the very bottom of it. Your room is brutal cement on all sides, except the ceiling. You choke down the harsh aftertaste in tears, looking up at the gutted exposed-beam way some Americans leave the underbellies of their homes. The tears are mechanical, not sad.

The sink/toilet/shower are separated from the living area with a single wall and a shower curtain with red-and-blue polka dots, apart from the two Bosnian flags, the only color in the room. The futon faces the jittery family PC and a slick monitor on a stand and you drop yourself down in it and turn everything on, run the game disc, and scan its gaudy list of players on the screen. Your heart bangs, bangs.

LITTLE BUDDHA is not there yet.

You lean into your mini fridge: a tub of margarine (Beloved would have killed you for it back in the day), two wilted carrots loosely bound by wire, a can of diet ginger ale, and a jar of mayo. You take it all out and set it next to you, dip a carrot into mayo, and check the multiplayer list again.

Still no LITTLE BUDDHA.

You finish one and start on the other carrot, watching screen names appear and disappear in real time, thinking you should sue your employer for religious discrimination. It'd be hard to prove Muslimness with this habit, though. You scoop a fingerful of margarine into your mouth and see that you left the front door wide open. But who cares?

Still nothing.

One eye on the monitor, you drag over the closest Trader Joe's bag of unpacked past, Bosnian and American alike, and you pick through the pictures, Haris's child drawings, random pieces of paper, afraid a little of where they could take you. Instead of paying real attention to the items, you make potential "to keep" and "to trash" piles, feel a little swoon coming, let your eyes rest just for a moment, and wake up in pitch blackness, your throat raw from snoring into the night, your head a brutalist monument.

You jostle the mouse and stare at a piece of graph paper in your hand in the sudden beige light of the computer screen. It says:

CLOSE ME OR I'LL GASH YOUR HEAD IN, I REALLY MEAN IT!

You look around, at your open front door, back at the note, until it comes to you what it is. You remember peeling it from inside of your childhood home's kitchen cabinet door, the only thing you took with you that your father actually touched. Then you wonder if Haris has anything you've touched, maybe those pictures.

You look at the monitor and realize that, again, Haris will not be joining the multiplayer game, that ever since—in an attack of malt-infused love and self-pity—you disclosed on the message board that TELETOVĆ_33 is you, after months of playing the game and cautiously interacting with your boy, a kid who for the first five years of his life spoke nothing but Bosnian. From that day he vanished and you became obsessed with finding him in the gamescapes, even played—spent after work—set alarms for ridiculous hours, called in sick just for a chance to see those bright red letters spell out LITTLE BUDDHA, see him safe in the fake, orderly world you grew to know how to negotiate pretty well over time.

So when Haris fails to show up and no amount of booze or narrative seems to be able to silence the truth-sayer within, and the motherboard hums its low-pitched hum and you are tired of looking at the odd angles your knuckles make against the screen, you start to drink with rage and abandon and there is a shift in your awareness and with a click of a button you metamorphose into LI'L BUDDHA (named so after your son's moniker), also a female soldier about five-five in desert fatigues and a black beanie, face painted with grease, and in your hand is a standard M16 rifle with a grenade launcher and you happen to be on the blue team so you find the blue barracks on the map and head in that direction since those red bastards are swift motherfuckers and they are known to send red commandos right away to plant red satchel charges in your precious blue barracks and armories, blue bunkers and turrets, your blue mash tents and commanding centers, underneath your blue choppers and tanks, jeeps and planes, and your job is to hide in the dry grass of some ravine and defend what is blue against the advancing red rash and you lie there watching the blue flag twist and flap in the predictable wind as the horizon bubbles up with a distant shape of a man in a sneaky camouflage, reminiscent of a desert bush, and you know he's a red sniper sent to clear the way for his red commandos already approaching and you know your blue weapon is not accurate at this distance so you switch to a LAW which is a modern version of a bazooka and you aim at the base where his red silhouette meets the outline of the hill as your eyes fill with pleasant glee and you pray he doesn't spot you through his red scope and you send one flying and scramble downhill away from his sight and some two seconds after the discharge there is a distant explosion and the message appears in the top-right corner in your team's color "LI'L BUDDHA ENDED MARTHA STEWART'S MISERY" and one of your blue comrades that isn't your son sends you a "NICE ONE" message and you are proud of what you did and elated with a sense of blue purpose but there's still a job to be done and you get into the crouch mode and run to the blue armory and sure enough a hefty soldier with a patch of red on his arm is trying to sneak in there and in eagerness to de-fend, to stop the red enemy from their evil red intents, you forget to switch your blue weapon back to rifle and when you press the trigger it's already too late and a blue rocket is launched and although it eliminates the red enemy, it blows up the blue armory as well and kills you too in the process and the messages appear in quick succession "LI'L BUDDHA KILLED CANADIAN NINJA" and "LI'L BUDDHA HAS DECIDED THAT LIFE IS TOO MUCH TO BEAR" and you kick yourself for being so dumb and have to wait ten seconds to respawn where you started but the keys of the little Spanish-style house in San Diego, so long ago, are rattled in the lock of your still-open front door here in Vancouver, and Beloved comes back from work and you feel guilty and hurry to get out of the game but she's already hugging you from behind, asking, *Productive day?* and you defend your positions in a feeble, poorly articulated manner, trying to con-vince her that you're just taking a break and that it helps you concentrate but weirdly enough she's fine with it, or is it just a facade, and she goes on to tell you that she heard on NPR that the American soldiers lethargically looked on as the Iraq Museum was stripped of priceless pieces of culture by armed looters and how much she loves her Political Science teacher who grew up a Jew in Nazi Austria and envied the crew-cut boys of Hitler Youth and wanted to be one of them and what it all means and all you can feel is shame for blowing up your own armory and she senses your distance and says, *You just wanna play your game, don't you?* and your guilt makes you snap which opens up a whole can of worms of *I just don't know how you can play those games with everything you went through in Bosnia* and *Precisely because you didn't go through the same thing you have no frame of reference, my love!* and her *Fine!* followed by a door slam and you angrily grow pixilated breasts, grab a pixilated gun, and wait to join the ongoing war between red and blue, but when you appear behind the wall you see you are red now, and the bad blue boys are advancing up the dune and you fire burst after burst at the moving dots as an absurd part of you feels glad that you blew up that blue armory in the last game, you pat yourself on the back for the spy work you've done for the red cause and suddenly everything makes sense again as the messages appear LI'L BUDDHA KILLED I_ KILLED_SADDAM and LI'L BUDDHA ENDED MYSTERIOUS LADY COCK'S MISERY and another night is a waste.

Later, alone on the futon in Vancouver, you are inside a vivid memory, in San Diego. In it, you apologize to your beloved Honeybee for disassociating, but she won't kiss you because you haven't shaved and you say you want to be like that Wolverine from *X-Men* and she says that if you can make metal claws spring out of your fists she'll reconsider and you're reminded just why you're with her in the first place.

Who was I before I met my ex, Bill?

Sometimes I think I was always meant to wait for love, not chase it down. Every guy I knew in my youth went into life hunting, chasing, changing tack, testing out, being tested, tasting, being tasted, battling, falling, rolling with the punches, growing—living, ya know. I couldn't *do* that for some reason, couldn't get my body to. There was an abyss between my desire and the agency required to take real-world action to encounter it, let alone win it. I believed the only way it would ever come to me was through providence or chance. I thought someone would just emerge out of the crowd and love me forever. But nothing ever slows the plummet of time. It's a death game, a long-haul gamble, this waiting for the right one. Because at what point does waiting for someone become waiting for anyone?

I remember a girl I met when I first came to the U.S. I took a writing class at some kind of night school and one of the women in it asked me if she could give out my phone number to a girl in her daughter's class who was *from your neck of the woods,* she said, and who had problems adjusting to life in the States and wanted to converse with someone from the Old World. I remember a shiver overtaking my body, my heart squeezing and stretching.

It's HER! I knew it.

It's gotta be HER, I believed.

YES, I said to the woman in my class and went home to wrap my mind around it all, to prepare. From the start, before I even knew what she looked like, there was a prayer: please God, send me someone who will fit me, feel me, recognize me. Please, Universe! They say that intent translated into words (as utterances) eventually manifests reality, and then the Universe shifts to make it happen. She called and set up a meeting, her voice like songbirds at twilight. I could have shat myself, went into panic. Eric, my roommate, ever a surrogate father, told me, *You'll be fine but you can't go out like that. Here are my Doc Martens, here's a cool shirt, use deodorant, take my Zippo in case she smokes, all the high schoolers mess with cigs, and here's a cool trick you can do with a Zippo, just snap your fingers close to the mechanism and voilà—fire!* Primed in this fashion I drove to what used to be a bowling alley in Thousand Oaks and was now a big bookstore and goddamn if I wasn't ready to take her to the altar right then and there.

But in the proximity of her body, my mind's eye flooded with old naughty pictures that made me feel ashamed of thinking them, these intrusive images that left a salty taste in my mouth. I tried to stay in my body, busy it with a job. The Zippo trick worked at the bookstore's back entrance, made her smile. I saw the faces of our children in the smoke. It was impossible to look her in the eye without bursting into flames so I looked at her delicate hands, the strange Dacian bracelet made of copper wire that scaly-snaked up her forearm to end in a profile of a howling she-wolf.

She spoke like no one I met, like she was aroused by everything around us, the back stairs guardrail, the sun, the breadcrumb she plucked from my shoulder and ate. She talked about Salvador Dalí like he was her lover, witchy crystals in her pocket like they were living organisms, well-beloved pets. We started hanging out, waxing nostalgic about our childhoods in the Balkans, pained and ecstatic as they were. We compared poverties and hungers (and the richness they taught us), abuses and delights, our grandmas' houses, ways we were tasked to start winter morning fires in their icy hearths. Her eyes had shiny flakes in them like confetti, light brown and hazel in turn, and warm and frightened and cold and calculating too. Very werewolfy. I was both enamored and afraid, pulled in and repelled by her gaze.

She dragged me out on nature hikes and pointed to blossoms and snake skulls, grasshoppers and Butterfinger wrappers, with equal amazement and sensuality. She showed me a Hindu dance she learned at an ashram in Agoura Hills. We went to see a Meg Ryan film and I broke and asked her out but she said she had a boyfriend that she'd never mentioned before. I was devastated, ran away to Bosnia for the summer, licking wounds. I stayed in the friendzone for a while, giving her rides, eating meals, while pretending I didn't have feelings . . . until I decided not to anymore, until I met my wife, started calling her Beloved, started calling the she-wolf The She-wolf, the one that got away.

I should be more careful with the words I use, Bill.

Are You Now or Have You Ever Been

For three months after Beloved's first miscarriage, as soon as I opened my peepers, for the most part, I tried to remember where in the house I had booze, where I hid it, how much booze I had, what I had to "do" that day, how sauced I could afford to become and still go through the minimums of everyday, and never—not until I was already good for nothing—what I had to lose.

Next, after she'd fled for work, I tried to recall where the empties were, how much money I had, what in the house needed something new that warranted a trip to the store so that alongside AA batteries, laundry detergent, zip ties, or biodegradable compost bags I could slip in some rotgut, make it look on paper like an innocent grocery run.

Then it was standing up in order to ascertain where I was buzz-wise, beeline for the booze left over from last night, that dreaded first gulp, the hair-of-the-dog equalizer. This was to be found in sneak places of the basement and attic, in the cobwebs of the house's innards, the isolation *glass wool* of its crawl spaces, hanging in the inside pockets of dormant, long-unfitting suit jackets, squirreled amid dusty Christmas garlands, even stashed with stacked chopped wood on the side of the house.

Skipping the shower, the toothbrush, the shit, and the shoeshine, I'd gather the empties into a paper bag, crush the cans and collapse the carton wine boxes, leave the bottles as is, and harrumph them all into the car. I'd cast them en masse to the garbage in front of the groggy supermarket—a place I made sure never to patronize with Beloved so that nobody could make a connection and tell her what I was up to—saunter into the establishment for warmth, and thumb through Stephen King paperback sentences in the magazine section until it was close to six-fifty a.m. and, casual-like, like I'm just this guy, just this ordinary consumer, make my way to the beer and wine.

You can't buy booze before seven a.m. in Oregon; I found that out the easy way in 2008 when I knew I had become a habitual drunkard. There's a form of a vetting question that the U.S. government still asks of their immigrants to answer truthfully when they apply to metamorphose into Americans: *Are you or have you ever been: a communist? a habitual drunkard? and now, perhaps, a Muslim?*

No.

I became communist because one mostly had to in the former Yugoslavia. Muslimness, I was born into that special kind of communist Muslimness by chance of birth. But alcoholic, I became an alcoholic on the corner of Park and University in San Diego. I was hungover from the party the night before, some poet's burrow where people sat on stacks of dictionaries and snorted coke off Rachmaninoff CD covers and ashed cigarettes into unfinished beer cans and, when there was nothing else to drink, finished said ashy beers. We powered through to the dawn, drank instant coffee by the gallon, decided to walk over to Mama's Lebanese Kitchen for *sujuk* wraps. In order to function, to play my role of a garrulous immigrant, everyone's best friend, I popped into a store and bought a small bottle of vodka, downed it in the restroom, and rejoined the others.

Or, wait a minute; did I unconsciously lie on my American Metamorphosis application? Was I an alcoholic already back in Tuzla, in Banja Park with all the punks passing that green bottle of *shpirit* that made us all black out?

Or did it go even further down the DNA track to my grandfather and namesake who lived and died as a drunk, which I found out too late?

Was this what they meant when they asked: *Are you or have you ever been?*

When Beloved said she'd like to try again, I tapered off the meds that were delaying my orgasms and tapered on some other ones that made me feel like my head was a Rorschach lava lamp. I started going to North Portland six a.m. A.A. meetings in a brown-carpeted annex room you could have transported from an urban somewhere-in-communist-Yugoslavia's community center circa 1975, only with a little white Jesus doing his tragic gymnastics from a chipped relief in the center of the wall instead of the five-pronged red star.

Anonymouses sat with hands in their laps or hiding behind jumbo coffee cups, restless-leg-syndromed the row of the raw ones in front of them, or just jangled in the corners. Ones in pant and other suits crossed their legs with yoga-straight spines, clench-assing the meditation cushions. The baseball caps and black-under-the-fingernails leaned forward, their legs open, as if their genitals were free-range. The young ones rarely shared, primed by schools and churches in how to behave in the back rows of auditoriums facing proscenium arches. Some knitted beanies, some kneaded them in laps. One always inked another page of his comic book in progress. One slept and woke up, woke up and slept.

I made jokes and shared anecdotes, tucked in perfect little sidenotes even though there was supposed to be no cross talk, but nobody got upset with me. I learned about the difference between guilt and shame and a lot of new nomenclature, relapse prevention, self-love, higher power, all new tools to put in my toolbox, a somewhat lost metaphor on me who never could bang a nail straight into a plank. I auditioned possible mentors and applauded numerous anniversaries and welcomed the newbies with my lovable bullshit from the peanut gallery.

It works if you work it, we said.

Fake it till you make it, we said.

So, I worked it and watched, faking it until I made it do wonders for my life. Just that simple daily ritual, the crack-of-dawn fellowship, primed me to do the right thing that day or, rather, not to do the wrong. I started to feel more energetic. Beloved and I joined a gym and I rowed while she ran in place next to me, and then I fucked with the weights and watched smiley subtitled morning shows until she was done with her shower so I could take her to work. On the way home I would buy Diet Pepsis and Almond Joys in the same 7-Elevens where I used to get my Hurricane malt liquors, and even the Sri Lankan owner family seemed to treat me with more love.

Beloved loved me better, started to laugh, share, remember old times more often. She was not afraid to show how she felt, got on my ass for reasonable things, and I realized just how much work she had to do inside to be with me, how much she had to keep in while I was drunk.

On ovulation days we went at each other with extra care, and everything would get serious and meaningful and I couldn't handle it, so I'd joke, *Let's make Timmy,* and she'd laugh, say, *I'm not calling my kid a Timmy. Cornelius, then,* I'd say. *They can call him Cornholio at school.* She'd go: *Quit namin' kids, I'm losing my lady boner.*

I got my writing done, in time too, and then Hollywood started calling again, disembodied voices saying words like *brilliant* but paying no money. I flew down a couple of times on Horizon Air, and they served complimentary beer and wine, but I stuck to my Bloody Mary virgin mixes, all proud of my strength.

The night I was snuck into a mansion in Thousand Oaks, I watched people who wanted to be in the biz act like they *were* in the biz in front of people from the biz who put them in their places, loving every second of their false power.

By two a.m. there were shirts and skins, and fortunes were snorted out of innies and poured down gullets, dropper-dripped right onto eyeballs. I understood the term *bombed* and it was fitting to what I witnessed that night, having seen some aftermaths of actual bombings (shellings really, but let me have this).

But did I join? No. Remember, I was strong.

It works if you work it, I said, and I worked it.

Fake it till you make it, I said, and I made it, and right there, in hindsight, was the rub, in that second little verb in that second little sentence. That little *to make,* followed by that innocent-looking *it,* together forming—after *do it*—the most American of phrases perhaps: *make it,* this finite-seeming goal for Americans. It suggested that once you make it you're done having to fake it for the rest of your life—after all, you had it made. It suggested that the promise is the land you can inhabit, that the American dream is a state you can forever stay in.

Weeks after that test of tests, and a day before I was to fly to my screenwriting gig in Copenhagen, coming from my A.A. meeting, I stopped at the supermarket and got some airplane-size toiletries, a box of port, a regular nonelectric toothbrush, duck hindquarters and asparagus I was to cook

Beloved for dinner that night, chicken broth, a mango and serrano peppers for the sauce, and toilet paper and kosher salt for the house. I don't know who chose to buy the port but the choice to buy the port was made and the port was real and right there in my hand and I, of course, drank the port.

Hustle, this for sure, but not the good kind. More like drudgery. Richard, my screenwriting partner, got this well-deserved filmmaker grant and I wasn't doing anything, according to him. So I signed on. There was no real burn to do it, not really.

We did it, though, don't get me wrong: we got up early and made outlines and numbered our scenes and put them in order, googled Korean customs and tried to get into the minds of forged characters as if they were us. We wondered about their first times, the sizes of their boobs and dicks, their skeletons and secrets, relationships with groups and individuals, joy and heartbreak, pain and guilt. We concocted their pioneer memories, other emotionally heightened moments that made them *them*. We were open to the suits' notes, changes, switcheroos, and conflations. What if the protagonist's wife were an asthmatic or a lesbian, a fat spastic or a Tea Party conservative? What if the protagonist ate boogers and dandruff flakes on the sly? Does he need two sisters, or can one be both a worrywart and a devil-may-care spinster? Or should he have a brother instead? A dead one? Blind?

Richard was all but maddening with his healthy-living shit, pelvis-stretching as we conferred, sun-saluting the open Danish window, and down-dogging his ass in my general direction as I typed out our artless, horrible lines: our *besides* and *suddenlies,* our *you lied to mes.* He meditated on the hour every hour for two minutes, took ice-cold showers, rationed some special non-GMO, gluten-free loaves of foodstuffs he humped all the way from Los Angeles.

In contrast, every time he went to take a whiz, I took a swig from a bottle of Grant's in my luggage and watched the fat-looking pigeon-like birds stalk spring buds about to sprout right out of the tree branches, their beaks sideways-cocked.

Denmark was gray in April; its buildings were made of bricks and Danes had healthy thighs from all the bike-riding and dog-walking and some of their coins were holey. The place felt safe for existence. The Danes

I could see didn't cross the street when the street told them not to, even when there was no one else there to see them do it. Nor, I presume, did they eat boogers. No, on Sturlasgade at Islands Brygge in Copenhagen, the Danes had it all figured out somehow.

Richard saw me at the fruit bowl and started on the evils of the modern banana: the genetic engineering to enhance sweetness and curb bitterness, the treatment of banana farmers, the fact that there were better ways to get that essential potassium with or without carbonated footprints or something; I lost him there, somewhere. I forced myself to listen again. He said he had nothing against plantains because they were a naturally occurring fruit and I finished both of my bruised bananas in front of him and comically careened to the shitter, sock-slid, even though I didn't have to go.

The loft we were staying in belonged to a fashion stylist/art director friend of Richard's and there were touches of interesting and pinches of weird all over the walls, pictures of goose-bumpy models' asses you had to really figure out were asses and not other naturally occurring creases and crevices, and Senegalese masks, and a lot of owls in assorted art mediums not-blinking from their surprising perches. I let the water run in the sink. In the mirror my hated face looked cross.

I tried to focus on my face until I was okay with it—and I never was, not even as a kid, some punchable sadness there of the tears-of-a-clown variety—tried to will ease and calm into its bloated tissues, but just couldn't accomplish it, and so burst out instead with a strange brio in my legs, a shift like something from a character out of certain video games, this unspeakable inhuman switch from boredom to action at the push of a button, made to look so natural but failing to capture how we humans really start to run.

"I'm gonna go and dip my foot in the seas of Denmark."

"That'll wake you up," Richard said knowingly from the mountain stance. "Nothing like cold water to show you where you end and the rest of the world begins. Handle your business."

"Business? I haven't seen a dime."

"Just go do what you need to, so we can take another crack at this."

It was our screenplay about first-generation Koreans that needed that, another crack. We were writing it on spec for no coin, and I didn't want to go back into it, what he thought was crucial (wrong) and what I thought was crucial (right), so I went to my luggage and packed me a backpack with my secret Scotch, my books, my meds.

"You should go on like an eight-hour walk. You gotta find a way to fuck up that body, otherwise there's all that energy in there you don't know how to get rid of."

"Like you do. I should just be more like Dick."

"Hey, man," he said, shrugging like: *It's how it is.*

I considered falling apart until I liquefied into a puddle of ex-human sludge. Or unsheathing the Scotch from my backpack, showing him how it *also* was, but waited until I was out in the building's vestibule to do it on the granite steps among locked Danish bicycles. Why did I think that nobody should see this, my real-to-real?

But after a time, after mind-annihilating Scotch, I picked myself up into an armful, like a large load of loose laundry, and I dragged my shambles to the shore, losing socks and underwear en route, dragging shirt legs and pant sleeves on the dirt in the streets. I dropped the mess of me on some rocks, rested there assuming the shape of the rocks awhile, but had no guts to slump into the water and get it over with, piece by piece or otherwise. Instead, I looked for fish. I looked for crabs. I looked for soda cans. I saw none.

My phone sounded a text. Beloved said: I'M PREGNANT ☺

My battery was at one percent. I started to text back but it went black.

I looked around in sudden tears.

Three run-of-the-mill Danes showed up on the cement shore to the right with a bleached-looking dog with a yellowy head—a Labrador, maybe. They placed green cans of beer on the concrete blocks by their bench and the Asian-looking one of them produced a red Frisbee and rubber-wristed it into the air. The dog went for it—fuck its teeth! fuck its jaws!—but with its throat, like it wanted to inhale it not catch it; that's how it went for it.

I sobbed at the sight with my smiling face aslime.

It felt Abrahamic to see this dog demonstrate into reality what he (there was a great set of balls on him now) believed to be real life and he didn't find it absurd or monotone or heartbreaking that us creatures of the world had to perform and perpetuate the said world if we wanted to have one, exist in one. This was what he did, and he was so great at doing it, going after that rubber disc like his life depended on it, which of course it did and it didn't.

I got the Scotch out and thought of pouring it into the sea like someone in a movie would, faced with this news. But to my right another one of the Danes, a woman nerd, flicked the Frisbee into a tree where it got stuck. She and the others pushed at the trunk some and tried to shake it down but soon got bored with it and continued to drink beer and speak Danish as I watched the dog's beautiful verve lessen, his yelps quieting, his jumps stalling, until he just laid down, sniffling into the salty air.

I drank, not fooling myself that it was in celebration.

I didn't tell Richard the news because he hated when big things happened in real life to people he worked with because they surely as rain would filch valuable creative juices that belonged only to him, only to him and his project.

He even had this rule about not watching movies while writing one because he believed that other people's tropes and mannerisms would inevitably make their way into the subconscious and onto the page. But TV was okay and, at night, projected over the beige duvet cover hung from the pipe against the kitchen portion of the loft, we watched some bald American guy go around the world eating boiled duck embryos and fried cow udders, chocolate-covered ants and stick-skewered tarantulas. The guy described tastes with unimaginative made-up words like *mineral-y* and *organ-y*. At times it was obvious even to him that the locals were making up shit just to see him eat a narwhal urethra dipped in motor oil off of a hot Kawasaki engine.

"Cringeland," Richard said, sitting crisscross applesauce on the floorboards and measuring his pulse. "Like our first movie."

What he was actually referring to was my performance, I was sure of it.

I met Richard at UCLA when he was in the film school and I was in the theater department and I wrote him a short film about a traumatized Bosnian who becomes a hitman, loses his mind, becomes a liability, and is about to be taken out by his hitlady boss. But, in this character's head, this guy splits into two people and the fucked-up hitman persona is banished from the body by his innocent alter ego, the punk-kid Bosnian he used to be. The two personas hug it out in the end in an all-white corridor amid dry-ice smoke, the exit sign blaring green. I wasn't much of an actor and he was just starting to learn how to be a director, though he was quite a hustler and ended up securing enough money from novice producers to shoot the thing on 35mm at the weeks' worth of ABC's lot in Los Angeles, and got an international star to play the hitlady boss to boot.

We were glittering journeymen and it was so crystal to every professional on the set. I was so bad that it made me drop out of acting altogether and turn to dramatic writing, a safer spot where my failures happened offstage, where I didn't have to live inside of them corporeally.

I flipped through channels, putting the loft through an array of light-changes, stopping on the image of a monkey hobbling across a sandy beach, trying to carry a sloshing piña colada half his size with one stick arm, spilling and screeching at the spillage with lament that was eerily recognizable to me. A prickish docu-voice of a Brit identified these as vervet monkeys that were brought to the Caribbean during slave-trade days from West Africa, and continued on about this study conducted on them about their relationship with pilfered alcoholic beverages at resort beaches. Apparently, some of the monkeys were straightedge and didn't touch the stuff, some partook in the company of other drinking monkeys, and some were just like me.

Richard chuckled to himself because he had the same thought, I was sure of it. Fucking sure of it.

Fuck you, I thought at the back of his fakir head and walked to my makeshift burrow, rummaged through my knicks and my knacks, and, making sure my face was hidden from him—*WHY ARE YOU HIDING IT?*—snuck a big gulp of new Scotch. I got comfy, powered my laptop, and chose a random document on the clusterfucked desktop, an old script of mine in Bosnian, and moved words around.

For the remainder of the week, instead of working on the Korean script, I lost myself in my past, in Tuzla, Bosnia, circa 1995, and, when asked, claimed to be in the zone and was left alone to work.

The plot revolved around a sociopathic American journalist who, failing to amount to anything in the U.S., comes to wartime Bosnia and instead of reporting on the tragedy, orchestrates one of his own in order to gain an exclusive and make a name for himself. In the original incarnation he was a slut and a slob but I changed that and made him into a health nut and a snob for therapeutic reasons.

When Richard found out I'd made no progress on our project he had a conniption and took off with his luggage two days early. I drank out in the open then, saluted the pigeons, watched movies, ate bananas, wrote my script in Bosnian, dedicating it *To Timmy, with love.*

Picking me up from PDX, Beloved immediately knew exactly where I was at, drinking-wise. She drove us home—her lips a minus sign—as I overcompensated with gregarious tales of Denmark, thinking I was doing a good job acting not drunk. At home, as soon as we came in, she couldn't help but start crying, only this time with this resolute calm that took away my liquid confidence and balance, shut me down, had me slowly settle to the floor. She made tea in the kitchen, cried waiting for the water to boil, leaning on the counter. Something was coming. I sat on the parquetry, waiting for it. She let the quiet and the time do their thing. Then:

"I'm not doing this alone," she said, her hands cupping each other in front of her womb's entrance.

Off I went to this new-age, holistic outpatient program: five times a week, guided mindfulness meditations and support groups with yoga and the five-needle acupuncture protocol designed for addicts specifically and, that very first day, leaning back in what the acupuncture lady called the Lamborghini, as opposed to more modest chairs she labeled Toyotas and Pintos, I planned me a little relapse for the Christmas break. Just a little something to get me through the program, a little goal to work toward.

In the meantime I became a model client, on time, saying all the right things I learned in A.A. at appropriate curative times. Beloved came in to a few of the groups, was somewhat dubious at first but finally accepting of my new schedule, new commune. I lost weight, slept like a deaf cat, stopped yelling at inanimate objects when they didn't behave the way I thought they ought to. Within two months I was friends with fellow clients, the staff, the piss-checking interns, the whole damn lot.

Before and after and in between recovery work I wrote and, as with every other time I wrote, the bottle gaped at me from the back of my mind like a butthole, beckoning, *Come on, bud, you know where you belong! Come on in with us, in here where the refugee refuse is squeezed for the last of your nutrients. We want those last of your purse- and pocketfuls. What else are you gonna do with them? Don't worry about after. You'll be clenched or dribbled or sharted onto white American Standard porcelain, flushed into our great cities' bowels, and, why not, reincarnated.*

I didn't answer the call.

Instead, I buried myself under words, changed the structure of my Bosnian script, turned it into an ensemble piece, changed the journalist's name to Richard, and named his sidekick, the voice of reason in the picture, Tim—

Walking the streets of my hometown in 1994 this Richard hears music coming from the ground, explores and finds a clutch of teenage punks rehearsing in the basement of a municipal building. Duvachki Orkestar, they are called, the name of my high school band, which in literal translation means Brass Band but, in slang, more like a Band of Glue-Huffers. Their drum kit is fashioned out of UNHCR buckets, the bass is stand-up, the guitars acoustic, and their front man, based on my childhood friend Igor—insane. Richard and Tim listen and can't believe that these kids sound just like the melodic punk rockers popular back in the States:

We don't want this adolescence / weakness in the times of crisis / heads full of good advices / that we're too proud to take, snarls Igor into no mic in a surprisingly high but perfectly pitched voice, like he really did.

What do you know that we're not aware of / don't tell us that you're not scared of / the future / that's coming our way!

Richard becomes their manager, records his first story about them. It's a positive war piece about the unbroken spirit, of art in spite of violence, the youth of the country standing up against adult bullshit madness. We meet the rest of the band: Masni, the drummer with a Mohawk who at night plays locally popular Dzigera gigs for cash and has to part his hair in the middle to look normal; the bass player who's literally tied to his girlfriend (with a rope); the rhythm guitarist who is really me; and the solo guitarist whose whole family goes to the enemy side and he stays behind and joins the Bosnian army at seventeen out of spite.

CNN and BBC buy the story. Christiane Amanpour mangles the band's name. Letters of support pour in. Bono Vox donates music equipment. Duvachki Orkestar records a demo called *Scream of the Cockroach* on real instruments, plugged into a real electric grid. They make a simple black-and-white video for "Adolescence," their first single. Richard chronicles their every move, makes a separate story for each band member, their everyday life. We find out about the bass player's girlfriend's pregnancy, the drummer's heroin habit, Igor's homelessness, the solo guitarist's shell-shocked nerves, and my relatively normal everyday existence. European MTV premiers "Adolescence." The band is compared to Green Day and the Ramones.

Then war in Rwanda. Eyes of the world shift to Africa. Nobody wants to buy happy stories from Bosnia. Richard feels his success slipping from his hands.

He needs an ending to his story, his book, his documentary, and so he hatches a diabolical plan: he puts Tim on organizing Duvachki Orkestar's first concert in Tuzla's central park to celebrate the completion of the first album but behind his back reaches out to the enemy on the other side of the conflict, provides some maniac with the concert's coordinates, its date and time.

The day of the concert Richard hires several camerapeople to capture "the event" from all shootable angles but Tim, of course, finds out about the plan and even though he wants to warn the band that they need to cancel, that the whole town is in danger, he can't. Even though he is supposed to save the day, he can't. He's supposed to deliver the message and the band is supposed to cancel the performance so that nobody shows, but being true punkers with fuck-you attitudes, they're supposed to confront and kick Richard's ass, tie him to a tree in the park right in front of the stage, and play the concert anyway with this sick fuck as the only spectator, amid mortar onslaught, how punk rock would that be?!—but he can't.

He can't because the bass player's girlfriend is spotting now and they rush her to the hospital and the doctor calls it a "chromosomal catastrophe" and she loses the pregnancy once more. So, in act three they immigrate to the United States as refugees, settle in Portland, Oregon, in the house of their own.

He breaches their now definitely *maybe* and most likely *not* future nursery, their current spirit-yoga room, to reencounter it.

"Are you now or have you ever been Timmy?" he asks the yoga mat in tears. "Are you now or have you ever been a blood clot?"

Ill-prepared, panging for the soul that never made it into the world—don't forget drunk—he retreats then into an in-between room opening into their office.

Exasperated, she pauses, asks: "What are you doing?"

Bass player says: "This is what one does when one has rooms to walk through."

She groans, unpauses the screen, goes on watching *The Good Wife* by herself

—even though I was painfully aware that this was not and could never be a real story, a real film.

Dear Billy Star Wars,

Congratulations! You look good in a uniform, blasting people with a space gun.

That's the way to go, in my opinion, if one were to get sick of the fear, the pain, and the dark and wished to take a fast way out: suicide by a fictional character. I bet even the ultimate judgment afterward would be hilarious and take shape as some lame late-night-TV appearance or, God forbid, an awards show. How do you see it? What do you think happens when we die?

I know your stance on taking a bath, that there's no way for a man to lie there in that warm amniotic-like fluid without thinking of taking himself out, making that full circle. But then I also know your stance on dying in motels, and my little domicile used to be one. I wouldn't do that to you, or to my landlord. My mother believes that a death by drowning guarantees paradise. I think that entails that the drowning has to be accidental. But I don't know about that. My liver thinks one way, my heart another.

Don't worry, I'm not there yet. But there *is* a weird kind of calmness that has *descended* on me lately. I don't know if it's the isolation, the pandemic, the election, or the fact that an ice storm just blew out all the power towers in downtown Salem, and driving through the foggy city without any traffic lights, encountering convoys of raised pickup trucks wrapped up in blue-tinted American flags, that reminds me of the other war and making the full circle. And weirdly, I'm not afraid. I feel resigned. Everything just feels like a joke.

Here's the new thing I wrote. You might like it as I know how much you love James Lipton, hahahahahaha.

GFY!

Love, izzy

Inside the Actor

After the fear, the pain, and the dark—after the fear of the fear, the fear of the pain, and the fear of the dark, after the pain of the fear, the pain of the pain, and the pain of the dark, and after the dark of the fear, the dark of the pain, and the dark of the dark—after all that, it's you, somehow, it's still you somehow, standing in the wings, on collapsible legs, feeling the whirr and the throng of the auditorium out there, beyond the red velvet curtains, as if it's a hive in your own chest.

Not that there "really" is you again, not that those collapsible legs are "really" your legs, with the same gout-ridden feet you had before the fear, the pain, etc. It's still you because you recognize the sensation of having had a particular set of legs in moments of anticipation of facing the crowd, facing the music (as they say), which comes with the knowledge of their collapsibility, legs' not crowds', though entropy is Mother to all. You're you because you can tell *butterflies* from butterflies, because the sensation of them in your gut at this point (read: now) is "realer" than the fact that somewhere, somewhere out in the world, there are "real" butterflies who have their own fear, pain, dark, etc.

The throng in the auditorium reaches a controlled and respectable crescendo, like a salve of Portland rain upon the roof of your Prius, then quickly diminishes into a mist of expectant, manufactured silence. The universe hushes its innerworkings, allowing for a voice to be heard, introducing you in this celebration ritual. In the great scheme of things, it's a relatively quiet, token thing, the whole shebang, though to you it is everything.

Of course, the voice is patterned to be familiar to you, to put you at ease (lest your legs collapse), to streamline the process of assigning meaning to your fear, your pain, your dark, etc. Though plenty shamanic, the voice is tempered into a shtick, bombastic at one moment, self-disparaging the next, as if going from one end of the spectrum to the other within the same utterance contains the multitudes of its iterations and permutations. It doesn't, but that's how meanings are assigned here. You're uniquely designed to respond to it, and when it starts, you can't help but feel your face smiling. Again, not that there really is a face, but you feel a gleeful muscle tug of it, undeniably.

"Tonight's guest began his career in the very cradle of life"—and here the cultured, über-academic voice takes a knowing pause, acknowledging the ridiculousness of its own grandiloquence, teasing the audience, before it pretend-succumbs into becoming just like *one of us*—"his mother's cunt."

The crowd goes wild with *it's-funny-because-I-recognize-it* laughter, with some anonymous standouts hooting and hollering in that patent American way. The voice continues: "Studying with the legendary pioneers of 'real' life," and here the crowd reacts as if to footage of a puppy doing a somersault to something shown to them out there, perhaps on a big screen behind a seated host on the stage, "led him inevitably to 'real' life's biggest shrine of first breath, where he made such a mark that he is now at the helm of his own 'real' life, as both a producer and a star."

Upon the host's uttering of "where he made such a mark" you hear a cry of a baby screecher with walloping lung capacity, presumably you. You're not privy to what they can see out there, if "seeing" is what they are experiencing at all. But the way they coo and sigh, giggle and cluck, the way their noises stir the air? space? time? between you and them, charges it with unseen, unknowable meanings, which is exactly why, in your mind, you're sure they're watching grainy footage of your actual birth, which you know does not exist; nobody had taped that unremarkable occurrence some forty years ago at the Gradina hospital in buttfuck Yugoslavia, yet out there they are, cooing and sighing at it.

Don't get you wrong, you're okay with all of this. Fuck! you're actually grateful, though you're for the most part still out of the loop. You're thankful they've gone through the trouble, even though everyone gets one of these. Absurdly, you find yourself thinking about the logistics of such an endeavor. You can't imagine how hard it used to be to get through these ceremonies, back before the advent of moving pictures, when souls had to be eased into entropy by means of ancient symbols and collective transgenerational memory work. Nowadays, in the era of the individual, when people are self-created, self-written, self-designed, self-narrated, self-chronicled characters who sport their own soundtrack and catch-phrase, their own utility belt, these souls can be duly pacified with the simplest of flashbacks. Because there's nothing that a strategic flashback cannot demystify, including life itself. The psyche that's primed to see life as footage is worried only about *getting everything;* it doesn't matter what it *gets.* You've no idea how come you're able to glean any foreknowledge about any of this but that is suddenly not quite as bothersome as the butterflies.

"Ladies and gentlemen," the voice booms out, claiming space and time, milking every ounce of patience and goodwill from the universe. "Without further ado, I give you . . ." and everything in your head goes Klaxon and *whoosh.*

You peel off from the spot in the jittery wings and, guided by glow-tape, will yourself up one, two, three steps to the stage level, to the glowing slit in the red velvet separating the darkness from the light, you from the rest of you.

And, and this is important, even at this moment that stops all moments, your mind grasps for not being in it; it grasps to observe it, to remember it, to capture, store, keep, prolong, have in the back pocket, so to speak. Fuck the mighty hum of the universe beyond the curtain; the universe on this side of it still acts like it's the only one. In your case the only thing that *flashes* in your mind is a memory of a happened-upon Facebook exchange, not a screengrab or footage, mind you, but a piece of narration:

> *A Bosnian refugee living in the U.S. was complaining on Facebook to*
> *a relative who stayed in the old country—both of whom, in their own way,*
> *survived the war—about his anguish, his PTSD, his suicidal ideation,*
> *the boot-crunch he felt on his chest even mid-mindfulness meditations*
> *at his trauma group at the Y. To capture what he's going through, what*

it "really" feels like, he wrote that ever since the war ended, he felt as if he'd been tossed into a bottomless pit in the ground, this non-fiery sort-of hellmouth, that even now he's still falling, still tumbling ass over tit, bouncing off toothed edges, horrified to no end that there will be no end to this here free fall, no end to the boot-crunch against his chest, no end to never stopping, that he will never know anything but this.

There's a time difference between the U.S. and Bosnia so the poor bastard had to wait in this state for the sun to go around some. When his relative wrote back it was a quick note bedazzled with crying-laughing smiley faces. It said: You're lucky, cuz. At least you know you'll never feel that splat! Now, that *would* hurt.

It's a bit of abracadabra is all, of course. Of course it is.

. . . abracadabracabracadabracabracadabracabracadabracabracadabraca . . .

You part the velvet lips and step onto the boards and into the earsplitting light; you part the velvet lips and step off of the boards and into the earsplitting darkness.

A ghost of gout in each step still.

In the limelight, while it lasts, while it still lasts now, "everything was matter-of-fact and nothing hurt." The questions were posed and answered by the universe. The universe responded with nothing but all-encompassing understanding, followed by prompt forgetting of all the details of itself, awaiting that entertaining wrap-up, the button ending. Fear, pain, dark, etc. . . . were shown to be made of the same building blocks their opposites are made of: words, pictures, tropes, sounds, jokes, in other words.

Might-as-well-Jokes.

The universe asks itself: "What is your favorite word?"

"'Fuselage.'"

"What is your least favorite word?"

"'Reality.'"

"What turns you on?"

"Change."

"What turns you off?"

"Change, obviously."

"What sound or noise do you love?"

"What sound or noise do you hate?"
" "

"What's your favorite curse word?"
"*Pichka materina.*"
And other such horseshit.

Dear Billy, dear Izzy, dear God of dizzy, dear Mother, dear Beloved,

Let's shut up.

Let's just shut the fuck up with the letters, with the tinkering with
the old words, the old worlds, the old wounds, the old wombs, the
old vulnerabilities, draggled as decoys, the old medications, let's
nil by mouth, nil through mouth. Let's shut up the Lexapro, the
coping, the baths, the beet shakes, the stationary kayaks, let's just
lock horns with wistful, unflappable nows now. Noisy, noisy nows.
All that gets said, or put down, collapses in process, I start a page
of fiction and it crumples into trauma, the past, and I can't stop the
narrative and comment, say this is why I don't write short stories,
this is why the artist has to what they have to art, and write how
they have to write, that's how long these days I can sustain fiction,
I get in, I want to do like storytellers do, take you to a room, a
mountain, have people walk in, on, and say, do, stuff and within
minutes———this, this is how trauma enters art, work, thought,
feeling of a soft tum, skull, life, and I could *cute around* and change
the word *trauma* into *monkey,* and go on exploring that whimsical
chestnut, but to what? end? this is how real life enters fiction about
real life. I've allowed trauma, bad lessons, to come into my grace,
into my art, my world, and ruin my plans, my happy ends. Let's
shut up.

And still, a voice in the noise: *Don't forget to tell them about walking
into the ocean, getting saved by a Mexican man, then slapped for
walking into it weighted like that. Don't forget to admit the alcoholic
hepatitis was a suicide attempt too, prompted by a true-crime show
about a man who was killing Native women in Alaska by forcing
liquor down their throats and leaving them to die. Don't forget to tell*

them about the healing silence of that one drive back from Community Health, the silent premonition in the lab, the dead quietus of the ultrasound, the quiet, gentle nurse. Mention the throne you made out of wine boxes in the Womb.

Don't forget to indulge me and send the rest, you hack! Hit send now.

Yes, send all of it! You can't be trusted with any of it.

Send everything. Hit it!

Hit send!

Yes!

Go fuck yourself now.

Bunnylove Savagery, or In Place of an Afterword

The Shannon Opening

This . . . *whole thing* is . . . not going to be about Shannon, don't worry. Sorry, but it's important to me that you know what you're getting into. She's just a bleary enough figure from my back-then that I'm trying to use to give myself a task of *solving for her,* in order to dupe this puffy brain into doing the real work I need it to do—to remember, primarily, but also to put years of my malt-masked pain and psychosis into words, so that they in turn can be put together, lined up from left to right like this, into a record of . . . again, *this whole . . . whathaveya . . .* whatever this is I'm doing with what I'm going through right now, which is dying.

As you can see, these shamble-sentences are where lie my problem. My . . . (ugh!) *material* blurts out of me in fits and starts along with doubts: the facts, the fictions, of memory, the learned foreign language they all stumble out in, the stabs at arranging its shrapnel so that facts are facts and fictions are fictions, etc. But I don't have time anymore to fight the throng for the sake of less cumbersome, less pathetic prose for you (though this is the biggest fiction of them all). There's a method to this. It's like . . . when Gill Dennis, in preparation to write the script for *Walk the Line,* asked Johnny Cash to sketch the blueprint of the house he grew up in, and while the aging rock star charcoaled susurrant, wobbly blocks with his palsied hand, in his mind he was already inside a particular memory, squinting toddler eyes against the dust motes whirling in the shine through the slats, murmuring ominously to Gill, *And this right here, this was "Daddy's room." We weren't allowed in there.*

For Gill it was never about the sketch but what it stirs up, what breaks off, a building block for a story that is yet to upcrop. But I'm not writing a biopic here; *this* is not that kind of story and mine is not that kind of life. I've got my conciliatory designs on the synapses between life and story of life—my own timid, wide-eyed attempt at living it—which is why I'm compelled to leave *my sketches* in, to show the work, as it were. If you spend your time on Earth trying to understand how you fit in life instead of living it, then to you, trying to understand *is* living, and what you're reading is that hard admittance. If I hadn't sent you packing already, just you wait.

It took some scouring of my email history to arrive at her name. I knew it was something Irish, and then I remembered (as if through a film) a story that a California judge had let her rename herself at seventeen, following an emancipation from bonkers parents, her father specifically, some court-sealed or otherwise unknowable neglect and/or abuse, now that I think of it. See, had I not jotted the Johnny Cash anecdote—the Daddy part, I mean—it wouldn't have come to me about Shannon and *her father.* Gill's tactic works wonders on shot-to-shit brains, I'm telling ya! Beat into the process and already—

I'm at my 2001 Halloween party in San Diego again, watching Shannon doing this white man's shuffle in silhouette against the black-lit aquarium. She's drunk and dressed in tight-fit black slacks and a white button-up—a Mormon zombie, with horror makeup and short spiky hair—holding aloft a foam bicycle helmet. And it's gotta be past midnight, because I'm in the phase of party drunkenness in which I manifestly sonic-force what *I* like (the Pogues) on my poor guests and goers, and the song that's playing is— of course! but of course it is!—"The Broad Majestic Shannon" (though real Shannon could fit into a thimble) and that, right there, is how her name and the title for this section came to me in the first place, back when I didn't know how to start writing this . . . *horseshit,* which I then had to trek down the switchbacks of my thinking to capture.

If I had it in me to have . . . *naughty thoughts* about this person, that's when I would have had them, back at the turn of the century, when I still had life energy and a boner for daring to think of maybe, one day, having— in real life, and not just onstage or in theory—experiences unburdened by fear, by my repressed upbringing and immigrant *over*thought, but I didn't (have naughty thoughts about Shannon, I mean). Please note here how repression and fear are present in the very structure of the sentences, how every word grovels, how every clause *stanks* of unworthiness, how *boner* and *daring* deflate when chaperoned by *think* and *maybe* . . . by *one day*! for crying out loud! Just listen to this whirring throng of explanations and excuses. It's my liver that changes my voice, I'm sure of it. But I'm gonna let her. I owe her that much. No time to edit for performance anyway. I'm leaving it all in. This too is a male *American* voice.

The solitary reason Shannon was in my life at all had been because she was friends with my Beloved, in the way my shy twentysomething then-girlfriend, who had a hard time making friends in childhood, could be friends with a stranger. In reality (in tension) Shannon was coupled with Chris, my Beloved's first high school boyfriend, who Beloved insisted was now like a brother to her, and to Shannon by proxy, I guess, like a sister. Though they never hung out just by themselves, Beloved felt that, with her track record, she couldn't afford burning any bridges, ever, and that I should respect that and jettison my concerns. We did spar about it early in our relationship when I still thought I should tell her some of the crap my cousins back in Bosnia would have said and done to Chris if this was taking place in my neck of the woods, until I met her family and realized that it was all normal to them. Let's just say that natural pains and jealousies, weirdnesses of hanging out with exes and their new squeezes, any such asperities were at worst, at least, beveled in this bunch and, at best, crushed into dust and swept under the proverbial carpet, rationalized by couching them in this Nordic credo of progressiveness and maturity, calmness and status quo, in we-are-bigger-than-thatness. It took me a stretch of time, but I was the newcomer charged with assimilating, learning the new, right-er ways to be.

This rankled, though, the power dynamic, that only I was expected to grow, to transform. I felt that no matter how rich and hard-won my life experience, what I was bringing to the table was marked marred on arrival, proven unsuccessful (*I'm so glad you made it out of there*), old-worldly and thus primitive, *weird*, paltry . . . in need of putting together, mending, refinement, and enlightenment, in that order. My objections, defenses, pleas, aches of body and spirit, explanations of why I felt the way I did, why I didn't do things the way I didn't do them, the crippling delirium of my post-traumatic in-brain existence, the innumerable illuminating example-tales from my miserable upbringing, my interrupted youth, the ole buggery of escalating into personhood in the upside-down morality of war, all culminating into my writhing body sobbing on our bathroom floor, at least monthly, were all duly heard and noted by her, considerately nodded through, stomached with a stiff upper lip, and <u>survived</u>! I found out later (*Who do you think was propping you up?*). By bedtime the matter would be routinely, ever magically scrapped and, by morning, filed under "progress." I'd awaken purged and thankful, restored to equality (though bone-feeling those *lycanthropic* growing-back pains), and sometimes within two minutes of waking next to me she'd make an exasperated comment that'd knock me right off my equal standing, made me feel like I wasn't forming fast enough for her, that her young life was passing in wait, and I'd wonder who was that young woman who listened to me cry the night before, who was the one who heard me, eased my pain, marked my progress?

Take my hand, I'm singing along with the song that Halloween in 2001, and I guess I'm looking straight at Shannon, who's now looking straight back at me. Or was she looking my way first . . . but no matter now, because she's placing the prop bicycle helmet on the seat of an empty chair, singing: *Forget your fears, babe!* . . . and I don't believe my eyes—she *does* look like a zombie and the black-lit guppies glimmering around her head make me feel like I'm seeing stars, or like she herself is a cartoon fiction recovering from a frying pan to the noggin . . . and is there *beckoning* in the way she snaps her fingers at me, but zestier? And if *naughty thoughts* are to come, now, right now, it would be the time for them to come, but they do not . . . or perhaps they do, but they're not thoughts at all, and I don't know what to do with what they do to me, which is turn my head widdershins, causing me to turn them *into* thoughts, and as soon as they become thoughts, they are not naughty but wrong! wrong! wrong! My face locks into a shiteater and I flee out to the patio, where Chris is making crowd-pleasing cocktails out of the Box o'Fiesta, his and Shannon's portable bar, which is what he calls a cardboard box of booze he drives around in the trunk of their car, because they're a careful sort of young alcoholics, sharing their poison, caring about quality, measuring every ounce in public.

"BARKEEP!" I howl, then diminish it to a civilized decibel level as soon as I clock Beloved wince in the crowd in front of him, a Pavlovian response on my part, *look what a good boy I am, look how I learn, how I know better.* "Can you make an Irish Car Bomb?"

I seek Beloved's eyes, *did you see it? did you see it?,* just to see her avert them, distinguish in her mien her ever present embarrassment *for* me, which hurts more than any anger, any rage, any hatred, any disappointment, even. Disappointment would mean that she still believes us linked; embarrassment *for* makes me stand in it alone. I try to figure out if this is about my volume at all, or does she know what I did? *But I didn't do anything!* But maybe that's *exactly* why I'm no good to anyone, why I'll always stand out as the other in this country. There is no *ease of being* with us refugees. Our heads are always on a swivel, waiting for the other boot. Case in point, inside, through the patio door at a quick glance back, Shannon's shadow's still shuffling, so all of this could still just be nothing.

"Ah, wait yer turn!" goes Chris, more pirate than brogue, and I catch Beloved wangle an inscrutable, none-of-you-fuckers-is-ever-gonna-know-me smile, something that in my mind marks her free, free of me, even then, which marks me alone, now as much as then, and like that I'm back here typing: *and like that I'm back here typing:* **and like that** . . . and I'm failing to name what I'm trying to name, I'm failing . . .

By the way, calling her Beloved in these pages has fuck all to do with the world's-your-oyster *mis*translations of Rumi's mystic love or Morrison's similarly unspeakable one for the soul of a murdered child . . . though now that I see them side by side in the same sentence, blending together their aching yet unsatisfying unspeakabilities, maybe . . . scratch that, that's exactly why I'm calling her that. For from where I'm sitting now (at a provisional Formica desk next to the water heater in the closet) post-divorce, I can tell you that none of my feelings *toward* or *against,* nor memories *of* her, are just positive or just negative—or just *just,* to be fair—but they're these chew toys, loved down to a nub out of habit, chased down and gnawed at for yesterday's dragons, frayed and covered in my bacilli, and meaning things, all things and none, just to me now.

No matter how many times I excavate these moments that stick out from my past (and, for some reason, the theory's that they stick out for a reason), no matter how many angles I attack them from, whether I clean them up and serve them raw or slow-smoke them and add them to a jambalaya, whether I reduce them to who, where, when, what, why, or blow them up into *this . . . overwrought insanity* for meaning, what comes out . . . comes out just as meaningful as this fucking sentence.

Writing, this particular type of time travel, is a Ponzi-like scheme: you're losing all of now and some of when to gain a crack at a particular then, exchanging appreciating assets for a depreciating one, spending months on milliseconds, to capture what? For whom? To what end? To seek gains for writing through trying to seize what has been lost to it? To find out what was it in the way that Beloved loved me (I assume love, because why else would you *be* with . . . *this*?) that made her always seem miffed at me? To unmask who it was that she believed I would become if everything went her way, as I kept baring everything—screaming—*this is all I am! this is all I am!*? To pinpoint a private smile from early in our relationship some fifteen years ago and say yes, that's when our problems really started, that was when I really lost her, and all the time from that moment to this very one I had already been alone. But I've been insufferable enough for tonight. To paraphrase a real writer (N. Ibrisimović): something like, *no matter how many times I write* tears, *this paper remains dry.*

1. The Stormy Petrel

What the pot was (hot!)
At once was made known,
Not by the groan, but
the new brand on the lawn.

The phrase *naughty thoughts* sure clangs oddly in this unmoored text every time it appears; you're not alone. It needles in that *Nudge, nudge? Bob's your uncle!* kind of way, a jokey chestnut that serves to undermine the seriousness of what it stands for, but enough of a marker in the pseudo-imagistic flow not to go unnoticed. But this is how Gill's writing magic works: after you get through the opener, you go back over it and shake the dickens out of it, watching for what it gives you (in the man's own words): "what breaks off." This is a telling moment, let me tell ya! When the narrative crust fissures, all these chips fall where they may. Whichever one I pick up next will have to be *written into* further, which means going farther back into the undealt-with, digging up the untold, that will undoubtedly . . . crack me right the fuck open . . . and in this . . . state, do I dare?

Again, there's no time for that! *Nudge, nudge?! Naughty thought? Naughty thought?!*

"And if *naughty thoughts* are to come, now, right now, it would be the time for them to come, but they do not . . ." is what I wrote earlier about locking eyes with Shannon. What I didn't say was that, in my entire life, spanning forty-three years and two continents, this has happened to me *every* time I've been near a woman. It happens now still, and it still will too, for however long I have. Every time my pheromone drone-scouts tangle with the others' within the proximate fly zone around us, and I'm supposed to (what?) get a tingle, male-flare my nostrils, feel a tug in my shorts, whatever people feel in these situations, I do not. Instead, every time, my entire system wrong! wrong! wrong! crashes and I disassociate. It's not body snatching; nothing comes over me, no other entity overtakes. I'm the one who bolts, who fucks right out of the body, drops it like it's hot, and flees up into a thought bubble above, looking down abstractly, agonizing at seeing the perfectly capable shell, the only one I'll have, fail to connect and instead pour liquor into its mouthhole, because there's no one in there to deal with the tugs and the tingles, with the brokenness that happened way, way back.

Every time.

It happened even when I first met my Beloved . . . and though *this* seems like a thing that broke off and we're off to the races now, like what a great opportunity for an easy transition into a conventional narrative, this is but a tic. This is my brain trying to steer itself into the familiar flow, into a generative yarnspin (like it has time, like it too will not go down with the ship) and away from . . . *what I'm trying to fucking name here.* And though it seems from reading these sentence machinations that this *I* here seems to have an uncanny ability not only to jump out of the body it inhabits and claim not to be it, but to jump out of the brain as well, and claim not to be that either (right now it imagines its own brain a doomed spider stuck in a pocket of air in the corner of a spaceship, instinctually shitting out yarn, then spinning it into a sticky yarn <u>home</u> that will never attract a mate or hold any offspring, that doubles as a yarn <u>trap</u>, that will never catch any prey out there in the chilly universe, etc. . . .), but this too is but a tic, a tack, that needs to be abandoned for the sake of what arises but cannot be named by this mystical, realm-hopping *I*, so lo! back into the body it has to go (and at once my liver Klaxons, a tick-tock to my tic-tack, screaming: *this is* all *I am! this is* all *I am!*), back into the brain that's desperately trying to avoid putting down in words what is continuously plopping open in my mind's wrong! wrong! wrong! eye which is the sight of my first vagina, opening, opening, opening, on a loop.

And no, it's not a birth memory, y'all.

It's summer long ago, though, in the old-old country, on the Adriatic Coast someplace (Tučepi?), and the beach is pebble and pine, an imperceptible incline swallowed entire by a swarm of cheese-white, continental proletariat on that one annual seaside vacation. Their din is murderous, but out here, in the azure waters, it's fine. I'm afloat—tippy-topside drunk on the sun, the rest wearied by the cold soak below—watching Jana's sister (later they will call her Frida) bury her own goggled face into the water, survey the seafloor for not that long at all, then rush up for air with cautious panic, blowing her nose and mercilessly squeezing her nostrils, milking them for slime with one chipped-red-polished hand, and with the other dutifully holding in place a black inner tube containing the younger sister, Jana. When she inverts her goggles on her forehead, her eyes are already on me, blatant with suspicion, scorn: *Whatchyalookin'at?!*

Baffled, though I got this attitude from her before in the Auto Camp's fetid communal bathrooms, I playact it's not directed at me. I look offward, pointedly, then swivel my whole body away too, for effect—hoping for a pouty, righteous, turn-the-other-cheek dismissal of this attack on me for simply looking at them, just in case anyone was monitoring or watching this as a scene, from the side, like: *WhatdidIdo?Ididn'tdonothin'!*—a sort of just-in-case performance.

I've always done it, this kind of thing, perform in real life, imagining myself being under vague, unseen, and endless surveillance. The grandmother who raised me—who saw her imam husband almost sent to Yugoslavia's infamous Naked Island prison camp thanks to a rumor that his faith was political in nature—taught me to always be staunchly good, because *walls have eyes in this country and walls have ears too.* She also instilled in me that all protracted eye contact was evil, that a decent person had no business staring into other people's eyes, windows to their souls, that looking out and through them and into others' let some of both souls out, and that shaitan always waited at the lids, ready to snatch them in the moment of our human weakness.

So I turn away from the accusing eyes, offing-ward. The sky is painful from the shine, from the shimmer of its echo, in which bobbing heads of more daring swimmers look like blurry, personal blind spots, which beg me close my eyes. The pivot confirms just how chilled I am by the needy, squeeze-the-last-drop-out-of-this-vacation float in the sea. But I have a kink for that, a trick I do for pleasure: I dunk my head under the surface, let water into my ear canals, come back out, and as the chilling deepens, I wait for it in anticipation, the pleasure, keeping my head just so, prolonging it for as long as I can, letting the heat of my brain warm up the sea in my ears, and when I can no longer endure the cold and the wait, I look up into the heavens and the wet streak down the skin of my neck feels as incendiary as a fever touch, or as spilled blood would, as enlightenment would, and the shiver it engenders is the height of my ordinary ecstasy.

But I'm robbed of it this time. I manage to dunk my head under, let the water into my ears, but when I lift it out, it's to Jana's screams. At once I'm turned, I'm again watching, watching her erect all her limbs into the air like a fleshy beetle on its back, watching her torso sink through the hole in the inner tube, her bumped-off visor jumping ship and shoving off on its own, already a meter away. Her sister's face is weirdly old, disfigured with a mother's kind of horror already, her repositioned goggles all fogged up, her hands blindly splashing to grab Jana's hands lest she drop through.

Jana's mouth must go under because her scream's engulfed by a yip and a gag. It's the older one who's blindly screaming now, going, *Jana! What is it? Jana!* She chances on one of Jana's wrists, manages to shoulder her goggles away from one of her own eyes, and in the absence of more suitable candidates to offer help, locks that one eye on me, going, *What is it? What is it?* again, and in an eerie blur, somehow I'm already there, clutching Jana's ankles, yanking up, up, with all my might, kicking against the swell.

In an instance of seemingly ordained, almost choreographed luck, the sister and I end up with one of Jana's kitty-corner limbs in each of our right hands, at the same time our feet find purchase on the rocks below. We steady the inner tube with our lefts, and in ghostlike unison, like heroes, we pull the five-year-old's butt out of the hole. I see that she's a little blue, a little red-eyed, but mostly just frightened. I see her sister prop her up by the armpits, making sure the girl doesn't slide backward off the flotation device, as Jana realizes she's safe and coughs herself into healing tears. I see her sister, a fierce eight-year-old, blink at me blankly, then follow my gaze. I see her face change into a snarl, her eyes go from *Whoa-that-was-close!* to *Get-the-fuck-away-from-her!-Get-the-fuck-away-from-us!-Get!!—*

I see all of this only in periphery, because what I'm actually staring at is wrong! wrong! wrong! Jana's vagina.

I'm six myself that year, petrified to start school come fall, a year ahead of everyone else. The girls and I are from the same town, though they live on the west side of it, which might as well be Bangladesh. My father works with theirs at the company that manufactures dish soap and detergents. It has six campers at the Auto Camp and its workers' families sign up for fifteen-day shifts, from May 1 until September 15. They are in camper IV, we in VI. Their mother borrows my mom's paperback romances that she never returns. At night, the little Tuzla enclave gathers for pooled meals around their moody portable TV, perched on a collapsible table, to watch soccer, get drunk, and talk shit, while we kids play hide-and-go-seek, tell ghost stories, and play-fight in the pine needles. They all stick together at the beach as well, detoxing on bath towels even right now, catching Z's and failing to monitor us. Jana is the baby of their family, haughty and quick to whine. Her sister insists on being called—

Isn't it funny how all of this readily just poured out of me right after my admission, all this context and info, all this yarn, all of it in a rush to assuage you, a gush to get you on my side, to protect myself against your judgment, to explain that I'm just six at the time, that I've been around naked little kids before, boys and girls, that I've noted the differences, that I know that I'm a boy and that they are girls, that I'm aware of the other-side-of-the-coin connection between the two, of some kind of attraction that I can see manifested in coupling all around me, but that I cannot, for the life of me, understand, so much so that I feel a need to switch to a third person here to get at it. I have an urge to make clear exactly what this clueless little boy saw, standing there sternum-deep with Garfield arm-floats on, holding on to an ankle of a spread-eagled little girl, staring at the sudden reality between her legs, its stark anatomy opening into . . . a wound.

If he were a type to fight, he would have reached for it to bandage it, to try and save her life from whatever eely monster hurt her from the depths. If he were a type to flee, he'd already be whimpering back to camper VI, his hand between his legs. Instead, he just stood and stared, and stayed in this . . . *thing* that cannot be satisfactorily named, this . . . *flinch* that lives on still, reigns still, stupefies still, this . . . *forever/moment* that refuses to be *lived through,* to be filed under "past," or at least under "progress," but that keeps on starting anew, again and again, throughout the years.

He might have been lost to it entirely had he not felt the familiar splash of warmth on his neck, the herald of his ordinary ecstasy, which brought him back into his tissues—an incendiary reminder that he was a warm body in a cold sea *as well.* And standing there on the verge of his private little pleasure, feeling a stiffening in his trunks because of the shiver that was surely coming, up his spine, any moment now, lifting his eyes from the puzzling wound and up to the female eyes that hissed fear and accusation directly into the core of him, and disdain, and yes, hatred, to be frank about it, he could only stand in it. And as the look started to burn harder, so did his neck skin, because it wasn't the hot sea from his ear that brought it on but the light fondle of a common jellyfish.

And even if I could somehow show you the body-cam footage of it, as it loops in my mind's eye now, and the corresponding recordings from the sister, from Jana, from any random onlooker that afternoon—from the fucking alien eyes of the jellyfish itself—I couldn't convince you . . . I couldn't convince *myself,* of this boy's innocence.

It was me, my inopportune, stupid little pleasure that was causing all of this wrong! wrong! wrong! fear in her eyes, all of this pain in all three of us, and all of *my* confusion.

What all will consciousness latch on to in the absence of actual agency?

2. Finding Your Story

I am, at this juncture, amused to report that ever since I've set that particular little shame of mine down into words, I do not seem to *see* it as vividly
in my mind's eye—the loop. As soon as I named it, as soon as I capitulated and in the act of gross approximation called it a *loop,* I made it—my
experience of it—strangely finite. Well, not *finite,* per se; it didn't stop it
from looping. I made it somehow *more* observable, allowing for more de-
tailed and more abstract scrutiny, from-the-side-like. And as I invited this
kind of observation of it, another unnerving image emerged from my past,
from an intro to an educational TV program about language, broadcast
on national TV at that time in my life, featuring a kid seated at the head
of a long table being forced to speak. The footage is choppily edited stop-
motion and this boy opens his mouth under some perceived duress and an
enormous red felt tongue rolls out of it and down the entire length of the
table, in the way one can stylize arterial bleeding in a theater production
by using a red ribbon. Alongside the table are numerous adults in boxy
costumes systematically lifting up and bringing down mallets, hammering
upon the representation of the tongue. What I find unnerving here is not
necessarily the visceral reaction to seeing that which should be kept wet is
so very, gag-inducingly dry, nor that this boy's organ is being tenderized
by committee (there's no pain on the boy's face), but that all of it is so . . .
vital for communication.

It's vital to expose our shame (and fear, and joy) to the community, one
way or another. Unuttered, our shame latches on to us where we're the
warmest and the wettest, on the inside of us, leaching out life and guz-
zling our time, defiling every other contiguous experience of life. Uttered,
it has to go into sleep mode, has to shut down all but its vital essence to
survive outside in the environs. Without a host it cannot live other than as
an abstraction, a word. All is made out of bits of possibility that meander
through a spectrum until they're observed into particularness, until they're
named. It's like when Gill Dennis, when I first met him, in a class that
shares the title with this segment, invited us wannabes to share instances
of our fears, joys, shames, all these heightened human emotions, and make
them known in plain language, the way we would tell the story to a friend,

and had the classroom take copious notes, and days later tell us our own fears, joys, shames back to us, in the language they heard us tell them in, remembering details not necessarily the ones that we thought necessary at the time of telling, but details that became meaningful in the discussion nonetheless, crucial, even. Honoring the gag order, all each of us could do was sit at the head of the table and watch our fears, joys, shames being discussed as fodder for literature, nothing that was just ours anymore. And in *seeing* them as such, *seeing* our shame as a story meant for another, we realized that this was how we fit in the world, this was *our* service to others, this was why we feel these things so hard in the first place.

The only difference was that Gill made the classroom full of people a safe space, and typing away in the total solitude of my crybaby cubbyhole next to the water heater now isn't the same thing at all. In isolation, like in a dream (if we were to interpret it), the kid who's compelled to expose his tongue and the adults who hammer away on it are one and the same person. Mine is a hostile environment for . . . what I'm still *sadly* attempting to do before I go, which serves me right for always chasing the past dragons, trying to catch moments, reinhabit them, do over, understand. And now that there's no more wrong! wrong! wrong! time anymore, no more . . . liver, no more life, I still sully the purity of the page with this facsimile of my livid in-brain existence, thinking it will come close to capturing my lived one. And it kinda does; hence the churn, the sense of being written into a corner, the philosophizing, the repetition, the bellyaching, the voice that harasses itself, shits on itself, the soul that accuses itself, that calls out the self-pity in the midst of living in it, giving it breath. If we're to write what we know, why is this disallowed? Why is a sudden shift into third person called a choice, a whim, even, when broken brains disassociate on a daily basis to survive their own thought-making, which is the only thing that keeps them sputtering, keeping the shell alive?

This page break has been brought to you courtesy of a mental breakdown. In my (snort!) "real" life, I'd made a plan to visit a poet friend of mine in Portland. I woke up on time, packed a lunch, and even brought a piss jar just in case, went out to the Prius, and found the battery dead. I sat there depressing *start* like I was stuck on an elevator, sobbing. How? The? Fuck? Because just yesterday, I'd driven over to South Salem to buy a used video game console from my youth as a present to myself, but no, it wasn't yesterday at all. That was a month ago. I lost a month this time.

When I came back to myself, to these pages, it was all there in the document, the evidence of what I'd predicted was going to happen in the first paragraph of "The Stormy Petrel." I fucking called it! "When the narrative crust fissures, all the chips fall where they may," I said. *This* "will undoubtedly . . . crack me right the fuck open," I said. Well, the crust fissured all right, all over the document. Above, on this very page, right below the place where I broke it, and decided to interject this jackass indented interlude, I found thirty-three pages of notes and false starts, all the chips of my narrative, all the dandruff. Something in there caused my break with reality. And before I go through the detritus to try and distill it, I have to put down the following little epiphany that occurred to me and just leave it right here.

Here's the thing. I've written about the events from my life as well as my in-brain existence even before *this* effort. The manuscript I wrote was in want of definitive shape so I asked for help. It was in Gill Dennis's class, when asked to share my greatest shame (and fear, and joy), having heard other participants spill real guts—one shared about giving up a kid for adoption just to, decades later, receive news from the agency that the kid became a victim of an unconscionable crime—I shared a share of my shames in those pages, and fears and joys to be sure, but not the greatest, it turns out. At the time, I swear to God, I was convinced that I was exposing it all, unwringing my soul, deep-elbowing ardent knots of trauma, releasing healing toxins . . . and the result was a manuscript that, when I gave it to Beloved, she read with deep trepidation and couldn't stomach the ending.

Why do you have to go so dark, so mercilessly into ambiguity?
Why do we die, you mean?
There he goes. Fuck you!
The trick is to imagine the worst possible outcome, make it as alive

in you as you can make it, flesh it out, and make peace with every last goddamn little detail of it. Then, whatever actually happens . . . you know? Dreams are like this also, our subconsciousness scouring the wealth of ancient lessons buried in the DNA, devising scenarios to prep us for what might happen.

You just love *that, don't ya? Fuckin' A!*

My little . . . hack? Yeah! What else do I have?

Dreaming your life away!

Who isn't? Aren't you dreaming a life with a sunnier me? Or sunnier anyone?

Nah, nah! you don't turn that on me. No. With you . . . it's like you're praying . . . like you're wishing for it?

What's the alternative? Praying against it?

Be careful what you wish for.

I wish you'd see me as I am.

But perhaps she did. Perhaps she read what I wrote and saw me exactly as I am, and ran for the hills for exactly that reason. Because I'm broken. Or worse, because I'm unabashed about my brokenness and willing to extrapolate and follow the pattern to the inevitable conclusion, chronicling every broken move I make, predicting them, even, dreaming up a groove for a broken life into which I'm allowing my "reality" to flow, dragging her in tow (she fears). It's not lost on me that a lot of what happens in that manuscript has already been happening to me in real life. The tragedy of all of this is that all those New Agers are right, you *can* manifest whatever you wish for. The problem is that some of us are broken—we came from the broken and/or we were broken by the broken—and because of that we "wish" the worst for ourselves, which is what we end up manifesting in the world at large: brokenness.

Brokenness, neither bad—just brokenness—nor good, just a lust. A given. For we were broken back in heaven, when we knew just not-brokenness. Then just a lust to break from heaven, to break, be broke n. A lust to know how shit works "for real," with no apparatus to handle "for real," just this roiling shit of life that soils "real" hands, souls, ovaries, testicles, in the process. In-betweenaries.

In-betweenticles. Broken, brokener, brokenest is in the cards for all of us. So, do break bread and into laughter, crack a *slime*! Lie! you broken piece of shit; it's fiction! Lie, why doncha? Tell these pages you're okay! Go ahead! Tell yourself you're okay! Okay! Izzy, you're okay! There you go.

But, let me guess, this's not allowed, going nuts like this, midstory, just cutting and pasting from the hodgepodge of notes, writings. God forbid letting the broken write from within the brokenness. No, to be heard, the broken, we have to present ourselves as whole, pretend that we are put together. Even if brokenness is the subject it has to be shown in terms of wholeness, wholeness lost, or wholeness gained. The broken have to assure the whole they're like them to be heard equally. Otherwise, why read the notes from the cracked brain, when all that does is show how brittle meaning is, how badly the shards once broken off want to remain broken, out of sheer inertia which is the law of the land, so to speak. And how breaking apart is easier than gluing together, especially when, in the mind of *this* broken one, the latter can only be conceived of as *breaking* of self *together,* or perhaps *gluing* of self *apart.* Ha! No, let this cracked guy lead you to the mountaintop! This guy, who can't remember a month of his life; let *him* put it together for ya! Look, he'll even switch back to—

But back to the so-called loop. Studying the thirty-three pages of these notes, it seems that my first instinct was to blow by it once again, establish this loop as a fact of my life, and go on telling stories. As I sifted, I looked for a *through line,* or an echo of what had been set up in the next paragraph, and found two more passages in a similar vein and I'm tacking them on as well. Do notice how summarily the matter of the loop is put to bed with an offering of a juicy admission in the first:

"It happened even when I first met my Beloved," I wrote, though that time, in the black-box theater of our junior college, was the first time in my life I was ever able to withstand its freezing effect on me and remain in the body just long enough to make a connection, which is *why* Beloved be-came Beloved. Not *how,* mind you, but *why.* Had I written *how* instead, it would have implied a sort of magical connection, a time when stars aligned and I met someone special in whose presence I was able to conquer "the loop" which turned my life around. But no, like I said, the loop is still in effect now and *I* haven't *conquered* liquidy shit. What I did was I temporarily hacked it by . . . *becoming* someone else, by coming up with and *performing* someone different than me, someone who appeared already assimilated, already *grown up*, someone not enslaved by his own interiority (hahahaha and look at me now, Grandma! just look at me now!).

And—and there's no mincing words here—Beloved became Beloved in the same way I became this new American—out of *Hail Mary* necessity. This is not to say that Beloved was and is not be-loved, that she was and is not special, that the moment when it happened wasn't and isn't magical—they were and they are; I wouldn't be going after these intricacies in this way if they weren't/aren't. But at the core of it was this necessity to become someone who could survive this real, *outer* world.

Before meeting her, in my adolescence and youth, whenever the loop made me jump out of my body, that body had somewhere to belong, somewhere to sleep. That body was relatively safe. But on that day when we met, during icebreaker warm-ups of Intro to Acting, I was still a pretty-fresh-off-the-boat refugee, newly estranged from my American relatives, who quickly invited and just as quickly disinvited me from living with them, existing paycheck to paycheck in a rented room with one mattress, one bookshelf, and a nightstand made of a cardboard box with a pillowcase draped over it, on the bias because it looked fancier that way. I was alone, half the world away from anything familiar, starting a second semester of my theater major, and part-time selling organizers and Bic pens at a failing mom'n'pop stationery store.

I could easily go on developing this, perhaps inform you that, at the time, I was also reeling from a semi-freshly broken heart, a girl I met after on my first trip back to Bosnia after the migration who, in her own right, just wanted to hook up, but who I, because of the loop, turned into full-blown love object on my part. When it all unavoidably, long-*distantly* went sour, I almost killed myself over it on the very campus where I met Beloved. It wasn't the betrayal so much but my . . . sense? knowledge? that the loop was my destiny, my force majeure. There was no going back to live in Bosnia after that. If there was to be life it had to take place in the New World; in my head it was my only option. And, being a theater geek since childhood . . . if I could breathe life into characters onstage what was stopping me from doing the same in real life? And there was Beloved, smiling from the crowd, who took the class to get out of her shell, to shed inhibitions, to make friends, to experience new things . . . was I not in the same situation, so to speak? What was not to love?

But again, I don't have time for excursions, which is evident even in the way these more evasive attempts fizzle out throughout the rest of the notes. It seems that my instincts had been not to write prophetic aftermaths but to search for the ever elusive point to this anguish . . . or the cause of it further back in the past.

My "loop" first returned, full-fledged, that very first fall in my elementary school when I started to like a dark-haired girl in the back of the classroom because she knew all the answers. Back then the grown-ups taught us to call this early bunnylove *having sympathies,* among themselves winkingly meaning *designs.* And as I was already primed to be petrified to make eye contact, I found solace in the syrupy poetry my mother championed around the house, these love sonnets about achy apprehensions, about the virtues of not going for it (love) but instead enjoying a cloud of possibility from afar. I didn't dare look and God forbid! make my feelings known, so I yielded to *beaming* intention, to *emanating* my love outwardly while keeping my gaze unfocused. She was my secret *sympathy.* Not once did I ever lock eyes with her and still, when our comrade teacher told her she had her pick of a partner for the *class walk* up to the meteorological station, the dark-haired girl crossed the circle and walked right wrong! wrong! wrong! up to me. I actually swooned, not from bunnylove (though I was feeling it, I was hopping with it) but because it came with *the loop.* It was the proximity, the charge of it, that brought it on, and in the instant Jana's vagina swelled and plopped open in my mind's eye—before I could even imagine its staying power in my life—I knew the dark-haired girl would see it too the moment our eyes met. I knew the devil waited at the lids, just like she *knew* she was my *sympathy* even without me betraying myself by looking.

She'd know, I knew; she'd see, and all the accusatory fear and disdain that accompanied the original loop would beam out of her brown eyes just like it did out of Jana's sister's gray ones, back on the coast. So I bailed. I bailed out of the moment, bailed out of my life, for the very first time. I don't know where I went, but when I came back to the body, walking up the hill, paired up with my best friend at the tail end of the column of students, I remember my ears were burning real hot.

This attempt in the notes about the dark-haired girl also fizzles out, just as the notes themselves do, except for one prominent chunk written in the third person, whose typographical position at the very end of the notes suggests that it could be the reason for my breaking with reality and losing a month of my life:

. . . it's this boy's sixteenth birthday and his high school friends come over and bring him a present. In a war year, mired by shortages and hunger, this is entirely unexpected. It's a big box, heavily taped up, and when he tears it open, there's a smaller box in it, and a smaller one inside that one, and like that, dot-dot-dot, all the way to a matchbox containing a single wrapping of condom. He laughs and rolls his eyes, pretends he knows all about these things, though he's never seen one in his life. He's seen porn so he can wrap his mind around its function but he has never even smelled a girl's hair, and his friends they know this, and they know that he knows that they know, but it's how it's done, so he takes the jeers, takes the jokes, the japes, lets them punch themselves out, and eventually finds a way to maneuver the night's focus toward other common interests. He stores the prophylactic in the front pocket of his Levi's jacket, takes it out intermittently from then on in the rare moments of solitude, dreaming of the day he might get to use it. He doesn't open it because he knows he doesn't have it in him to ever go up to a grown-up and purchase one himself, and he's resigned that this is going to be **the one**, when the time comes. Months pass and, unbeknownst to him, his mother stumbles upon it in one of her I-was-just-cleaning swoops (snoops) through the kids' room, makes her own horrendous assumptions, and being her mother's daughter (*Walls have eyes! Devil's in the eye!*) enlists his father (because her husband's a man, and it's easier for men to relate to boys, it's not a woman's job, etc.) to give him and his brother **the talk**. Some twenty years later, sitting on a terrace of his brother's house and talking childhood snags and sorrows, his brother brings up **the talk** and he (me!) calls bullshit on it, insists there never was **the talk**, that he'd remember if there was one, but when his brother starts setting it up, he realizes that he does remember the scene in question, and that they are both right in their own way.

I'd give you the scene here but the chunk already ruins the joke, which was that our mother sent my father to give us **the talk**, that he skulked into our room, a highly irregular occurrence, which made both me and my brother sit at attention. He asked us how we were doing, another once-a-blue-moon clunker, so rare in fact that we both remembered the nothing day. We answered, then tried to ignore him, but he stooped there squinting at the twitching of Jim Carrey on a mercilessly rewatched VHS tape. *Is this a movie you're watching?* he asked, all absentminded-like. We rolled our eyes; we quipped. He acknowledged the weirdness of the moment with only a small look but didn't do anything to alleviate it. Instead, maintaining the becloudedness, he asked: *Is it American? Yeah,* we moaned, super-annoyed now. He watched the colors on the screen change for about ten minutes in all, looking as uncomfortable as he was making us, calculating how long a conversation like this might take regular humans in real time, and when that much real time lapsed, he slunk out, closing the door behind him. *That* was **the talk**.

This is all that could be salvaged from the notes I've written in the month that I lost, every recognizable string of possible narrative. There were other curious snippets about how life is an ambiguity becoming a particularity and death a particularity becoming an ambiguity, about hallucinogenic mushrooms showing us how everything (plant, animal, mineral) is alive as we are alive, in the same knowing way that we are alive, etc. But in terms of what caused me to break, the above chunk seems to be, more or less, it. But it's just a lame little memory; I don't understand. Maybe it only set up the break. Maybe the throng of the download continued on but I was too nuts? too scared? too ashamed? to catch it, to record the truth that came. Maybe I refused to write it and only spoke it, my truth, out loud to myself, and for myself only, only to forget it again, push it away again. Or maybe I let it tell itself inside my head, in that fuzzy, unmanifested, wave-without-particle, word-without-utterance way. How can something that big be so elusive from the spotlight of my mind while entirely saturating and shaping my body, behavior, biorhythms?

Going into all of this to . . . remember, to find an explanation for the anguish staining every smile of mine, every touch, every closeness, that makes me slink away or avoid your eyes, and yours, and yours too . . . to disinter what my brain has been burying, to find my story, **the story** if you will, all the while dreaming . . . *ridiculous dreams* of healing, of becoming whole, I'm realizing that, just like **the talk** is labeled the talk, even if it contains no talk at all, so does **the story** end up being any story that springs up when summoned, even a failed, scattered one.

It's about writing *into* it.

And I found it now, most of it.

I know enough, some of it.

3. We Haven't Moved Any Farther from the Start, Mrs. Snail Says to Mr. Snail

The yellow flashes just as I flick the blinker. I can make it—there's no one coming opposite—but I catch the urge and ease the Granmobile to a smart(ass) complete stop. Having snuck two stiff ones on my lunch, which was two and a half–three hours ago, I'm not taking any chances with the coppers out here.

The burb lights take forever so I stick out my elbow like I belong, turn up the cassette, try and lean back and look around the pristine light gray interior like it's really my own, an old-lady church sticker on the dash, hardly a punker's ride despite the current jam from the speakers. My fiancée made me buy the white Camry off her dad for five grand (I/we didn't have) when her grandma lost her driving privileges, hence the moniker. Gran only ever drove it in third and *maybe* as far as the post office and with my greasy sheen and floppy blue Mohawk at the helm of a faultless limousine like that, *I'd* pull me over. I can't wait to slap some stickers on it, though, real-life it up a little, escape some jams in it, puke in it, drive it over at least a pylon or two, but I still owe him for half of it and both his daughter and I are living under the man's roof, for the time being, we all keep telling each other.

Life out of college wet-socked us both across the face, me for my theater and my Beloved for her poli-sci bullshit. We were sentenced to move out into someplace we could afford and get into the working-and-paying-rent business, but she thought we should move in with her parents to regroup, marry, maybe apply for grad school or look for better jobs—and I remember this part being important to her—without a drop in the standard of living. Having no one else and no plans of my own other than to be with her, I said yes, let's. That was five months ago. I'm still slugging sausage and cutting frozen turkeys and she still works at a factory where just fucking yesterday some coworker of hers had his arm and head sucked in by the roiling engine of an industrial machine.

I make a smooth left on green, coast up the delightful hill, all the while clenching in the private jitters of anticipation. On rare occasions when I work the mid shift, like today, there's a chance I might arrive to an empty house and have a half an hour or so to myself, make a guilt-free drink, stretch out within the bounds of my Bosnian body, and rib-breathe from my Bosnian diaphragm.

Please, please, please.

The neighborhood is nice, the evening sky still blue, the houses patriotic, the yards lush blue velvet. Only the song is in Bosnian. Trucks and SUVs garland the street, tarped boats, even, despite double garages abounding. I hold my breath to crest the hill and I can see my soon-to-be father-in-law's house on the left now, with his tremendous palm up front, an arboretum specimen with its own fancy footlights. And yes! the driveway is empty, and so are the spots in front of the house, and all my jitters vibrate down to a warm elation in my increasingly Bosnian-feeling chest.

Yes, yes, yes!

I can't but smile until—on the final stretch of the approach, navigating around a neighbor's dormant camper—I see Shannon's beige blah sedan parked in my spot by the cacti. I disassociate, wondering why my lips are curled when inside I feel like *this,* why the music doesn't match the surroundings. I pull up behind, staring at the back of the car, waiting to see if it is real, if it's really there, if it makes sense that it's there or, opposite, if it makes sense that *I am there,* here, pulling up to *this* scene. It gnaws at me, bites, not to park in my spot by the cacti, and this obsessive compulsion seems the only thing that argues for my right to be there at all. I secure the brake, having no alternative; I shut everything off.

I don't see anybody in the car. Without my soundtrack it's easier to place myself, and despite this small awakening, a part of me still hallucinates a wishful scenario in which I get out and, upon inspection, I find, inexplicably, that this is not Shannon's car (despite the dusty shamrock on the rubber rim of her license plate), or that *it is* Shannon's car but that she, Shannon, is not there and that I can still have a little time alone for myself inside the house where I put my head down, where I keep my clothes, papers, my only home—Beloved's childhood room, complete with a painting of a unicorn that, if it existed the way it was rendered with both of its left limbs midair, would already be tumbling down the inked mountainside.

I get out of the Granmobile with my backpack on, trying not to slam the door or make a ripple in the fabric of the evening (that still feels like the afternoon), reeking of small prayers, dying to get away with a measly wishful Bosnian vacation. Though my future in-laws never lock any doors out here, it's my immigrant compulsion to secure, to lock up, to stash, even if it means giving up my position. In my head, I'm aware that if I acted like I belonged, if I simply walked into the house without locking the car, I'd get what I want. But I just *have to* press that button; there's no universe, no dimension of any universe, in which an immigrant wouldn't.

The Granmobile announces its devoted compliance, and though its two-tone tweet is so reassuring, even relaxing in part, it also brings Shannon's driver's seat up from the reclined position. She slips into groggy consciousness and sees me through the glass, slaps on some immediate sunglasses, one foot out on the asphalt before the sound of the car door opening even hits my ear.

"I was wondering which one of you'd be home free first," she goes, crooked-smiled, coming in for a wrong! wrong! wrong! hug.

I avoid hugging altogether but if my circle of personal space is breached by impromptu intimacy, I hug people like my life depends on it and a lot of times huggers and people who appreciate hugs call me a good hugger and linger in the hug. Shannon's a titleholder in that, but out in public and one-on-one like this, I'm sweating *the loop*.

Looking down, I see I still have on my butcher's rubber booties that prevent one from skidding in blood. Here's an out, a thought forms, but even before it does, I hear myself say:

"Shannon," watching my hands do this Steve Martin *Three Amigos* pistol thing with my index fingers, "I wouldn't, I'm literally schmeered with turkey fat."

I don't know what she feels behind the sunglasses but the way her hands abort coming up, and break into back-and-forth flipping of a set of keys with a can of Mace on the key chain, tells me everything. Deterred, her body loses confidence and halts in the middle of the street, pivots, looks about.

"Is it okay if I . . . come in? I mean, I know you guys are probably . . ."

"No, no . . . I mean, yeah! yeah! Come in! Of course, of course . . ."

". . . sick of me by now. Aw, thank you so much, you . . ."

". . . I don't see why not. She'll be home in like . . ."

Shannon's been over a lot, third-wheeling. *A lot* lot, like three–four nights a week, and despite Beloved's hints, her increasingly chilly announcements about how tired she is or how much sleep she needs to be efficient, etc., Shannon, in her particular grief, could not seem to—or cared not to—really hear it. Following a spectacular life explosion that severed her from her barkeep boyfriend, Shannon too couldn't afford San Diego prices on her own and, like us, retreated to the old stomping grounds, but sans the family help, sans any emotional support other than us. Last week, when she drove over here midday on her break from work to drop off a truly random lemon meringue pie (an excuse?) and went to use the little girls' room, my Beloved— in a stunning move I'd never expected from her in a million years, because this is a woman who gags at the word *spittle*—reached over the coffee table and picked up Shannon's Starbucks cup, lifted the lid, and smelled the contents, then took an actual sip using Shannon's straw, and then whispered, not without a good dose of righteous pleasure either: *Of course it's wine.*

I'd noted the moment with sincere reverence for Beloved, for her investigative prowess, her quick improv, willingness to take chances to discover what's hidden, while, at the same time—being a stasher, a hide-in-plain-sight immigrant, faced with this level of commitment to track down what's what—I also noted it with fear, letting it settle that in this game of assimilation I was but a cub. This was shit of a higher echelon and I'd have to up my own game considerably.

"Need help?" I ask now, kicking off the rubber booties, holding the door open for her so I'm partly behind it (always making sure I am between people and my backpack), but, having been invited, Shannon has no qualms about coming in, carrying her customary box of booze from her car, her only inheritance from the snuffed-out San Diego life.

The pool's animate reflection greets us, a splash of shimmer over the living room wall, and when Shannon's initial coos turn to intelligible speech, celebrating its lighting effect and asking about the possibility of having a soak, her tone pays obeisance to the shimmering. I gladly tell her (what I've been told as well) to feel like she's in her own house so I can excuse myself to drop off the backpack in the bedroom. There, I first secure the door, then take a new fifth of vodka out of my trusty hump, pour it into an empty bottle of Aquafina that is still attached by a plastic ring to a six-pack with five sister bottles containing actual water. I put away the now tainted pack in plain sight, in the drawer on *my side* of the bed, making sure the boozy culprit is all the way in the corner and least likely to be chosen. There's cheer in my heart, yes! cheer, that thanks to Shannon, I don't have to tear into my own supply immediately.

The empty vodka bottle smarts in my hand as I inch back through the house, but I slacken, seeing Shannon's out by the pool, and glide through the living room, the kitchen, the garage, and out to the bins where I bury it underneath some slimy real trash. After witnessing Beloved take that snoopy sip, I'm not even fucking with trying to recycle these.

I cut to the backyard from the side of the house, and as I step into the shine, I catch Shannon checking herself out in the French door, slipping the blade of her hand inside of her blouse, pulling some skin out of the bra, pushing her shoulders together, and I turn toward water. I somehow must *have to* turn toward water.

The sun is a burnished yolk rippling on the surface of the pool and I'm in a memory. And . . . Jana is the baby of her family, floating on the inner tube, haughty and quick to whine. Her sister is . . . and here I jump memories, and her sister is a teenager now and insists on being called . . . Frida for some reason, a punk-rock moniker with a 'tude to match, that made her an icon in the streets. But I make that connection only *way later* when—at a wartime New Year's party (Tuzla, 1994), looped up into a truth-telling frenzy on DIY war-booze—I witness this icon, *the* Frida, bully a childhood friend of mine for his inexperience at *being a man,* and I call her out by her real name, shake her off her high horse for a sec by reminding her that we used to summer together as kids, that we're all still only just teenagers, pretending to have lives in this . . . what passes as youth in our circumstance, hapless nimrods really, every last one of us, and I watch her eyes narrow with her household disdain first, but then . . . spring open in . . . something else, a kind of true recognition.

Frida calls me *that little creep* but instead of getting angry, she starts following me around her apartment all throughout the gathering, bullying still but friendlier, allowing for an actual back-and-forth. And gaining on midnight, as around us the TZ PUNX steadily black out from the poisonous spirits, Frida and I find ourselves in the throes of a stupor, inhabiting a doozy of a conversation where things of thought and things of utterance are neither thoughts nor utterances, nor things at all. Pinned by gluggedness to the same patch of parquetry, I hear her *laughingcrying,* spitting out details of her childhood rape to me, and I hear her laughing through the rape parts and crying through the parts about the willful denials of her loved ones to ever really hear what she wants them to fix, as my own hilarious mind keeps on hallucinating her sister's vagina in both halves of Shannon's sunglasses, where my reflections should be.

"Where did *you* go?" Shannon says, offering me a red plastic cup, which I snatch at once and start to chug. Vodka stuns the footage into emotion and I turn away to hide the tears. "What are you, trying to get it over with?"

If not careful, I will surely unreel.

"I feel you," she says. "By the end of the day I'm so sick of prosecco."

I don't know what she means. Shannon sways over to the water, her sway a bit too on point, holding her cup all sexy by the lip down almost at her knee. She toes the surface for temperature (she'll have me believe). The instant she turns around I get busy *behaving.* I make a point of pouring myself a casual neat, of leisurely parking my ass on a lawn chair, trying to keep my legs in a correct aggregate state. I feel her looking for my eyes but I keep mine on the mountains out there, like the ones in the opening credits of *M*A*S*H*.

"What's up your woman's ass?"

"She *used* to be fun."

"Seems like she's all business now, just like fuckin' Chris."

"*They* should have stayed together."

"Cheer up, man."

"You know I always found you attractive."

Shannon says all of these things, with varying pauses in between.

She also . . . approaches, incrementally, with varying pauses in between.

"Does the body good," she says almost into my ear, but I'm through the French doors in an instant, stammering my go-tos about smelling bad, some shit about lamb casings, and there's a crackling burn in my abdomen, burning wrong! wrong! wrong! as I whimper a sorry after sorry to her, even though I'm all alone now, naked in my American shower belonging to my almost family. Because shower follows *smelling bad* in this country, and a foreigner, *this foreigner,* only has to follow these little rules to fit in, a piece of cake, especially when they get him off the hook like this, when he can hide behind them to allow a pigheaded hallucination to pass. But, leaning in the steam with his forearms against the tile and submitting to the scalding ray of water scanning his face like a barcode, washing away the waves of vomit as they spurt out of his Bosnian nose and mouth and down his Bosnian chest, boner, feet . . . he sees *the loop* at last for what it is.

A dam gives in his mind, slowly to start, and he flashes first to the wrong! wrong! wrong! goddamned taste of the flesh of his recurrent memory, which is an impossibility. He never tasted . . . *WhatdidIdo? Ididn'tdonothin'!* But the taste's so real and it doesn't give a damn that it doesn't make sense to him. It's his lips next that suddenly remember the gristly relief of the sex, the heat and the stickiness on his chin, the quick cooling and hardening of stickiness away from heat. There's tang on his tongue, hot salty liquid pooling in his mouth, and it can't be wrong! wrong! wrong! Jana, it isn't/can't be Jana that he's tasting, though the loop remains the loop as it always was while the sensations of taste remain what they are until he encounters—*in his mind's eye? with his mind's tongue?*—the rasp of pubic hair being combed by his childhood tastebuds, and who ever heard of five-year-olds with pubic hair? which exposes the loop for the fraud that it is—his mind's stand-in for another . . . *earlier* vagina.

Same seashore, different town, different summer, a year prior perhaps, hide-and-seek with the younger kids with . . . (what is her name?) Body odor, rasp of voice, older girl with zits, sixteen perhaps, much bigger girl in charge of entertaining and safeguarding the rest of us. Big football game's on and the adults are drinking under the communal tent set between campers . . . Her brown lipstick, too-close-together eyes . . . Big-assed girl, with glasses and fat grown-up chest, inside her trailer (*our cubbyhole,* she said), and a sudden gunk of black hair down there and that beam of hers, that vehemence and pain in her eyes. Eyes so adult and cold . . . so other(under)worldly they froze you from the tippity-toppity fringe layer of the electrons of your epidermis *in.* Inside, as she pressed, you were cooking. Her sex was incendiary, maw-scalding. *I made you!* she said to the kitchen area, not you. *You were supposed to be my joy!* she cried to the kitchen area, grinding her gunk into your . . . into my face.

Oh boy! is right . . .

Poor Jana. I cursed her so over the years. My psyche cast one of the most innocent creatures of my life as my original shame because it was too afraid to uncover the real offender, lest I lose myself completely way too early, lest I go nuts trying to deal with this rape when not yet ready. What strange, beautiful brains we have. Even stunned and broken, they serve to save us. Thank God for that.

If I could go back in time to when I first met Gill, to that class in the High Sierras, to that Tuesday when it was my time to share my biggest "shame" with the room, I wish I'd really heard his question. I wish I'd picked . . . *this shame* and not the lesser ones I'd already (un)covered in the previous manuscript. Working title: "How I Learned to Ignore the Loop." What a missed opportunity, to get at this grody little culprit secretly shaping my life with yesterday's energy, yesterday's drive. But hell, even in *Walk the Line* Hollywood didn't (couldn't) go for the early versions of Gill's script with Johnny Cash's <u>true</u> biggest fears, joys, shames either, because, you know, biopics need to uplift in the end and one has to think about Americans and what they can take, forgive. Choosing the way I did, perhaps intuitively, I too might've simply wanted to just be taken in, by my Americans, and be—fuck forgiven! fuck read!—just fucking . . . held.

4. The Shannon Closing

I never told Beloved.

I mean, I did tell her about Shannon making a move on me and me running away . . . and to take a shower!—*I did good, didn't I? Two birds, at the same time too! Despite naughty thoughts! Naughty thoughts! Right? Right?!*—and I did it the very same night it happened, after Beloved, fed up and sauced herself, had finally histrionic-yawned the (by then) garbled Shannon out of the house at one a.m. She'd excused herself with a curt, definitive wave and left me to see our friend out, help carry her *boozebox* to the trunk. It took Shannon so long to pick the car key on her key chain and that whole time she never even looked at me, never acknowledged that anything at all took place, before driving off. I stood in safe shame for a long time, this Bosnian under the unlikeliest of palm trees, under a foreign sky, this guy.

After hearing me out, Beloved first asked if I was sure that was what had happened, given my track record of never knowing what's a come-on and what isn't (as she only knew about *the loop* as my symptom). Yes, I was sure. She wrestled with it for a time and landed on deciding to see the situation from Shannon's point of view, understanding her pain, understanding that breakups can lead to *acting out*, that after losing Chris the poor girl had no emotional support to speak of, that it's better it happened within the safety of a friendship where it *Thank God* didn't amount to anything, didn't cause any *real* damage, and . . . I had neither the right nor the heart to tell her about my epiphany. Couldn't ruin what she valued, this beautiful taking of the high road.

And even when Shannon showed up a week later to apologize for always crashing our meals, insisting on cooking *us* a salmon dinner (which she proceeded to drunkenly burn), Beloved *understood*. Even when, days after, my future mother-in-law received two all-swag-included tickets to the Coachella festival that she hadn't ordered and, stunned, called Ticketmaster to be informed that it's their policy to always mail to the billing address, then called the number from which the order was made (kindly guided by the representative to where it was printed on the ticket itself), to get Shannon's cell phone's outgoing message, then scrambled through the drawer in the dining room hutch, looking for an emergency Mastercard to find it not in its secret stash, then called Mastercard to report it stolen, and in due course got a written list of purchases made on it, which included a fortysomething-dollar charge at Trader Joe's on the day of the salmon dinner, and a three-hundred-dollar charge at BevMo! (which explained the relative inexhaustibility of Shannon's Box o'Fiesta) and even when Shannon swore over the phone to Beloved that she didn't know what the hell happened, that she's outraged, and that she'll be at the house first thing after work to get to the bottom of this, and then proceeded to drop off the face of the planet and was never heard from again, even after all that, both Beloved and her mom, they worked through it pretty quickly and arrived, again, at an *understanding*. They said, *Poor woman*. They said, *No police*. They said, *Her predicament is punishment enough. Poor woman*, they repeated. They hinted at all this previous knowledge of what Shannon survived in her childhood, her resultant troubles with the law. *Relapse*, they called it. *I hope she's okay*, they said, *I hope she makes it out okay*.

All that *understanding* going on. All that forgiving. It sure was reassuring.

I was the only one silently convinced that her coming on to me was a ruse, a tactic, that she wasn't into me at all. I hadn't known anything about her criminal past, but she *had* been acquainted from the start with my wilting always at first flirt, my ossifying at every unavoidable hug, my looking away at a mere *feel* of a look. Shame recognizing shame? She had seen mine the way all the rest pretended they didn't (at least that's how I always felt) and she'd counted on it, and used it to her advantage, however untoward. She knew how to get rid of me to give herself time for a thorough snoop, to hunt down that hidden, never-used credit card like a pro while I puked in the shower.

But how come mine hadn't recognized hers? Why couldn't my shame give me any secret power, any outlet, however untoward? Is it all always about fight, flight, or freeze? And if you're in the frozen category, does it mean that you don't get to exorcise *any* of it, ever? That you just have to take it, breathe it in, breathe it out, live in it, be of it, and what? *be it?* Be the shame? But it has to do with nurture too, right? and thinking way, way back, I did recall one of my grandmother's custom caution-tales about the evil powers of direct eye contact. She told of the not uncommon occurrence in her day of encountering a certain kind of unsavory villager, men exclusively, squatting bare-assed in public, in plain view, like at a bus stop, but without ever really being seen shitting. Like, really, *actually*, seen. One would encounter them, she'd say, and somehow . . . not see them, simultaneously.

How's that possible? I'd ask. And she'd grab my chin in a clamp of her raspy peasant hand and look directly into my soul, and no matter how much I didn't want to, I couldn't look away, and she wouldn't say anything for a maddeningly long time, letting me stew in unreality and *chinpain*, enough for me to start shaking from fear, and she'd let go then, and say, saucily:

Because that's how *mushkinje* (malekind) would look at you, beaming their shame, their thoughts, at you, so *you'd get* scared, and *you'd get* ashamed *for* them, and that's why you'd always look away, you'd always keep always looking away. Pretend you don't and didn't see anything, while standing right there in front of it, being part of it. Erasing it from common reality, not thought. Using thought to ignore the reality away. And *mushkinje*, they'd use that time to wipe their ass with a leaf and go on with their day.

But you're not like that, she'd say then, winking, half-smiling, hoping it was true, but shaking her head too, a bit, her mouth trying on doubt then belief, then doubt and belief.

After Shannon vanished, closer to Beloved's and my wedding, I gave Beloved a ride home and when she stepped out of the Granmobile, in my spot by the cacti that had overtaken the hill, she spotted a glint out there. I watched her face scrunch up, like that time when she sipped from Shannon's coffee cup to find wine. She trekked up the hill like a junior investigator to discover several empty prosecco bottles (Shannon's) and five months' worth of small vodka bottles I'd been chucking up there upon coming *home* from the third shift at the meat department.

Of course, wrong! wrong! wrong! they were all Shannon's, the bottles.
Right? Beloved asked.

Right? I aped.

There was a silence in which we were tricking ourselves, and each other,
Beloved and I, knowing we weren't tricking anyone at all, just feeling that
fuck! fuck! fuck! of life once the ride is already mid-roaring-plummet and
allowing for this . . . ride, I don't know what to call it . . . allowing for whatever that same allowing allows to occur.

And then we got busy cleaning up the arid hill of "Shannon's bottles,"
recycling the evidence, erasing things from reality, making them fit the
plot. It's insane . . . it's fucking impossible what humans all are and aren't,
in turn.

It's a lucid dream, being an immigrant in the U.S. For others in
it (*The Matrix*, anyone?), it is crucial that the American dream is a
real thing, while you're always conscious of it *only* being a dream,
a dreamed-up thing, a concept, and to buy into it as into a reality
would be abstruse for you, taking into account what happened to
your old reality, the old-old family, the old-old country that these
supposed so-called Yugoslavs *allowed* into sundered smithereens,
which is why you're in this here red-white-and-blue dream in
the first place, weighing meager (no) options with the rest of us.
And it's that lucidity that makes you the other, the fact that to
you the spotlight is always on the artifice of the dream and on the
corresponding inability to buy into it hook-line-and-sinker, the way
a dream needs to be bought into, the way it needs to be sold to be
made into a real brand.

This is why you're frustrated reading this. Every time someone
interrupts one individualized world to tell you of another means
work for you. Nobody wants to hear about another person's dream,
for one. And two, nobody likes to be awakened from their own life,
especially into another, just as loosey-goosey and tentative as the
one they have to perpetuate to stay in. You're trying to pinpoint
where this is written *from*?

I don't know what to tell ya . . . if I bring this guy back . . . does this help?

Throughout my whole time with Gill, until he passed away, I was in the program, either *crushing it* or fucking up so much that he never really knew, at any time, whether to offer me a beer or not. After I'd accept or decline, he'd shrug and shake his head at the thing we've been discussing from the start. Ever since we first met—I remember that Sedaris's quip was in, the one about writing about drinking and drinking about writing—Gill's point was that, in his experience (and he hung out with some of the greats), those who couldn't stop died of it and those who stopped died of cancer later. I'd balked at it at the time, though I'd *recognized* it, in my core, in my very breath.

Later, at this place called Lucky Lab's, weeks before he died, I was off the wagon and crying about how Beloved and I were fighting, how she wouldn't read anything I'd written because *it was too hard,* and that it felt to me like being denied a voice (since this was the only way I knew how to make my feelings known), and Gill asked me about my earliest memory, perhaps to take me back into my childhood, into happier times, and, instead of the loop, I told him of a night when Grandpa was watching a black-and-white film in the dark, and that it was winter, and that I was supposed to be asleep but wasn't, that Grandma was snoring in the room behind me, which smelled of slow smoke and even slower snow outside, and that the story reflected on the fogged-up double-paned windows was subtitled and about a*(n American?)* writer who was trying to write a book called *The Bottle,* but how he had to stop drinking to write such a book, but how, when he stopped drinking, he couldn't write *The Bottle,* and, with the bottle, he couldn't write at all, and that the scene with which the memory ended was of this guy tearing his house apart, trying to remember where he stashed the bottle his dipsomaniacal mind was a hundred percent certain was somewhere around there, and about his agony of not being able to tell whether his mind was correct or whether his reality was, which led to him coming to terms with not knowing, and, having no alternative, eventually sitting back down at his typewriter, and turning on the light to write, realizing, by the shadow on the wall and ceiling, that the missing bottle was stashed in the lamp the whole time, and that there was no reason to start writing just yet.

Then I admitted to Gill that I didn't know who I was nor what to do with that, that when I came to the U.S., I had to invent *someone else* to become, someone new, someone extroverted, a persona that could withstand the environs, and that everyone loved that guy way more than me, that putting him on required insane amounts of delusion and energy (powered by drink), and that I couldn't keep doing him anymore, but that everyone missed that guy and hated me for not being able to maintain him, to keep him conjured up, and Gill simply took me by the elbow, nodding, and said, smiling: *Well, yeah, welcome to the fold!*

I'd be remiss if I didn't say that it was the only time, in all of my lives (lived, dreamed up, and/or remembered), when I didn't feel like *the other*.

If you start with joy and end with shame, it's a tragedy.
If you start with shame and end with joy, it's a comedy.
But what is it, given all of . . . this?
What do you want it to be?
What a strange, American question, Gill.

In their open-access article about my first manuscript, titled "The Silenced Narrator and the Notion of 'Proto-Narrative,'" Marina Biti and Iva Rosanda Žigo attempt to ". . . establish the concept of a narrative subject whose voice emerges from the deep zone of their 'proto-self' . . . to be weaved into a distinctive narrative form . . . a proto-narrative."

Actually, here's a whole chunk:

". . . as the narrative progresses, the narrator moves more and more away from the objectivist memoirist approach, allowing entrance to the imagery that blurs, to the point of elimination, the line between the real and unreal. As the novel progresses, an intradiegetic voice increases in presence, undermining the memoirist frame and claiming the narrative 'I' to disappear and turn into 'you' and does so, in some instances, even at the cost of disrupting narrative coherence. This garnishes the memoir with elements of an obscure internal reality that seems to be fully submerged within the experience of trauma.

"The complexity of the narrative structure that involves not only multiple levels of diegesis and various diegetic combinations discussed by Genette but also an unusual correlation between verifiable reality and fiction, invites theoretical speculation primarily concerning elements that can be qualified as 'disruptive' to the memoir, related to trauma. We will, therefore, explore the actual, diagnosed mental state of the character—the posttraumatic stress disorder (PTSD)—and attempt to trace narratively detectable symptoms of the character's/narrator's illness across the text, as to shed light on the transgressive power of trauma that affects both the form and the content of the overall narrative, and on the ability of trauma to garnish narrative reality with 'realities' that it creates in the mind of the traumatized subject."

To Corresponding Author:
Iva Rosanda Žigo
University North
Trg dr. Zarka Dolinara, 1, 48000 Koprivnica, Croatia

Dear Ms. Iva Rosanda Žigo,

I hope this package finds you healthy and happy and tired in the best of ways, that you're keeping sane as much as possible in these COVID times. I'm writing to thank You and Your Colleague so much for writing your article on my work. I came upon it by accident when I googled "Prcic," looking for ever elusive evidence of Prcic once being a solid, regular person and real in the world. Reading it, I felt seen for the first time in *my* life. You Two seem to be the first people to *really* notice me, to, in fact, "hear" my voice in the very noise that is this writer's narrative.

Let's just say that I find your concept of the Silenced Narrator absolutely fascinating, and it's because—and I know this will sound batshit crazy at first—I believe I am . . . it. Not the broken guy I'm using to type up this letter before his liver explodes, but me who dwells within him, who keeps keeping him honest about his brokenness, at each and every turn, in real life or on the page, night and day, without respite. I'm the one who ruins his every attempt to connect or fit in, or to write a simple, naturalistic ending of a chapter, the one who shows him that he has no business ordering or making sense of anything, especially not his life. Because it isn't his, his life.

I'm a little annoyed at these *broken artistic types* pretending they'd survived me. They never give props where they belong. *I* run their life and *I'm* the one who gets them all in the end; *I* win every time, yet they all go on writing these . . . books in which they manufacture themselves changed or whole, whichever tack they employ. They put themselves together on paper and they think that'll change something.

This is why I'm really liking the recent push out there, in academia and culture in general, to get me out of the shadows and let the scar tissue get some vitamin D. Not enough populace likes to face me, though, actually look at me, and know me, which is why I have to be a ghost in the machine, so to say. But by noticing me, and naming me, you allowed me into this existence. You went as far as giving me a voice. Agency, however, I took that off the lot of you. I'm buzzing louder and louder, bleeding through the grouting—as you've noted. I'm learning to enjoy the attention too, and changing with the times . . . sliding in for a winning goal right after which the referee calls the game (a game that really doesn't matter) and basking, a little mischievously, why not?

The days of me being only symptomatic are over and you must have sensed that shift in me. I did help you out by being the only part of this writer guy that is not afraid.

Still, I appreciate You and Your Work immensely. When everyone else was going on and on about "narrative coherence" you were like, "Fuck narrative coherence, what about *the dude is broken* don't we understand!?"

Again, I appreciate that eternally. You seem to comprehend that all this . . . *bookwriting*, all this storytelling, actually hides the truth, the way it really is, that to hear this truth one has to, like my close friend Geever says, *sometimes read with a feeling of found text, that even within an author in control, there is that element of a voice screaming alone, that is then somehow collected by an outside force, and not an editor, more of a treasure hunter of trauma and loss who presents these found texts not in an attempt to provide understanding or purpose, or order, but to deny the attempt to hide truth behind story.* Also, *being* this guy, inside of this guy, having danced the dance of that anguish, *I don't want to deny the broken the further chaos of anonymity or silence.*

I don't trust his broken ass (though) to get much more done than this, which is why I'm sending you this manuscript in its entirety in hopes that it will further aid you in *your* work of chronicling my rise from the collective unconscious.

If I don't directly hear from you in time, don't worry—I permeate, like a childhood. If not from this one, I will keep in touch from other hosts.

Or I'll just holler at you from your inner ear.

I know you can hear me.

I'm that shit that, right now, you're trying not to think about.

I'm that shit you *so* don't want to think about, that your own soul has conspired to make me inaudible to you.

Now you're trying to figure out if I mean the addressee of this letter or *you* you. C'moan, people, who do you think I mean?

Don't wait to name my existence into the world lest, silent, I gorge here on *your* love, *your* nerves, *your* time, *your* sweat of brow.

Lest I mine the very marrow of *your* mind for the limelight of my own.

There is no inner life and outer life, people.

You big forgetters, you big forgivers of selves.

There's no inside and outside voice.

These are all utterances, not thoughts in words.

That I'm not right here, screaming at ya!

you're sitting there, pretending again,

izz

LINER NOTES

The Bachelor Party 2.0

×

I am a writer, I guess, by any means now. And I have some friends.

×

I used to be an actor. My role was, I could drink all day. But the key to having memories is remembering them. You have to remember to have memories and friends.

×

I used to be married. The weekend before the wedding me and a couple of other guys went camping—a bachelor party or, let's face it!, *instead of.* It was Eric's job to plan it, but he never did anything like that before, so at the last moment he deferred to my redheaded bride-to-be who made trips occur with clicks of her magic mouse.

We trashed one another, as *real men* did in the late '90s, early aughts, though none of us could've been mistaken for one, *a real man*—whatever that is—dicks and adequate hobo skills notwithstanding. We were young-ish *male people* who made decent but ambitionless boyfriends and poor third basemen. Talking macho comedian shit was an act, funny because it was so unlikely coming from us. Especially me, the immigrant. *Tree (3) pussies in the voods,* I'd said with my accent, and they cackled, asked me to say it again and again.

Two of us barely left the campground for the duration. Of the four of us, two drank every day, all day. Eric waited to drink, tried to last as long as he could, at least until the dinner preparations. The fourth guy did not arrive until the last evening, so he wasn't on any kind of drinking schedule. We had no soap. One guy's pants ripped all the way down the seam the day we went home.

×

The wedding a week later was great drinking. Eric remembered the most. Me and my new bride, we had seen him a few times since. Remember this? Remember that? Remember when Ryan was throwing those cups?

I laughed, so hard, because I didn't. At all. I am supposed to be a writer, from my own experiences, no less. I figured someday I'd write about that important weekend. But how?

Later I thought: We all have memories of our lives, despite the nothing of life. We all turn the nothing of life into something to remember. I decided to write *into* the space where the memories would be residing now had I not drunk. And since I don't remember anything but what Eric wrote down in *The Bachelor Party*, I couldn't help but let myself be free to imagine and intuit my way into the soul of the story. I even added a monster in mine. A werewolf.[3]

×

Before all that, I have to say that I know . . . I *do* remember what we all were/are. We all remember that.

I'm a groom-to-be, a brand-new—certificate in hand—American from Bosnia, a refugee, and because of that they keep calling me Tom Petty, in-

---

[3] *The Bachelor Party* is a bound document comprised of a blow-by-blow nothing-narrative of the aforementioned real-life trip of ours, interspersed with choice copied photos from a point-and-shoot camera of mostly Ryan and me, all lovingly written and designed by Eric Carlson and given to me as a wedding gift (one of) for the sole reason that I could one day write about it, using his memories, his language. Eric's version starts with: "I'm not a writer, by any means. I have some friends who write. My role is different. The thing is, I can't drink all day." Do note the echo from the opening of the augmented version of the story you're actually in the process of reading, and it will give you an idea of what I did here, what I'm doing with his version to make my own right in front of your eyes. Do not look at me like that; this document gives me explicit permission to use it as I please. Facsimile of it is available upon request as proof.

sisting that nicknames invite mascot status, and that Americans love mas-
cots. I'd seen some fucked-up shit back in *the old before* and I thought I had
to somehow counteract my resultant brokenness to be taken in. After the
initial fits and starts, I constructed a persona in a loud burgundy jacket à la
Wild and Crazy Guy from *SNL*—a mascot, let's face it!—so that I could
be loved. Pieced together in this fashion is how I met my bride in these
American suburbs, where "nothing happens in a good way," as in better
than before, as in anything is better than *the old before*.

Eric is the best man, the keeper of the narrative and the one who en-
sures that everyone has equal amounts of fun. He's married himself, five
years, and with a two-year-old son and an office job at the time. Though
eccentric up the ass in his own hilarious right, he takes great pains not
to act on it or at least not to murder people with it (like some people
I intimately know), to sacrifice it to count-your-lucky-stars reality. We'd
become roommates when I was in a lurch with a family member and he
helped me stay in America by signing that lease. Way later, when his bride
moved in, it made me make my own move at having a bride as well.

Ryan—I know Ryan from the world of college theater. When I first
met him, in a corridor of a black-box theater, he was having an involved
and heated conversation with a wooden wedge. The kind you scotch vehicles with or prop open the venue doors. Naturally he is a somewhat
reserved conversationalist but that afternoon, in the break between classes,
he saw a stranger sitting in the audience and enacted for me an entire love
affair with this wedge—balancing it on his knee—from infatuation to pur-
suit to connection to affair to the fight to the makeup to the dredge to the
brokenness. He did it as a greeting or a mystical offering and really knew
how to stretch the subtleties of every phase. You would watch this guy sort
out mail for an hour and a half; he was that good.

×

The day of the trip, the three out of four of us converged at Eric's house to
take one car. It was promptly clear that Ryan was in brand-new shambles.
He stepped around the yard arm-danglingly stunned, with a face of a baby
angel. We pressed him till he divulged that the girlfriend he had lived with
in Burbank for years had gotten herself shacked up with some naughty

photographer up north, instantly engaged. We breathed in through our teeth, clapped Ryan on the wings, packed the meat and the booze into the minivan, and promised him hijinks to keep his mind off her.

My future bride called before we left, asked if we had sunscreen. Eric said *he* did. I told her he had brought some, and she loved me and wished us all safety and a good time. Eric then said something like: *See, it starts before it even starts!* and drove us toward a McDonald's inside a Walmart, the last hurrah before he had to brave my food.

My Pepsi bottles had vodka in them, premade, and I offered one to Ryan in the back because I was excited at becoming husband material and wanted to scream my hard-won *americaness* with my fellow Americans. They were both very used to their own, though, so much so that they didn't seem to understand what I was so riled up about. To my chagrin, Eric refused to play Tom Waits until the atmosphere matched some innate inner feeling of his, which was already met in mine. But he was doing all the driving, and it was fine, and I understood. I drank, buzzing, watching farmlands devolve into plazas and businesses.

×

I was hungry to belong, which in my mind meant Hollywood shenanigans, which meant private jokes in English and unexpected encounters with real-life *characters*, strange little things you don't see in front of your house every day. I wanted the augury of seeing my American memories present themselves to me openly in the present, natural as gravity. The key to having memories was remembering them; that much was true, if you were a writer. But before that, when you were in the middle of acting in them, before you attached meaning to those moments, you had to be in them without knowing what they meant. You had to let them or make them happen, inhabit them in flesh and lung.

Isn't *that* fucked?

That constant goddamn *now* we all flip out about—the presentness of life passing with nothing happening, the panicky freedom of it—seemed right there in each boozy nothing-breath, commingling with the inner commentary that recognized it as an *experience*, categorized it and filed it somewhere as an organic abstraction. I didn't know how to wrap my mind around any of that. Was I supposed to wait or do? *Don't just sit something, do there!*

×

Eric advocated for the everythingness of Walmart. We all remembered ice. I remembered skewers. Ryan bought a bottle of Jägermeister. He had bad luck freaking out on substances often and was always trying to faithfully duplicate some last best experience. He remembered a great night on cold *Yager,* a deep cut from the time before he even met Elsa. It was through trying to remember *around her* that trip, that he remembered Elsa a lot. That and through freakin' Ben, of course, later, when *he* showed up.

I felt like an understudy in another person's life, going: *Wait! Was that my prompt? What's my line? Am I fucking this up?* I was bent on something to occur, though, all these aggregating nothing-seconds to cohere into something akin to a beat, at least, let alone a scene, but the only thing that happened was that while waiting for his McNuggets meal, Eric found a crumpled fiver in his pocket on which some moron had scrawled: BEER'S ON ME, FAG! and decided no way would he part with such hilariously defaced currency and paid instead with his card. When he showed me the five, I hacked out a laugh so unhinged that other folks in line turned ornery and stared arrows at my person, and the friendly McGirl with bangs that stood straight up, like a yellow tsunami, gulped in fear.

But audience was audience.

×

We cruised the 118 out of Simi Valley, to the 5 North and into what Eric called Clyde Country. He went on about the old-school Clint Eastwood of the era when he rode around in a pink coupe with an orangutan and what it brought up in him. He'd grown up in a desert town in Arizona, so small-town America that he once proved it to me by googling its weekly paper and sharing that week's front-page headline, which read, and I quote here: "NOCTURNAL ANIMALS RARELY SEEN!"

He played the Pogues and the Dead Milkman and got us through a stretch around Bakersfield where all the street signs whizzing by seemed random: *Avenue 142* was followed by *First Street*, which was then followed by, like, *Road 133*, then it was back to the avenues. The air was hazy from far-off fires. Hills were smoldering on the side of the freeway and a couple of cars too—seemingly unrelated-like.

Whatever incendiary soul-thrills I thought I'd be feeling on this drive, I had to will and keep alive inside.

×

We drove up into Sequoia Park and through a maze of trails, under what Eric kept calling the Goodnight Moon, his kid's thing. We found the anchors of the campsite #43—the picnic table, the firepit, and the bear box—and conjectured our tents far, far from the last. All three of us were shitting being eaten alive, though a few shots would surely abate that fear.

Ryan, he knew about *taints*. I kept calling tents *taints*, a joke from a beloved *Mr. Show* skit, trying to up the mood after all that driving. Under Ryan's leadership we had all three up and perfect. Our confidence was gaining. We took a rest down by the minivan. The alcohol, the last to be loaded, was the first to come out. Brandy and cola for me and Ryan, from red plastic cups like back in college, and Eric cracked his Mickey's Big Mouth and a broadening sheen alighted in his smile, finally.

Silence faded in until we began to hear sounds in it. A trickle.

A creek?

We took our flashlights and took off after it. It was fast, no mere trickle, flowing with elemental, unremitting intensity. We got quiet in front of it. Our shadows loomed large on the trees. *Bosno moja!* Even I forgot what non-landscaped trees were all about, non-lit-up skies. In the narrow ribbon visible from the spot, there was galaxy dust up there between the few visible stars. Between stars, stars between stars.

Then Ryan waded in. It felt right to all of us. Wished *I'd* thought of it, but he was magnificent in his role. His silhouette resembled that deep ocean fish with a light atip its goad. He bent at the waist and nuzzled that bottle of Yager in the current, securing it with rocks. Going after that cold. When he suddenly took the flashlight out of his teeth, he looked like he had collapsed upon himself, going out with a slight delay, like an incandescent spotlight.

×

We couldn't stay in the magic, couldn't make it last. Ryan might have been able to, thanks to his fried-eyed heartache; his heart was broken enough. But even he cracked, hugged his elbows at the gust of wind, did one of those big sighs, as in, *The moment is over, right?*

"One, two o'clock, what do you guys think?" Eric asked, and we knew he had responsibilities we didn't so we took off back to the camp.

"I have to figure out a way to call the wife at some point," he let us know.

We sat at the picnic table with a lantern and drinks. Portable CD player played Waits on low. *Better off in Iowa against your scrambled eggs / Than crawling down Cahuenga on a broken pair of legs.*

"Vhat about dinner tomorrow," I said to say something, "chicken or steak?"

"Chicken's what your wife makes when you're out of spaghetti," Eric fired. He couldn't resist making all the same marriage jokes that bitter old fucks said to him before *he* got married, because most of them turned out to be true. But then he caught himself, said: "We'll have the steak."

Gorgeous forest moths started landing, furry, capable of purring.

"Pardon the beef curtain," Ryan said out of the blue, and Eric lost it, laughing.

I filled my red cup to the lip with Christian Brothers brandy, fuck it.

×

Every sound we made was amplified, to my drunken delight. My hard-working countrymen and countrywomen, mature people with jobs, lives, and itineraries, were down for the count in their trailers. They'd be up in a few hours to get it all done and I understood that, but in my mind, I wanted to be heard tonight, I wanted them to know I was also there, one of them.

Eric shhhed me every thirty seconds and I'd be back at full volume within ten. The pattern repeated for an hour until someone finally called out:

"Can you guys please keep your voices down?"

It was exactly what Eric was dreading, always, that he was somehow preventing others from doing what they needed to do. That sheen came off of his regard. Ryan grimaced into a cup and I was belligerent and righteous and the show had to go on.

"Pardon my beef curtain!" I called back out. "This is America!"

"What is it? You want Dark Side points?" Eric said, some unknowable *Star Wars* reference, I bet. "Shut the fuck up—it's the right thing to do!"

I was pissed, though, flipping off and whisper-yelling at a dude who just wanted a peaceful night's sleep. The mood fell. Conversation stopped. I ended up winding down to introvert. Sack time was the only option.

Before we went to our tents, Ryan said: "It's parting."

"Huh?"

"It's parting . . . It's *parting* the beef curtain."

×

. . . that night, in the tent, listening for bears, listening with my eyes, my skin, I changed, and I smelled her in her mossy grove there, smelled her scratching her lucky crystals and batting her brown eye and howling, hitting upper harmonies to a flora-wail of a bolt-burnt, hollowed-out oak out there, holding on to the earth by a curved shadow of cindered bark and yearning, but greening still above, still breathing, wailing his ancient love at the she-wolf below, and it was as if I felt her through his soaring scar, through the singed wound of it in which she had stashed her crystals and can lids and bits of dental floss and two plastic googly eyes and a fertility candle she never lit, her precious things that had to be kept secret, where no one would ever look to think, inside this sad sanctuary, an organism that's on a precipice and has no choice but to live, give with every cell, and I have to find her now, to see what she'll do, and the path of the scent is clear, straight out of this tent, between a man pissing into a water bottle from all the beer, feeling weird, and a man dreaming of a girl who just throws herself into a pile of laundry that he's folding, takes him by the neck, and kisses him hard and away from the rest of them creatures and down the slope through the resin wind, to the grove, to the wailing oak, but as I round the mossy stone and I see the river's edge I know I'm not a local wolf which means I'm not privy to all the magic here but her scent is not from here either and is that Balkans that I hear, is that my home?

×

A green tree limb hissed under the pan, frothing at the burn. I was making breakfast. All the campers around us had gone out, or had already come back, even.

Some late-in-life Ernest Borgnine waddled into view and was going by us in slow, measured steps, with four glistening fish at his hip. He grunted in a meandering way at our own shifty-eyed nods, keeping an eye on his forward momentum. But . . .

"Nice work!" Eric said. The silences were always killing him. "Where the hell did you get those?"

The way the man decelerated at the question was a clinic on exasperation, or evidence of unimaginable *bone*pain. I turned to the sizzling hash, scraping nonexistent bits off the bottom with an offset spatula. In scenes with a lot of characters, it was crucial to have business. If I messed with the taters, I was contributing to the naturalism. Look at these little movements of my arm filling up the reality of the moment, stuff you can later remember, or have someone remember for you.

"Just over there," the man said, "in the river."

"The creek?" Eric went, indicating the opposite way from where the man was indicating.

"No," the man punctuated. "The river. Over. There."

The river? I flipped the portion of taters, saw that they weren't browned enough, and flipped them back.

Eric's voice became higher: "There's a river over there? Like, within walking distance?"

I flipped the hash again, left it flipped, saw my hand pick a plastic cup from a stack. I was ready for my first of the day, I guessed. I turned back to the scene and caught the old man's brow feel bad for his cadence. Like, he didn't seem to have meant to be that gruff.

"Couple of real nice fishing holes there," he offered.

"Whoa!" Eric took it and ran. "Guys, we should be ashamed of ourselves!"

The red plastic cup next to the water canister on the camp's table had four fingers of brown liquid in it from last night, and I couldn't wait a second longer for Borgnine to fuck off so that I could cut it with something. So I didn't. I went for it; I set my new cup down, put the cup with four fingers of Christian Brothers brandy inside it, picked up the two cups together, and drank the whole thing like it was pop.

In Hollywood it was the opposite, I thought, you had to drink soda pretending it was booze.

×

Eggs and hash turned out rugged chic and only Ryan and I ate them because Eric knew his stomach. Ryan, dressed like a hipster in light blue slacks, an olive T-shirt, and a scally cap, cooked the two of them some bacon. They scarfed it all down, saying: "You poor sonuvabitch, you don't know what you're missing." But I was on a buzzway to drunkville, playing power chords, a B then a G, a B then a G. It was a safe spot in inebriation, where anguish was a dullard and the faculties were capable of inspired feats.

×

Eric tried to make coffee in this old camping pot he borrowed from his in-laws—*freakin'* made for primitive brewing situations like this, by the way. He set it on the flame and when it started to burn, when the silver underside started to turn black, he freaked out, thought he was destroying a family heirloom. Granted, knowing his in-laws, they would have been polite when he told them, but inside they would have been very, very upset. I don't know if he believed me that it washes off, but twenty minutes later, he was sipping coffee and loving it, asking should we try and go somewhere, there were waterfalls, and I said you guys can go ahead but I'm opting for a slow and careful survival until it's time to steak.

×

A park ranger came over to verify our reservations, talked up the bears. Eric asked him where the nearest pay phone was. There was apparently a general store. That sold generals, my brain thought. Its cells were hurling themselves off the cliff, fearless of error.

"Are there wolves here?" I asked, though I didn't know to pronounce it with the fancy z sound at the end there and the ranger looked gobsmacked trying to understand me. Eric kindly translated. The guy started getting back into his vehicle.

"We don't *get* wolves out here. Coyotes, uh . . . black bears, muskrats, uh . . . deer. Bats . . . Oh, beavers! Uh . . . bighorn sheep! Not many of those left, unfortunately . . . Yep! . . . Mountain lions . . . Fishers . . . from a weasel family . . . Badgers! . . ."

His voice got tinier as the utility vehicle moved on, waved. I felt incrementally forsook.

×

Ryan's demeanor never changed—he always seemed a little pleasantly drunk. I was already semi-belligerent, poking the fire with a tire iron, throwing small branches in to keep it in flames. I was magnetized by the thingness of the contrivance in my hand. With each poke my shoulders stung from running in my dreams.

If Eric drank too early, he'd need a nap, would be a grumpy ass upon awakening, and he just didn't want to miss anything. But he looked mighty shifty at the picnic table there, watching the two of us winos feed the fire. At some point he joined us at the pit and we stared at its crackle, listened to it, enjoyed the satisfaction of a bright burn.

Then Eric lit up: we'd need more wood! A task! Boom! He led us. We foraged nearby for usable wood, as we had a full day and a half left, and two more late nights. Sticking to our territory at first, we cleaned the forest floor of twigs and sticks, logs and rotten bark, broken trunks, and humped it all back and into a healthy pile by the firepit. We ventured across the creek toward the highway, grabbing everything manageable, then circled around, passed a perfect family playing horseshoes in their own territory. Perfect parents waved and perfect children emulated. We perfectly did the same. Part of me thought: don't people ever tire of the need to be made to feel pleased?

×

Eric and Ryan took turns picking out stuff from their portable CD collections they thought the other would like but had not heard. I had nothing

Bosnian to offer to this dork fest, except to bust in with rusty power chords in the pauses between selections, play a B then a G then a D then an A and sing the only line in English from a Bosnian song that I could remember, one that went: *Come on, darling / I'm not Bob Marley / Come on, sweetheart / I'm Captain Beefheart*, until Eric actually played Beefheart's *Safe as Milk*, and I heard in its drumming and its mad wailing just how right I'd really been.

I put the guitar down and jerked my hammered forefingers into the air, in my mind thinking I was slam dancing up a storm, coiling my hind-quarters and pretending to leap. Things begun to get silly-goosh.

×

Eric brought out a pair of random Salvation Army goggles, and when Ryan put them on, he slipped into a personality that came with them. He jabbered about memory-foam prices and hoarding, saying clichéd American phrases and making them sound like he was their originator. *I got a bag of goodies, right here. You better believe it. Oh, yessiree!* In the middle of a sentence, he'd throw whatever he had in his hands at the time: a cup, a CD cover, even a tire iron; he'd just toss it behind him or to the side of him with zero regard where it would land, what it would do.

Eric and I were in awe of this behavior and took turns trying to capture the act in a photograph, but half the pictures ended up smudges of Ryan's saintly sneers and blur-motion arms. We could never predict in what direction the objects would fly.

By four p.m. the activity had matured into a knife-and-skewer-throwing contest. Some of these actually stuck into the bark, like in ninja movies, making us feel good in the chest. But when the blades started twanging and bouncing off and projectile-whispering into our ears, Eric put an end to it all by ceremoniously opening a fancy beer with a rooster on the front.

"How about that steak dinner now?"

×

I had premarinated the flatirons in Key lime juice and Vegeta, so all I had to do was lower the grate over the roar to get it piping, slice thick onion rings, and oil up the hatch peppers. Again, the veg were for Ryan and me, as Eric mostly murdered bread and meat.

Ryan thought of his Yager and he and Eric went to trek it down. Eric humped his twelve-pack of PBR cans with him, and from what I knew of that creek, and from what I knew of PBR cardboard packaging, I surmised well enough that a few of those cans would *whoops* downstream and out of Eric's reach and would have to be let go of.

At the bear box, Christian Brothers brandy was depleted, so I took the Slav route next and snapped open a handle of Popov. It was stark clear to me that Ryan would find—chilling—remnants of Elsa in that creek as well.

×

. . . alone, I drank like I was free, like I was getting away with something, when this strange breeze sideswiped me and I heard it whoosh *Slavenskaya dusha!* in my father's drunken croon from *the old before,* grating against any sense in this my circumstance, but weaseling still its age-old lineage's language around the trunks of these New World conifers, slaloming through the spaces between realms, and I knew its gush on my face—the very mossy poof-puff that displaced my hair—carried on it *her* scent even before I swooned darkly again, and changed form to get to dream-see her, and feel her in my electric musculature, in the light of my strange wolf-knowledge of her, but her windborne particles don't land the same on the old receptors now . . . like the she-wolf's blocking me today, choosing to hide in her green den, it being daytime and all, but what grief is this in her scent? what's this maddening Balkan under-hum my own membranes recognize, overrun? (I must have missed it in the novelty of nearness) and I scent-see her nuzzling her own womb, trying to intone of everlove but watching the love-charged air exiting her get snagged on that bone in her throat, that old thing, of course, always with the old thing and never done, always off-throwing the pitch, making each sonority dock with a painful howl and a part of me can't take being the hearer of this pain, the witness of it, a man inside me wants her not to feel it so hard, wants to *go* something, *do* somewhere, like men do, lovehack the reality so she doesn't feel this so hard, but me-wolf gnashes teeth at the silly wants of the man, a warning growl that everything is for people and for beasts alike, we're already made of it, grief and desire, pain and love, and life, and death is for people, and people are for people, and to help is not to *do* but to be(am) and to let be(am) and be(am) let, so I take off past the creek, past the man on the shore, itching to make a Honey-I'm-not-dead phone call, and the man *in* the creek, panging, thinking, *Really, Elsa? Really?! Oh, God!* and lunar as fuck down the slope I go, to the grove, I make the *'grimage* to her hollowed-out oak, both of me shows up in incurable one, and I guard her sacred medicine with silly fang and claw. I *do*.

But—*and*—for an awakening, I beam what I am too. *New.*

×

It came that I saw Ryan say something and saw Eric laugh at it (it was darker now!), and it came, amazingly, that I was *also* already dying laughing about it too, literally under the camp's table, without knowing why that was. What Ryan had said was: *Feels kind of good, actually!*

"Feels . . . kind of . . . good!" I repeated, fighting the somehow unstoppable roll of *ongoing* spasms in my abdomen. Privately, *simultaneously*, I made to lift myself onto the bench, to gather what the hell I was actually in the middle of. What had this body been performing in at this American campsite while I was . . . but *where* was it that had I been?

"Hey, I'll try it!" Ryan announced, and there I was again, doubled over in senseless merriment already in progress. And it kept on like that, one-liners each.

"Let's go through it," Eric said, and it kept on.

"What? I'm fine," Ryan said, and it kept on.

"C'mon, guys, that's not funny," Eric said, and it kept on.

"I'll go first!" Ryan said, and it kept on.

"Let's go over *here!*" Ryan said, and sidestepped, intently-like, but arbitrarily too, just four inches to the left.

That one sent us roaring, crying, fighting for piney breath.

That one was the high point and Ryan sensed that—the crescendo vibe about it, perhaps—and the intuitive master thespian that he is, he, kind of, threw his body into the pile of wood and garbage by the pit, and lay there like an inverted tortoise in a stiff tableau, offering himself as kindling, as visual fodder that our nerve endings could then forever sear into our collective memory, fooling us or proving to us that we were there, seeing and feeling all of that, being in and of it.[4]

×

Eric disappeared for a spell of timelessness and then returned with presents in the early night: novelty shot glasses, a twelve-pack of Newcastle in bottles, a plastic miner's helmet with a light on the front (which immediately appeared on Ryan's head and became a fixture for the night). My shot glass had a glued baby bear with a hat on, hugging it. Eric thanked me for the luscious steak I didn't recall cooking or eating, and then launched into a narrative of his trip to get in . . . heheheh . . . *in wife with his touch,* how the ranger was right about the general store, like where it was and all, but that he failed to mention the *people running it were dicks!* that he went there, didn't know how to pay for the pay phone using his credit card, tried everyone collect but no one answered, *knew* he couldn't call wife's cell phone collect *anyway,* and how the cord to the receiver was very short and he had to lean his forehead against the top of the booth to use it, how right there, in front of his face, inches away, were more of those giant furry moths, collected around a bare fluorescent light, and a few hollow corpses of them lying around as well, *needing haircuts, for Christ's sake,* and how he thought, like, you know, why wasn't anyone home? didn't someone care that he wasn't dead? but that he then smoked a menthol to collect himself, saw that the staff were watching him through the glass, went in and purchased a twenty-dollar calling card which the cashier couldn't figure out how to activate, kept trying more and more cards until finally making the call up the ladder and subsequently informing him, *Sorry, the whole system is down,* that he then went back outside and collect-called my future mother-in-law of all people and that she, class act that she is, picked up and agreed to call both Eric's current and my wife-to-be to tell them that none of us are dead up here, that he also gave her the number of the pay

---

4 "We started making lists of 'Famous Last Words,' things someone would say just before they died." From **The Bachelor Party** by Eric Carlson.

phone to give to his wife so she could call him and stood there for half an hour, waiting for it to ring, just to see a local kid walk by and say, *You don't need money for that phone*, that *It's free*, that *You can just dial out*, and that he did, that he called his wife's cell phone and that she answered on the third ring, and that when he turned to look at the greedy bastards in the store they were pretending not to see him passing out wolf tickets, wanted to pop his head in and yell, *Fuck General Sherman! and all of your water-falls!* but that he just went across the way and got some gas instead, and I thwacked him on the back and was like, *We all should do a shot from our new shot glasses*, to celebrate the task accomplished, but he said he couldn't mix, and only Ryan and I shot shots, and yipped like Nicholson in *Easy Rider*, and the guy who yelled at me the night before was playing Kid Rock louder than I ever talked, comfortable in his americaness.[5]

×

Our fire really came to life late in the night when it was the only one left. We fed it wood, songs and trash, lint from our pockets and loose hairs. It was our muse and audience, our TV, phones, strippers. It fucked with time(lessness) but not in the way booze did; it had potency to stretch instances into enduring impressions, moments out of the realm of mere occurrence—memories, I guess, finally.

But because of the booze I wasn't there in full. A child in me never liked what I had to do to pretend to fit into the big world, and chose the free rein of the etheric, the astral. And ogling this moment for truth from that orbit, I could glean that none of the three men could take the tender quiet; the quality of the instant they were in made them uncomfortable. They weren't used to anything like the present.

I watched Eric try, God help him, to give in to low crooning along with Ryan and the refugee, to stretch himself, to open in his own belief about

---

[5] Actual conversation between Eric and his wife that night, as per **The Bachelor Party**: E: Hi! W: Hi! What have you guys been doing? E: Not much. I don't know. Nothing. We made breakfast. We have a fire going. W (in a tone usually reserved for kindergarten teachers): Are you having fun? E: Oh yeah. Totally.

his own future room for more moments like this. His yearning for it was ancient, self-evident. Eyes closed, he let go of fear, striving to psychically embrace any goodness he was entitled to, and hold it, hold it, at least for a chorus, *Hey little bird, fly away home / Your house is on fire, your children are alone,* only to break the spell and peek out from beneath his brow at reality, positively terrified that it would not be there when he did, and upon seeing that it was, immediately disappointed that he gave in to doubt.

×

. . . in the tent as in the pit the beloved fire wouldn't go out all night but I did, I split as before, and I let my half of feral nerve keep patrol, and be my eye, my snout, my snarl, my goad, my tongue also, while in the tent, like her oak, my own stump with a heart in it spoke the way a torso would, with no mouth, no lips, no elbows to kiss, and while my wolf-half watched her crystals it was to the tent that the she-wolf sent her pent-up dance, to let me know how she felt, striding through the ancient woods that didn't smell like home, of the tactile panic in her whisker scraping mossy stone, joints buckling against the hard loam, clicking into hip as she dove or sank, mock-falling gait not learned by rote, but that in that abandon, her arch-soul, the frenzied aesthete, she gave meaning to the air she moved through and love to its charged poise, theatricalized blank ferns into gasping to perform, as she paused and took a pose, smiling back, batting brown eye, meaning: so what if you never catch me, *love will alone,* what you love will never leave you, isn't the chase back *enough*? and that in my suspension, with my senses elsewhere employed, in my disambulatory intuitions bereft of any expressive tool, I knew that she saw me, that yes, yes, it is, and that of course it is, but that the wolf will not stand for (just) it upon return.

×

Waking into hungover skins in the morning, corseted into almost-rigor by the *cold, cold ground,* we went back to feeding our baby, staring at its every stir. We fed it everything we could: more wood, paper plates, packagings, Ryan's broken sunglasses, entire box of matches, and all the CDs that skipped. We cooked another breakfast on it, same as the day before, gave the leftovers to a scrounger blue jay, and planned on not making plans. Except to wait for Ben.

The more vodka I drank, it seemed, the closer my new dream lore came to bleeding through. I could sense it just below the here and now, the same stretched-out realm from which *the old before*, from time to time, reaches for me from behind the furniture. But I couldn't let myself pass out in front of my friends, no matter how much I wanted to find out who the she-wolf was. The act of maintenance to stay between the worlds was delicate and technical, and required nothing short of abandon to achieve.

Ryan wrapped his short coat around his face like a babushka and I didn't know if he was tapping into something in my psyche or chasing his own thing. He cracked a tiny bird egg that he found in the dirt into a frying pan. It had two baby-Advil yolks that didn't cook like regular eggs but kind of, just, gelatinized.

×

Later, one of the two CD players stopped working altogether and could not be revived. We held a small service and I watched Eric situate it in the fire. I didn't see that coming. It burned with revolutionary force, spewing acrid smoke and stench. When the flames took its inner hub, they were *wrong*—some color between green and turquoise—not of this world. Might've been the batteries. We were stupid and ashamed but, as it sometimes happens, most of the campers were gone. It was a Sunday. Even a real fuckup like this turned out to be nothing much. *But the she-wolf would know, her poor nose!* Ryan swung a short coat around like he was signaling for help, trying to fan the gray smoke away, made a gorgeous spectacle of it.

From our site to the bathrooms the air was hazy with tiny particles of music for all occasions.

×

Ben found us in his little white car, all skinny now and in a sensible button-up and with his head near-shorn. He looked nothing like trench-coat Ben of yore and I gave him shit about it and didn't pat his back back when we hugged, just wouldn't let go. He said, *Whoa-whoa, let me get into it.*

"Wait till you see our fire!" we said.

"Yeah, that's a fire, all right," he said, looking for the magic we were insinuating was there.

"No, but look at it!"

He looked, but *for* it.

×

I was fire-roasting butterflied Cornish game hens on skewers, and coal-baking bell peppers and eggplants in foil, because Ben was now a vegetarian. And I drank hard and listened, somewhat, to him, spine-straight, presenting even more aspects of his new life to us, utilizing professional lingo, saying how he moved to San Fran to be closer to the people he knew in the self-help industry, that he doesn't drink anymore but that he'd make an exception for us, for me, that he was learning how to control his chaos, empowering people by teaching them how to walk over hot coals and broken glass, that he was *honing his powers,* trying to be a natural alternative to the Generation Xanax.

Old Ben's heart was such that he never met a devil he couldn't advocate for, which he often used to become the measure of every conversation, even the ones he had no business or acumen being in. In the old days he used to show up at three a.m. at my and Eric's door, beaten and bloodied from defending SoCal's random underdogs. If-Batman-was-a-hobo, we always teased him, for his restless night-driving in search of adventure, people to meet, help, save. One time he had jumped into a circle of bodies in Oxnard to help a kid from being kicked apart, not knowing it was a gang initiation—helped the guy earn his stripes instead.

While we were closer, he always both hated *and* was endlessly trying to figure out a way into the established world, and always through the side hatch or the shaft of a dumbwaiter and never through the so-called proper channels, which he deemed froth with assholery and bullying and stacked against people like us, like him. Because of that he'd always been a short-term everything: a telemarketer, a barkeep, a psychic, an extra, a Tweety

Bird or a Ninja Turtle at some rich little shit's birthday party in Sherman Oaks. And every time the established world flexed its bullshit rules, Ben would nuke the bridge, moon his bosses from the parking lot, or break someone's arm or get hilariously fired or repeatedly punched and thrown into a dumpster, just to get back up and try another way.

He was *on a mission*, he said—taking one of the tiniest sips of beer I had ever seen—to become NLP-certified because nothing gets him more excited than *getting people to overcome their obstacles*.

In my belligerence I thought he was putting us on, doing a character. I had cast him in my community college plays for his capacity to make a scene, make a hero or a fool of himself, but also for his gift to handle the sort of mind-numbing repetition and nothingness of rehearsal and/or life with grace and humor. That's why I'd thought he would get the fire.

But then I saw him look at his watch.

. . . and with the very next breath my nostrils flared, and I knew she was near, skulking through the brush away from eyes, ears, but being dogged in her advance to be the witness to this, to what? my human brain asked, and I had to choose with which half to think then, while my senses looked beyond and through a shimmer saw her trot up to my tent, snuffle the worn tarp, lick the rig's peg, just to arch her back and unfurl her spine, knowing I could see, then sit tall like the priestess of the Lycan court and set her eyes on mine, finally, then tilt askew her lupine face to make me wise, said, *ce crezi tu ca faci?!* and I looked through my human eyes to divine that . . .

Ben felt me, caught me judging, but when he looked at me, when he saw me and saw what he saw, which was a great blow, he didn't seem to judge, to pity, he . . . cared, yes, that's what it was, he cared, but from a distance, from the safety of his new conviction, from the aura of clean and energized poise and knowledge. He cared from his newness, *What would it take for me to become someone like this?* and the newness was plain in the eyes, in the changed body, its determined movements, its carriage of a person who lived his life with purpose. And newness, *What would it take for me to be true?*, wasn't that what the new me was promising to the elusive Balkan she-wolf? So I turned to my tent, somehow knowing that Ben would think me ashamed, but I wasn't. I was just looking to see what she'd

. . . show me, and despite her crystalline, fortress-like posture, there was sadness in her brown eye for me, and foreboding fear and love that bore down hard on me, for the pain of life that was coming, and I beamed at her my turmoil, mystification inherent in breath: *Ko si ti?* and with her heart she said I'm The One but you are The Two, and I beamed, *Sto me ne pustis blizu?* and with her heart she said you're already in my tribe, in my very flesh, in the body of my wisdom, my love, and *wisdom tells us we're nothing, while love tells us we're everything,* and I said out loud, *Al' sto me onda ne pustis zaposve?* and again with her heart, the language I could only glean, she said, *You're cleaved and can't yet be simultaneous,* you'll have to learn it, on your human skin, no shortcuts, burn through your nerves and organs, and face every fear, every wrong, let them in and groove on them and pour them drinks, until they can't teach you anything else, and in her heart I saw what the next chapter of my life would be, what americaness really means in apartments and houses up and down the coast, alongside a woman I will love to the bitter almost-end, who will encourage my desire to fit in and wait for my transformation and never meet the mol/////////////////
//
//
//
//
//
//
//
//
//
//
//
//
//
//
//
//

//////////////////////////ested child, waking up before her every time so that he could breathe and dream, as well as going to sleep last for the same reason, and keep the overgrown skin of what passes for a man and arrange it over the back of a chair for easy access, so that upon awakening of the world he could slip into it, and wear it like a drape'n'cape on Halloween, and costumed thus, plug himself into the American dog-and-pony of it all, and perform a man in this performance-sustained world, showing love and deference to its splendid artifice, blow out its prewritten lines, and wield its artisanal props—its performers its own audience, its common twists unfurling out of the commonness of its very prayers, its commonsense blueprints—and sustain his energies throughout by spewing truth words disguised as dramas and lame jokes and by vodka and self-pity up the ass—and rarest, saddest seconds of grace in the sun! and NO! *Take me with you?* it was too much to know, and I couldn't take it, couldn't countenance, abide the horror, that old formula for how to grow a monster, no I couldn't, and I turned my gaze from it, from what the she-wolf was showing me, and I shook my head NO! so hard it rattled the swollen brain into blotchiness and when next I looked toward the tent it was like the she-wolf had never been there, its tarp *un*interfered with, the rig's peg *un*licked, and I glugged the panic, and picked up on the vodka, and I must have said, *Povedi me, molim te,* because my friends asked me what is it that I meant in Bosnian, by this *powedeeme voleemte.*

×

What was shown to me—I had to slug it down instants before my insides tried to upchuck it. I had to keep it down and in. Nobody could know.

The guys were getting personal with life stories in the presence of a neoprene life coach. Eric talked about his wife and kid, his gun-crazy in-laws.

I gawped at a paper plate where my bird was relegated to bones. Was of a mind to stand up and feed it to the fire but didn't need attention. If I'd moved or spoken, I knew I'd have faltered. So I kept swallowing, and breathing in between. A mark of ketchup on my plate looked like a drunken *zvijezda petokraka.*

×

Ryan remarked on Elsa with a crick between his eyebrows, on the fact that some of her stuff was still in his Burbank apartment, and how it gutted him so to bear it there, and Ben wanted to know more, like why was it making him feel that way, *'cause* gutted *is a serious word, man,* and Ryan wasn't really in the humor to open up about all that, till Eric and I nudged him, *Why not? It was prime time, was it not?* and Ben pledged he had a technique that was guaranteed to take the edge off that word *gutted,* that if Ryan allowed himself to relive this painful memory just this one last time in words, that Ben could vouch that the next time he remembered it, it would not be as painful, that, in fact, it would diminish with every future remembering and never ever be the same again. We were all sitting at the picnic table, Ryan, Eric, and I wondering how in the fuck would Ben do this? But it was dark enough, quiet enough, intimate enough—we had certainly spent enough time together—and Ryan was prying enough to give it a try.

And I can't write down the details of the story Ryan told because Eric was scanty on them in the original as well, but you can imagine: four years of intimacy, living together, acting together, holidays, family gatherings, then a cast party for some Brecht show they were both in, and Ryan catching Elsa flirting with some douchebag from San Francisco, then finding a way to disappear into a room with him, etc.

The moment Ryan's face showed that *gutted* look, that said perhaps acid was rising in his stomach, Ben untied his Doc Marten shoe, encouraging him to continue. *Oh, really? And then what?* He managed to look sympathetic but was way less emotional than me and Eric.

Ryan resumed with *guttedness,* feeling it, when Ben coolly lifted his leg onto the picnic table, pulled off his white sock, and nodding at Ryan and saying, *Yes, go on!* took his bare foot in his hand and started to suck on his big toe.

"Hmmmm, hmmmm," Ben slobbered. He paused and took the toe out. "And what did you do then?"

Ryan kept going somehow, no longer looking material in his flesh. He was . . . kind of grinning.

I looked at Eric, hand clamped over my mouth, trying to keep from laughing, interrupting. And Eric, he was knuckling his eye sockets as if they didn't contain his precious only eyes.

×

All four of us tried continuing the conversation afterward but it was no use. The night was spent. Three of us were touched and weirded out by what we had witnessed. One of us was wasted and confused and announced his plans to retire to his tent, lit the way to it with his son's miner's helmet. One of us explained the philosophy of his approach twice, second time as if he were presenting it at a conference. Two of us nodded at it all, then said casual good nights. One of us took the bottle into the tent with him and blacked out trying to conjure up a mystical love coach in his heart.

As for her, she wouldn't come back until years later, after my divorce, after the plagues hit.

×

She wouldn't come that night. And I split myself and I called her and I howled at the moon when I couldn't find her at the grove, her treasures gone from her sacred oak's hollow. I split the halves of me then, halved the splits too, ad infinitum like Zeno, *paradoxed* myself into corporeal waves and ghost particles, and sent these *myselves* everywhere, listening for her scents, sniffing for her yip-yelps, hallucinating her off-balance hip-clicks against my stubbly skin—a tactile spook of a memory, or a dream, a shivery glitz, this. I drank straight from the bottle, a desiccating liquid for sure, and when I woke, I only had her gelatinous, engulfing portents to guide me.

×

It was warm, our last morning. I could barely stand, keep my head up top from rolling away. The lizard brain was cooking the leftover meat on the grid: tri-tip, lamb necks, sausages, and we ate it all, burned up the plates and the bones, the trash and a few more last things, for old times' sake, some jean shirts, more gas-station sunglasses, Ryan's pants that split down one side. We packed up the dregs and took down the tents. Eric would miss a part of this part of the story because he slipped out to take what kept refusing to be his final piss that morning and that's when Ben found a hunting arrow in the brush, which inspired him to practice honing his healing powers again. And having cured Ryan already, he turned instead to me and said:

"Do you know that I can teach you how to break this arrow with your neck?"

"Why?" Ryan and I scoffed.

"Your brain can be tricked into happiness. You can break it in like you would a horse."

"Don't they break horses' spirits when they do that?" Ryan asked.

Ben nestled the back of the arrow against the bark of a nearby trunk and aimed the tip in the hollow between his collarbones. He smiled a winning smile, explaining himself as he went on, tensed the cordage around his upper chest, visualized how he was going to *walk into the arrow with intent,* and then walked into the arrow with intent to break, and I saw the arrow bend and strain, and Ben stopped to check on his thick skin, then walked into it again, and again, the arrow refusing to crack, and that's when we heard Eric go, *What the fuck are you doing, man?!* and *Do you know how far the closest hospital is from here?* and Ben laughed when he saw that this was a professional animal-killer's arrow, not of wood but, in fact, manufactured so as never to break at all.

×

She-wolf didn't appear that morning either. Nor any other, for a time. But something of her aura infused my being, gave me a way to see in or, perhaps, through a moment.

Eric was over it and eager to leave, having said goodbye to the picnic table, the empty bear box, the signpost #43. Goodbye to the fur-moths, wherever they slept during the day. Goodbye to leftover-egg-eating blue jay cannibal motherfucker. Goodbye to the shards of kindling that never made it into the fire. Goodbye to the fire, and this nothing-bachelor trip, and no shower, and the dip into depression without the kid, and the inflatable mattress that did nothing but deflate, and keeping this drunk immigrant from advertising it like a noob, out in these woods, with all type of stranger lurking about, our little group so vulnerable, and the drinking all day especially, goodbye and fuck all that!

I could feel him.

I could feel Ben needed a win after the arrow setback. He returned from his car holding a small board. The way he held it, we knew he wanted someone to break it. Eric was visually upset but held it in, said we had time for one more quick ritual *but then it's time to get into the vroom-vroom and GO go, right, guys?*

But Ben was now having fun, getting to practice his budding craft. He even gave me a Sharpie to write on the board, five negative things about my life that I wanted to strike at and five positives that I wanted to break through to. I held the board and the Sharpie, looking beyond him, scanning the surroundings for the she-wolf. I'd give anything to know what I wrote down on that board, but not even Eric remembered that. None of these made it into the chronicling, these hidden traumas that needed breaking, these strivings that needed to be broken through to.

I could feel Ryan and Eric exchange glances: *Aw, fuck! This could take a while.*

Ben gave me breaking instructions, tried to give me confidence, said:

"This is to empower **you**, to show you a way that **you** can hack your own brain and show it that **you** are the boss. It has to learn that it is not in charge, it is a tool. You don't have to live in the past, in the misery, in pain."

"Vhat happens to the reasons, then?" I said. "Of the misery, pain?"

"You can train your brain to be happy."

"Yeah, but for vhat reason is happiness . . . important. Vhat about truth?"

"Well, don't do it if you're not ready, it will really hurt your hand."

I was gonna do it.

I paced. I shook my hands around. I hyperventilated.

I kept hearing the she-wolf . . . *you'll have to learn it, on your human skin, no shortcuts . . .*

"I am to break myself in, like a horse, to be happy. I have to break my own spirit, my soul, for the goal of happiness. I have to trick my eyes, to trick my brain, so that my body would be pleased? This is a way to live?"

"It's okay," Ben said, holding the board. "Whenever you are ready."

ACKNOWLEDGMENTS

First, I'd like to thank You, the Reader, inside of whose heart, mind, and guts all of these strangely arranged symbols get alchemized into feelings, meanings, and portents. I did what I could, left it all on the page. This writing with intent to heal. Thank you for your attention and willingness to go there, for your time, patience, and courage. It's hard work, this, on both sides. And it has to be done.

Writing to save a life, John Edgar Wideman called it; I'm paraphrasing here. Lofty-sounding thing, which is exactly why I want to extend my thanks to Bill Burr at this very spot, unabashedly by the way: his work helped me get through the worst of my gutter days. Comedy to save a life, for sure.

My unbounded gratitude goes to my agent, PJ Mark, and my editors, Lauren Wein and Amy Guay, for believing in me, for their encouragement and fortitude as well as the rest of the gang at Avid Reader for the hard work that went into delivering this book into the world; to the editors and the staff of journals who published early portions of it as standalone pieces: "Curfew" first appeared at IdentityTheory.com; "At the National Theater" and "Nimrods" appeared in *McSweeney's Quarterly Concern* (cheers! Jordan Bass, didn't forget you like last time); "Slouching Toward Pichka Materina" at *New England Review*, and a segment from "Homo Homini Home Est?" appeared in *Faultline* as "Seeing Red;" to my fellow instructors and students at IAIA, New Mexico, for listening to me slur these pieces out loud into a mic back in the days when I was in the grip of the grape—your love for my dumb ass at my lowest remains unmatched.

I'm so grateful to Alan Grostephan, Justin Rigamonti, J.M. Geever, Mona Ausubel, Matt Sumell (hey, I spelled it right this time around), Eric

Carlson and Ryan (the-Sensuous-Man) Higgins for reading many drafts of this book, or portions of it, each time illuminating my mistakes and pointing out clunkers without making me stab myself in the eye with a pencil. And to Cpt. Carlson for remembering, so graciously and abundantly, my own bachelor party for me.

Thank you to Villa Lena and Portland Community College's Carolyn Moore Writing Residency for their hospitality and the best lodgings ever! For these same reasons and for friendship and partnership to boot, I thank my old *drug* Malik (*Malik-na-govno-si-nalik*) Vitthal. Shout-out to Jaya and Sri for putting up with me in the Airstream behind the house!

My love goes to mom, brother, my families, friends, Bosnian and American alike. And to Melissa, for all the days, with Love.

ABOUT THE AUTHOR

ISMET PRCIC was born in Tuzla, Bosnia-Herzegovina, in 1977, and immigrated to America in 1996. His first novel, *Shards,* was a *New York Times* Notable Book, a *Chicago Sun-Times* Best Book of the Year, and a B&N Discover Great New Writers Selection, as well as the winner of the Sue Kaufman Prize for First Fiction and the Los Angeles Times Art Seidenbaum Award for First Fiction.

Avid Reader Press, an imprint of Simon & Schuster, is built on the idea that the most rewarding publishing has three common denominators: great books, published with intense focus, in true partnership. Thank you to the Avid Reader Press colleagues who collaborated on *Unspeakable Home*, as well as to the hundreds of professionals in the Simon & Schuster advertising, audio, communications, design, ebook, finance, human resources, legal, marketing, operations, production, sales, supply chain, subsidiary rights, and warehouse departments whose invaluable support and expertise benefit every one of our titles.

Editorial
Lauren Wein, *VP and Editorial Director*
Amy Guay, *Assistant Editor*

Jacket Design
Alison Forner, *Senior Art Director*
Clay Smith, *Senior Designer*
Sydney Newman, *Art Associate*

Marketing
Meredith Vilarello, *VP and Associate Publisher*
Caroline McGregor, *Marketing Manager*
Katya Wiegmann, *Marketing and Publishing Assistant*

Production
Allison Green, *Managing Editor*
Jessica Chin, *Manager Copyediting*
Kayley Hoffman, *Senior Production Editor*
Alicia Brancato, *Production Manager*
Carly Loman, *Interior Text Designer*
Cait Lamborne, *Ebook Developer*

Publicity
David Kass, *Senior Director of Publicity*
Alexandra Primiani, *Associate Directer of Publicity*
Rhina Garcia, *Publicist*

Publisher
Jofie Ferrari-Adler, *VP and Publisher*

Subsidiary Rights
Paul O'Halloran, *VP and Director of Subsidiary Rights*
Fiona Sharp, *Subsidiary Rights Coordinator*